Top Honors
For
TONY GIBBS
and
His Suspense-packed

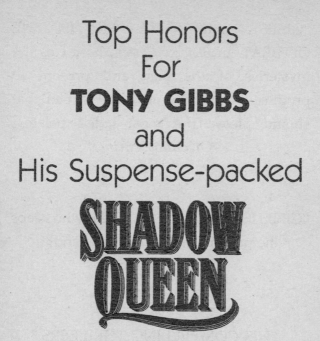

SHADOW
QUEEN

"SATISFYING . . . Tony Gibbs combines an historical whodunit with contemporary suspense, laces it with a bittersweet romance and a touch of the occult, and comes up with a tasty and satisfying dish."

—*San Diego Union*

☆

more . . .

Also by Tony Gibbs

Fiction

Dead Run
Running Fix

Nonfiction

Practical Sailing
Advanced Sailing
The Coastal Cruiser
Cruising in a Nutshell

Tony Gibbs
SHADOW QUEEN

THE MYSTERIOUS PRESS

New York · Tokyo · Sweden

Published by Warner Books

 A Time Warner Company

MYSTERIOUS PRESS EDITION

Copyright © 1992 by Tony Gibbs
All rights reserved.

Cover design by Jackie Merri Meyer
Cover illustration by Kinuko Craft
Hand lettering by Carl Dellacroce

The Mysterious Press name and logo are trademarks of
Warner Books, Inc.

Mysterious Press Books are published by
Warner Books, Inc.
1271 Avenue of the Americas
New York, NY 10020

A Time Warner Company

Printed in the United States of America

Originally published in hardcover by The Mysterious Press.
First Printed in Paperback: February, 1993
10 9 8 7 6 5 4 3 2 1

For the family:

Elaine, Eric and Lisa, Bill and Michelle,
Jessica, and Megan

HISTORICAL NOTE

In 1565, the twenty-three-year-old Queen of Scots, Mary Stuart, took it into her head to marry her nineteen-year-old cousin, Henry Stuart, Lord Darnley. The marriage united two of the principal strands of the House of Stuart, but the bride and groom also figured prominently in the succession to the Crown of England, and many contemporaries felt that the Catholic Mary had a better claim than did the Protestant incumbent, the childless Queen Elizabeth. Mary's marriage to Darnley was stormy and brief, culminating in his murder two years later. While most observers agreed that Mary's lover, the Earl of Bothwell, was certainly one of the killers, opinions were divided about Mary's role—until she allowed herself to be "kidnapped" by Bothwell and then married him.

This new marriage raised a storm of outrage in Scotland and beyond, and Mary was shortly deposed in favor of her and Darnley's infant son, James (or, in reality, a council of regency dominated by Mary's bastard half brother the Earl of Moray). She was imprisoned on the island of Lochleven, where she miscarried twins, and Bothwell escaped to Scandinavia, where past indiscretions caught up with him; he disappeared into a dungeon, never to emerge.

But Mary managed to charm her way out of captivity and, in a moment of supreme miscalculation, fled to England, claiming refuge with her cousin Queen Elizabeth. That ruler, torn between her dislike for rebels against a sister monarch and fears that Mary loose on English soil might trigger a Catholic uprising among her own subjects, put the ex–Queen of Scots in polite confinement while considering what to do next. Typically reluctant to make the decision herself, Elizabeth summoned a council of her nobles and turned the question over to them. Mary was not allowed to appear before this assemblage, but the Earl of Moray and his fellow rebels were. They claimed to have removed Mary because she had helped to murder her husband, Darnley, and they produced documents to prove it.

These papers, known to history as the Casket Letters (they had been discovered in a silver-gilt casket), consisted of eight letters and a long poem in several parts, all supposedly written by Mary to Bothwell. Nearly everyone who has read copies of the Casket Letters agrees that if Mary wrote them she was at least an accomplice in Darnley's murder and possibly a principal. The question, of course, is whether she wrote them. At the time, no verdict was reached, but Mary continued to be held in English prisons for two decades, until her own desperate intrigues and English fears at last forced Elizabeth to execute her.

In the four hundred years since, the question of Mary Stuart's guilt has remained open, and her enemies and partisans, absolute in their conviction, have multiplied with each generation. Only the Casket Letters themselves, subjected to modern scientific testing, might decide the matter— but the original documents vanished in 1584, very possibly at the instance of Mary Stuart's son, King James the Sixth of Scotland, who three years later allowed his mother to be beheaded with only a token protest. James's restraint, which still seems cold-blooded to many, may have stemmed from pure dislike of his mother or, more likely, have been part of his successful campaign to become Queen Elizabeth's successor, as the first ruler of a nominally united England, Scotland, and Ireland.

STIRRINGS

1. East Elmhurst, Borough of Queens

Marie glanced up from the book as her mother shuffled cautiously into the living room. The old woman's rheumy eyes were fixed on the dully gleaming staff she was holding before her, balanced across her upturned palms. She halted a few feet from the spavined couch, and forced her shapeless body into a contorted half crouch.

"I'm a little stiff today," she said to Marie. "You must assume that I'm kneeling."

"That's all right," said Marie, head lowered again. She glared down at the arid, gray pages of *Marine Pollution Law and Public Policy,* but she was aware only of the spongy wheeze of her mother's breathing. Still not looking up, she retrieved the half-eaten tunafish sandwich from where she had discarded it on the coffee table's scarred surface, took a deliberate bite, and forced herself to chew and swallow.

"It's time, dear," said her mother. And then, in her other, ceremonial voice: "Your subjects are waiting, Majesty. You must remember, promptness—"

"—*est la politesse des rois.* Not that *l'exactitude* did poor old Louis much good." The words sprang from Marie unbidden; startled her so that she found herself meeting her mother's astonished stare. "Louis XVIII," Marie mumbled. "The one Napoleon chased out. He used to say that a lot." But how did I know?

3

"How did—" her mother began, in her everyday tone. Caught herself: "Your Majesty, please." She held the staff out to Marie.

"Oh, all right." Marie set down the sandwich, closed the book with just enough force to suggest annoyance. At her side, Old Ruthven the cat stretched and rose, accordioning his spine. His single yellow eye regarded her sandwich, but he made no move toward it.

Marie pulled herself free from the sofa's broken-spring embrace and stood—feet together, back straight, head high. Extending her hands, palms up, between her mother's, she lifted the metal staff from her. The *scepter,* she reminded herself. As always, the sheer weight of it caught her attention, and the way the lead pellets inside shifted slightly with every movement. The knobs at each end still had an aureate gleam, but along the rod's length the thin brass plating had worn away, revealing dull streaks of gray metal beneath.

She cradled the scepter in the crook of her bent right arm, her hand cupping the knob, and waited.

"This way, Your Majesty," said her mother, backing crabwise toward the stairs across the room. Marie allowed a faint, condescending smile to shape her mouth. She gave the old woman a barely perceptible nod and took a measured step forward. From the corner of her eye she saw Old Ruthven watching her. Tunafish was the battle-scarred tomcat's favorite, and as soon as they were out of sight, Marie knew, he would sidle over and claim his prize.

Marie's mother had sagged to one knee, head bent, at her daughter's stately approach. Marie paused for a moment at the foot of the stairs, to give her imaginary attendants time to straighten her nonexistent train. Usually, she had to drag the smelly old quilt, safety-pinned around her neck, but this time her mother had seemingly forgotten it.

Marie ascended the narrow stairway, from which the banister rail had been removed so she would not absentmindedly reach for it. A queen, Mother had told her firmly, did not grab at handholds. Behind her, she could hear the muted, gasping struggle as the old woman heaved herself to her feet. A part of Marie's mind noted the slithering crash as the stack of books by the banister toppled over, but by now the familiar ritual had her in its grasp. Under her feet, the splintery steps had turned to marble, dished slightly by centuries of use; in her hand, the section of brass curtain rod had become massy gold; jeans and sweatshirt were jewel-encrusted satin robes.

Her mother was panting audibly, grunting with the effort of mounting each step. Marie thought she might be dying, but it was hard to know for sure: Thousands of dusty books lay in heaps everywhere around the house, but few of them were medical texts and even fewer dealt in the practical details of death. Not that death itself was a stranger to Marie; from time to time one of the cats would disappear, to be revealed, pungently, a few days later. Marie wondered if the same thing would happen to her mother. Somehow, it seemed unlikely.

At the top of the stairs Marie paused while she counted to five, then paced down the dark, musty hallway. The only light came from the bedroom she shared with her mother, but that was not where she was going. She stopped at the small, closed door, turned to face it, and waited. At last her mother achieved the top step and scuttled, wheezing, down the hall. She bobbed obsequiously past Marie and flung open the door. The odor of mildew rolled out, spiced with a faint tang of decay.

Marie stepped forward, and the scepter slapped lightly against the door frame. The knob at the end clanged to the uncarpeted floor, and the sound of metallic hail echoed down the hall as a cascade of lead pellets rained down. *"Merde,"* snapped Marie.

"Marie!" The girl flinched, but not quickly enough. The old woman's hand caught her across the cheek with enough force to send her, off balance as she was, to her knees. "Marie Stuart McIntyre! I'm ashamed of you."

Marie looked up apprehensively. Her mother's sagging features were blotched with rage. "But Mother . . ."

"Silly, clumsy girl. I've done everything to prepare you. Everything. And you waste it."

The old woman paused, momentarily breathless. She raised her hand to strike again, and Marie felt, from somewhere deep within, a black surge of fury. It must have showed on her face, because her mother took an unexpected half step backward, her hand falling.

Or perhaps it was only the weakness that had been creeping over the old woman lately. Her fits of anger came on as fast and strong as ever, but more and more often they tapered quickly off to panting, gasping tears. Now she had begun to wheeze, racking breaths that left her wordless. Shaking her head, she leaned against the wall, her heavy breasts heaving beneath the stained housedress.

Marie, still on her knees, began scooping up the lead pellets, pouring them back down the mouth of the tube. The nearly uncontrollable rage that had seized her was gone as fast as it had come, leaving only the determination that her mother would not strike her again. Not ever. She found the brass knob that had fallen out of the tube and jammed it tightly back into the opening. Some of the shot was missing, and what was left rattled noisily inside.

In a single, liquid motion Marie rose from her crouch. Fully erect she was inches taller than her mother, herself a tall woman. She couched the scepter again in the crook of her arm and waited. "Let's get it over with," she said. "This charade." *Charade*, she repeated silently, savoring it. A good word—but where had it come from?

"You have to know these things," her mother said slowly. "A person in your position."

Marie recognized the olive branch and rejected it. "My position. That's so stupid." But she turned toward the two chairs that faced her across the cramped, bare room.

As Marie took a slow step forward, her mother whispered, "Acknowledge your consort, Majesty."

Marie inclined her head toward the small chair on which Darnley sat, unblinking and rigid, staring at her. "My lord," she said, hearing the condescension in her tone. For an unsettling moment she thought she saw life in Darnley's wide eyes, but it was only a reflection of her own movement in the glass. One of the other cats had been at Darnley again, she saw—a chunk of gray fur was missing, and sawdust was leaking out the hole.

She smiled graciously, as if Darnley had indeed offered her his duty, and turned toward the other chair, the one that would have dominated a far larger room. It was of some black wood, its carved back as high as Marie's head. The arms ended in crudely carved lion's heads, and the legs in paws, but the effect was marred by the legend burned into the back in Gothic letters four inches high: "Ye Olde Rathskeller."

Marie halted, facing the chair—the throne, as it was now—while her mother moved about behind her, miming the rearrangement of her train. When she sensed the old woman had finished, Marie turned slowly, facing an invisible throng that stretched away over the mind's horizon. Slowly, gracefully, she sat; back straight, face expressionless, she held the position for half an eternity and, just as her silent count reached 185, sneezed.

It broke the spell. Her mother reached forward and took the drapery rod, handling it gingerly. "Very good, dear," she said. "A little more . . ." She groped for the word. "A little more *warmth* when you look at your consort, I think."

"It's hard to be warm to a dead cat," Marie said. "Especially when his insides are dripping."

"Oh, I know," said her mother heavily. She made an ineffectual attempt to push Darnley's stuffing back into the hole. "You just have to pretend, though. For when it really is your consort."

Marie snorted. She knew her mother hated the sound: unladylike. "When's that going to be?" she demanded. "I've been cooped up in here since you took me out of school. Three whole years." A recollection of school flicked her memory—jeering classmates, condescending teachers; when she wasn't hating them she was terrified of the place itself. "When?" she said again. "That's what I want to know."

"Soon." Marie's head snapped up. She had been expecting the usual answer—"all in good time"—and this response was wholly new, with implications that stretched far beyond her vision. "*Very* soon," her mother said. She seemed to be trying to smile, but her eyes were wet.

"What do you mean, Mother?" Marie asked, wary.

"I've had another letter from Ireland," her mother replied and, noticing Marie's puzzled frown, prompted: "From Miss Orme. You must remember about Miss Orme, Marie." She paused, her eyes clouding. "Or did I write from the library? Yes, I think I did, because of their nice pens. I don't know why it's so hard to keep pens in this house, but they seem to disappear . . ."

Launched on one of her monologues, she might go on for half an hour and end in midair. Marie interrupted, pitching her voice to cut through her mother's monotone. "*What* letters, Mother? Who is Miss Orme? Oh." Suddenly the mental image came to her: an immensely thick paperback with a brightly colored cover—a young woman on a white horse. A young woman whose pale face resembled Marie's. *Queen Betrayed,* that was the title; and below it, "A Novel of Mary Stuart, By Patricia Orme."

"See? I knew you'd remember."

"But it was such a *dumb* book," Marie objected. "Why'd you want to write to Patricia Orme?"

"I know you didn't like it," her mother said, with a glitter of malice in her eye. "But if you'd been patient enough to finish it, you'd know why."

"Tell me. Please, Mother."

She waited a long minute, enjoying her small triumph. "I'll give you a little hint," she said. "Lochleven."

"Lochleven?" Marie knew the name, of course: the island prison where Mary Queen of Scots, whose name she herself bore, had spent several long months before her flight to England, Elizabeth, and the headsman. But what was important about Lochleven? Slowly, Marie looked up: "The twins," she said. "That's what it is, isn't it? What did she write about them? Come on, Mother—tell me."

"No," her mother replied, smiling.

Sale vache, the words leaped without warning into Marie's mind, so strongly propelled they almost escaped her lips. Now it was she who was trembling with fury, but her voice, she noticed, was quite calm: "Why not? It's my right to know."

"Day after tomorrow," her mother said. Without warning, hoarse, racking coughs shook her thick body. Marie moved quickly to her, eased her into the high-backed chair. After a while she was able to speak: "She's coming here, Patricia Orme. From across the sea," she added, "just to meet you." A sly smile spread across her face. "My little baby," she said, reaching out to embrace her daughter.

"That's not all," Marie said, twisting quickly out of her grasp. "I can tell. What else is she coming to see?" The old woman was large and heavy, but Marie hoisted her to her feet in a single motion. *"Dites-moi!"* She snapped. She saw the answer in her mother's eyes. "No," she said slowly. "That's not for outsiders. *Jamais. Tu m'avais . . ."* She shook the intruding French out of her head. "You told me so yourself."

"It's time," her mother gasped. "Time for the world to know." She pulled herself free from her daughter's hands. "Who better to tell them than a famous writer?"

A smutty-minded *romancière*, rather, Marie thought. A fool who'd seen the Queen as no more than a slave to her appetites. But still . . . what had it said on the back? *"10 Months on the Best-Seller List!"* People would listen. She was wrenched from her reverie by a grunt of pain. "What's the matter?"

"My side hurts," her mother said. Her face had gone yellow, and there was sweat on her forehead. "Help me into the bedroom, Marie."

When her mother finally subsided into a fitful, twitching slumber, Marie went thoughtfully downstairs. As she had expected, the tunafish sandwich was gone. Old Ruthven was stretched on the sofa, and his insolent, one-eyed stare brought her back to reality: Nothing was going to happen; she was going to stay in this house until her mother died, and then . . . Then what? She had no idea. Despair clutched at her heart and she sank to the sofa.

Courage, ma petite. Marie started, looking wildly around her: She had heard the woman's voice plainly—deep, warmly affectionate, yet a tone that commanded instant obedience.

Around Marie the stuffy living room was unaltered, yet completely changed, as if the still visible walls, with the awful flowered wallpaper, had fallen away. She felt a light-headed freedom that was wholly new to her.

She became aware that Ruthven was on his feet, back arched, every hair on his body fully erect. His single yellow eye regarded her with what could only be terror.

Marie returned his unblinking stare, her lips curved in a cold smile. "Off with your head," she said softly.

2. Manhattan: 47th Street and Fifth Avenue

"But Haskell—we can't wait till Diana comes back from vacation," said Judith Sanders, in her most plaintive voice. "I already explained: Patrick's flying all the way from Ireland, but he'll only be in town a couple of days. He wants to nail this down, and we've got to tie him up before some other publisher does." Judith, whose title of executive editor carried its usual publishing-industry connotation, *valuable but unpromotable*, was a tiny blonde with a chest so large it made her look foreshortened. She had carefully positioned herself by Haskell Rose's office window, so the afternoon sun silhouetted her from the waist up. It was, he reflected, the kind of pose she assumed automatically, and perhaps he really was getting old, because these days it scarcely deflected his mind at all.

"Even so," he objected. "It looks like we're trying to pull a fast one: an unscheduled editorial meeting with the treasurer out of town. And for something like this."

"You're the editor-in-chief, though. And that makes you acting head of Wild-Freeman Publishing."

"It used to," said Haskell. "These days, I wouldn't count on it."

"You told me you could okay up to a half-million advance, Haskell," said Judith, ignoring him. "I know Patrick will go for that. On signing, anyway."

"Generous of him," Haskell said. "But why don't you tell me what the book's about?"

"Haskell, *dear*," she said, swinging away from the window and propping herself on the corner of his desk. "You'll hear all about it tomorrow. And you can take my word for it: This is the biggest book of the decade. Maybe of the century. When we get it, Random House and S&S will be positively *green*."

"I seem to remember the last big Patrick Sarsfield idea," Haskell reflected aloud. "The love story of Saint Teresa and the King of Spain."

"This one's not *like* that, Haskell," she insisted, leaning forward to give him a better view. "Not even remotely. You have to remember, dear: This is our own author. Wild-Freeman's biggest seller. Surely we ought to give him the benefit of the doubt."

"His sales have been slipping," Haskell remarked, thinking that sounds directed down a cleavage of those proportions ought to produce some sort of echo.

She straightened up so quickly he felt a surge of vertigo. "Well, that's *it*," she said, as if he had just reinforced her argument. "He's getting stale writing bodice rippers. And he's tired of writing as Patricia Orme. He told me it makes him feel as if he's . . ."

"In drag?"

"Whatever. But this is nonfiction, under his own name. And Patrick's a good technician. He's been researching it for a couple of years. It has everything, Haskell—sex, love, violence, intrigue, royalty. And it's all true: You've always said how important that was."

"I suppose I have," Haskell muttered. He'd been through enough discussions with Judith Sanders to recognize when the ground was slipping from under his feet.

Suddenly her scent seemed much stronger, and he knew she was moving in for the kill. Maybe greed did something to her glands. Still, she was Wild-Freeman's most successful editor, a considerable technician herself, both in and out of bed. "Look, Haskell dear. Patrick will absolutely allow us to bring in any expert we like to vet the project. We can credit future royalties on all his published books against the advance—he's that confident."

"Sweetheart, you know as well as I do that his published titles have already brought in most of what they're going to make. And besides, I still don't like going behind Diana's back."

"You sure its *her* back that's worrying you, Haskell? It wouldn't be Chairman Rajah who's on your mind, would it?"

Well, of course it would. Six months before, when the billionaire entrepreneur Roger—inevitably Rajah—Channing had acquired Wild-Freeman as lagniappe to his purchase of a much larger firm, he had instantly fired the treasurer and president, replacing the former with his hard-nosed satrap Diana Speed and leaving the latter job empty. Dangling. At sixty-three, Haskell Rose wanted two things—the presidency of Wild-Freeman Publishing and a number-one best-seller. If Judith was right, this might be his last opportunity for both. If she was wrong, on the other hand . . .

Judith had been reading his face: "Listen, Haskell, dear, this is your big chance to score. Bring the Rajah a marvelous, moneymaking coup, *and* show him you're the kind of decisive person he wants to head up the house."

She was right, of course. And as always her timing was perfect. That very morning he had received a long, ominous questionnaire from the pension committee. "Okay," he said. "We'll do it. I'll have Diana's secretary run up a special agenda tomorrow."

"It's already taken care of," Judith said. "The mailroom will have it on everyone's desk first thing in the morning." She had absolutely no right to do such a thing, and Haskell was on the point of saying so when she continued: "I didn't trust that O'Donnell snip. She's probably got a direct line to Miss Diana Spy."

"Diana will find out, you know," he said.

"By the time she does, it'll be too late."

"She'll insist on vetting everything. And she'll probably be even tougher than usual."

"Let her," Judith replied airily. Feeling victory, she was clearly prepared to shoot down objections for as long as he raised them.

He heard his resigned sigh, realized he had been sighing a lot lately. He wondered if Judith had already typed up the contract, but found he lacked the spirit to ask her.

3. Lower Manhattan: Duane Street

"For the hundredth goddamn time, Larry," Pearse said, "you've got to make those Frogs realize that if they don't put the labels on each and every wedge, customs is going to hold their goddamn Roquefort right there on the pier till it turns to goddamn *penicillin*."

The receptionist–telephone operator at the front of the big, crowded room looked over her shoulder. "For you on four, Mick," she called.

"Damn it, Dorrie," said Pearse, putting his palm over the mouthpiece, "I'm already on the phone."

She put the incoming call on hold before she said, "It's that guy who sounds like Vaseline, Mick—Mr. Galmoy. You told me—"

"I know what I told you," he snapped. Then, into the phone: "Larry? I'll call you right back. Got a crisis." He punched up line four. "Pearse here." Listening to the slippery voice at the other end, he thought, Vaseline, indeed. That's one for Dorrie. But aloud he said, "Look, Mr. Galmoy, things are kind of hectic here today. I can't just walk out of the office and go to another phone. Can I meet you after work? I'm afraid it'll be seven at the earliest, the way things are shaping up."

• • •

The bar was one of the last survivors of old Third Avenue, a distinction the proprietor reinforced with bad lighting, muddy black-and-white framed photographs of the Elevated, floors covered with sour-smelling green-tinted sawdust, and a handful of regulars who looked as if they'd been propped in place at the end of St. Patrick's Day and left to rot. Pearse sat by himself at one of the three small tables, ignoring the bartender's steady glare and nursing his glass of bad white wine. He desperately wanted something to eat, but was damned if he would order one of the leather-edged ham sandwiches that places like this held ready for the foolhardy.

Galmoy was already a half hour late; this was so usual that Pearse had as a matter of course armed himself with a pencil and pad before he left the office. As he sat, his mind on nothing in particular, the pencil in his right hand sketched in signatures. *Oliver Wolcott*, said one, in bold letters, and under it a skillfully crabbed *Button Gwinnett*. Warming to the work, Pearse essayed an oversize, florid *John Hancock* and, pleased with it, added the requisite flourish beneath, crossed twice for emphasis. From the corner of his eye he saw Galmoy's white face peer in the steamy window and then dart away. Pearse sighed, knowing it would be at least ten minutes before the man himself came in, and then only if he had convinced himself that no one was following him. *G. Washington*, he wrote, then angrily crossed it out. It really was enough to drive you up the wall, wasting a perfectly good evening in this smelly rattrap, trying to make sense out of James Parnell Galmoy's paranoid fantasies.

Before becoming a customs broker, Pearse had spent five exasperating years dealing with other people who felt they had to veil the simplest action in a cloud of double-talk, and he knew it was futile to ask Galmoy to abandon his beloved little rituals. It had been bad enough when Pearse was dealing with the Puzzle Palace, but at least they'd been paying for his time. The man who called himself Galmoy was even more elliptical, and he wanted it all for nothing. The worst of it was that he had Pearse by the balls and knew it.

The saloon's door opened, so hesitantly that he guessed instantly who it had to be. He looked up from his sketch pad and feigned elaborate surprise. "Hey, James," he called. "Never expected to see you here. How's it going, man?"

It sounded suspiciously silly even to him, but the sodden barflies never twitched. Galmoy drew the corners of his mouth into an awful smile. "Hello, Michael," he said. "What a surprise."

• • •

"Let me see if I've got it straight," Pearse said, half an hour later. He was nearly rigid with boredom, exasperation, and hunger. "You want me to vet some kind of old manuscript, which might be worth a whole lot of money, only you don't have it and you won't tell me what it is—damn it, Galmoy, I *am* whispering—or who's supposed to have written it. You got me out here in the middle of a December storm for that? New York's full of manuscript experts. Nobody with anything really valuable's going to come to me for an opinion; I'm just your friendly neighborhood forger. They'll go to Patrick Hamilton or somebody. I would."

"Still, you *are* an expert, aren't you, Michael?" said Galmoy, his voice breathy and earnest and almost inaudible. He looked like one of the talking pastries in TV commercials—a round, doughy face and eyes so small and beady they strongly resembled raisins—but the effect was marred by his hair, which had been drenched and hung in damp, mouse-colored tendrils over his ears. His cheap plaid tie had run, tinting his white shirt blue and red and yellow. "You could tell if some documents were handwritten by a particular person. A historical person."

Pearse shrugged. "Maybe. Sure I could—if I can have validated samples of his work to check against." He paused. "This an *important* historical person?" he asked, keeping his tone uninterested.

"Perhaps. Does it matter?"

"It might. In the old days, before typewriters, important people had secretaries to write even their personal stuff. Napoleon used half a dozen at a time."

"You see?" Galmoy sounded delighted. "I didn't know that. You're just the man we need."

"So what do I do?" Pearse said. Suddenly, he felt a million years old. The prospect of being jerked around by Galmoy one more time made him want to hit somebody.

"Nothing," said Galmoy. "I've got everything set up. The people who have these documents will get in touch with you. Just sit by the phone."

"My phone, I suppose." Galmoy nodded. "You know, the office doesn't pay me to stay home and wait for the phone to ring. They pay me to come to work and get import food through the goddamn New York Customs House. I can't afford to sit around waiting for some friend of yours to call."

"I'm afraid," said Galmoy, in the precise voice he would sometimes assume, "that you haven't any choice. This is very important to us—to the cause. And you happen to be indispensable."

"Have I told you lately I don't give a fiddler's fuck for the cause?" Pearse said, mimicking Galmoy's prissy tone.

"That's too bad. I hate to have to drag in the you-know-what."

Pearse sighed. He knew it was going to come down to the bomb. The only one he had ever made, and only because he'd been juiced up at the time, unwilling to admit there was anything he couldn't do. "Call me Pierre the bomb builder," he muttered, but Galmoy apparently didn't know the old joke. "It didn't even work," he added unhappily.

"It worked well enough to blow the heads off two valuable men," said Galmoy. "Comrades," he added, giving it the long A.

Goddamn idiots, not comrades. He knew he had lost. "Give me some details."

"You'll do it?"

"I just said I would. But I can't operate in the dark. What's the deal?"

"Do you know a book-publishing house called Wild-Freeman?"

"Just heard the name, that's all."

"Small, old-line, respectable," said Galmoy. "You should be getting a call from them tomorrow or the next day. Probably from a woman named Diana Speed. She's their treasurer."

"She's my contact?"

"Absolutely not. She'll be your client. She's being touted onto you. Your contact is her secretary, Catherine O'Donnell."

"One of our own, bedad," said Pearse.

"A very devoted young lady," Galmoy said. "The granddaughter of our oldest and most faithful member."

"Her legs any good?"

"I've no idea." Galmoy was visibly angry. "Pearse, she's only eighteen. Her first job out of parochial school."

"So you're teaching her to double-cross her employer. That's class." He waved Galmoy's objection off. "Never mind. Tell me the rest."

"There's nothing to it. You take the job, look over the documents, and form your best opinion."

"Only I call you instead of my so-called client," said Pearse. "Is that it?"

Galmoy pushed his face into a rubbery smile. "As you see, there's nothing to it."

Pearse wondered what it would feel like to throw Galmoy over the bar and into the mirror behind it. It would, he decided, feel damned satisfying. "I'm not real fond of working for you people," he said quietly. "I didn't mind"—in a pig's ass—"doing you the odd favor, but I can't go on like this forever. It's got to stop here, Galmoy."

If there was one thing he hated most of all, Pearse thought, it was Galmoy's indulgent little smile. "And it will, Michael. This is the last request. Absolutely the last. You have my word on it."

"Seems to me I've heard that word before," Pearse replied.

"It's a pity," said Galmoy, "that you can't appreciate the cause. You're Irish; it should mean something to you."

"I'm fucking American," said Pearse. "But I grew up here

on Third Avenue, so I know about the cause, all right. You know what the cause is? 'Here's to the ould sod, and may I never have to go back there.' That's your cause—I've heard it all my life, from old farts too drunk to stand."

"England out of Ireland, that's all we're fighting for," Galmoy said quietly. "I'm sorry you can't see it." He pushed the chair back and got to his feet with a squelch. "Why don't you have another drink, Michael? Give yourself time to calm down." He swung toward the door, his feet hugely misshapen by the clumps of wet, green sawdust that stuck to his shoes. "Bartender," he said, "a Bushmills for my friend here. Make it a double," he added grandly, as he pushed out into the rain.

The bartender brought two brimming shot glasses to the table and set them down deliberately, right on *John Hancock*. "You don't want water with this," he said.

Pearse eyed the golden whiskey gloomily. As the bartender stood over him, he emptied one and then the other down his throat.

"And that'll be six dollars," the bartender said.

4. Manhattan: Lincoln Center

"Nessun dorma," the chorus sang softly, from offstage. And again, *"Nessun dorma."* Diana Speed leaned forward in the box, her fists clenched with apprehension. The Calaf had been in trouble right from the first scene, straining for notes that were well within his normal range, and she wondered that he had lasted this long. Every time he forced his normally limpid tenor over a dry patch, she felt a sympathetic abrasion in her own throat. Now he stepped forward into the spotlight, and her breath caught. Beside her, even Alan Troubridge, the eternal cynic, was still as a stone.

A hand touched her bare arm, and she jumped. "Miss Speed?"

She glared her answer.

"Telephone for you." The whisper was just audible. "Mr. Channing."

When she slipped back into the box, the aria was over. "Did he make it?" she whispered to Troubridge.

"Just barely. Men have got the Victoria Cross for less." He eyed her curiously, but waited until the curtain was down and the applause had ebbed before he spoke again. "Your peerless leader, I presume."

"You're not so dumb, Troubridge—for an Englishman. How'd you guess."

"Elementary, my dear Speed. Only the world's thirteenth richest man—"

"Seventeenth richest."

"Not according to my sources, love. As I was saying, only one of the world's *very* richest men could have got you out of your seat just before the climax of *Turandot*. And the Rajah is, as far as I know, the only very richest man you work for."

Diana got to her feet and allowed him to hold the mink for her. "Rich," she said, as if the word were bitter on her tongue. "Just rich doesn't make me jump."

Like so many tall, thin Englishmen, Troubridge affected a slight stoop. Though he was surprisingly attractive, in his angular fashion, there were moments when he reminded her irresistibly of a heron. Or was it a crane? In any case, it was at these moments when she almost felt she loved him. He leaned forward, his mouth right at her ear: "My dear, I like to think that I alone know exactly what makes you jump."

And then, just like that, he could make her want to kill him. She felt her ears burn. "You're a cocky bastard, Troubridge."

"Alas."

"Not even an apology?"

"Speed, I apologize—none quicker—for error. But never for insolence."

As they descended the staircase to the lobby, Diana was aware of the covert stares, reveled in them. The long, black dress emphasized her height and the perfection of her skin, and the mink was open to show the d'Arcy Vert, the emerald her mother occasionally let her wear, on its plain gold chain around her throat. Troubridge, who always wore black tie to the Met (setting an example, he said, for the colonials), was the perfect backdrop, subdued but elegant.

"The thing is," she said, "I owe him a lot."

They had had this conversation before. "Your exalted position, you mean."

"A chance to show what I could do," she replied. "You don't know how hard it is for a just-divorced woman of thirty to find a decent job. Even with a Wellesley BA and having run a successful congressional election campaign . . ."

"Not to mention your years at State."

She looked at him quickly, trying to catch him watching her expression. "Eight long ones. And you know the jobs I had to take?"

"I believe you've mentioned a few."

"Receptionist," she continued, unswerving. "Switchboard operator. Office temp for *lawyers*, for Christ's sake. I was at the bottom."

"And then, the summons from Olympus," he said, holding the door for her.

She smiled at the memory. "Not exactly Olympus. Grand Central Station."

"The private railroad car. I'd forgotten."

The faint boredom in his tone made her defensive. "Well, it's been three fantastic years. And the Rajah did it for me."

"I wish I could make you realize you did some of it yourself," said Troubridge. They were at the curb. He turned his unexpectedly boyish smile on her. "Speaking of private cars, madam—Her Majesty's own." It was not, thank God, the ambassador's limo, which she found grossly showy, and it certainly beat hailing a cab. The driver looked over his shoulder, one eyebrow barely raised, and Troubridge gave him a slight nod.

"Forgiven?" he asked her.

"Perhaps."

"What did the Rajah want, anyway?"

She felt the annoyance sweep over her again. "A revolt among the nerds," she said.

"I beg your pardon?"

"My loyal opposition. The editors at Wild-Freeman. They apparently have some huge, dizzy project going, and they're going to try and fog it through while I'm on vacation."

"Really? I thought nothing could fly without your signature."

"The Rajah lengthened their leash. He told Haskell he could approve up to . . . quite a large amount. On his own."

"And that's what he's doing? Sounds like it's in his brief. What's the crisis?"

His tone was elaborately casual, so much so that she automatically edited her reply. "It's a lot of money—a lot for W-F, anyway. The Rajah's going to be overseas for a few days, and he wants me to check it out."

"But you're on vacation," Troubridge protested.

"I *was* on vacation," she said. "Tomorrow morning, bright and early, I'm back to being girl executive." The car pulled silently to a halt. She glanced out the window at the deserted sidewalk and the brownstone beyond. "I'm not going to ask you in tonight," she said, opening the door.

He was faster than she'd expected, out of the car and on the pavement beside her. "Still angry?"

"Oh, that? Hell, no." She grinned at him. "Besides, you were right."

"Then why the curbside dismissal? D'you know what this will do to my reputation at the consulate?"

"Just another small chapter in Britain's long retreat," she replied. "Actually, milord, I don't feel up to it, with tomorrow to worry about."

"I'll behave," he said. "Surely the embassy's box seats are worth one tiny glass of port."

She reached in her bag and extracted a formidable key case. "The operative words are *one* and *tiny*," she warned.

Inside, she settled into an armchair, pointedly avoiding the couch. On one knee at the liquor cabinet, Troubridge asked, "Where is it?"

"The port? In the fridge."

He was visibly shocked. "You put my Cockburn in the bloody icebox, woman? What kind of savage are you?"

She shrugged. "I like it cold." Still muttering, he brought the two glasses. "If you really want it warm," she suggested, "try giving it a fifteen-second jolt in the microwave."

He stared at her, beyond words, until he saw the blandness of her smile. "Here's your poor, desecrated booze, Speed. God knows how I put up with you."

She accepted the glass, kicked off her shoes, and put her feet up on the glass-topped coffee table. Looking around her, she was conscious as always of a pleasantly warm sense of security. The apartment, furnished with the doubly sweet money her ex-husband had thought she could never retrieve, was her nest, her fortress, her eyrie; no one else, not even Troubridge, had a key. It wasn't large—a living room that fronted on East 50th Street, bedroom overlooking the back yard, kitchen and bath off the corridor connecting them. But every stick and thread was exactly right, the result of her own unrelenting perfectionism. Perched on the edge of the couch, and looking more like a long-legged bird than ever, Troubridge had just finished saying something. "Sorry," she said. "Not paying attention."

"You didn't really miss anything, not hearing the *Nessun dorma*. Heroic, yes, but otherwise unmemorable."

"I suppose." The mirror over the fireplace was crooked again.

"Still can't get over the Rajah, though," Troubridge mused. "I don't suppose he told you why he was in such a flap."

Now that was definitely odd, she thought. Troubridge never pressed her about what went on at W-F. Quite the opposite. Perhaps it was just a legacy of paranoia, from those years in the back rooms of State Department Intelligence. She found herself wondering again exactly what Troubridge did "on the cultural side" of the consulate; decided, on an impulse she could not name, to make a couple of calls and find out. Without answering, she got to her feet and went over to the newly installed marble mantel. She moved the mirror a careful half inch, stepped back to check it. If I had a slightly less hawklike beak, she thought, I would be beautiful.

"The dial from your wall safe projects too far," said Troubridge from right behind her, "It's pushing the mirror out. A little to the left. There, that's better." His arms were around her, his lips just behind her ear. "Very much better," he said, several minutes later.

His legs were too long, his knees absurdly knobby, his hands and feet too big. He excited her desperately, and scared her sometimes as well. "Oh, all right," she said. "But you'd better be right about making me jump."

• • •

Lying beside him in the dark, Diana felt the wild hammering of her heart gradually slow. He had done it again, damn him: Her iron self-possession was the attribute she prized above all others, and he was the only man—the only person—who could wrench her out of it. In the delirious moments of ecstasy, nothing else mattered; afterward, she found herself blushing to recall the things she'd done and said. He was so still she knew he must be awake.

"Contessa?" It was the nickname he used when feeling contrite; she had never told him that the reference—to the forgiving Countess Almaviva of *Figaro*—annoyed her.

"Yes."

"I rather lost control. *Perdóno.*"

"So did I, Troubridge. No pardon required."

"Are you sure you have to go to the office tomorrow?"

"Later this morning," she corrected him. "I'm afraid so."

"The Rajah must really be concerned about that project. What was it again?"

There is no such thing as a third coincidence, she thought. Damn.

THURSDAY

One: Diana

She rolled over at seven, instantly awake. Troubridge had gone, of course: One of his attractions was a talent for unobtrusive disappearance. She lay staring upward for a few minutes, replaying last night with him, feeling the excitement galvanize her again. What she let him do to—with—her was her own business, she told the ceiling firmly. In the crisp light of morning, postcoital embarrassment was only mawkish. Anyway, there were more immediate things to think about. Up and at 'em.

She bounded out of bed, resolutely ignoring the tall, nakedly pink figure that flashed across the mirror. As she moved about the bedroom, picking up pieces of clothing that had been tossed here and there, Diana considered the plotters at Wild-Freeman who'd cut short her vacation—who thought they could put one over on her—and allowed her irritation to fan itself into a controlled smolder.

While washing her hair, she toyed with entrance lines: "Gotcha!" had the twin appeals of triumph and brevity, but she favored the more subtly demoralizing: slipping into her regular chair at the meeting with a demure "Hope I'm not late." That should set everyone nicely off balance. She could almost hear the liquid click of dropping jaws as she entered the room.

Her sense of anticipation heightened through breakfast. It

was no more than her usual—fresh-squeezed orange juice, two scrambled eggs and three strips of bacon, hash-browned potatoes, a couple of slices of buttered toast with homemade (by her domesticated sister) beach plum jelly—all washed down with two mugs of coffee barely off the boil, and fervent thanks for the hyperactive metabolism that allowed her to eat like a halfback while gaining not an ounce.

She set the third big, steaming mug on her dresser while she surveyed her walk-in closet for the appropriate costume. After some thought, she settled on a tweed suit with lapels edged in dark velvet. Tweed because it was book publishing, and dark velvet because they would be talking about money. A restrained white blouse that buttoned to the throat—she had no intention of competing with Judith Sanders in the Embonpoint Sweepstakes—and, on her lapel, her great-grandfather's heavy gold fob seal, the only jewelry she wore at work. The resulting effect ought to be formal enough for the lesson she had in mind to teach, but not so heavily symbolic as to make her look like the Queen of the Night.

It was, after all, barely a year since the Rajah had installed her as Wild-Freeman's treasurer. ("Shoved her down our throats," as one senior placeholder put it, shortly before his termination.) For some months thereafter, she had been treated like the natural daughter of Simon Legree and Lucrezia Borgia, but recently the staff seemed to be getting used to the ubiquitous presence of a driving, efficient, intolerant, capable financial officer—or if they weren't completely won over, at least they no longer flinched against the wall as she strode past. Though she would never have admitted it, being feared had no appeal to her.

She considered herself in the full-length mirror and approved the result. As her mother so often pointed out, *le bon Dieu* had, for His own inscrutable reasons, made Diana six feet tall, so there was nothing for it but to stand up to every inch. Troubridge had compared her features to those of an elegant bird of prey, and once she accepted the idea she found it pleasing. Her gray-blue eyes could, she knew, seem chilly to an observer, and her lips were not as full as some women's, but her skin was still nearly perfect, and the frown lines that had begun to form between her brows seemed in recent weeks to be fading. Her ash blonde hair was short and straight, which she found convenient for the brushed-back style that suited both her life and her cheekbones.

The editorial meeting was scheduled for ten-thirty, or so the Rajah's informant had said. (Diana wondered who it might be; knew there was no point in asking—the Rajah never revealed his sources to anyone.) No Wild-Freeman editorial meeting had ever started on time while she had been there, but to be on the safe side she cut one game out of her regular squash match at the Princeton Club, to the transparent relief of her gasping male opponent, so that she could shower and relax and still arrive exactly on the instant, icily unflustered.

At ten-twenty-five she stepped aboard the elevator, acknowledging the uniformed starter's obsequious greeting with a smile that did not reach her eyes.

Someone's going to get it, the starter thought, quickly pressing the button that closed the car's doors and sent it wheezing upward. Thirty seconds later, the elevator alarm bell began to ring. "Oh, shit," the starter said. "It's going to be me."

At twelve-fourteen, Diana climbed through the escape hatch in the elevator's side and into the car that had been positioned in the next shaft. Slender as she was, the opening was narrower still, and she stepped aboard embellished with a streak of grease down one sleeve of her new winter-weight raincoat. The starter, who had supervised her rescue, was foaming apologies, but Diana cut him off. "Sixteenth floor," she said, between clenched teeth.

She exploded from the car with such force that the receptionist's copy of *Spy* was blown right out of her hands. "Miss Speed," she gasped. "I thought . . . your coat . . ." Diana swept down the narrow hall, whose walls some long-gone office manager had covered with a tweedlike fabric that always made her feel as if she were traversing a nubbly esophagus. On either side were the cubbyhole offices of editors and their assistants and their assistants' assistants—tiny, windowless chambers stacked with dusty manuscripts and unanswered correspondence. At the end of the corridor, the door to the conference room was open. A vagrant wisp of cigarette smoke, caught in the light, floated into the corridor.

Inside, it was deserted. Chairs had been casually pushed back from the long oval table, and scraps of paper littered its surface. As Diana stood in the doorway, a discreet cough behind her made her start. It was one of the maintenance men: "Good morning, Miss Speed."

"Morning, John."

He moved past Diana and began scooping crumpled papers into the plastic bag he was carrying. Diana watched him, her lips pursed, for a few seconds, then turned on her heel and stalked back down the corridor, through the reception area, and into the territory of the Sales and Promotion departments. She stopped at a closed door; a chastely lettered plate at eye height read MISS AARON, and under it a trained hand had added "drinks a little" in 24-point felt-tip Times Roman. Diana knocked and walked in. The woman behind the big, cluttered desk was tiny and wizened, face like a marmoset's, fringed with thin white hair in violent disarray. Her deeply lined face was heavily made up, but the penciled-in eyebrows were a good quarter inch above the stubble of her own, and the lipstick was only approximately over her mouth. Her fingernails were thickly painted and bitten off short, and she held a cigarette in one hand and a half-full glass—brandy, by the smell—in the other. She watched in silence as Diana entered, tore off her coat and threw it in the corner, swept a pile of papers off the room's only other chair, and hurled herself into it. Silently, the older woman held out her glass. "Here, love—I think you need this more than I do," she said, in a deep, hoarse voice.

Diana managed a weak smile. "No thanks, Milly. I will steal a cigarette, though."

Milly Aaron's left eyebrows rose, more or less together, and she held out the pack of unfiltered Camels. "That bad, is it?"

Diana took one, lit it, and drew in deeply. She felt the satisfying stab all the way down to her lungs. "So what happened?" she demanded.

"At the meeting? It was a tour de force, a super-deluxe Judith Sanders production number. They swallowed it whole." Milly paused and drank a longshoreman's swallow of brandy, which set her coughing. Diana watched in silence as the spasms subsided, knowing better than to make any comment. At fifty-five Milly looked seventy, and the only question was whether her lungs or her liver would give out first. (The mailroom had set up a pool on it, and Milly herself had put a hundred dollars on cirrhosis.) She was also a publicist of genius, able to stagger faultlessly through the minefield that separated her natural cynicism and the wide-eyed credulity her job required. She was the only person at Wild-Freeman whom Diana fully trusted.

"How big was that whole?" Diana asked.

"Half a million advance on signing. Straight fifteen percent royalty, and no foreign rights for us. Guaranteed promotion budget I don't even believe myself . . . You sure you want to hear the rest?"

"That'll hold for me for the moment," Diana replied. "I suppose somebody was going to write a book in return for all this largesse. Could I see the TI sheet, please?"

Milly's grin uncovered a palisade of huge, yellowed teeth. "No Title Information sheet, love. No written specs at all. A verbal presentation by the author himself—one of your favorite authors."

There was, Diana thought, no question that Milly had a connoisseur's taste for disaster; she was clearly relishing the details of this fiasco. Diana, on the other hand, was thinking of the Rajah's reaction. "Just feed it to me bit by bit, Milly. Start at the beginning, go on to the end, then stop."

"Right, Your Highness," Milly replied. "The author, as Judith took great care to point out, is Wild-Freeman's biggest seller . . ."

"Not Patricia Orme."

"The very one," Milly agreed. "But under his true colors: Patrick Sarsfield."

"Son of a bitch," breathed Diana, in genuine surprise. The identity of Patricia Orme, author of a dozen panting titles whose heavy-breasted covers decorated airport newsstands across America, was perhaps the only genuine secret in book publishing—a secret so artfully manipulated by Milly Aaron that it had propelled a run-of-the-boudoir historical novelist into a perennial best-seller.

"Oh, he's a son of a bitch, all right," Milly agreed. "And a tacky one, too, with a ghastly fake Irish accent. But he's got one hell of an idea this time."

As Diana well knew, Milly's profession made her peculiarly vulnerable to off-the-wall proposals, but the older woman was also a shrewd judge of what the public would swallow. Her judgments in that area were always worth hearing. "Tell me about it," said Diana.

"Mary Queen of Scots," Milly replied. "Sarsfield says she's the biggest romantic drawing card in history, and he's right—she puts Marilyn Monroe back with Tugboat Annie. There've been movies, plays, even an opera written about her, not to mention a dozen successful books."

"One of them by Miss Orme herself," Diana put in. "Did Judith's heaving bosom make you all forget? *Queen Betrayed*, wasn't it—or was that about Berengaria and Richard the Gay? Anyway, I do recall we printed 125,000 copies and had to eat 50,000 of them."

"What sharp claws you have, dear," Milly said. "There was a decent paperback sale, as I'm sure you also recall. Which W-F split. Likewise a Guild selection."

"Only half of a dual," Diana corrected. "Still, I take your point: I do have a little trouble being fair to Judith's projects. But the basic question remains—why another Mary Stuart book?"

"Thought you'd never ask. The big thing about Mary is that she's still so controversial, even after four hundred years. You can't write about her without taking sides, and it always boils down to the same thing: Was she a noble, embattled queen surrounded by rotten traitors, or a sex-crazed dimwit who helped blow her husband to pieces."

"Strangled," said Diana. "Darnley wasn't blown up. He was strangled, and the explosion—"

"Shut up, dear—I'm telling this. The point is, Mary's an enigma, a mystery. Readers love a mystery, but they love the answer even more, and Sarsfield's got it."

"In a novel?" Disappointment swept over her in a wave. How could Milly have fallen for so pathetic a pitch?

"No, of course not," Milly snapped. "What kind of sucker do you think I am? This is a true-life mystery, and the clues are those letters Mary wrote to her lover, what's-his-name. Sarsfield's got the originals, and we're going to run glossies of them as a sixteen-page signature."

"Bothwell. Mary's lover was Bothwell," said Diana absently, her mind racing back to her college history classes. "Wait a minute. Weren't those letters—the Casket Letters—forged? Mary said so herself. And anyway, the originals disappeared. Burned, most likely."

"But they *weren't* burned," said Milly triumphantly. "Sarsfield's found them. The original Casket Letters, plus one nobody knew about. And he says he can prove they're real."

"Oh, he does, does he?" Diana replied, her suspicions at full stretch. "How can he do that?"

"That's not my department." Milly shrugged. "You can ask him yourself."

"He's still in the building?"

Milly glanced at her watch. "If you hurry. Sarsfield and Judith and a couple of others were going to the Four Seasons to celebrate the contract, but they're probably in Haskell's office."

"Celebrate, is it," said Diana, getting to her feet. "I'll give them celebrate."

Outside Milly's door Diana turned left, back toward Editorial, then stopped in her tracks. The Rajah: She should probably call his office to pass on an interim report. No. It would sound to him like an excuse or a cry for help, and he would never hear either one from her.

•   •   •

Someone had produced a bottle of champagne, and the noisy group in Haskell Rose's office were splashing it into little paper containers. Diana paused outside the open door, unnoticed, just as Judith Sanders raised her cup, crying, "I've got one! I've got a toast!"

"Hear! Hear!" said the big stranger who must be Patrick Sarsfield—a solidly built J. Arthur Rank country squire, with wind-roughened face and white hair brushed straight back; a generous mouth and a nose slightly askew, and bushy brows that nearly hid his close-set blue eyes. He was facing Judith and, over her shoulder, the door. As he caught sight of Diana, his eyes widened slightly and one corner of his mouth seemed to twist in amusement.

Judith, whose striking figure was just beginning to erode (though not quickly enough to suit her many enemies, all female), was famously protective of her authors—always ready to grant the ultimate favors to anyone who might advance their cause or to savage those who, like Diana, got in their way. Flushed with triumph and emotion, she rose on tiptoe and cried, "Here's to the dragon slayers! Here's to *us!*"

Diana caught the reference instantly and so, to judge by their pained expressions, did Haskell Rose and Maury Thomas, the sales director. No such awareness showed on the faces of the two others in the room—Tim Mark, Wild-Freeman's youngest editor and Judith's adoring protégé; or bulky, graying Brand Ellison, the managing editor and one of publishing's sizable cadre of self-destructs. As Maury Thomas tipped his paper cup up to drain it off, his eye fell on Diana, his hand clenched automatically, and a gout of champagne rose several inches in the air before collapsing over his heavy silver ID bracelet. Haskell Rose's gaze, following the momentary fountain upward, locked on Diana's; his face turned a surprising shade of gray, rather like wet cement, and he muttered, "Oh, Christ."

Judith, staring at her colleagues, was clearly bewildered. "What is it?" she asked, and swung around.

Diana stepped into the silent office, just as Sarsfield remarked, to no one in particular, "Enter the dragon."

* * * *

Five minutes later, the frozen tableau had reconstituted itself, with Diana seated magisterially behind Haskell's big desk and the others in a semicircle of uncomfortable chairs facing her. She concentrated on radiating calm authority while she quickly added up the faces before her.

Brand Ellison sat with his eyes unfocused and his mouth slightly open. Even before lunch his mind was already fifteen minutes behind what was happening around him; he was not a factor. Maury Thomas, that buttery smooth old bandit, was looking pleased with himself, which gave Diana pause; Maury had been in publishing since slightly after Gutenberg without ever reading a book, and he had yet to be caught on the wrong side of any issue. Haskell was attempting to look unconcerned, but when he lifted his hands off his thighs, oblong damp spots remained on his trouser legs. Judith, predictably, was radiating eager defiance, righteous indignation, and just a soupçon of wariness around the whites of her eyes. Standing behind her, one hand lightly on her shoulder, Tim Mark clearly envisioned himself as the young Perseus, ready to leap in front of his Andromeda; Diana could barely look at his stern, unlined face without feeling the urge to put him over her knee.

And then there was Sarsfield. He had appropriated the only chair with arms, which seemed to give him an obscure moral advantage. If he was guilty, frightened, defiant, or defensive he gave no sign of it. His manner, Diana observed with amused annoyance, managed to align him with her against the others. *We are the two who matter,* his calm assurance told her. And of course he was right.

Diana unveiled her most winning smile for him. "I do hate to impose on you, Mr. Sarsfield," she began, "but perhaps I might ask just a few questions about your project, before everyone becomes too self-congratulatory."

"It's *our* project, Diana," Judith put in, her voice quivering with anger. "We voted on it at the meeting. Unanimously."

One of Judith's great strengths, Diana had early discovered, was her willingness to start a shrieking, top-of-the-lungs fight in any setting whatever. People—men especially—would go to extraordinary lengths to avoid setting her off. It was, however, quite possible to sidestep her: "I beg your pardon, Judith," Diana replied, all sweet surprise. "I wasn't aware that a meeting was writing the book. I thought Mr. Sarsfield was the author."

"Well, of course . . ." Judith began, but Sarsfield interrupted her.

"I'd be delighted, Miss Speed." A modestly self-deprecating laugh. "I'll do the whole presentation again, if you like—I've not had such a grand audience in years."

"I'm sure that won't be necessary." Diana's smile was almost genuine. "Let me just see if I've got the deal straight: As I understood it, your book is to be based on the Casket Letters, which you yourself have, and which you've determined are genuine. Right so far?"

"Oh, dear." Sarsfield's face was a mask of mock dismay. "Surely I never meant to put it quite like that. But yes—the book will rest on the original letters that Mary Queen of Scots wrote to her lover, James Hepburn, Earl of Bothwell. I haven't been able to test the actual letters for genuineness, though of course we'll want to do that. But their source—their provenance, if you will—convinces me beyond the shadow of a doubt that these are the real thing. And they show, again beyond any possible doubt, that Mary Stuart was . . ."

Had that ellipsis been evasion or accident? Diana interrupted before Sarsfield's rhetoric could sweep them both away: "But you have them yourself. The letters."

"That's the very thing that's brought me to New York," he answered smoothly. "To pick them up."

From the corner of her eye, Diana saw Judith's head snap around. "They belong to someone, then?"

"Well, of course they do," said Sarsfield. There was a momentary flash of nerves under the joviality, but it was gone as quickly as it had showed. "That's what makes the whole thing so remarkable. The owner, who lives in this very city, is able to provide an exact pedigree for the letters, every step through four centuries and more."

"I see," Diana replied.

Before she could continue, Judith interrupted: "But Patrick, what about those letters you faxed me? I thought you had the originals."

"Photocopies of the originals," he said, and turned quickly back to Diana. "They're what I've done my outline from. They're complete and entirely readable."

"But you've not seen the originals, either?" Diana put in. "Who's verified them?" A vibrating silence filled Haskell's office. Patrick Sarsfield smiled apologetically at Judith. "Just so," said Diana.

"As I see it," Judith began, "it's a question of whether—"

"No," Diana said. "I'm afraid not."

"We've started badly," Sarsfield put in. "It's my fault, of course—I was too eager. Perhaps it'd be best if we just called the whole thing off."

He seems to mean it, Diana thought, as all the editors began gabbling objections at once. Is it a bluff? Sarsfield was attempting to calm Judith, who had burst into angry tears, but he darted a quick, sharp look at Diana.

Partly a bluff, she decided. She raised her hand for silence, without result, then brought her palm down on Haskell's desk with an echoing smack that cut through the raised voices.

They were quiet, except for Judith's suppressed snuffling, and Diana addressed Sarsfield: "No need to become apocalyptic, at least not yet. Did you say the contract was already signed?"

"Why, yes," Sarsfield said innocently. "I was quite

surprised when Judith brought it to the meeting." He grinned. "Usually, it takes you people a month or so to answer a letter, never mind write a contract."

He was right enough on that score, Diana thought. Judith's snuffling had shut off abruptly, and she was watching Diana with wary, red-rimmed eyes. "What about the advance?" Diana asked.

"I have the check right here," Sarsfield replied. He pulled an envelope from his inside jacket pocket and held it out. "Would you like it back, Miss Speed?"

"Oh, that won't be necessary, Mr. Sarsfield." She let him wait for a moment before she continued: "Why don't you just hold on to it until everything's resolved?"

"To be sure," he said, repocketing the envelope. "And just how shall we—as you say—*resolve* the situation?"

She had not fully worked it out, but she knew the first step at least. "A manuscript expert," she said. "That's what we'll want right off. How quickly can you get hold of the originals?" She let her voice emphasize the last word just enough to get a tight smile from Sarsfield.

"A couple of hours," he replied, with easy confidence. "I can take a cab out to . . . go get them right away, and your expert can start on them this afternoon."

What expert? Diana thought. Aloud: "And ruin your expensive lunch? Certainly not." Out of the corner of her eye, she saw Haskell looking nervous. "Now you just toddle off and celebrate," she continued. "I have a few things to do, and then I'll come by your hotel . . ."

"The Algonquin," he put in.

"Where else? Five-thirty, in the lobby?"

"Splendid," Sarsfield said. He was on his feet, leaning over Haskell's desk with his hand extended. "A pleasure doing business with you," he said. "I know we can work this out."

One way or another, she was thinking, as the others babbled their way down the corridor. One way or another. Maury Thomas had hung back and was clearly waiting for a word with her, but she picked up Haskell's phone and dialed her own extension. "Cathy? It's me. I'm coming down in a couple of minutes, but I want you to do something right away. Call Mr. Harms at Fidelity and tell him I'm temporarily stopping a check we issued this morning." As she spoke, Maury's cherubic face lit with amusement and mock surprise. "Five hundred thousand dollars—yes, that's what I said—made out to Patrick Sarsfield. Get the check number from Accounting. Harms may be stuffy about accepting the stop order from you, but tell him that if his bank cashes that check, I will personally feed him to my pet stoat. S-T-O-A-T. It's a kind of weasel, Cathy. Now go to it." Putting down the phone, she matched Maury's smile. "Just playing it safe," she said.

"So you don't trust our star author?"

"Not when he's surrounded by Judith Sanders," she replied. "A bottle of Veuve Clicquot and she might get a clever idea."

"Oh, I don't think she'll try anything foolish," he said diffidently. "The book itself is too good to risk it."

"You think so?"

He hesitated, turning her question over, as his smile dissipated. "Yes," he said at last. "Yes, it is. There's no top to this one, Diana. It could go all the way."

He was in earnest, and she suddenly remembered that Haskell Rose wasn't the only Wild-Freeman executive aching for a blockbuster best-seller—or for the big chair in the empty president's office.

"Of course," he added, "it all depends on those letters being real."

"Doesn't it?" she replied.

•   •   •

The previous treasurer of Wild-Freeman had been a desiccated gnome who wore the same shiny blue suit every day and inhabited an airless burrow just off the Sales Department. The only decoration in his office was the printed motto WHEN THE GOING GETS TOUGH, THE TOUGH GET GOING, hung over his

desk in a plastic frame from Lamston's. His rectitude was as
legendary as his penny-pinching, and the Wild-Freeman staff
were baffled when he was one of the first to be let go.

Diana, whose management style was closely modeled on
the Rajah's, had laughed aloud when she was shown his
office, and claimed instead the fifteenth floor's only corner
suite, then occupied by the advertising director. The main
room was large and airy, with a superb view up Fifth Avenue
and a frequently unnerving vista into a dentist's office across
47th Street. Diana promptly voted herself a ten-thousand-
dollar decorating budget that not only put an ankle-deep beige
carpet under her vast teak desk, and new drapes around the
windows, but also hung a framed Stobart print on the wall
facing her and placed beneath it an elegant second desk
whose roll top concealed her computer.

Diana's computer was a smaller version of Cathy O'Donnell's, which with its sound-shielded printer occupied the
entire surface of a large steel table in the anteroom. Cathy's
own desk stood just outside Diana's office door, as if
symbolizing the watchdog aspect of the girl's job. But as
Diana walked into the office, Cathy was standing beside it,
looking miserable.

"No problem with the bank?"

"No, Miss Speed. It's all set."

"Then what's the matter, kiddo?"

Catherine O'Donnell was a short, fat, blotchy girl from the
uttermost Bronx; Diana had hired her right out of parochial
school, sent her at company expense through the best
secretarial course available, and even staked her to speech
training that moved the apparent source of her voice a little
further away from her adenoids. She was bright enough, but
an incurable romantic—probably because (as Troubridge
unkindly pointed out) her appearance precluded firsthand
experience. Now, as she struggled to answer Diana, her eyes
filled and her nose began to run. At last she managed to blurt
something out, and after a long two seconds Diana decoded
it: "This morning? You mean the meeting?"

Cathy gulped convulsively and nodded. She blew her nose

twice, stood stiffly upright. "I tried to get you, Miss Speed. I tried and tried. But I only found out at nine-thirty there was even going to *be* a meeting, and you were already gone."

"Oh, that's all right," Diana said. "Really it is," she insisted, seeing that serious reassurance was required. "Not your fault at all. Don't even think it."

The girl began to glow through her tears, and Diana wondered, not for the first time, if a devotion like Cathy's might be more trouble than it was worth. Why on earth, Diana asked herself, did she—a woman who despised the gibberish of "nurturing" and "supportiveness"—spend so much time holding her secretary's head above water? Noblesse oblige was the tempting explanation, but Diana's mother, noblesse to her marrow, would have dispatched a dozen Cathy O'Donnells to the Bastille without a second thought.

Troubridge had a theory, of course. He'd started to trot it out one evening, had got as far as "suppressed mother instinct" when the icy anger on Diana's face had dried him up. It was the only time he'd breached the unwritten rule that kept their conversations off the dangerously personal.

Cathy seemed to have slipped into a mute, adoring daze, something that never failed to exasperate Diana. "I've got another job for you," she said.

The girl's mouth shut, and she picked up her pencil and steno pad.

"I need to find a handwriting expert," she began, thinking as she spoke. "Fast. Someone who's good but not too well known."

"Here in New York?"

"Definitely. And someone who knows . . . who's familiar with the handwriting of historical figures. Sixteenth-century figures."

Cathy looked puzzled, and Diana decided to amplify. "You heard what the meeting was about?"

"Not exactly, Miss Speed." Which meant, Diana knew, only that the mailroom messenger had not yet made his noon round. "Some big project."

"That's right. A book about Mary Queen of Scots." She was on the point of explaining, when Cathy's expression told her it was unnecessary. "You've heard of her."

"Oh, yes. The nuns told us about her. She was a very beautiful woman, but she lived a very wicked life. Because she was brought up in France," she added.

"That's all it takes," said Diana.

"But she was all right in the end," Cathy continued. She saw Diana's look of surprise and elaborated: "She died for the Faith. She was a martyr."

"Oh. Well, the author of this book claims to have some letters of Mary's, but before we put the company's cash on the line, we have to know if they're real."

Cathy was writing busily again. "I see," she said.

"I suppose you could try the public library for starters. Maybe the Metropolitan Museum. But I need someone as soon as possible. So make me a list, with qualifications, of six or so. By three this afternoon."

"Six by three," Cathy repeated, writing it down.

"Don't tell anyone you talk to that it's about Mary Stuart," Diana warned. "Sixteenth-century handwriting, but don't say whose. Go to it, kiddo."

"Right, Miss Speed," she replied, turning quickly away to her desk. Almost, Diana thought, as if she didn't want to meet her boss's eye, but that was ridiculous.

Two: Pearse

By the time his telephone finally rang, Pearse had forgotten he was waiting for it, and the bell made him jump. Annoyed at his own reaction, he snatched the phone up. "Yes?"

"This is Mr. Swallow's friend," said the girl's voice. Mr. Swallow? He groped for a second before he remembered, with a sour grin: The name was so perfectly un-Galmoy—who less like a darting bird than the doughy little man?—but it told him at once who he was talking to.

"Hello, Catherine," he said.

"Oh. Is it all right to use real names?" She sounded disappointed.

"It's a lot easier," he replied. "All the best terrorists are doing it."

Silence. Well, of course—she thought of herself as a patriot. An idealist. *England out of Ireland,* he reminded himself. "Come on, love: Speak to me."

"I have some information for you." Her voice was chilly.

"Shoot."

"The book that Patricia Orme is writing: It's about Mary Queen of Scots."

She seemed to expect some kind of response, so Pearse allowed her a brusque "Right."

"The author says she has the letters Mary wrote. The

original Casket Letters, you know? Miss Speed—my boss—has to find out if they're real before she goes ahead with the project."

Oh, for God's sake, Pearse was thinking. The oldest chestnut in forgery, and Galmoy's grabbed for it with both hands. He tossed the girl another "Right."

"She told me to get her a list of manuscript experts," Catherine O'Donnell said, sounding more animated now. "Experts on sixteenth-century handwriting. I got five real names, and yours."

He bridled silently. "Where are you telling her you found my name?"

"Well, that's it. I don't exactly know."

He had foreseen this contingency. "Tell her that Mr. Galmoy . . ." He paused, waiting for her reaction.

"G-A-L-M-O-Y?" Her tone told him she didn't recognize his real name. Something to remember.

"Right. Of the New York Graphological Society. He recommended me. Give her Gal—Swallow's number. I'll call on ahead and get him prepped for it."

"Hey, that's sharp," she said, brightening. "But what if she double-checks the number herself?"

Not as dumb as her awful accent made her sound. "She won't find a listing," he replied. "Anyway, doesn't she trust you?"

"Yes, she does." Guilt and defensiveness, in about equal portions, he thought. To his own surprise, Pearse found he felt sorry for the girl.

"It'll work," he reassured her. "Just be cool. Wait—who are the other five names?"

She read them off, all of them men Pearse had heard of, with formidable backgrounds. "Honey," he said, "that's a terrible list."

"What do you mean?" she demanded. "Miss Speed wanted the best."

"Maybe so, but what *we* want—you, me, and Mr. Swallow—is for your Miss Speed to choose Michael Matthew Pearse. My qualifications are okay, but not quite in that

league." He was fumbling, as he spoke, through a tattered
directory with scuffed cardboard covers. "Now, I'll give you
five names to replace those you've got, with quick sketches
of each of them. When you give her the list, put my name
fourth."

"You really think of everything, don't you?" The girl
sounded quite sincere, and Pearse found himself warming to
her tone.

"I'd better."

"Mr. Pearse," she began, and dried up.

There was clearly something on her mind. He took a deep
leap into the dark: "Look, Catherine, don't worry. I'm as
good as any of those others. You won't get stuck with a
turkey."

"It's not me I was thinking about, Mr. Pearse," she said.
"Mr. Swallow promised me that Diana—Miss Speed—
wouldn't get in trouble . . ."

"And she won't," Pearse said, willing her to believe him.
"You know how Mr. Swallow values his promise, I'm sure."

"I guess it's all right," she said, so dubious that he
wondered if she knew the doughy man as well as Pearse
himself did.

"It will be," he said. "You have Mick Pearse's word, too.
I'll look out for your Miss Speed."

"Thank you," she said, her voice small. "Thanks a lot,
Mr. Pearse."

"My friends call me Mick," he said. "And I'll presume
and call you Cathy. We're fighting in the same line, love, and
for the same good cause."

"Yes, we are," she said. "Tell me those other names,
Mick."

•   •   •

He dialed Galmoy's number, self-disgust bitter in his
mouth. How easily the Gaelic drivel poured, once it started.
No wonder old men fell under the spell. And just how much
good did it do Mick Pearse to know better?

Galmoy answered on the second ring, his voice breathy and indistinct, as if he were talking through a handkerchief. For all Pearse knew, he might be.

"It's Pearse. Now listen carefully." He ran quickly through his conversation with Catherine O'Donnell.

"I see," Galmoy said, his speech clearer now. Pearse could picture the little man, crouched over his scarred desk, in that amazing rubbish heap of an apartment he inhabited, out in Park Slope. "So you want me to pretend to be this—" he paused, perhaps consulting his notes— "New York Graphological Society. Won't she be suspicious that it's a 718 area code?"

Pearse had not thought of that; he was momentarily annoyed with himself but dismissed the objection: "Brooklyn's still part of New York, last I heard. Anyway, it might even sound more authentic: small, scholarly institution in an outer borough; too much integrity for a fashionable address; ultimate authority in handwriting information. That kind of thing." As he spoke, his words made the deception come alive in his head.

"I guess it'll work," Galmoy said slowly. "It'll have to: We only get one swing. Now, what exactly *are* those qualifications of yours?"

Pearse had already assembled them. When he was finished reading them off, slowly enough so that Galmoy could take them down, he waited. There was no reaction at the other end, and he heard himself saying: "It's all real, you know. I took those courses, and passed 'em all. I did those research jobs, and the people I worked for will say so."

Still silence. At last, Galmoy said, "We need something more. Something dramatic, to nail it down."

"Like what?" Pearse said. "I just gave you the works." But warning bells were going off in the back of his head.

"I'm afraid we're going to have to mention what you were doing in Washington."

"Fuck that," said Pearse flatly. "Those people don't love me anymore. Besides, it won't do any good. You know how they are: 'We don't even exist, therefore we cannot confirm or deny anything.'"

"All the better. Leaves a nice sense of mystery." Galmoy was obviously enjoying himself, and Pearse gritted his teeth. "I can drop a couple of hints—hush-hush service to the nation, vastly important expertise . . ."

"For Christ's sake," said Pearse, "I was only vetting papers for spooks. And how did you find out, anyway?"

"Never mind, my boy. The point is, she won't be able to check, and it sounds impressive. Just leave it to me."

"I guess I'll have to." He was trying to recall his few conversations with Galmoy; surely he had never mentioned the Agency. And surely the mingy Provos couldn't reach into that super-secret hive.

"I'm glad you agree," Galmoy was saying. "Now, what about the papers themselves? These Casket Letters."

Pearse felt a fierce amusement in letting Galmoy have it, full strength: "They're utter bullshit. A political fake, set up by Mary Stuart's enemies to discredit her. And the so-called letters all disappeared for good once they'd served their purpose. Obviously, nobody wanted them around anymore."

He could hear the dismay Galmoy was trying to hide. "But Sarsfield knows all that. He may not be a historian, but he's written great, fat books about the period."

"Wait a minute. Who's this Sarsfield?"

"Oh, that. Patrick Sarsfield is the real name of the person who writes as Patricia Orme. And now that I've told you, forget it: When you talk to Miss Speed, I dare say you'll never hear that name from her."

"Whatever you say. But it's still a fake. I'm not going to say the letters are real if they're not."

"I've never asked you to," said Galmoy. "If they're forgeries, then feel free to say so. And I'll deal with Mr. Patrick bloody Sarsfield."

"Probably not even forgeries. There were copies made at the time, and copies of the copies still exist," Pearse said. "I bet those are what this Sarsfield's got."

"You seem to know a good deal about it," Galmoy observed.

"Well, they're famous. And they are in my line of work," Pearse replied.

"Manuscript research," Galmoy agreed.

"No. Forgery."

●　　●　　●

The conversation had ended on a satisfactory note, Pearse decided, though he still felt a nagging unease at Galmoy's knowledge of his past. He got up from the big desk that filled most of one side of the living room and walked into the kitchen. As he fixed himself a sandwich and then hunted up a cold beer to wash it down, it occurred to him that he ought to be informing himself about sixteenth-century Scotland. Even if those letters were the most obvious fakes, there was still a consulting fee in it for him.

Pushing half a dozen unopened bills and a couple of ink bottles to one side of the desk, he set down the sandwich and the beer bottle, turned to the bookcase that filled one wall and whose weight was gradually pushing the floor out of plumb. Big books and small ones, most of them dusty. Sheaves of loose papers in cardboard binders tied with ribbon. Pearse had always filed his books according to where they could be jammed into a gap, and it took him five minutes to locate what he wanted. He propped the book up against a lamp, found the page he wanted, and began to read.

Twenty minutes later, he realized he had not taken a bite. Instead, he gulped half the beer without tasting it and turned back to his reading. It was foolish, even crazy, but he felt the old excitement creeping up his spine. The odds were still very strong that the Casket Letters were forgeries. But there was a small chance that at least some of them might really have been written by Mary to her lover. Foolish, headstrong, lonely: She had been all those things, and even her advocates could not deny it. And she was one of those women who had to have a man. Pearse's lips curled in a small, contemptuous smile. There was nothing that said a queen couldn't be just another hungry broad.

•   •   •

The phone rang again at half past four. This time, Pearse was ready for it. Almost too ready. He forced himself to take a deep, steadying breath. "Michael Pearse," he said.

"Mr. Pearse? My name's Diana Speed, and I've been given your name as a manuscript expert." He prided himself on his ability to read voices—women's voices, especially—and he knew instantly that this lady was no pushover.

"Oh, really?" he said, thinking: I am a busy man. I am a man who doesn't chase jobs. I am hard to get, but not too hard. "Might I ask who recommended me?"

"Mr. Galmoy, at the Graphological Society. He said you were very sound on the northern Renaissance." Was that a touch of amusement in her voice? He decided to play to it, just a little.

"Which means, of course, that he and I agree about it," Pearse said. "But that is a period I'm interested in."

"Northern Renaissance—what area does that include?"

"Well, northern Europe generally," Pearse tried to sound as if he would enjoy discussing the term at some length. "The Scandanavian countries, of course. And Great Britain . . ."

"Scotland?"

"Yes. It was an independent nation until the beginning of the seventeenth century, and a great center of culture a hundred years before that."

"And it—manuscripts from that place and time—they'd be familiar to you."

"Yes." It was the moment, he judged, to be unequivocal. "What do you have?"

"I can't be too specific over the telephone." Clearly, she had rehearsed this part. "Letters. A dozen or so. I want to know if they're genuine."

"I see. Well, it's not too hard to test the paper and ink, but as for genuineness . . ." He let her hang for exactly a second and went on. "Besides the materials, there are three considerations, really. First is context: Is the text itself reasonable, given the period? Second is the style of hand: Was it the way people wrote then? In the period we're talking about, there were two handwriting styles used by educated people, and the same individual might have used both, at different times in his life. And then there's comparability: Are there authenticated samples of the person's hand? Might I ask," he went on smoothly, "if the supposed author left other, authenticated documents?"

"I expect so," the woman said. "Signatures, anyway."

Pearse sighed gently. "Oh, dear: signatures. Not all that conclusive, especially with well-known people. I dare say your supposed author was well known."

"Definitely. Look, Mr. Pearse, I think we ought to talk this over in more detail. If I brought the material to your office, perhaps you could give me a quick yes or no, and if it turned out to be a maybe, then we could discuss terms."

"Well," Pearse replied, "I don't know. With documents as old as the ones you apparently have, there's no such thing as a quick yes, and if they're even second-rate forgeries, a quick no isn't all that likely, either."

"Fair enough. Let's take the maybe for granted then."

"The kind of testing I do takes time," he said. "And time's money—even for a scholar." He allowed himself what he hoped sounded like a scholarly chuckle.

"Then the sooner we get started, the better," she said. "How about this evening?"

"This evening? I'm afraid—"

"An hour of your time for five hundred dollars, regardless of the verdict. Shall we say at seven?"

He let a genuine annoyance creep into his voice. "Miss, uh . . ."

"Speed."

"Miss Speed, I'm in this line of work because it fascinates me. But I'm my own employer, and I dislike being pushed."

Her contrition sounded real enough: "I do apologize, Mr. Pearse. I'm in a terrible time bind—but that's my problem, not yours. You'd be doing me the most enormous favor if you could carve an hour out of your schedule this evening. Please."

It was, he decided, a very nice voice, when its operator wasn't trying to rule the world. "I think I can manage it, especially for five hundred dollars."

He put down the receiver and regarded the phone thoughtfully. So far, so good. This Diana Speed was going to take some special handling, but she was under the gun and knew it. He looked around his living room. I'd better clean this place up. No, he decided on second thought: It'd be more believable if I spread some props around. But a beer bottle isn't one of them.

In the kitchen, he was amused to note that his mood had changed. There might be some fun in this game. And what—just what—if she really had something?

Three: Marie

She was sitting in the lotus position, in the middle of the living room floor, trying to empty her mind. The walls around her had faded to a uniform blur, and she no longer saw the dusty volumes that jammed the floor-to-ceiling bookcases, relieved here and there by tinted lithographs of long-dead royalty thumbtacked to the shelving. She was equally oblivious to the three cats who sprawled across the couch, motionless in the fifty-watt gloom, or the justifiably nervous canary on the coffee table, who was pecking at a rock-hard piece of whole-wheat toast. Marie's thought processes had stopped; only a sense of herself remained.

Herself and another: the watcher. Marie first sensed the other's presence some uncertain time ago. Weeks rather than days, she thought, though in the unvarying semidarkness around her the difference between day and week scarcely existed. But she hadn't been aware what was bothering her until she caught herself, for the third time in as many instances, looking quickly over her own shoulder.

Nothing there. Or nothing, at any rate, that was not part of her ordinary life: books, mostly—in sagging, bulging shelves, and tottering piles, and drifts where the piles had collapsed—and stained and dusty furniture, torpid cats, voracious birds. But she knew from the start, without knowing why she knew, that the watcher was no bird or cat, and that it was female.

On the face of things, that knowledge led inescapably to the watcher's being her mother, but Marie was used to being watched by her mother. This sensation was in some respects the same, and also very different.

Now the room had come back into focus, and Marie abandoned her mental exercise for a new one: Make a list, she told herself. No, two lists. First, what was the same about this new surveillance and her mother's? The awareness of being weighed, appraised, considered; in every action, every motion. All that was familiar enough.

Then what was different? Unlike Mother, the Watcher (she had earned a capital letter, Marie decided) was inescapable and omnipresent. She hovered in the bedroom, in the bathroom. She was there even—especially—when Marie was asleep.

There was no getting past it: The Watcher was inside Marie herself. That being so, it was no wonder she was invisible. And yet . . . Marie unfolded her long legs and eased to her feet, willing herself not to allow what she was doing to take shape in her mind. She mounted the stairs, her feet raising small puffs of dust at each step. She concentrated on the act of climbing, lifting one foot and then the next. Concentrated on the pile of books (twelve of them) at the head of the stairs. Three steps down the hall and then quickly left, and she looked up.

The face in the mirror looked back at her without expression. Intently as Marie stared, she could see no one else behind her own eyes. What she did see, through smears of dust, was a tall, pale, big-boned girl with a round face under long, dark red hair. Watchful eyes that were momentarily hazel and then some color less easily defined. Behind Marie was the big bed she shared with her mother. Rumpled sheets and dirty blankets, and the inevitable cat—this one watching her with something approaching interest, for the moment.

The telephone downstairs rang. It was the third call since Mother had left that morning. Three calls in the same day was an almost unique occurrence. The one time it had happened before had been years ago, but the memory was still distinct: The child Marie had picked up the telephone and listened. At first she thought the person on the other end must have been running. After she said hello several times, the person spoke, in a deep voice, using words she had never heard before. It was not a very interesting conversation, though the speaker seemed quite excited by it, and after a while Marie hung up. A few minutes later, the phone rang again, and when she answered she heard the same voice, and the same questions. She assumed it was a game, though the point of it eluded her. When the phone rang the third time, she didn't bother answering it. She had, however, remembered the phrases, and tried one of them on her mother, when she was making dinner: "Mother, do I want to fuck?"

It was, Marie supposed, a valuable lesson, though she was black and blue for two weeks afterward. Now, of course, she knew what *fuck* meant, at least in principle. It was something the boys in school had talked about all the time. Some of them did it, too—to some of the girls. Or at least they said they did. A couple of the boys had even asked Marie if she would, but by then she'd learned to recognize the opening stage of another cruelly teasing game.

She wondered sometimes if men were different from the boys she had dreaded and loathed. If men in this age were different from the men of Mary Stuart's time—Bothwell, say, or Moray. Darnley, of course, had been only a boy.

The ringing telephone stopped. Marie, broken out of her reverie, began to turn away from the mirror, but something held her in place. She found herself facing the glass again, her hands tugging at the faded sweatshirt she wore. "Don't," she heard herself whimper, but it did no good. In moments her clothes were a heap around her feet; her hazel eyes, never more watchful, regarded the image of her stripped and shivering body. At last, she felt herself released. She pulled her clothes back on, careful not to look at the mirror until she was fully dressed again.

"Who are you?" she demanded, her voice shaking. "You can't pretend you're not there."

No answer. The Watcher had seen what she wanted and had retired, for the time being. Marie wandered down the stairs, her mind spinning. I suppose I must be crazy. That's the obvious explanation. The books she read made it clear that the life she and Mother lived was unnatural. It had always felt normal, but she supposed that crazy people seemed normal to themselves—or did they? It was an important question, and she remembered where she might find the answer. The book she wanted was one of the oldest in the house, discarded years ago by the library where Mother still worked. Marie had not seen its cover—purple, with faded gold stamping—for some time, but her memory's eye told her exactly where to look, in the middle of a row that marched across the kitchen table, held in place by a cupboard at one end and the toaster at the other. *An Outline of Abnormal Psychology,* that was the title. She pulled it out, dropped into the kitchen chair, and began to read.

•   •   •

By the time Marie heard her mother's key grating in the front door lock, she had decided, upon weighing the evidence carefully, that she was not a victim of *dementia praecox.* The decision relieved her mind considerably, since the only treatment discussed in the book involved chaining the patient to a wall and hosing her down periodically with cold water. Marie was quite familiar with the sensation of cold water on her skin—the water heater had been broken for three years now—and she disliked it intensely.

The outside door shut with a crash that brought Marie's head up. She heard the key scrape around the edges of the inner lock and then drive home, but several seconds passed before she heard the lock click open. Her mother's feet shuffled into the hall—from the uneven pace, she was limping badly—and then she called out, "Marie, are you there?"

The voice was that of a far older woman than the one who had left the house that morning. Marie got up from the kitchen table, leaving the book open, and went into the cluttered living room. Her mother, still wearing her coat, was sitting on the edge of the couch, hunched over as if in pain. She was panting, and when she looked up, the whites of her washed-out blue eyes were edged in yellow.

"What's the matter, Mother?"

"I'm all right."

"No you're not. You look awful." Marie paused. Nothing in her reading had told her how to ask the question that was forcing its way to the surface. Just the same, she had to know the answer. "Mother, are you going to die?"

Her mother's eyes fell. She shook her head, still panting, then met her daughter's questioning gaze. "Not yet," she said.

"Oh." The Watcher's attention—if that was what it was—had returned with new strength. Marie felt as if her very eyes were under the other's control, shifting and focusing to an alien command. "How long?" Marie heard her voice ask; it was her own voice, but the words had formed by themselves and the tone was peremptory.

"I don't know." Her mother had not noticed, apparently. She was staring dully across the room. "Oh, God, I'm so tired."

She is dying. Marie's realization was almost synchronous with the Watcher's: Two thoughts with but a single mind. She had an almost uncontrollable urge to cry, but heard herself say: "You must show her—me—the proofs, then."

Her mother's vacant eyes widened in surprise. "What? What proofs, Marie?"

Vous savez bien, Madame, the Watcher's voice said, with a snap, as Marie's mind echoed her mother's question.

"Let me rest a little, first."

Lips and tongue shaped the word *vite*, but Marie clenched her teeth and held it in. After a moment, when she was sure she could command her speech, she said, "Tell me where they are, Mother. I'll bring whatever it is to you."

Her mother was shaking her head again. The panting seemed to have subsided, or perhaps she just had it under better control. "No. Help me up."

Marie heaved her mother to her feet, and the two of them stood for a long minute, swaying slightly, with the old woman's arm over Marie's shoulders. "Where are we going?"

"Cellar."

Marie felt a sharp stab of apprehension. Unlike outside, where Marie no longer went, the cellar was a place she had never even seen. She knew, however, where the entrance was: a solid, locked door right under the staircase. The two women lurched across the room, and Marie's foot caught a book lying on the floor and sent it spinning. Her mother fished the key ring from her coat pocket, but her hands were trembling so badly that Marie had to unlock the door. Behind it, the staircase fell away into the darkness. The top two stairs—scarred, unpainted wood—caught the dim light, but the rest were in shadow.

"String. Pull the string."

Marie freed a hand and groped above and behind the open door. She felt the dusty grasp of spiderweb; something ran quickly over her fingers. She yanked on the string, and the staircase was bathed in a yellowish glow.

After the first two steps Marie mastered the trick of standing one step below and allowing her mother's soft, heavy weight to sag over her. Even so, it took them a full five minutes to reach the bottom. The surface looked firm but the edge of Marie's bare heel sank into it. After a moment's panic, she realized it must be dirt. She looked around her. It was a low, square chamber, about twenty feet by forty, entirely empty except for a square of ragged carpet in the center, and lit only by a single bare bulb hung from the ceiling. The walls were uneven white stones, fitted one upon the other and edged with cement. Every protrusion carried a thick cushion of dust on its upper side. Marie became aware that her mother was pulling feebly at her arm.

"Over here." She fumbled at a stone that was noticeably

larger than the rest, trying to work it from side to side. Marie
let her go, felt her start to collapse, caught her in time to
lower her to the ground, where she sat with her back against
the jutting stones, her head sagging to one side and her eyes
closed. In the yellow light, her skin looked like wet wax.

Marie grasped the stone in both hands and pulled. To her
surprise it slid out easily, with a soft, grating sound, and fell
heavily to the dirt. She reached into the dark cavity until her
fingertips touched cloth. Incredibly smooth and cool. Silk,
she knew. But she had never touched silk. How . . . but of
course: The hands within her hands knew silk. The cloth was
wrapped tightly around something large and square and hard.
Marie's groping fingers found a narrow strip of silk that had
been used as a tie, grasped it and pulled. At first there was no
give at all; Marie took a better grip and pulled again, harder.
She felt it shift, and then it slid toward her. Almost a cube,
and so heavy she had to take it in her arms.

"Unwrap it," her mother gasped.

Obediently, Marie set the object down and began to untie
the strips of white silk that secured its covering. Beneath was
a solid-looking wooden chest, strapped with rusty bands. It
looked to Marie very old, and its surface was tracked with
scrapes and scars, also very old except for one, a bright gash
across the thick iron hasp. Incongruous even to Marie's eye
was the shiny padlock that secured the lid. Without a word,
her mother passed over the ring of keys; Marie selected the
smallest and newest and fitted it into the lock. As she turned
the key and the padlock sprang open, she felt the presence of
the Watcher more strongly than ever, consuming Marie with
her own impatience.

The chest's hinges squealed as Marie lifted the lid and let
it fall back. She was ready for nearly any contents, but not for
the gleam of plastic sheeting that met her eye. She looked at
her mother, whose eyes were open now, the whites yellower
than ever, watching her intently. No question was necessary;
her mother nodded, and Marie groped under the plastic.
There were three separate, tightly wrapped bundles, one

much lighter than the others, and she set them in a row on the dirt floor.

Her mother's hand, shaking badly, tapped the largest bundle. "That one first." It was triple-wrapped in plastic, sealed and resealed with wide, silver-colored tape. Through the coverings, Marie could feel it was a book, but a book like no other she had ever handled. When at last she had pulled off the tape and unwrapped the sheeting, she saw an expanse of thick, cracked leather that had perhaps once been a royal purple. Embossed in blackened metal up the left-hand side of the book's front cover ran a looping, many-branched vine. Here and there in the vine were cuplike metal sockets, empty except for one which contained a dark stone split across the middle. Leather straps with tarnished buckles held the covers closed. Stamped deep into the leather were the two words *Holy Bible*.

Marie saw her own fingers working at the buckles with such eagerness that one of the straps ripped free from the leather. Her hands, entirely outside her control, opened the book near the back, to a creaking sigh of protest from the ancient binding. The left-hand page was blank and the one facing it was also unprinted, but someone long ago had written across it, in a hurried sprawl, words that were almost impossible for Marie to decipher. She leaned forward, all her will focused on the faded lines. Words formed in her mind before she could read them on the page, but they were the same:

A Marie Royne dEcosse et son mari le comte de Boduel
en sa pryson Lac de Leven, le 2 septembre 1567
deux enfants Iames et Marie

A wavering line was drawn through the name *Iames,* and as her eye fell on it Marie felt a pang of sorrow so intense that it made her gasp. Her mother, misinterpreting the sound, said, "You understand! I knew you would."

Marie shook her head. If only she could think it through, she knew the meaning would come to her, but she was being

rocked by surges of raw emotion—sadness, rage, triumph—
that swept over her in waves and made it impossible to
concentrate.

Her mother saw her bewilderment and lashed feebly at her,
a blow so light Marie scarcely felt it. "Foolish girl!" the old
woman snarled.

Suddenly the words seemed to shift on the page, and the
writing was clear to her, as if it had become modern English:
"To Mary Queen of Scotland and her husband the Earl of
Bothwell, in her prison at Lochleven, September second,
1567, two children—James and Mary."

She was looking at a birth record. Mary's premature twins,
who orthodox history claimed had been born dead. But this
writing seemed to say that one at least, the girl, had lived.
Lived, but not to be a queen. Never to be heard of again: her
life as obscure, for all her royal birth, as Marie's own. She
began to close the book, careful not to force the ancient
binding too quickly, but a voice in her head said, *La
prochaine page, ma petite*. No, not a voice, Marie's brain
corrected. The thought itself, but in French. And as she sat
frozen, her mother spoke from her side: "Turn the page,
Marie."

This is too much. It's bad enough being ordered around by
Mother, but by my own . . . My own what? she thought,
but she turned the page anyway.

The next right-hand page was covered with inscriptions, in
half a dozen different faded inks and archaic handwritings.
Her eye went to the topmost, which was dated 1579 and
noted, in a careful, illiterate hand, the birth of a daughter
named Anne to "Marie filz-Iames callit Balfor" and her
husband, Willie Crawford of Glenside.

"Queen Mary's daughter?" The question was only halfway
to Marie's lips when the answer formed in her mind:
Naturellement.

She moved her eyes down to the next entry, made two
decades later. Now that she had the hang of it, the writing
was easier to decipher: to Anne and her husband, David
Scott, a son who died. And then a daughter, Marie, who

lived. Captive now, she followed the entries down to the bottom of the page, and over to the next, and the next. Eleven generations—nearly two hundred years—until the writing stopped short, halfway down a page, late in 1743: to Mary and Patrick Ogilvie, à girl they named Joan, dead before her second birthday. And right beneath it a notation—the only one—of a marriage: Mary Ogilvie again, to Captain Michael Donovan; June 16, 1745.

"Ogilvie was killed at Culloden." The voice was her mother's, but faint and dreamlike. "She went to find his body, and the Irishman called out to her. He was lying wounded in some bushes nearby. One of the Wild Geese, of course. His head was forfeit if Cumberland's men found him. She needed another husband to keep the line going, so she took him instead of Ogilvie, there being so few men left. They fled together, to the New World."

Slowly, Marie closed the Bible. Without being told she knew where the trail was inevitably leading. As she unwrapped the second heavy parcel, she found herself wondering if those other men and women had been watched over, had felt the same passionate, imperious presence inside them. Inside the wrappings was a second Bible, also very old, its covers gone and half the Book of Genesis eaten by mice or rats. She knew now where to look, and sure enough the tale picked up, on the unprinted pages after Revelation, with another birth, to Michael and Mary Donovan, in the city of Philadelphia.

The Donovans had moved west, and their son's child was born in Fort Pitt. From there, the trail led south, ending with the Keillors of North Carolina. No, not quite ending. At the very bottom of the final page, in what Marie recognized as a stronger, youthful version of her mother's straggling hand, was the inscription:

To Joe Thomas McIntyre and Flora Keillor McIntyre
a daughter, Marie Stuart
Jamaica Hospital, County of Queens. 12/8/74

Marie rocked back on her heels, feeling the Watcher's satisfaction warm her own veins, and regarded her mother. The old woman was sitting up, her eyes feverishly bright. Two spots of color burned on her pallid cheeks, but somehow they made her look even more unhealthy. She seemed angered by Marie's calm. "Don't you see, child?" she demanded. "Don't you realize who you are?"

"Well, not exactly," Marie replied, after a moment. "I mean, I can follow all that genealogy, but what does it make me? What did it make *you*, Mother?"

Shocked, her mother could only sputter: "What? What did it make me? A guardian. An acolyte. A keeper. Open the last package."

It was far lighter than the first two, and loose. Its surface was the expected plastic sheeting, and inside that a plastic envelope. Marie struggled with the heavy tape that sealed it, finally pulling it open. Inside was a small pile of papers, sheets of different sizes. Some of them were very thick and stiff, scarcely like paper at all; others were cobweb-light, almost transparent. With great care, she drew the topmost sheet from the envelope, until she could see the first words on it: "Having departed from the place where I left my Heart . . ."

Without warning, a sensation of dreadful loss swept over Marie. She felt tears streaming hot down her face, blinding her, and she quickly pushed the page back into the envelope. She had read the words before, many times, and she knew them by heart, but never before had she heard them: The voice, vibrant and warm and passionate, resonated in her inner ear. She felt her own lips moving, but knew no sound was coming from her mouth, as they formed the letter's loving, damning close: "God forgive me, and God give you, my only Love, the hope and prosperity that your humble and faithful Love desires unto you, who hopes to be shortly an other Thing to you, for the reward of my irksome travails."

"You *do* see." Her mother was smiling at her. It had been so long since Marie had seen her smile that it took her a moment to realize what the expression was. Slowly the smile faded, first from her eyes and then from her lips, to be replaced by a look of mild surprise. "Oh," she said, and a little saliva trickled from the corner of her mouth. Her head fell back against the stone with an unpleasant thump, but after a moment Marie realized that she was beyond feeling it. Or anything else, ever again.

Marie stretched out a hand toward her mother. *Let her go in peace*, ma petite. *She has served her purpose.*

Fear and calm, bewilderment and certainty, emptiness and eagerness—Marie felt as if the entire universe were swirling inside her. "What shall I do?" she cried aloud, despairing.

Suivez-moi.

Four: Diana

She arrived at the Algonquin a good half hour early, and would have been earlier still had she not forced herself to dawdle along Fifth Avenue. Warm air from the south had swept in the night before, and the temperature was more like early autumn than the first week in December; the animated Christmas displays in the department store windows and the weirdly amplified bray of carols seemed even more premature than usual.

Diana's own ambivalent feelings toward the season combined, she supposed, those of both her parents. Her mother openly detested *cette fête bourgeoise* and fled annually to her family's smaller château, in Provence, immediately after Thanksgiving, staying there until mid-January, when the holiday madness had ebbed so that it was safe to return to Park Avenue. Diana's father had adored everything about Christmas; he would spend hours bumbling around the edges of the largest pine tree the living room could hold, loading it down with ornaments until the lower branches sagged to the floor. It was appropriate, Diana thought, that when he caught the pneumonia that carried him off he'd been standing for two hours in ankle-deep snow, staring transfixed at a diorama populated by mechanical elves under the supervision of a clockwork Santa Claus.

The approaching holiday had disfigured even the Algonquin's high, paneled lobby: An immense, overdecorated tree occupied a space in front of the dining room that might have accommodated four or five cocktail tables. Most of the people milling in front of the main desk, however, were dressed for the sun, in puffily ill-fitting garments that lacked only "Rodeo Drive" spray-painted across the padded shoulders. Behind them a seven-foot glass and mahogany partition, hung with swags of red-ribboned pine bough, cordoned off the cocktail area, an artful maze of overstuffed chairs and divans, and low coffee tables each with its push-bell (firmly secured to the surface, against souvenir hunters). It was not yet five P.M., but the daily influx of performers, impresarios, authors, and other would-be *mâchers* was already well into the afternoon ritual that Milly Aaron sardonically called the Refueling of the Arts.

Diana stood for a moment irresolute, glancing over the crowd without really seeing them. She had planned to spend her spare minutes ensconced in one of the Algonquin's lobby chairs, reading the "Page Six" column of the *Post*–a secret vice she had so far concealed from even Cathy O'Donnell, and one she was not about to practice in front of so many people. Suddenly, her eye was caught by a too-familiar puff of honey blonde hair, alongside a pair of rounded shoulders she knew equally well. Judith and Haskell were deep in martinis and heated conversation, but they looked up as the chunky, tweeded figure of Patrick Sarsfield loomed over them. Sarsfield's heavy shrug was as eloquent as the frustration on his face, and he hurled himself into a chair across from them. Diana discarded almost instantly the impulse to stalk them through the crowd—her height put urban stalking out of the question—and decided instead on confrontation. She set the *Post* down on a convenient tabletop, froze with a glance the man who mistook her gesture for an overture, and began to pick her way among the crowd.

Haskell spotted her first, and waved her on while at the same time saying something under his breath to Judith. Watching the other woman's face, Diana was surprised to see the kaleidoscope of expressions end in what looked strangely like relief. Sarsfield, on the other hand, was smiling with a determination that roused her instant suspicion. Returning the smile, Diana glanced about her for an empty chair and saw one at the next table, which was occupied by a pudgy little man with indeterminate features, sitting alone. "Are you using this?" she asked.

The man shook his head. "No, no," he said, his voice urgent and breathless. "By all means."

She pulled the chair up and dropped into it, alert to the undercurrents that swept around the table. Something, she decided, was very wrong, but she would let them tell her about it themselves. "I'll have a kir, please," she said to the water who appeared at her elbow. "Straight up, with lemon peel."

The other three exchanged glances, and Sarsfield cleared his throat and spoke. "About the letters . . ." he began.

"Yes?" She waited for him to continue, but it was Judith who picked it up.

"Mr. Sarsfield's run into a little problem, Diana."

Diana noted the realignment in Judith's use of names, and so, clearly, did Sarsfield.

"It's nothing," he snapped. "A small delay. Annoying but temporary."

"Oh?"

"The owner of the letters," he explained. "I'm having some trouble getting through to her."

"Patrick's been calling her home since before lunch," Haskell put in. "She doesn't answer."

"So what?" Diana asked. "She's out at work—she has got a job?"

"Oh, yes," Sarsfield replied absently. "But someone's always at home. Always." He answered the question on Diana's face. "Her daughter, Marie. She never goes out."

"What, *never?*" asked Diana, expecting the customary cliché in response.

"Absolutely never," Sarsfield said. "She's, well, a little odd. They both are, I gather. I've never met them—just talked to the mother twice on the phone. And corresponded, of course: That's how I heard of the letters in the first place."

"The girl's mother wrote to Patrick, after she read *Queen Betrayed*," Judith interjected.

"That was how it started," he said. With the recollection, his spirits seemed to pick up slightly. "Of course, she thought she was writing to Patricia Orme, and I've not disillusioned her."

"What did she say?" Diana asked. "When she first wrote, I mean."

"Oh, the usual thing," Sarsfield replied. "How she loved my sensitive treatment of Mary—I saw into her heart—only another woman could have done it." He grinned at Diana, who could almost admire his transparent satisfaction. "She said I must have been able to understand Mary's soul, because she could, too."

The waiter chose that instant to return, bearing Diana's kir and a bowl of the nibbly snacks that looked as if they ought to be fed to large birds. Judith, her gaze fixed on Sarsfield, scooped up a handful and began devouring them.

"Well, I wrote her the standard answer—it's on my mail-merge program, I use it so often—and forgot all about it. About three weeks later, I get another letter from her. A great, fat one. She's been rereading *Queen Betrayed*, she says, and she's even more struck by"—his lips pursed, a small moue of self-deprecation—"by my obvious identification with this deeply wronged woman." He paused and took a lubricating swallow of the golden brown liquid in his glass. "Well, hell, I almost didn't finish reading it; I could see what was coming, and I'd no intention of setting myself up as a transatlantic Dear Abby. But, to make a long story short, I did read it, and what she wrote nearly knocked me off my chair."

Diana glanced deliberately at her watch.

"She got right down to things, once she'd made up her mind," Sarsfield continued, picking up her pace. "She had the Casket Letters. The originals. They'd come down in her family, eleven generations without a break."

"But how did her family get them?" Diana asked. "If they

were real, I'd have thought the English government would have them squirreled away someplace. If they were fakes, somebody certainly would've had the sense to burn them after Mary's execution—in fact, I thought that was what happened."

"True for you," Sarsfield replied, beaming. "One set of letters did vanish, late in the sixteenth century. But there were several sets of copies made of the originals—they didn't have the blessed Xerox, poor things, and hand-copying was the best they could do. The originals were apparently stolen by one of Queen Elizabeth's many double agents—"

"The first Queen Elizabeth," Diana interrupted.

"Gloriana herself," Sarsfield agreed, nodding. "This agent, a Scot, may have been suffering pangs of conscience, I don't know, but he gave them as a sort of legacy to Mary's daughter."

"Whoa," said Diana. "What daughter? I thought Mary had only one child, who became King James the First."

"The unspeakable James," Sarsfield said. "Sixth of Scotland and First of Great Britain. Mary's son by the unlamented Harry Darnley. But she also had a daughter by Bothwell," Sarsfield replied. "A legitimate daughter, because by then Mary was married to her husband's murderer. This daughter was the survivor of premature twins born to her at Lochleven, when she was a prisoner of her own nobles. The births are well documented, though the survival of one child is only rumored."

Taken suddenly beyond her depth, Diana buried her nose in her kir and mumbled a noncommittal "Um."

"Anyway," Sarsfield went on, "the baby was named Marie and lived out her life in obscurity. Which was probably why she was able to live out her life at all."

"A danger to the state, I suppose," mused Diana, who was beginning to be intrigued by Sarsfield's tale.

"More than you could possibly realize," said Sarsfield. "Besides the Casket Letters—"

"Why're they called that?" Haskell put in. Diana realized

he had been snuffling up martinis as she and Sarsfield talked, and he was more than a little drunk.

"They were supposedly found in a golden casket—a box," Diana said impatiently. "It was Bothwell's property, but one of his servants turned it over to Mary's enemies. They used the letters as evidence against Mary, after they pitched her off the throne. Evidence that she and her lover, Bothwell, had her husband, Lord Darnley, murdered." She turned back to Sarsfield. "You were saying?"

"Besides the known Casket Letters—and there are different purported letters in different accounts of them—my source has one letter that postdates the others. It was written by Mary on the night of February seventh, 1587." He was looking at Diana for a reaction and, getting none, he groped under his chair and produced a large manila envelope. "These are the photocopies," he said. "Right now, I want you to see just this one." With a care that suggested reverence, he extracted a single sheet and handed it to Diana. The writing was surprisingly clear and legible, and the first sentence leaped out at her: "Tomorrow I shall see my God face to face."

Diana's fascinated gaze galloped down the page, and she could feel a sensation like cold lightning prickle her spine. When she had finished, she went back to the beginning and reread it, right down to the bold, uncompromising signature, "Marie Royne dEcosse," at the end. She looked up at Sarsfield: "It's awfully farfetched," she said.

"But is it? Darnley would've subscribed to it. He did publicly, more than once. And it certainly explains why King James was so delighted to have his mother silenced forever. Not to mention why Mary and her illegitimate half brother, the Earl of Moray, became so hostile to each other, after having been so close."

"A deathbed accusation," Diana said slowly, more to herself than the others. "Mary claims that her son, James Stuart—King of Scotland and shortly of England, too—was a bastard."

"Worse than that," said Sarsfield.

"A good deal worse," Diana agreed. "She says that James was actually her son by her own half brother, Moray. Incestuous as well as a bastard. Which means . . ."

"That the whole English royal family is grounded on a lie, and a mortal sin," said Sarsfield delightedly. "All those divine-right Stuarts, all those pompous Hanovers, all those self-righteous Windsors. It's gorgeous."

"And an abso-fucking-lutely guaranteed number one bestseller through the next decade," Judith exclaimed.

"If it's true," said Diana.

"I'm sure it is," Sarsfield said, his eyes glittering. "Positive."

"Anyway," Diana went on, "you hadn't finished your story. The child Marie got the letters—then what?"

"She lived and died in obscurity, in western Scotland," Sarsfield replied. "Married and had her own offspring, who in turn received the legacy, and kept it secret. And so on until the middle of the eighteenth century."

By now, Diana was used to his rhetorical pauses, and she waited for him to go on.

"The '45," he said, after a moment. "What does that mean to you, Miss Speed?"

"Bonnie Prince Charlie," Diana said immediately.

"The birth of Drambuie," Haskell added. "Calls for another round. Same for everybody?"

"Princes Charles Edward, to be sure," said Sarsfield, ignoring him. "And the Götterdämmerung of the Stuarts, at the battle of Culloden. Mary's legitimate line was almost snuffed out there—her many-times great-granddaughter lost her husband. But the girl found another husband, one of the Irish mercenaries who fought at the Highlanders' side. The two of them fled to America."

"With the letters," said Diana.

"Right you are. They arrived as impoverished fugitives, and they stayed impoverished, I gather. Down to the uttermost generation, now resident just a few miles from where we sit."

"The lady who doesn't answer the phone," said Diana, in whom renewed doubt was rising fast.

"She and her daughter," Sarsfield agreed. "But I'm not such a fool as you apparently think. She has the names and places and dates of birth in each of those generations, four hundred and fifty years. Written down. I called her up, pretended to be Patricia Orme's confidential secretary, and had her photocopy all of it and send it to me. And then I proved it out."

"How?"

"Parish records, tombstones, tax rolls," Sarsfield replied. "The first two hundred years were all in Scotland, and the Scots are demons for keeping records. Took me ten months, nonstop. It was much harder doing the same thing over here, on what was then the American frontier. But it's all there. Every step is documented."

"Seems to me we haven't quite got that far," Diana objected quickly. "Written down, yes. Documented . . ."

"Any expert you like," said Sarsfield. "You pick him."

"I have," she replied. "Do you know a man named Pearse? Michael Pearse?"

"Pearse, is it?" Sarsfield said, with an odd look at Diana. "Now that's an offbeat choice—but never mind. Pearse you want, Pearse you shall have."

Something in Sarsfield's voice rang just a quarter note off-key. "What's wrong with Pearse?" she demanded. "His credentials sounded good to me."

"Oh, credentials. I dare say they're fine. It's just that he's such a contrary bastard—or so I've been told."

"All the more satisfying when he backs up your letters, then," Diana replied. "And the sooner we get under way, the more satisfied we'll all be. I've made an appointment with him tonight, as it happens."

"Splendid," Sarsfield replied. "Here, take these for starters. I know they're not the originals, which he'll have to see, but at least he can begin on the handwriting."

"You're not coming?" said Diana, surprised. "I'd have thought you wouldn't miss it."

"To tell you the truth," said Sarsfield, "I'm dead on my feet. These transatlantic leaps catch up with you, especially as the years go on." A small, patently artificial grin. "But I'll absolutely have the originals for you tomorrow. Now, if you'll excuse me . . ." He hoisted himself to his feet.

"By all means," Diana said, thinking that Sarsfield totally lacked the stunned, absent stare she associated with jet lag. If anything, he looked pleased, like a man who had just accomplished some difficult trick. And his smile was less forced than it should have been, for someone whose half-million-dollar advance had faded back into limbo. *What am I missing?* Diana thought. *Why do I feel as if I'm being taken for a ride?* She slipped the big manila envelope into her shoulder bag. "Have a good rest," she said, to his departing back.

"Do we have time for a quick bite before the appointment?" Judith asked. "Haskell and I are coming with you, of course."

"What? Oh, of course," Diana agreed. The lobby throng split momentarily, and she caught a last glimpse of Sarsfield, on the elevator. As its door closed, he caught her eye and quickly looked away.

"I hope this won't take too long," said Haskell blearily. He grasped the arms of his chair as if to rise. "I have a dinner date."

"You have a dinner date with *me,* silly," said Judith, putting her plump hand on his shoulder. The brightness in her voice had a trace of brass under it. "Why don't we all have some nice coffee?"

Five: Sarsfield

He was unaware that anyone had followed him off the elevator until the breathy voice behind him said, "You don't have to hurry, Mr. Sarsfield. I'm not there yet."

Sarsfield spun on his heel. He had never set eyes on the short, pale, pudgy man in the ill-fitting suit, but the voice was painfully familiar—flat Belfast accent, with an underlay Sarsfield couldn't quite place. "Mr. Galmoy, isn't it? Sorry I'm late, but I couldn't get away—"

"I know. I was watching. Let's get out of this hallway, shall we?"

Once in the room Sarsfield went to the bureau and took a pint bottle from beneath the pile of undershorts. He poured three wide fingers of Jameson's into a glass from the bathroom and drank it like medicine; refilled the glass and offered it to his guest, who declined with an abrupt gesture. "What progress, man?" Galmoy asked.

"Progress?"

"With the documents," he explained. "Weren't they what you gave the Speed woman?"

"Only photocopies." Sarsfield dropped heavily into the room's only armchair and regarded Galmoy, perched on the edge of the bed. "She hired your man Pearse," he said after a moment's thought. "In fact, she's going to see him tonight.

73

With the copies I gave her, he can start vetting the handwriting style and content."

"But what about the originals? You were going to have them by this afternoon, and my associates are all on tenterhooks."

Sarsfield found himself annoyed by Galmoy's almost apologetic tone and his whining persistence. "Your associates will have to hang a little longer, I'm afraid."

Galmoy was watching Sarsfield closely, his head tilted to one side. "Why is that?"

"A slight delay," Sarsfield replied. "It'll be cleared up soon—don't you worry."

"Oh, *I'm* not the one who's worrying," Galmoy said. "But that's what you were saying yesterday. I think you want to be sure that my friends don't start worrying."

"Well, we couldn't have done anything until you had your manuscript expert in place," Sarsfield said firmly. "I gave Pearse's name a reluctant okay, the way you told me to." A thought struck him: "How'd you work that, anyway? It was pretty clever."

Galmoy's creaseless face wrinkled into a tightly self-satisfied leer. "That's my little secret. I've slipped Pearse in under the Speed woman's nose—now you provide him with something to read."

"Tomorrow," Sarsfield said. "First thing in the morning, I'll go out"—*to* changed awkwardly into *and*—"and fetch them myself."

"Will you, now? Is it far? Perhaps you'd like company. Just in case."

"No," Sarsfield snapped, and Galmoy's face darkened. Sarsfield realized he had spoken too sharply. "It's just that my source is very antisocial. She'll deal only with me. Alone."

"A wise policy," Galmoy said.

"You realize it'll still be a couple of weeks, at least, before your—our—friends see any cash," Sarsfield went on. "Miss Speed has to be satisfied the letters are real."

"She will be," said Galmoy. This time his smile looked

quite friendly, but his hands were locked white-knuckled in his lap.

"I wish everybody else was as confident as you." He saw Galmoy's eyebrow raise, and continued: "I mean, I am of course. But how can Pearse know . . ."

"He doesn't. In fact, he's near as damnit convinced himself they're fakes." Galmoy paused, as if to enjoy the effect of his remark. "You see, Mr. Sarsfield, I've got other sources of information. You'd be surprised."

He was tired, and this game of innuendo was giving him a headache. "Maybe you'd like to share them, since we're both going in the same direction."

"We are, aren't we?" said Galmoy, sliding off the bed. Even standing, he was not so much taller than the seated Sarsfield. "At least," he added, "I trust we are."

"Your friends back in County Mayo have my word," Sarsfield replied. "Ten percent of my advance, and then our relationship's over."

Galmoy nodded. "Fifty thousand you owe us so far, isn't it?" He saw the look Sarsfield tried vainly to suppress. "There's very little I don't know, my friend. You might as well get used to that."

"Then you're aware I can't cash the check quite yet," said Sarsfield quickly. "I'm not holding out on you."

"Oh, I know," Galmoy replied. "But I'll know when you *can* cash it, too. Probably before you do." He shot his shabby cuff and glanced at his watch. "Well, I'll be leaving you now, Mr. Sarsfield. If you decide you need help tomorrow—an escort service, perhaps—you have the number to call."

•　　•　　•

The drink Sarsfield had poured for Galmoy was still untouched, and he slugged it back in a single swallow. On his way to the door, he picked up the nearly empty pint and poured another. The bottle's neck chattered against the glass. Outside, the hall was empty. Sarsfield double-locked the door and then went to the phone. He dialed the number in Queens and heard it ring twice before the receiver clicked. "Hello?" he said urgently. "Mrs. McIntyre?"

The voice that came on was female, and a stranger's: "She's not here anymore."

"What?" He stared at the handset in stunned disbelief.

"She's gone away." Before Sarsfield could speak, the line went dead.

It wasn't possible. He dialed again, and this time the phone at the other end just rang and rang, as it had done all day, the dozen times he'd called. When he hung up, his hand was shaking so badly the telephone overset and crashed to the floor. He let it lie there while he tried to collect his shattered wits.

Whoever had answered, it wasn't the McIntyre woman, whose thick, almost breathless wheeze was unmistakable in itself, not counting the remnants of a Southern drawl overlaid by decades of Queens twang. This voice was young and clear and cold as ice.

Had the crazy old woman changed her mind and run away? Or had the Provos somehow got to her first? Bugged his phone and traced the number maybe? With exquisite care he dialed one last time, checking each digit. Instead of a ring, the dull buzz of a busy signal. Damn her soul to hell, she'd taken it off the hook. He slammed the receiver down.

I've got to do something, he thought, and the words repeated themselves in his head over and over, the emphasis changing each time: *I've* got to do something . . . I've *got* to do something . . . I've got to *do* something . . . He lurched to his feet and flung open the closet door, grabbed his heavy sheepskin coat from a hanger.

Outside the hotel, on 44th Street, the brown-coated doorman flagged down a passing cab. It was considerably warmer than it had been back in Ireland, but just as damp and raw. The sky was already inky, featureless between the looming buildings. Sarsfield had said "Penn Station" when he got in, loud enough for a bystander to hear, but as the cab approached Fifth Avenue and edged into the right lane to turn south, he leaned forward and tapped on the Plexiglas partition. "I've changed my mind. I'm going to Queens."

"You crazy?" The driver demanded. "Not Queens." He spoke with a deep, guttural accent.

"Queens," Sarsfield said. He took out a piece of paper he had prepared. "This is the address. It's straight out Queens Boulevard."

"Not Queens," the driver insisted, looking straight ahead.

"Look, my lad," Sarsfield said, between gritted teeth, "you can go to this address in Queens, or we'll find the nearest police officer, with whom I shall file a complaint and have your arse on toast." The driver gave him a frightened glare in the rearview mirror; perhaps, Sarsfield reflected, his voice had not been as calm as he thought it was. Sitting back, he produced three ten-dollar bills and held them up. "Let's get started, Mr."—he glanced at the name card next to the meter—"Mr. Dolgoruky."

Tires squealing, the cab leaped across the intersection of 44th and Fifth, toward Grand Central. At Madison, the driver turned north into the heavy rush-hour traffic. "Fucking Queens," he muttered, loud enough for Sarsfield to hear, but he kept on going.

Sarsfield unrolled the tightly furled copy of the *News* he had brought from his room, but it was already too dark to read. He made himself sit back and watch the teeming streets of midtown Manhattan inch past, as the driver worked his painful way north and east, toward the East River and the bridge to Queens. The two-block stretch of 59th Street between Lexington and Second avenues seemed to endure for an eternity, the passing eons marked only by the flicking of the meter, as it worked its way up to a fare that Sarsfield calculated at something like a dollar for every ten yards of forward movement. He realized he was tensely poised on the edge of the seat, actually holding his breath each time the cab eased forward, as if any movement on his part might somehow diminish the minuscule advance.

At last the taxi oozed across Second and up onto the 59th Street Bridge ramp, where it picked up a little speed, tires whining on the metal grill roadbed. Below, the East River surged down toward the harbor, and off to the left a scarlet cable car swung upward on its wire toward Roosevelt Island in midstream. As the bridge traffic loosened still more, and the whine of the tires edged up the scale, Sarsfield felt the tension mount inside him.

He was so close to his goal, the target he'd been aiming at for two years. Two wearisome years tracking old Mrs. McIntyre's family back through the centuries. Several times the trail had dried up or vanished under the debris of years, but always a new source would reveal itself, as if some benign force were looking over his shoulder. He had overcome all difficulties or found paths around them, and now his line of research was complete; he knew beyond doubt that Mary Stuart's letters had come down in one family, from hand to hand, over four hundred years. And he knew the letters' content was far more explosive than he'd imagined it could be. Their publication would be the capstone of his career—perhaps not the equal of Schliemann's discovery of Troy, but every bit as good as the pyramid of Tutankhamen.

Fame. Solid fame, far beyond the secondhand adulation that Patricia Orme received from clapped-out old biddies. The thought of it, rendered specific by fantasizing, made his heart race. What a pity the United States had nothing like a knighthood, though honorary doctorates would fall on him like snowflakes. He would have to hire someone to schedule his TV appearances. Why not a TV series?—after the film, of course.

And the money. Patricia Orme had made Sarsfield rich, but the royalties never seemed to be quite as much as expected, and they evaporated like fairy gold. Buying that damned castle had been a mistake—he knew that now. Now that he was up to his ass in debt, and worse. His mood abruptly darkened. How in God's name had he let himself get entangled with those Provo loonies? Sure, his family was dimly, distantly Irish, but it was not an inheritance that made any difference to him. *England out of Ireland* indeed. Except for the taxes, what Ireland needed was a good dose of England, or maybe Japan.

He'd been aware, one level down from consciousness, that he was being sucked in. Even as he was savoring his lord-of-the-manor role, even as the locals were playing up to him, Sarsfield could sense the mockery—their sly, elusive, never-absent delight in the preposterous. But he had accepted the cap doffing at its face value, just as he had accepted the earnest, respectful admiration of the young men who had courted him, first for political advice, then for material help, until they had boxed him in from all sides.

They had not cared at all where his money came from, which was in a way gratifying: It was one thing to be an author, but it was quite different to be a man who hid behind a woman's name in order to write silly, breathless effusions that were read only by maiden ladies, most of them well past a certain age. And while Sarsfield's pseudonym had by now graced more than a dozen hardcover books, he could seldom (especially alone in front of the mirror) think of himself as an author, and never as a Writer. It wasn't modesty, merely the sense of unreality that had grown in him since his first novel manuscript had been accepted—tentatively, with many editorial provisos—by Judith Sanders.

Judith had made him, there was no denying it. She had taken nearly a thousand pages of undigested pseudo-history, assembled during odd moments on the word processors that Sarsfield was supposed to be selling to customers who never came, and had carved and molded the turgid prose into a coherent story of half its original length. She had showed him not only where the vital sex scenes went, but exactly how far they went (limits the two of them could ignore in private); how to retrieve the heroine from the deepest, most insoluble perils in the nick of time to secure the vital happy ending; just how much genuine history was needed to make the rickety vehicles lurch forward . . . And, finally, it was Judith who had hit upon Patricia Orme, that mysterious pseudonym so skillfully manipulated by W-F's drunken old dyke of a publicist.

It was a long time since he had been amused by the mythical Patricia Orme, even though the speculations about her identity (fueled, of course, by Milly Aaron's discreetly indiscreet lapses) had successfully floated such unlikely candidates as a Prime Minister of Great Britain, an antipodean soprano, and an émigré tennis champion. Famous, all of them, and eminent in their own professions, but all women, a fact that Sarsfield felt increasingly sensitive about.

Well, his own name would go on *The Letters of Mary Stuart*—a title that would itself be a welcome change from the likes of *Hoyden Princess* or *Avaunt, My Heart*. Wild-Freeman, who owned the name Patricia Orme, could keep her or kill her off, as they chose, but one thing was for sure: Patrick Sarsfield would never again have to creep about the literary landscape in drag. Or never, that was to say, as soon as he had charmed old Mrs. McIntyre out of her crocheted booties.

Mrs. McIntyre: Once she'd settled for talking to Patricia Orme's secretary instead of the great woman herself, they'd got along like a house afire. A hundred and twenty-five pounds' worth of collect transatlantic calls from the library where she worked. She was expecting to show the actual letters to Patricia Orme—how would she react to Sarsfield popping up on her doorstep? But what else could he do?

Once through the caterpillar maze of traffic on the far side of the bridge, the driver darted left off the main roads. Earlier in the day, between abortive phone calls, Sarsfield had carefully studied a Queens street map, but after half a dozen turns he was hopelessly lost. "You sure you know where you're going?" he said.

"Oh, sure yes," Dolgoruky replied. "I live out here. Terrible place. More people under ground than on top." The cab shot across a broad avenue lined on both sides with depressed-looking semi-industrial buildings. "We almost there."

Up a slight rise, into a street of small, red-brick houses, each with its chain-link fence protecting a plot of dead grass around a leafless tree. They passed two cheaply pretentious apartment buildings whose side-by-side awnings announced them as the Lord Byron and the Lady Caroline, and then the cab turned right so abruptly that Sarsfield slid halfway across the rear seat.

The street had even fewer lights than the one they'd just left, and it was fully dark where the driver braked to a sudden halt, in front of the only completely unlit house in a row of nearly identical two-story structures. "Okay, mister. Here we are."

Sarsfield stared out the window, trying to suppress the strong impulse that urged him to leave this place immediately. He didn't consider himself a sensitive man, but he couldn't ignore the neighborhood's aura—stunted hopes, dull resignation, an inward-turning listlessness—that was not a great deal different from parts of Dublin or, for that matter, East Los Angeles. The house before him was shabbier than the rest, and windblown scraps of trash in its tiny yard emphasized its air of abandonment. But there was something more, something he could not quite define. The little house was no more than fifteen feet from its neighbor, but it seemed completely isolated. Sarsfield shivered without knowing why.

"We here," Dolgoruky repeated emphatically, tapping the meter.

"Yes," Sarsfield replied. He looked about him. The street was deserted. He took out his wallet and extracted an additional ten, which he added to the three he was holding. Rolling the four bills into a cylinder, he pushed them into the tray that was recessed in the thick Plexiglas partition. "Wait for me, please," he said. "I'll only be a few minutes." Slowly, reluctantly, he got out and shut the door. He had barely released the handle when the cab took off with a screech of tires and a blurt of half-combusted fuel. Sarsfield watched its brake lights come on; it took the corner fast and was gone.

He picked his way up the footpath—cracked circles of concrete subsiding into the gritty mud—to the front door. He pressed the doorbell, hesitantly at first and then harder, and heard the incongruous clang of chimes from inside. For a full minute he pumped the bell, and once he could have sworn he heard something move inside the house, but no one came to the door. No one home? Desperation was knotting his stomach. He had come three thousand miles; he was meant to enter.

The front door lock was old and feeble, and resisted his pocketknife for half a minute at most. He pulled open the door, winced as the smell inside hit him across the face with the force of a blow. Not long enough ago, something had died in this dank, narrow hallway, and for years something else—quite a few somethings—had been using it as a bathroom. In front of him was a glass-paneled door, with what looked like a heavy blanket hanging behind it. Through a worn spot in the fabric Sarsfield could see a glow of light.

This door, too, was locked. He tapped on the glass, first softly and then, using his pocketknife, more loudly. He found himself quite unsurprised that there was no answer, and he felt in his pocket for a handkerchief. Closing the outer door behind him, he wrapped the cloth twice around his knuckles, cocked his fist, and punched out the glass rectangle alongside the doorknob.

He thought he was prepared, but the sour, penetrating miasma that rolled through the broken pane in a nearly palpable cloud was like no odor he had ever encountered. As his hand groped through the opening for the lock on the other side, he forced himself to separate the smell into its components. Cats, he decided almost at once; a great many cats that lived wild. And food of various sorts, in every stage of decay. His square, powerful fingers found the knob of the lock and turned it, as the list continued to form itself in his head: old woman—correction: sick, not very clean old woman.

As he pushed open the door, he saw in the light of a single bare overhead bulb the source of the final combinative odor that had been eluding him: damp paper and rotted cloth, from hundreds and hundreds of books. Books in cases that lined each wall from floor to ceiling, that lay heaped on the filthy couch, that were piled in stacks leaning perilously against other stacks.

On a chair facing the couch, an immense orange-colored cat with one eye stirred lazily, radiating the insolent air of possession that only very senior felines ever master. It watched Sarsfield step quietly into the room and then deliberately turned its back on him. "All right: be like that," Sarsfield heard himself say aloud, and recognized the remark as a sign of his own nervousness.

A pair of glass doors with several panes gone from each separated the living room from a gloomily shadowed dining room whose sole piece of furniture, a big oval table, was piled with books and papers. Sagging bookshelves covered the outside wall of the room and blocked the space where its only window must be. Here and there, tacked to the shelving, were faded, curling pictures that must have been scissored from books or magazines. Sarsfield glanced at the nearest, which showed two costumed women in an open field looking complacently down at a sprawled corpse in armor. Not far from it was a colored engraving that Sarsfield recognized: the climactic moment of young Queen Victoria's coronation.

Shaking his head, Sarsfield turned his attention to the papers, most of which appeared to be household bills; they lay in dusty windrows that went back a dozen years. The only scraps that were not bills appeared, on quick inspection in the dim light, to be the voucher halves of salary checks, issued in derisory amounts by the Queens public library. The name on both bills and vouchers was the same—Mrs. J.T. McIntyre. At least, Sarsfield told himself, I've broken into the right house.

Turning away from the table he stumbled, in the half light, over an old-fashioned dial telephone lying on the floor. He picked up the receiver and listened, but it was dead. Then he saw why: The wires had been ripped from the wall jack. So that was why his last call hadn't gone through. But who had done it, and why?

On the far side of the dining room a swinging door opened into what turned out to be the kitchen. It was exactly in key with the rest of the house, right down to the dripping sink faucet with the rust-stained hollow in the porcelain below it. As Sarsfield entered, he felt rather than saw a quick movement up above his head. He pulled at a cord that hung from a ceiling light fixture. The bare bulb—no more than forty watts, he judged—illuminated a fluttering, chirping, hugely shadowed shape that darted across the room, barely missing his head, and shot through the closing door behind him. Birds as well as cats, he shuddered; but no people.

The kitchen, too, contained its own impromptu library, ranged with backs up along the counter next to the sink, and propped at one end by a bulbous old toaster. The badly singed volume touching the toaster had been elegantly bound in oatmeal-colored cloth with a black leather spine, on which *Hard Times* was stamped in peeling gilt. A less imposing book—thin, with a faded, stained purple binding—lay open on the counter, and Sarsfield picked it up and glanced at the title page: *An Outline of Abnormal Psychology*. He grimaced, set it back down and opened the refrigerator door, holding his breath. The contents were surprisingly ordinary, mostly half-empty cans of food. Some of it was moldy, as he had expected, but some still looked relatively fresh.

As he stood in thought, staring into the refrigerator, he heard a muffled thump from overhead. Upstairs: of course. He returned quickly to the living room. A narrow staircase without a railing led up into the gloom, and he mounted it two steps at a time. Three closed doors fronted on the landing at the top. The center door opened into an unheated bathroom, whose chipped, stained tub was filled with lathing and fragments of wet plaster that had apparently collapsed from the ceiling. A couple of toothbrushes and a single ragged towel were the only signs of use, and he closed the door and tried the one to his left.

His hand went out to the doorknob, and he became aware of an odd scratching noise coming from inside. As he turned the knob he realized what the sound was, a half second before the cat on the other side of the door forced its way through and between his legs. Part of Sarsfield's mind registered the cat, but most of his attention was fixed on the double bed whose head was against the far wall.

Amid its rucked-up sheets and blankets, a human figure lay, illuminated at head and foot by guttering candles jammed into the necks of dusty bottles. He moved a reluctant two steps forward and saw the figure was a fat old woman, wearing a dark, heavy sweater and a pair of ill-fitting double-knit tights. Her wrists were crossed on her breast, but her head had fallen to one side so that her gray-skinned face—mouth sagging open, eyes mercifully closed—faced him. Even from five feet away, Sarsfield knew she was dead.

For several futile moments, he tried to tell himself that the dead woman wasn't Mrs. McIntyre; she'd been fine only a couple of days ago. But his memory perversely reminded him of her dreadful wheeze, the not-so-subtle allusions to failing health that she had dropped into their phone conversations. Besides, this woman was the right age and her body in the right place. There was no getting past it: He was looking at the corpse of Flora McIntyre. And the corpse of Patrick Sarsfield's bright future, too.

He couldn't—wouldn't—accept that. The damned letters must still be here someplace. He stared helplessly around the dimly lit room. Toppling piles of books, as in the rooms downstairs, and a waist-high breastwork of yellowing newspapers. Unasked, his memory tossed up another fragment of the old woman's rambling monologue: "Don't worry," she'd said, when he asked where she kept the letters, "I've got them in a safe place."

A safe place. What in God's name would seem safe to a crack-witted old recluse? Not out in the open, that was sure. Tucked into a book? Inside a stack of newspapers? Under the damned bed? It could take days to search this terrible old place thoroughly, and Galmoy wasn't likely to hold his hand for that long. Heart sinking, Sarsfield knew he was beaten.

Wait: the daughter. What was her name? Marie. She must know where the letters were. But where was she? Old Mrs. McIntyre said the girl hadn't been outside the house since—

how had she put it? Oh, yes: "Since her training started." He hadn't asked, training for what. Hadn't wanted to know.

Still, she might be here someplace, maybe cowering in her bed, not knowing who to call and too scared to run. And there was another room on this floor, one he hadn't been in yet. Sarsfield flung out of the dead woman's room; the other door was directly across the hall, and he wrenched it open.

Near-total darkness, but something in it moved. Sarsfield felt the hairs at the back of his neck prickle. "Hello?" he heard himself say. "Is that you, Marie?"

Not a word of response, but he heard the whisper of cloth drawn across a hard surface. His fingers groped along the door frame and touched a light switch.

The occupant of the huge, high-backed chair was sitting bolt upright, looking straight at Sarsfield, but she gave no sign that she saw him. A young woman's body, he found himself thinking, but a girl's face, blank with shock. She was huddled in an ancient, disreputable quilt that was safety-pinned about her slender throat, and under it she was wearing something nondescript and dark. Even in the dim light, he could see that her bare feet were crusted with what looked like earth.

Sarsfield took a cautious step through the door, his senses taut with anticipation. Unlike the other rooms, this chamber was bare, save for the thronelike chair and a smaller one beside it. The air was close, dusty, still.

The young woman blinked—greenish brown eyes, he thought, and then he was not so sure. The color seemed to change as he looked into them. She was very pale, with a redhead's milky skin but lacking the freckles that so often went with it. Her hair was long, filthy, and tangled. A compelling face, if not beautiful: Her nose, though straight, was too long, and her mouth too small. He had seen that mouth before—but in a picture, not on a living person. He thought of the dead woman in the other room; no, the features were not hers.

The girl was watching him, and he sensed expectation.

"My name is Patrick Sarsfield. I've come to see Mrs. McIntyre. Your mother."

The girl regarded him silently. He could see no sign of fear in her eyes. No sign of anything at all. Even so, he had the sense she was about to speak, and to encourage her he said, "I've come from Patricia Orme. About the letters, you know."

Her face closed, and as it did the resemblance suddenly came home to him: If you concealed the reddish hair with a white coif and drew a lace collar up under her chin, what was still exposed would be the pale, reserved, secretive face in the portrait that the world knew as *Deuil Blanc*—White Sorrow; the young Mary Stuart in court mourning for her first husband, the boy-king of France.

She was still silent, watching. He had no notion how to get through to her: "You must be Marie. I've come to help you." No reaction. Perhaps she needed a jolt to open her up. "She's dead, your mother."

Nothing, but he thought he could see the smallest movement of her lips. "She must've told you where the letters are, Marie. I'll take you out of here if you'll show them to me."

She moved slightly, and he saw she was clutching a cat under the quilt. Just as he was wondering why it allowed her to hold it so tightly, he realized it was stuffed. All at once Sarsfield decided he could not abide the awful house another second. At the same time, he didn't dare go without the girl: What if she had the letters and wandered off with them? What if someone else arrived, and Marie turned the letters over to them? No, he couldn't leave her, but he had no idea how to make her come with him.

Maybe he could call someone for help. A hospital, the police . . . No, that was out of the question. The last thing he wanted was a barrage of stupid questions about why he was there. He had to take the girl away. Once she was out of this dreadful place she'd come to herself. He would take her to the Algonquin, that was it; some of the Beverly Hills arrivistes thronging the lobby looked no more disreputable than she. He bent over and eased her to her feet. To his surprise, she moved readily, and once she was standing he saw she was his own height, or even a little more.

Shoes. He looked helplessly about the room, but there was nothing. Maybe in the other room, much as he loathed the idea. To his surprise, Marie let herself be led across the hall, still clutching the stuffed cat, which left a trail of sawdust from a ragged gash in its chest.

Five minutes' increasingly frenzied search through the bedroom forced Sarsfield to admit that, aside from a pair of down-at-heels slippers, the only footgear in the place was the cheap fur-trimmed boots on the dead woman's feet. The following five minutes would, he knew, return in his nightmares for the rest of his life. At least Marie was easy to maneuver. Had she struggled or even cried out, he might have fled. But at last she stood in the middle of the bedroom, shod and wearing what was presumably her mother's stained and ragged coat, from whose pockets Sarsfield removed a pair of books stamped QUEENS PUBLIC LIBRARY.

Down the stairs, Marie sleepwalking submissively, and through the living room. At the front door the girl balked. Her face was chalky in the gloom, and her wide eyes glittered with terror. (In his head he heard again her mother's thin voice: "Marie *never* goes out.") Gently, he put his arm around her shoulders. "Just close your eyes, dear," he said, keeping his voice matter-of-fact. "There's nothing to be afraid of."

It worked. Leaving the door swinging open behind him, he led her down the stepping-stones, walking beside her in the sour mud. At the curb he looked up the empty street and down. It was lined with dirty, nondescript cars on both sides, but not a vehicle in motion as far as he could see. Far down the street, an immeasurable distance, he thought he could see a brighter glow of lights. He took Marie's arm, turned her in the right direction, and set off slowly.

Six: Diana

The powerfully built young man blocking the apartment's entrance looked as substantial as the door itself. He seemed slightly bewildered to find three people where he had expected only one. "Miss Speed?" he said, addressing them collectively. He had an open, attractive face—snub nose and bright blue eyes, and a wide mouth that looked to Diana as if it smiled a lot. His hair was a tight cap of very short black curls that reminded her of her mother's favorite Persian lamb wrap. Diana stepped forward, and the young man's direct gaze focused on her. "Good evening, Mr. Pearse," she said. "I'm Diana Speed."

"How do you do?" Pearse said, his politeness automatic.

"These are my colleagues—Ms. Sanders and Mr. Rose. Mr. Michael Pearse, the manuscript expert."

"Diana, dear—of *course*," Judith gushed. Without appearing to move she had placed herself immediately in front of Pearse; she was short enough and close enough so that for him to acknowledge her at all meant looking straight down into her formidable décolletage. To make the decision easier for him, she thrust her hand practically into his stomach.

"Uh, hello," said Pearse. His hands did not go with the rest of him, Diana thought. They were not much larger than Judith's and rather more feminine—smooth skinned, with white, slender fingers, whereas hers were blunt and square-tipped, despite the camouflage efforts of New York's most expensive manicurists.

"My friends call me Judith." She had a way of staring at a man that left no question about what was going through her mind. Under that hot-eyed appraisal many men would virtually snort and paw the ground, but Diana was amused to see that Judith at full strength seemed to make Pearse merely uncomfortable.

"Mick," he said, coloring. Judith released his hand reluctantly, and he glanced down at it, as if counting the fingers.

"Haskell Rose," said Wild-Freeman's editor-in-chief, putting out his own hand. Diana was pleased to see that three cups of black coffee had restored his coherence, although he still had a tendency to sway a little.

"Pleased to meet you," Pearse replied. "Well, I guess you'd better come in."

The living room of Pearse's apartment-cum-office was cheerfully untidy, dominated by a huge leaded-glass window that filled most of one wall and overlooked a maze of fenced backyards three stories below. Immediately under the window was a big desk, flanked by a pair of low steel filing cabinets. The desk's surface was scarred and stained, but a new, unmarked blotter under a sheet of clear plastic sat in the middle, with an oversize, high-powered magnifying glass on a swing arm to one side, and a pair of gooseneck desk lamps on the other. The tops of the two filing cabinets were covered by stacks of what appeared to be correspondence. From the unnatural neatness of the piles, Diana had the feeling that the papers had been arranged for effect.

Besides the desk and its adjustable-height artist's stool, the room's only furniture consisted of an armchair upholstered in cracked red leather, a reading table next to it, a cheap wooden coffee table, and a big, ugly sofa that clearly got a lot of heavy use.

Pearse took his visitors' coats and piled them on the stool. Motioning his visitors to the sofa, he sat down in the chair facing them and nodded at the large manila envelope Judith was holding in her lap. "Those the documents you wanted me to look at?"

"Oh, these." Judith looked down as if surprised to find the envelope there. Ever since the letters' authenticity had come into question, her manner toward them alternated between possessiveness and detachment: If they turned out to be real she would have been their sponsor and guardian, but if they were fakes she would merely have been carrying them as a favor to others. Diana had witnessed similar performances, both in Washington and in the Rajah's various boardrooms, and she had to admire Judith's interpretation of the theme.

"These are just photocopies," Diana said, as Judith held out the envelope and Pearse took it from her. "I know you'll need the originals, but I thought you could at least get started with what's here."

Pearse nodded, his eyes on the envelope's contents. He spread the sheets out on the coffee table, then began picking them up one at a time and holding them under the very bright reading lamp beside him. "Well," he said, after several silent minutes. He seemed at a loss how to continue, and as his three visitors watched him, he carefully restacked the photocopies in the center of the table. Finally, he looked up at Diana: "You know what these purport to be, of course."

Had there been a stress on *purport*? No, she thought not. "The Casket Letters," she replied.

"So you know the odds against them being real."

"Not precisely, but I hear what you're saying."

"I bet you don't," Pearse said abruptly. He paused, clearly ordering his thoughts. "Look, most of the time, when you're working on a historical document that may have been faked, the dirty work—if any—took place centuries after the original. So a lot of your most important testing has to do with paper and ink and penpoints and stuff. If you can prove that the piece is physically as old as it's supposed to be, then you're more than halfway home.

"With these"—he nodded dismissively at the papers in front of him—"the chances are that it was a fake from the very beginning. You see what I mean? Even if the ink and paper and all turns out to be unquestionably sixteenth century, it hardly means anything. You could have the absolute originals that helped pitch Mary Stuart off her throne, and all you've got are genuine, sixteenth-century forgeries."

"I'm afraid I'm a bit lost," said Haskell apologetically. "Do you suppose—"

"What Mr. Pearse is saying," Diana interrupted, "is that most authorities think the Casket Letters themselves were faked. In the fifteen sixties, by Mary's Scottish political enemies."

"Or maybe by Queen Elizabeth's intelligence people," Pearse added. "Provocative forgery was a specialty of theirs."

"You see," Diana explained, "the letters turned up much too conveniently. After the murder of Mary's second husband, Darnley, she almost immediately married his murderer, the Earl of Bothwell. Mary's nobles revolted against her and her new husband, imprisoned her and chased him out of the country. The supposed letters, in a locked casket, were found when the rebels picked up Bothwell's servant—"

"—Geordie Dalgliesh," said Pearse and Diana together.

"—Geordie Dalgliesh," Diana repeated, as Pearse flashed her a quick smile. "He was retrieving the box for his master. He said he didn't know what was in it, only that Bothwell, who was on the run, wanted it and its contents. It just so happened that those contents were exactly what Mary's enemies needed to make her look unfit to be their ruler: proof that she and Bothwell had not only been lovers while she was still married to Lord Darnley, but that she had been an accomplice to Darnley's murder."

"But why did anyone care?" Haskell asked plaintively. "I really can't untangle the minutiae of Scotch history, but weren't they always murdering and betraying each other?"

"Maybe the nobles weren't upset, but the common people were," Pearse said. "Common people sometimes get pretty uptight about their rulers' behavior. And anyway, to a lot of Scots Mary already had three big drawbacks. First, she was openly a Catholic, when most of the Scottish nobility had gone over to the Prots; there were still enough Catholic nobles in power so that a Catholic monarch could have started a bloody civil war. Second, she was only half Scottish: Her mother was a member of a French family, the House of Guise, that was more powerful than the kings of France themselves. Mary was brought up in France, so she *sounded* French. A lot of Scots didn't like that. And third, she—"

"—was a woman," Diana interrupted. "A lot of the same people didn't think queens should reign without some man at their side."

"True for you," said Pearse, "but what I was going to say was that Mary had already turned out to be a real loose cannon. Once her nobles had pried her off the throne, they decided to make it permanent. They had a replacement—her infant son, James—who was too young to make trouble. If Mary wouldn't cooperate by dying, she had to be kept in prison or slapped into a convent. These letters proved she was a whore and a murderess—" He saw the look on Diana's face and hastily added, "In contemporary terms, that is. Not a proper Scottish queen. And when Mary escaped to England, and tried to get help there, the same letters helped convince the English to pop her right in the slammer. Which was what they wanted to do anyway."

"So the letters were too good to be true," said Judith, who had been waiting with visible impatience to get back into the conversation.

"They were too convenient not to be suspicious," Pearse corrected her. "That's one reason not to accept them."

"There's others?" said Haskell, whose enthusiasm seemed to have vanished.

"Afraid so," Pearse replied briskly. "For one thing, you've got no accepted text to check against. Even though the letters were flashed around a lot while Mary's enemies were putting her down, nobody seems to have made a single, authenticated copy of everything that was in the casket. It's like Shakespearean texts, only far worse: We've got several collections of copies of the letters—some of which are poems, by the way—and no two are alike, even as to number. One copy is in English, another in Scots, which was a different language then. And anyway, lots of people feel that Mary would've written something as personal as a love letter in French, since that was the language of her girlhood, and Bothwell was educated in France." He tapped the stack of papers in front of him. "Most of these are in English, by the way."

"Did your quick look tell you anything else?" Diana asked. The way Pearse put the case, it was sounding as if the whole mess might better be quietly buried right now.

"Well . . ." He was obviously reluctant to give a more detailed opinion, but after a moment's hesitation he said, "I can tell you a couple of things for sure. First, you've got two items that aren't in any way part of the Casket Letters. I didn't really bother to look at them, but they're not letters at all; lists—some kind of family birth records, I think; the photocopies make it look like the originals were bound into a book. Second, among the letters themselves there's at least three different handwritings I can spot right off. Beyond that, I don't want to say, without the original papers."

"Let me ask you one more question," said Diana. "Should we walk away from this right now?"

Pearse hesitated, but Diana was sure his mind was already made up. "If it was my decision," he said, "I'd stick with it a little more. Sounds like I'm contradicting myself, but I'm not. Look: You're paying five hundred bucks for an hour of my time, and that's down the pipe." He grinned at their several expressions. "But the originals of these stats are probably worth twice that much, even if they're fairly recent fakes. Just for their curiosity value. For another five hundred, I'll check out what's here—the photocopies—and give you my best opinion on the writing itself. You can decide where to go from there."

Diana could sense that Haskell, who was barely paying attention, had already written the project off. Judith, for whom things and people existed only as absolutes, was clearly uncomfortable with such an extended maybe. Diana reached into her bag and took out a plain white envelope, which she passed over to Pearse. "By tomorrow evening?" she asked.

His delighted smile was as broad as she'd expected it to be. "This time tomorrow," he agreed.

At the door Haskell and Judith were muttering uneasily to each other, and Diana turned to Pearse: "What kind of odds are we talking about—a thousand to one?"

"Oh, much worse than that," he said cheerfully. He had stuffed Diana's envelope into his hip pocket without even looking inside it. "About the same as picking the New York State Lottery." He let her digest that one for a moment, and then added, "But the prize is about the same, too."

●　　●　　●

The taxi dropped Diana off first, and then carried a subdued Judith and a querulous Haskell off to whatever delights they had planned. Wearily, Diana climbed the stone steps to her brownstone's front door; as she reached the top step, she was sorting through her keys when from the edge of her eye she caught, in the tiny vestibule between the outer and inner doors, a flash of movement. Only a couple of weeks before, one of Diana's fellow tenants had been mugged in this same constricted hallway. Without a pause she slipped the keys back into her bag and palmed the illegal stun gun she had recently acquired as a substitute for the container of Mace so many New York women carried. Pulling the outer door wide, she held the electrically powered gun, ready for anything.

Ready, she decided an instant later, for *nearly* anything, but not for the sight that greeted her. Pressed back against the inner door was Patrick Sarsfield, his arm around a large, vaguely female heap wrapped in a filthy, odorous raincoat, its face pressed into his shoulder. For several seconds Diana stood frozen, her mind running through the varieties of male sexual peculiarity. Sarsfield's mouth opened and closed several times, like a landed fish's, before he said, "It's me."

Slowly, Diana lowered the stun gun, but kept it at her side. "So I see," she said. "You want to introduce your friend?"

"This is Marie," he replied. "I could explain better inside." In the light from the single overhead bulb, he looked cold and exhausted. The woman had not moved, and Diana wondered if she was conscious.

"Marie?" Diana repeated. The head on Sarsfield's shoulder stirred and then turned. Diana found herself looking through a rat's nest of stringy red hair into a pair of terrified hazel eyes. "Why, she's just a kid."

"Her mother has—had—the letters," said Sarsfield, dropping his voice to a whisper. And seeing Diana's look of blank incomprehension, he repeated, "The *letters*."

Some of the fear had ebbed from the girl's eyes, to be replaced by what looked, through the curtain of hair, like awe. "I guess you'd better come in," said Diana.

•　　•　　•

". . . I couldn't get a cab for nearly an hour," Sarsfield was saying. "And when I did, he made us get out after just a few blocks." He looked at the girl, who was crouched unmoving on the edge of the sofa, her head down and the horrible raincoat pulled tightly around her.

"I bet he did," said Diana, who was breathing through her mouth in spite of the wide-open living room windows. "What is that, anyway—cat?"

"Mostly cat," Sarsfield agreed. "I was going to take her to the Algonquin, but then it didn't seem such a good idea."

"A wise decision. Bellevue's more the ticket, from the looks of her." At the word *Bellevue* Marie's head came up; her expression of despair cut like a laser through years of emotional armorplate. Diana's hand went out automatically, and Marie flinched away.

Not too fast, Diana told herself. She forced what she hoped was a reassuring smile, and Marie seemed to relax. Diana lowered herself cautiously onto the couch, let her hand lie, palm up, on the cushion between herself and Marie.

Sarsfield picked up the glass of Scotch she had provided and inhaled half of it. Setting it down, he leaned forward. "Diana, those letters are in that house. I'm sure of it. And Marie's the only one who knows where they're hidden."

The letters. Diana forced herself to consider the situation as the Rajah would have done. The letters were probably fakes, and the girl was probably a nut, and who said she knew where they were, anyway? But what if the million-to-one shot paid off? What if the letters were there, and Marie knew their hiding place?

Diana felt a cold, trembling hand take her own, clutch it tight. She turned to Marie, who was watching her with desperate intensity. She didn't look all that crazy, just dazed and scared. If one tenth of what Sarsfield said about the place she lived in was true, she must be petrified. Diana shook her head briskly. "Okay," she said, getting to her feet, still holding Marie by the hand. "Come on, kiddo. Let's get you cleaned up." Marie gave a faint sigh and rose.

Sarsfield breathed something that might have been "Thank God," and Diana spared him a glance. "I think you'd better leave us alone," she said. Firmly rejecting the thought of fleas, she put her arm around the girl, felt her taut body yield infinitesimally.

"What?" Suspicion dropped like a cloud over Sarsfield's face.

"Oh, relax," Diana snapped. "I'm not going to double-cross you. But this is nothing a man can help with. You go back to the hotel and have a good dinner, and I'll call you in the morning."

Sarsfield looked from one woman to the other, smiled weakly. "Maybe you're right. First thing tomorrow." He picked up his coat. "Good night, Marie," he said. She turned away from him and pressed her face into Diana's collarbone.

Seven: Troubridge

What's this, then?" said the dough-faced man across the table, poking suspiciously at his hors d'oeuvre.

"It's called *Bundnerfleisch*," Troubridge said, with resignation. "It's just beef, Carr. Thin-sliced, air-dried beef. It's very popular in Switzerland."

"Doesn't look like beef to me," Carr muttered. "Looks like the dog's breakfast."

Troubridge groaned internally. He had hoped that a civilized dinner with Carr might grease the wheels of their forced collaboration, but already the evening had the earmarks of a four-course disaster. Carr, whose professional forte was said to be social invisibility, had for some reason decided to impersonate a Cockney tough guy. Troubridge had the uncomfortable feeling he was being baited by the fat-faced little horror; the mere possibility was ridiculous—Gordonstoun and Oxford outfaced by Ilford Grammar and the Police College?—but the hostile challenge was clearer by the minute, just beneath Carr's scruffy exterior. And, worst of all, the paper-thin slices of reddish meat *did* have a slightly predigested appearance.

"Plonk's not bad, though," Carr was saying, through a mouthful of half-chewed hard roll. "Any more in that bottle?"

The ruby tide of Dôle de Sion rose in Carr's glass. Almost

before Troubridge could pull back the bottle, his guest had sluiced half the glass down his throat as if it were beer. He pushed away his nearly untouched plate and lit a cigarette. Through the initial smoke cloud, his tiny, bright eyes glittered like polished stones. Troubridge took a leisurely sip of his own wine and noted that Carr's short-fingered hands were trembling very slightly. His nails had been bitten down to the quick, and he had acquired, since their only previous meeting, a habit of rubbing the tips of his left thumb and forefinger together, as if to smooth the skin.

Our nerves seem to be a little raw, Troubridge thought— and no wonder: Almost five years spent burrowing into the entrails of the Irish Republican Army's Provisional wing had taken Carr from Belfast to Beirut to Amsterdam and now to New York, and placed those gnawed fingertips right on the IRA's fattest overseas artery. But if the Provos ever found out that the man they knew as James Parnell Galmoy was a Special Branch agent . . .

The waitress, having removed their plates, was standing expectantly over them. Troubridge asked his guest, "Do you like veal?"

"I suppose it's the nearest they come to proper meat." Carr was oblivious to the large young woman, but Troubridge could feel her bristle.

"Zwei Geschnetslets, bitte," he said to her. *"Rosti und . . ."*

He could not remember the word he wanted, but she supplied it: "The creamed spinach, sir?"

"Please. And a bottle of the Fendant, I think. Les Murailles, if you have it."

Carr was watching him, the little mouth tight. As the waitress turned away, he said, "You know the one great advantage we have over the Yanks?"

"What's that?"

"Americans can't work together unless they like each other." He paused, forced a tiny smile. "But we Brits actually get off on mutual dislike."

Startled, Troubridge asked, "Who on earth said that?"

"Me. Herbert J. Carr." He lowered his eyes as he lit a new

cigarette from the glowing stub of the old. "It's true, anyhow."

Troubridge supposed this was Carr's oblique way of beginning a substantive discussion. He considered and rejected several conciliatory remarks, and asked bluntly, "What do you want from me?"

"Cooperation."

"It'd help if you were a little less Delphic," Troubridge replied. "I thought we'd been cooperating."

"Not really," said Carr. "We've been going through the motions, and that's been enough. Our assignments haven't crossed, until now."

It was late, and the tables on either side were empty. The waitresses were conducting their own murmured conversation at a serving hutch across the low-ceilinged room. Troubridge leaned forward slightly and dropped his voice: "I'm not entirely sure what your assignment is," he said. As he spoke, their own waitress appeared with a bottle in a silver-plated bucket half full of chopped ice. Troubridge and Carr watched in silence as she presented the wine, uncorked it, and poured a small amount into Troubridge's fresh glass. He took a sip, savoring the nutlike taste and the faint prickle of the Fendant's natural carbonation. "Good," he said to her. When she had poured the other glass and gone, he turned back to Carr: "I don't want to know any more than I have to, of course."

Carr emptied his glass of red wine and followed it with a noisy gulp of the white. When he set the glass down, he appeared to have come to a decision: "All right," he said. "I was sent here—to this bloody awful city—to do something about the funding the IRA are getting from their Yank cousins. We've tried exposing the American connection, we've tried appeals to Washington, we've tried everything. And none of it has any effect. The Provos just send another fresh-faced, blue-eyed assassin over here, and the good citizens tumble all over each other to give him their money."

"And you're supposed to cut it off."

"The instruction was to document the flow of cash and arms, expose it, and let the publicity wither it."

"You don't think much of that policy," Troubridge said, carefully neutral.

"I don't think about policy at all," Carr corrected him. "I'm not allowed to. But I know when something doesn't work." On the verge of continuing, he drew back as the waitress appeared with their dinner. She spooned out the veal in cream sauce, the crisply browned potatoes, and the pureed spinach. The mingled smells seemed to defuse even Carr's anger. The little man applied himself to the food, hesitantly at first and then more and more eagerly. He glanced up at last and saw Troubridge watching him. "'S not bad at all," he said. "Don't see why they can't let you cut it up yourself, though."

Troubridge recognized a pro forma grumble and ignored it. He speared a fragment of veal on the tines of his forkful of *rosti* and regarded it thoughtfully. "Must be frustrating," he said. "Following a policy when you know it's futile."

"Easy for you to say," Carr replied. He pulled the bottle of Fendant from the ice bucket and poured himself another glass. "That airy-fairy connection of yours. Not even in a proper department. Fucking medieval survival's what it is." He glanced up from under his sparse eyelashes at Troubridge's face. "Doesn't bother you, my saying that?"

Troubridge's wry smile was almost genuine. "Why should it? You're largely correct."

"But things work out nicely for those as belong, right?" Carr cocked his head to one side, and Troubridge saw that the agate eyes were slightly unfocused. "A tidy K.C.V.O.—neat but not gaudy—and a company directorship at the end of the trail. No wonder you love 'em. I love 'em, too. Loyal subject, that's me. Though underpaid."

"My heart bleeds for you," Troubridge replied. "Some of your colleagues have done rather well—rusticating in the Australian sunset, counting the proceeds from their best-selling memoirs."

"Although not for sale in the UK," Carr agreed. "All we have to do is live to write 'em." The barbed exchange seemed to have mellowed him, at least for the moment, and Troubridge decided he could press forward with caution.

"You said that our assignments had crossed. Just what did you mean?"

"Crossed," Carr repeated, drawing an X on the tablecloth with his finger. He touched the intersection of the two lines. "Right there. Patrick Sarsfield and those 'posterous old letters."

"I beg your pardon?" How much did the awful little man know?

"Don't lift that expensive eyebrow at me," Carr snapped. "I know what you're up to, my lad." Suddenly, he sounded quite sober. "I only want to know one thing, really: Are you supposed to bring the letters home to Mother, or just destroy them?"

An interesting question for Carr to ask, Troubridge reflected. "If they're genuine, they belong to the Crown," he replied, trying to sound uninterested. "What difference does it make?"

"A financial difference, that's what." Carr lit another cigarette, as the waitress materialized to remove their plates. She returned almost immediately and took their order for coffees and, on Troubridge's recommendation, framboise. The hiatus seemed to give Carr time to shape his thoughts, and Troubridge decided that the other man was groping nearly as blindly as he himself was. "It's about money," Carr continued. "Same as always. Sarsfield's promised the Provos that those letters of his are going to be a gold mine, and they're to get ten percent." He laughed without humor. "What he doesn't know is that I've had instructions from Belfast to get hold of it all, as soon as he's paid."

"*All* being how much?" Troubridge asked.

"They're counting on a million. American dollars."

"A million," Troubridge repeated, thinking that the IRA were selling themselves very short indeed. "But they don't want the actual letters?"

"Whatever for?" Carr sounded genuinely surprised. "No,

they want what the letters will bring on delivery to a Yank publisher. And they want it in cash."

Troubridge took a sip of coffee to clear his palate and followed it with a much smaller sip of the clear, sirupy liqueur. A raspberry-flavored flame seared pleasantly down his throat. "And you're to pick off the cash, is that it?" he said.

"I'm to ensure the Provos don't get it, that's all," Carr said. "I gather—I'm not supposed to know this, mind—that the Micks have already made some heavy commitments on the strength of the million they're expecting. If it doesn't turn up, they'll be considerably—"

"Embarrassed?" Troubridge suggested.

"—besides not having the guns. But my bosses don't care what happens to the letters, as long as the Provos don't have 'em." He paused, as if waiting for Troubridge to say something, then went on: "Right. Now, I've shown you mine; suppose you show me yours, as the Americans say."

"Do they say that?" Troubridge replied, trying to decide, as he spoke, whether he had just been made an offer. "I'll be totally honest with you," he began, and realized immediately that his opening had been a mistake, had sounded exactly like what it was—an admission that he was about to tell his guest as little of the truth as he could manage. "From our perspective," he said, "everything depends on whether the letters appear to be real."

Carr emptied the small liqueur glass, and Troubridge was amused to see his eyes widen at the impact. But he caught the distinction quickly enough: "*Appear to be*, not *are?*"

"*Videri quam esse*," Troubridge replied. "In this case, appearance is what matters. The appearance of genuineness is all that's required to make headlines."

"What sort of headlines?" Carr asked, squinting as if he could see them in the blurred distance.

"Oh, like the ones the so-called Hitler diaries made a few years back. Pure visual noise, at first—but attention-getting."

"And then?"

Shouldn't have left himself open for that probe. But, he told himself, perhaps it was as well to get the nub of it out in the open now, rather than let Carr hear it through Sarsfield later: "It's not just that they're letters from Mary Queen of Scots. Not exactly," he began, feeling his way through the raspberry-tinted haze.

"Well, what are they, then? Exactly." Carr was watching Troubridge with desperate concentration.

"Trouble, perhaps." Troubridge flagged down the waitress and indicated their empty glasses, as he framed his reply. "You know about the Casket Letters themselves, I expect."

"More or less."

"You know there are several lists of what Bothwell's casket contained, no two alike?"

Clearly, this was news to Carr, but all he said was "Go on."

"Our table of contents—the one I've been given—lists one letter that none of the other collections has." He looked at the featureless, utterly bland face across the table. How could he possibly make this poisonous dwarf comprehend? He found himself leaning forward, as if proximity could give his words extra force: "According to our information, the extra letter was written by Mary Stuart the night before she was beheaded, in 1587. It wasn't addressed to an individual, but to posterity." He was watching Carr for some reaction, but saw only a glazed attention. "In it, she disinherited her son, James, and all his line. Which is to say," he went on, as understanding crept slowly across the face in front of him, "she disinherited the remaining Stuarts, by extension the Hanovers—"

"—and the bloody Windsors," Carr whispered.

"Who are only Hanovers Anglicized," Troubridge agreed. "And chief among whom is our gracious sovereign, Her Majesty Queen Elizabeth the Second."

"But that's mad!" Carr said, jolted into a squeak of protest. "How could Mary do that? Her son—James, wasn't it?—he got the English throne from Elizabeth Tudor."

"True enough," Troubridge said. "He got it as Mary's

legitimate and only heir. But what if his mother said, in writing, that he was a bastard? And what if there were another child, one she said was legitimate?"

"Is there?" Carr demanded, then caught himself. "Oh, damn it, man—even if there was, he'd be dead for . . . for centuries."

"Of course." Troubridge found himself feeling oddly vindicated by Carr's distress. Vindicated, yet eager to spill the remaining bad news on another victim. "His—or her—descendants would be down to the eleventh generation by now."

Carr's open mouth snapped shut. He took a deep breath. "That's a great pile of speculation," he said. "Not to mention a hell of a lot of descendants."

Troubridge smiled. "All it takes is one documented descendant—"

"—better one than a bloody horde—"

"—who's an American."

"An American?" Carr looked stupefied.

"We're not certain, but that would account for several things that don't make sense otherwise."

"An American wouldn't be—what's the word?—eligible," Carr protested.

Troubridge picked up his framboise glass, saw it was empty, and reached across the table for his guest's. "Eligibility's not the question here," he said. "We've been tracking the possibilities for some time now, and we think that Mary Stuart's last legitimate descendant may be a female American."

"A woman?"

"An *American* woman," Troubridge emphasized. Unbidden, a picture of Diana Speed, crowned and robed, sprang into his head. She looked quite natural, he was not surprised to find.

"Parliament would never—"

"Of course not," Troubridge said. "But in terms of the potential trouble such a person could cause . . ."

"Now I see what you mean: appearance, not reality," said Carr.

"Exactly. Suppose it *should* turn out to be a young American female. Call her Cinderella, because that's what you'd be dealing with. The present crop of royals doesn't need that kind of competition, nor does the nation need to have every lunatic north of the Tweed up in arms again for an independent Scotland."

"Oh," said Carr. "And how do you know about this last letter of Mary's, since no one else has ever heard of it?"

There was, Troubridge thought, no real harm in telling him that part of the truth. "We've always known about the Casket Letters," he began. "In fact, some of them were ours in the first place."

"Ours?" Carr said. "You mean they were written by the English? Then they *are* forgeries, after all."

"Don't be so quick off the mark. I said *some*. The casket itself was quite genuine, and so are most of its contents. Back then, nearly every Scottish noble except Bothwell was taking money from England, so it was easy for us to add a few things."

"D'you realize," Carr exclaimed, "that you're making all this sound like it happened last Wednesday, and it was—what?—four hundred years ago?"

"Four hundred and twenty-odd," Troubridge said, obscurely pleased by Carr's reaction. "But it'll be another four hundred before we're done, if you keep interrupting."

"Sorry. You were saying that some of the Casket Letters were real."

"No, I said that some were English forgeries. *Most* of them were real letters, or love poems, written to Bothwell by several different ladies. Souvenirs of his active love life, you might say."

"All right," said Carr, brows knitted. "So Mary's turfed off the throne, runs to England, and gets popped in prison. What happens to the letters then?"

"They're set aside—filed," Troubridge replied. "For

twenty years, till Mary's execution, at which point her last letter is added to the collection."

"But why keep them?" Carr asked. "Especially if some were forgeries. They'd served their purpose."

"Part of their purpose," said Troubridge. "Remember, James was King of Scotland and heir to England. The letters—especially that last one—would help keep him on the straight and narrow, at least from England's point of view." He caught the waitress's eye, scribbled on air, while he waited for Carr to catch up.

"But after James got the English crown, too," Carr said, apparently thinking aloud, "then the letters were definitely surplus to requirements."

"Surplus to King James's requirements, yes," said Troubridge. "Once he was King of Great Britain, he scarcely needed a reminder that his late mother had been a proven murderess—of his own profligate father. Or that he himself was illegitimate."

"You're saying someone else preserved the letters, is that it?" Carr asked. "Who? Why?"

"One has to consider the situation," said Troubridge. "James was still a very young, very foreign ruler, an unknown quantity. It was felt he might be a bit more controllable if he had the letters hanging over him. And if he didn't work out as king, that final letter might be quite remarkably useful."

Carr's rosebud mouth extended in a tight smile; Troubridge saw that this was the kind of thing he could appreciate. Then the little man's forehead wrinkled. "This *it*," he began. "As in 'it was felt.' I don't suppose you're referring to—"

"You called my people a . . . what was it? Fucking medieval survival," said Troubridge. "I can't speak to the copulative participle, but the *medieval* is near enough: My masters have been in business a long time, ever since some ruler realized there are some actions that must never, *never* attach to the royal family itself."

The little man's face had acquired a satisfying expression of stunned respect, and Troubridge pressed on: "After a bit,

James was firmly on the throne, and demanding to have the letters turned over to him. But they were gone— Oh, he received *a* set of letters, which he promptly burned, but the real ones had vanished, along with the man directly in charge of them. A Scot named Balfor, who seems to have been playing both sides at once. Not uncommon, then as now. Our people expected he'd eventually offer to sell the letters back to the Crown, but the years went by and they never reappeared, nor did he."

"D'you have any idea what happened to him?"

"We do now. Twenty-twenty hindsight. Balfor was a functionary at Lochleven when Mary was imprisoned there. He knew about Mary's baby daughter by Bothwell—he may have helped smuggle the child out. Years later, after Mary's execution, Balfor married his own son to Mary's daughter—a sort of long-term investment, I suppose. Gave the children the Casket Letters, plus the last letter, as a legacy."

"But if you knew—"

"We found out for certain only last year. Actually, it was Sarsfield who put us on to it. He'd been asking all sorts of people about the Casket Letters, and then suddenly he stopped. But he made some quite visible ripples in the Public Records Office, which drew our attention, and from there he went, for no obvious reason, up to western Scotland and started poking about in parish churchyards. It dawned on us that he was following a trail we couldn't see, and since he seemed to know what he was looking for, we let him run—even helped him over one or two hurdles. When we finally saw where matters were leading, we thought we could head him off easily enough."

Carr's pale, round face opened into a horridly knowing smile. "Head him off—by dropping you into his publisher's bed, wasn't that it?"

Carr was right, of course. Whatever Sarsfield found out was bound to become a book sooner or later, so where better to place an observer than Wild-Freeman? Troubridge's superiors had set up the introduction, while blandly allowing Troubridge to convince himself that what happened in

Diana's bedroom had nothing to do with the reason he was in her life at all. He had long since come to terms with the doublethink required. Or thought he had, until confronted by Carr's smirk. Now he realized that he'd just blocked himself from thinking about it. "Diana Speed's not your concern," he snapped, all too aware of the pompous weakness in his tone.

Carr's coup de grace came with a surgical precision that Troubridge might have admired, had it been administered to someone else: "She's still in the hatch, your wife."

"Obviously, you know she is," Troubridge replied, too off balance to fence with the little man.

"You could divorce her, if you wanted to," Carr went on, more to himself than to his host. "The bloody Archbishop of Canterbury would handle it, if your relations asked him."

"You overestimate my connections," Troubridge snapped. "In any case, we don't divorce in my family." The defiant inanity hung in the air like lead, as an expression that could only be delight lit Carr's face.

"'We don't divorce in my family.' That's lovely. But I've heard it before, and you know who I heard it from? From a fucking wife murderer, that's who, back when I was in the CID. But I don't care that your wife's a doper and a nut case, Troubridge. In fact"—Carr's bloodshot eyes were knowing—"I don't even care if it was your kinkiness that sent her round the bend . . ."

Through the red fury that nearly blinded him, Troubridge could see the sudden alarm in Carr's face, hear his voice backpedal quickly into smooth ingratiation. But the pudgy man's words were lost; all Troubridge's mind could absorb was that the lie he had left England to escape had followed him here. And nothing had changed: His helpless rage felt exactly the same as it had the first time he'd heard—at fourth or fourteenth hand—what Lavinia's relatives were whispering about him. Whispers as elusive as mist and as impossible to crush, even when one knew the source.

He realized that Carr had stopped and was eyeing him with cautious expectation. Troubridge raked his memory for what the man had been saying. Something about money. Carr apparently read the expression on his host's face and said, "I was asking how much those letters are really worth."

It required more self-control than Troubridge thought he possessed, but his response was a model of detachment, even in his own ears: "It's impossible to say. I should've thought you'd have figured that out by now. The letters themselves are just the beginning; it's what can be made of them. Even without that last letter, there are books and films and syndications . . ."

"Millions," Carr said. The triumphant venom was gone from his manner; he might have been discussing the weather.

"A good many millions," Troubridge agreed. "If they're the real ones—and that's still a big if. Only experts can determine that."

"Oh, experts," Carr said, dismissing the problem with a wave of his hand. "I've already got an expert on it. A damned good one, too—he used to be a top forger for the National Security Agency."

"An American?" Troubridge was stunned. "You know this whole exercise has *got* to stay away from them. God knows what would happen if Washington heard about what I'm doing—or about your Irish enterprise, for that matter."

"You mean the FBI? They're not as paranoid as they once were. We can do a little business from time to time: We throw them a wog, they toss us a Mick, that sort of thing. But I found my American expert myself." Carr let his self-satisfaction show for a moment. "And tamed him myself."

"I trust he'll stay tame," Troubridge said.

"No fear," Carr replied. "I got him to make me a small bomb, and it went off prematurely. Sent a couple of our gallant lads to glory a bit before their time."

"You rigged it, I suppose."

Carr smiled. "Accidents happen. I arranged for your Miss Speed to hire my man to check the letters for her. So we'll have the news even before Sarsfield himself does. And if they're real . . ." Carr let his words trail off into a meaningful silence.

"Those letters are Crown property, Carr. Don't forget it," Troubridge snapped.

"Tell that to your lady friend," Carr retorted. "She doesn't strike me as someone you can warn off by waving the Union Jack in her face." He hesitated, choosing his words: "Just out of curiosity, how *do* you plan to square her?" He saw the look on Troubridge's face and shrugged. "Me, I go by the Herbert J. Carr motto: *Strike or be stricken*."

"You've a nice choice in sources," said Troubridge. "That was Elizabeth Tudor's motto, too."

"Was it? I guess our minds work the same, then." Carr grinned cheerfully. "But that's what it comes to in the end—strike or be stricken. You mark my words, lad."

Eight: Diana

Marie was seated at the bathroom sink. Diana, standing behind her, was rinsing the girl's hair for the third time when Marie finally spoke: "The letters are mine now." Her voice was low, uncertain, and slightly hoarse. She paused and looked up at Diana's image in the big mirror. "Aren't they?"

"I suppose so," Diana replied evenly. She picked up the hand dryer and fiddled with the controls as she constructed a reply. "So that really was your mother. In the bed."

"What? Oh, yes," Marie replied. "She died in the cellar, but I got her upstairs." She seemed uninterested, her mind clearly elsewhere. "Mr. Sarsfield says he's writing a book about the letters."

Diana turned the dryer on low, and Marie watched it nervously. "It's just to dry your hair."

"Yes," Marie said, feeling the warm air. "I've seen pictures of them. In the newspaper." She had an unusual accent, Diana thought—pure, nasal Queens, but underlaid with a soft drawl. "How can Mr. Sarsfield write a book about the letters if they belong to me?" Marie demanded suddenly.

"Well," Diana replied, working the comb through the girl's long, tangled hair. "Don't you want him to write the book?"

"I didn't say that," she shot back. "It's just that Mother always told me I had to be careful, someone in my position."

Her hair really was quite beautiful, a deep, smoky red that seemed to make her white skin even whiter. "What position is that?"

"Being the chosen vessel," she said. Her tone made it clear no further definition was required.

"That has a number of implications," Diana replied. It was a phrase Maury Thomas used often, and Diana had noticed that people to whom it was addressed always seemed eager to explain the implications.

"You understand, then," said Marie, satisfaction in her voice. "I thought you would."

Shit, Diana said to herself. As she groped for a new approach, she picked with the comb at some of the more complex tangles. Whoever had last cut Marie's hair hadn't bothered to comb it out first; and they had used blunt shears. "You and your mother lived alone?" she said.

"Oh, yes. My father went away years ago. Just after I was born."

So much for Daddy. "And your mother worked in a library?"

"Always. It was suitable."

"For a lady of position," said Diana, taking a chance on the phrasing.

"And there were the books, of course," Marie added.

"Sarsfield said you had a lot of them," said Diana.

"The library gave them to Mother." I'll bet they did, Diana thought. "Eight thousand, two hundred, and fifty-three."

The old woman must have been stealing them for decades. Aloud, she said, "You read them all?"

"Of course. They were my training."

"Mostly history, I suppose," said Diana, feeling her way with increasing confidence.

"Those were the good ones. Then there was international law." She wrinkled her nose in distaste. "Economics. Political theory. I hated those."

"I can imagine." Diana set the comb down; the hair would have to do, for the moment. "Subjects like that must have been pretty tough to understand, without teachers."

Marie, who had been regarding herself with obvious pleasure, looked startled. "Oh, I don't *understand* them," she said.

"You don't?"

"Certainly not. I memorize the important parts. For later."

"You memorize them." Diana was stunned. "Eight thousand, two hundred, and whatever it was?"

"Fifty-three. Are you finished with my hair?" She saw Diana's expression and laughed. "Just the important parts, I said. Would you like to hear?"

"I'd be fascinated," replied Diana, with total sincerity.

Marie stood—she was Diana's height to within an inch—and addressed the shower curtain, her voice dropping several notes: " 'These great officers of state precede all peers of their own degree: the Lord Great Chamberlain, the Lord High Constable, the Earl Marshal, the Lord High Admiral . . .' That's Boutell on precedence," she added, in her own voice. "Or how about, 'Tar water is of a nature so mild and benign and proportioned to the human constitution, as to warm without heating, to cheer without inebriating.' I never did find out what tar water was, though. Or, 'Tuning the lyre and handling the harp are no accomplishments of mine, but rather taking in hand a city that was small and inglorious, and making it glorious and great.' Themistocles."

"I see," said Diana slowly.

"Mother chose them," Marie said, revolving in front of the makeup mirror and watching Diana's second-best robe swirl around her body. "This is very beautiful."

"I'm glad you like it." A sudden abdominal pang brought Diana back to earth: "Have you had any supper? Neither have I." She led the way to the kitchen, her head still spinning, and opened the refrigerator. "Mostly breakfast stuff, I'm afraid," she said. "Maybe something frozen . . ." Though the kitchen was small in terms of floor space, its equipment was both complete and up-to-date; the freezer was a full-size model, and it seldom contained less than two dozen complete dinners, since Diana often worked late and dined alone.

"The curry's not bad," she muttered, fingering a foil-wrapped package. It was, in fact, excellent—Troubridge's one culinary specialty—but it was spiced to an Englishman's idea of Indian taste, and might well produce third-degree throat burns in the neophyte. Probably some plain-vanilla junk food would be a better idea. "Pizza," she announced. "Which would you prefer: sausage, mushroom, or plain?"

Marie, who was standing in the doorway looking bewildered, shrugged.

"Mushroom, then," Diana decided. She opened the box, thrust the contents into the microwave, punched in the setting. "And to drink, beer or Chianti—I ought to warn you, the Chianti's not cold."

"I don't know," Marie confessed. Her lip quivered for a moment, and then she burst into tears. "I don't know any of it," she wailed. "Not pizza, or beer, or Chianti."

Diana took the girl in her arms. "It's all right, kiddo," she said, stroking her back. Marie was thinner than her round face suggested; her shoulder blades were sharp, as were her hips, but she was big-boned and full breasted. "You've had to take in a hell of a lot all at once."

Marie took the paper towel Diana handed her and blew her nose hard. "Thank you," she said. Her eyes filled again, and she managed a watery smile. "I can tell you what a habergeon is, or an order in council, but I don't know the difference between that"—she pointed—"and that."

"Well, the big one's a microwave . . . You know what that is? And the small one's just a TV, so I can watch the news while I'm making breakfast."

"A TV." She leaned forward, eyeing the small, blank screen eagerly.

"Would you like to look at it?" Diana asked, guessing that this was another piece of modernity Marie had never encountered.

"Oh, yes! May I?"

The girl's attitude was so genuine, so unforced, that it dissolved what was left of Diana's detachment. "Sure," she said, grinning. "But why don't you try the one in the living room? The screen's a lot bigger, and you can watch it while we eat."

She left Marie sitting on one of the chairs at the small parson's table that Diana used for solitary meals, but when she returned a few minutes later, bearing the pizza on a big serving platter, she saw that the girl had moved down to the floor and was sitting, cross-legged and transfixed, with her face no more than two feet from the screen. Diana thought for a moment of suggesting she move back, then decided it would be pointless. Instead, she passed slices of pizza to Marie and watched the girl ingest them unconsciously while she watched, enthralled, a sitcom of numbing stupidity, interspersed with soap and insecticide commercials which seemed to delight her even more.

About halfway through the show the phone rang, and Diana, swept by a feeling of reprieve, carried her own piece of pizza and glass of beer into the bedroom, to monitor the answering machine. She stepped through the door, kicking it closed behind her, just as the machine finished its recorded announcement with the customary beep. "Diana, are you there?" said a familiar voice, blurred by the small speaker. "Hey, cannonball to musket. Come in, please."

She set the pizza slice down on the notepad beside the phone and picked up the receiver. "Hello again, Xenie. What's up?"

"I've got some more answers for you, if this phone's all right."

"It's clean as far as I know," Diana replied. After nearly four years away from Washington, she found it hard to remember that any telephone might be tapped. And anyway, Xenia Dawkins, her friend and former State Department colleague, had always been obsessive about telephone security.

Clearly, the obsession was still operative: "I won't use names, if that's all right with you."

"That's fine."

"There's nothing else on the first subject you asked me to check. This call is about the other one."

Troubridge. Diana felt a slight acceleration in her pulse. "You were able to find something, then."

"It took longer than I thought it would," Xenia acknowledged. "Most of it wasn't even in my computer, it was that obvious."

"Tell me anyway."

A silence from the other end, and then: "Honey, is this one business or personal?"

Diana's stomach tightened. "Does it matter?"

The answer was drowned by the long-distance operator asking for more money. Quarters clanged, and Xenia continued, speaking quickly now. "You'll have to decide that one, hon; I'm just raising the issue. Here goes: His job at the consulate's real, and he's connected back home like you wouldn't believe. Cousin to a couple of dukes, and his wife's father is a baronet."

Wife. Well, she'd been almost certain, and now she knew. But Xenia, after a discreetly meaningful silence, was running on: "Younger sons in his family have always been in government service, mostly in the military. The motto on their coat of arms is *Tout pour le roi,* and they seem to mean it. Your man's grandfather, Sir Guy, was equerry—whatever that is—to the Duke of Windsor, before he abdicated. And that much you could've got from Debrett, if you weren't bone-lazy."

"But you make laziness so worthwhile, sweetheart," Diana replied. "Now tell me what's not in Debrett."

"Two things." Another pause, and Diana reflected that hesitation was very unlike her old friend. "The wife's been in and out of the funny farm for years. Almost since they were married. The official word is depressive schizophrenia, complicated by cocaine. But there's some very faint whispers—hey, you sure you want to hear this?"

Apprehension carved a hollow under her ribs, into which her heart was sinking. "I'm sure."

"It's hardly even rumor," Xenia said, her voice apologetic. "I mean, it never made *Private Eye,* or anything like that." Diana could hear her take a deep breath. "Rough stuff.

Sexual rough stuff. They say it was what sent his wife up the wall. And just before your man came here from England, he had a real round-and-round with his brother-in-law. Beat the living bejesus out of him. But at least he's straight"—her laugh was unconvincing—"I mean, he doesn't nuzzle into sentry boxes or anything."

Was it possible? Diana had felt the heat banked under his supercooled exterior, knew it was the wildness in him that inflamed her to a sometimes frightening intensity. There had been moments when he could have done anything to or with her, as he must have known. Sometimes, afterward, she was embarrassed to recall her own vulnerability. But she could let herself go because she knew, beyond the possibility of doubt, that she was safe in his hands. In less than a heartbeat, she had weighed the accusation and discarded it, and heard her voice say, lightly, "That's not really what I wanted to know. Is there anything spooky about him? Anything at all."

"Funny you should ask. Langley wondered the same thing, but they couldn't find a connection to any group on their records."

"That's equivocal enough," she mused aloud.

"Sorry, hon."

"Oh, not you," Diana added hastily. "You've been a tremendous help, especially on the first guy."

"He was easy," Xenia replied. "Name on the payroll, report in the file. It's the old-boy network that gives you fits. Anything else?"

"Just a big, wet kiss for Woodie."

"You come down here and deliver it yourself," she said, laughing. "You're the only girl he knows that he has to stand on tiptoes to kiss."

•   •   •

She stood in the living room doorway for a while, watched the flickering light from the TV screen illuminate Marie's rapt features. Xenia hadn't said why the CIA had bothered to check Troubridge out. It could mean anything or nothing—

and so could their clearance. The whole report was completely typical: fragments that might be fact, inflated by wishful thinking into whatever shape the hearer most feared.

Once, not so long ago, Diana had been an expert at untangling the skeins of raw intelligence, knitting apparently unconnected bits of information into a seamless garment that revealed the shape of an enemy (or an ally). Besides having a good analytical mind, she'd been armed with the far rarer quality of true detachment: The problem itself was what intrigued her, not the antagonist. But when she tried to consider Troubridge, she discovered her detachment had evaporated.

The bastard's got under my skin, she thought. Since her divorce, she had been careful to keep her men at emotional arm's length. It was surprisingly easy, once she'd broken the essential code: Men simply weren't interested in anyone but themselves, however carefully they disguised it. Once Diana learned to filter everything men said and did through the screen of their self-absorption, they became almost completely predictable. And, she soon found, almost completely boring, too. Troubridge, however, was different—he flaunted his egotism with so stunning an openness that it was funny. And he could laugh at it himself.

Even now, when she looked back to their first encounter, she felt herself smile. It had been . . . where? A PEN cocktail party, or maybe the National Book Awards. One of the seemingly numberless publishing nonevents that could fill a room with short, overweight, untidy men and plain, earnest women with disastrous hair. Free drinks and the noisy reinforcement of their prejudices drew them together, and Diana almost immediately felt out of place in every way—for being six feet tall; for having taken some care with her appearance, for having no interest in fuzzy causes; most of all, for being a stranger in a world everyone else seemed to have been born into.

She had spotted Troubridge across the room, which was no great feat, since he stood out like a lighthouse; and a lighthouse wearing a dinner jacket at that. She didn't know who had caught whose eye, but their rueful grins met halfway between them.

They hadn't talked, though. Diana had allowed the party's horizontal currents to carry her toward him, but when she arrived he was gone. She didn't see him for a couple of weeks, and then they suddenly found themselves face-to-face at the Metropolitan Opera bar during intermission. Diana was alone, the last-minute beneficiary of a decent orchestra seat from a friend of a friend unable to use it. (What friend? Her checkbook might remember—she made a mental note to consult it.)

Somehow, the fact that they had missed contact the first time made their second encounter easier, more natural, and both were crestfallen when five minutes of civilized chat were interrupted by the signal for the curtain.

"Would you care to join me?" Troubridge asked. He was sitting in a box, it seemed. There was plenty of room, since the other consulate personnel who'd been scheduled to use it were working late. Diana hesitated only momentarily. Her seat was not as good as she'd expected, and the performance, Kiri Te Kanawa singing Fiordiligi, was superb. "Please come," Troubridge insisted. "I'd hate to lose you again." She braced, faintly disappointed, for the predictable compliment—"You've no idea how hard it is to find presentable women of a decent height . . ." As he paused, she saw his eyes were amused. "And I expect you have even more of a problem."

At that moment in her life—two months into Wild-Freeman—she was surrounded by bootlickers, some of whom had made it clear, in sidling, convoluted terms, that they were also willing to lick anything else she might suggest. Troubridge's casual arrogance came as a bracing relief, and his interest in grand opera (not to mention his access to box seats) spoke to her spirit. But what put him in her bed was their shared passion for elaborate, expensive food and drink. That, and his remarkable ability to maintain their relationship on the same exciting, essentially unstable level.

He used her shamelessly in his professional capacity (or what she assumed was his professional capacity), usually casting her as a delightfully shocking American to be trotted out for an endless procession of doddering VIP visitors. "You look so nearly normal, Speed—an oversize Sloane Ranger—and then you bite their throats out. They adore it." And they did seem to, which she put down as one of the more exotic facets of Brit masochism.

Of course she used him, too; not only as an escort at publishing parties and dinners (where he would lure the more humorless by trailing his Tory coat before them, then yank it from under their feet with an apposite quotation from some member of the American liberal pantheon), but also as a sounding board off which she could bounce the frustrations and disappointments she could share with no one at Wild-Freeman, not even Milly Aaron.

They never discussed their pasts, never entertained a joint future, and Diana had counted herself safe at last, except, once in a while, in bed. Shows how wrong a girl can be, she thought. And I don't know which would be worse—finding out I'd been suckered, or finding out I loved him.

"What's wrong?"

Diana snapped back with a start, to the sound of finale music from the TV and the sight of Marie's anxious face. "What? Oh, nothing. Nothing at all." She moved into the living room and lowered herself to the floor beside the girl. It had been years since she sat cross-legged this way; the position took her back to school assemblies. "The news is next, I think. Do you want to watch it?"

"Yes, please," Marie replied. Diana suppressed a sigh. TV as a treat—that was as good a definition of deprivation as she could imagine. But Marie seemed intelligent enough; it was bound to wear off.

"If we moved back a little, the screen would be easier to look at," said Diana, a few minutes into the regular evening slice of apocalypse. At first she thought Marie hadn't heard, but then the girl began to wiggle backward, never taking her eyes off the screen, until she was at a nearly reasonable distance. They sat in silence through the latest installment of municipal budget crisis (though Diana got up during the commercial to pour herself another glass of Chianti), and it began to seem as though Marie might be planning to spend the night where she sat, when Diana, who had been nodding, suddenly came fully awake.

". . . sordid death of a Queens recluse," the announcer was saying, his voice dropped three notes in tribute to the Grim Reaper. "Police, called by a neighbor, this evening discovered the body of a woman in this filthy, cluttered house on a quiet back street in Elmhurst." The damp street gleamed in the TV crew's lights, and was replaced by the overexposed face of a very young man in a white jacket—an ambulance attendant, perhaps, or an intern. "It's unbelievable in there," he said. "I've never seen anything like it."

Appalled, Diana reached past Marie to turn the set off, but the girl struck her hand down impatiently. *"Non,"* she said absently. "I must see this." The young man in white maundered on for several seconds, and was replaced by the studio announcer.

"Although the woman, identified as Flora McIntyre, was thought by neighbors to have lived alone—except for literally dozens of cats and birds—police say there are indications that another person may have shared the house with her." Diana found herself leaning forward as the announcer continued: "The neighbor who called police said that two people, a man and a woman, left the house early this evening. Their identities are not known—except, perhaps, to the solitary woman who lies tonight in the ultimate loneliness of death."

"Vulgarian."

"What did you say, Marie?"

"That man with the smooth hair," she said. "He has a great deal to learn about death."

Diana looked more closely at her. In the kaleidoscopic flickering from the screen, the girlishly round contours of Marie's face seemed to have hardened. "It doesn't seem to bother you, anyway. Death."

Still looking at the screen, Marie smiled. Her hand went

slowly to the base of her throat in a gesture that was half exploration, half caress. "No," she said, "death scarcely concerns me."

Diana eased her stiff legs, moving to a position where she had a better view of Marie's calm, absorbed face. "You don't seem very broken up," she said. "Considering she was your mother."

"*Ma mère?*" Marie's head half turned to meet Diana's eyes. An expression of surprise and disgust was already fading, but still unmistakable.

"You speak French?" Diana offered, when she was sure Marie had nothing more to say. It wasn't, she was thinking, that Marie's expression had changed. More the way she held her head, the way she sat. As if she had become both older and far more self-assured.

"*Bien entendu. Et tu?*"

"*Assez bien,*" Diana replied. "But not well enough to *tutoyer* my elders."

Whatever reaction Diana had expected to her shot in the dark, it was not a look of icy rage, followed almost instantly by scarlet embarrassment. "Oh!" said Marie. "Miss Speed, I'm sorry. I didn't mean. . . "

"*De rien,*" she said, smiling. "Really. And I think it's time you started calling me Diana, since we'll be sharing a bed."

The girl's eyes widened. "Are you sure? I can sleep on the couch. I don't want to be a problem—any more of a problem," she added, reddening again, "than I've already been."

"Nonsense. I insist. The bed's plenty wide enough for two"—she suppressed an unexpected giggle that Marie seemed not to notice—"and the couch would be too short for you, anyway."

"Oh, thank you," said Marie earnestly. "It's the most beautiful bed in the world."

"It's not so seedy," Diana allowed. "But Marie—are you sure you don't want to do something about your mother?"

Marie's bafflement seemed complete, untinged with any trace of grief. "Do what? She's dead."

"A funeral might be appropriate," said Diana.

"But I have no money. None at all."

"Don't give it a thought. Wild-Freeman will pick it up. You can pay us back later. You're going to be very rich, you know."

"I am?"

"The letters," Diana reminded her. "They're worth a fortune." Once we get them.

"But I could never sell them," said the girl. "They're not mine—that is, they are, but only . . ."

"In trust?" Diana suggested.

"That's it," Marie agreed quickly. "In trust. Until she comes for them."

Crazy as a bedbug, Diana thought. Just what I needed.

FRIDAY

Nine: Pearse

. . . pour navoir loisir estant ascheminee le Roy mon nari et moy contre nos rebelles—the big, sprawling letters galloped across the page—*ne vous fayray plus longue lettre que pour prier dieu quil vous doint madame ma bonne soeur en sante tres heureuse et longue vie.*

With a sigh, Pearse pushed back the magnifier in front of him and screwed his knuckles into his aching eyes. It was far too little on which to commit himself, but he had no doubts at all. In front of him on the desk were photocopies of two letters known to be in Mary Stuart's hand. The first, a breathless note from the Queen of Scots to her English cousin, dashed off in visible haste; the second, written five years later from an English prison, composed with caution (or what, in the Queen of Scots, passed as caution) for the hostile eyes of a jailer who wanted only her head.

Two languages, the writer equally at home in either. Pearse had little time for the affectations of graphology, but the writer of these letters was quite unable to keep her personality out of her hand: rash, emotional, exuberant; contemptuous of details of accent or punctuation (and maybe, by extension, of right or wrong). A woman men might admire—might even love—for her headlong gallantry alone.

He picked the topmost document from the stack of photocopies on the right-hand edge of the desk. The print that had a legal-size sheet of penciled notes in Pearse's tiny, meticulous printing paper-clipped to it. *O Dieux, ayer de moy* it began—a long poem, forty quatrains, whose soggily conventional sentiments quarreled on every line with its writer's impatience. Mary had written this, Pearse was certain; he was just as certain that the words were someone else's. He stared at the italic lettering, his mind in neutral, letting his eye sort resemblances from differences, and then the front door buzzer burred softly. Pearse pushed his chair back, got up, and walked to the intercom. "Yes?"

Through the echoing background of outside street noise the voice was clear enough: "Good morning, Michael."

Christ, Mr. Vaseline. Tops on my most unwanted list. He stabbed at the button that opened the front door downstairs. A minute later, as he stood in the open door of his apartment, he heard the elevator's gate clash, four floors below, and then the asthmatic whine of its motor. It stopped with a mechanical thump, and Galmoy stepped out. Even from thirty feet away, and under the pale yellow glow of the hall's overhead lighting, he looked terrible. As he came closer, Pearse's first impression was reinforced. "What was it—a night on the town or a pitched battle?"

Bloodshot eyes, delicately bagged in black, blinked at the bright light that streamed out Pearse's door. Galmoy slipped through, under Pearse's arm. "I was . . ." he began, and had to clear his throat. "I was in the neighborhood," he said, speaking even more softly than usual. "I thought I'd stop by for a progress report."

Pearse released the door, allowing its heavy spring to close it with a slam that echoed down the hall and crumpled the other man's face as if it had been struck. "Jesus," Pearse said. "I've seen hangovers, but—"

"A little indigestion, that's all," Galmoy said. "Nasty foreign food." He stepped into Pearse's living room and sank down on the sofa, shielding his eyes with his hand.

Pearse went to the sideboard, took out a bottle and poured three inches of its contents into a highball glass. "Here," he said, holding it out. "I don't want you upchucking on my nearly new rug."

Galmoy looked at the thick liquid and shuddered. His cheeks, white before, faded to a pale green reminiscent of the reverse side of a dollar bill. He shook his head.

"Suit yourself," Pearse replied, and poured the glass back into the bottle, his hand insultingly steady. "A progress report?" he said, his eyes on the thin stream. "Okay. What I'm looking at is a collection of thirteen discrete documents, of various lengths." He capped the refilled bottle and set it down.

Propping his buttocks against the sideboard, he continued: "Two of the documents are genealogies—one extended genealogy, really, running from the mid-sixteenth century in Scotland to eighteen years ago, right here in the U.S. of A. The handwriting in those two lists looks right for the periods it spans, but with something like that I really can't do anything without ink and paper tests, so I've set those pages aside. Of the rest, there are eleven different items in three languages—French, English, and Scots—including one very long letter with no salutation. The language and the spelling look to be right on the money for middle of the sixteenth century. They were written by four different people—three of them women, one much better educated than the other two. I'm guessing that the fourth writer was imitating one of the other three. Pretty good, too. The only thing he couldn't duplicate was—"

"Is any of it in Mary Stuart's hand?" Galmoy interrupted. "That's all I want to know, Michael."

"It's not that simple," Pearse protested.

Galmoy's slitted eyes bored into his. "But you think so."

Pearse took a deep breath. "Some, yes. Not all." He saw the next question and headed it off: "Five out of the eleven, I think."

"You think?"

"For Christ's sake!" Pearse exploded. "I'm working with two samples that are authenticated Mary Stuart letters. Just two, and they're both photocopies. I haven't any originals, man. Until I see originals, I can't commit further."

"But all the indications you have—style and language and whatnot—tell you that five of these letters were written by Mary Queen of Scots."

There was no point to evasion. "Yes," Pearse replied, then corrected himself almost instantly: "Four letters and a poem."

Galmoy sank back on the sofa, his eyes closed. "You might just have said so right off," he sighed.

Pearse regarded Galmoy with loathing. "If I said right off that the handwriting looked like hers, that's all you'd have heard." He reached out as if to shake the other man, and changed his mind. "Are you listening to me, Galmoy? The odds are still that these are a dud. Very heavy odds."

Without opening his eyes, the dough-faced man asked: "And if they're not?"

"What do you mean?"

"What are they worth, that's what I mean." Galmoy wrenched himself upright with a grunt. "What can"—Pearse sensed the slightest pause—"Sarsfield get for them?"

"Sarsfield?" Pearse blinked, then remembered that this was the author Diana Speed was fronting for. "Oh, you mean selling them, after his book about them comes out?"

"Selling them, yes. Leave the book out of it for now."

Pearse lifted one of the photocopies with the tip of his finger. "What makes you so sure they really belong to him? The originals, that is."

"You let me worry about ownership," said Galmoy, whose patience seemed to be fraying fast. "If someone had the originals of those documents, just the five Mary Stuart letters . . . How much would they be worth?"

"That's an unanswerable question," Pearse said, and rode over Galmoy's snarl of irritation: "—and I'll tell you why, if you'll shut up for a minute. Two of those five documents are almost beyond price: this very long letter from Mary to Bothwell"—he indicated a dozen photocopied sheets paper-clipped together—"and the very short one, that she wrote the night before they cut off her head. The first settles, once and for all, the most emotional argument in all of history: Did Mary knowingly have a part in her second husband's murder? Flatly, yes, if you accept the letter as real."

"They'll have to accept it," Galmoy said.

"Bullshit. You're talking about years of scholarly infighting, in several disciplines. You know how these buggers argue, Galmoy? In fucking quarterly magazines. It's like chess by mail, only three months between moves."

"I don't see—"

"Look: Let's take the Mary–Bothwell letter as an example. Say we line up half a dozen top handwriting authorities, all saying it's authentic. Boom! Headlines in the *Times*, magazine articles, big interviews with TV personalities who couldn't read the words on a Popsicle wrapper. The works. Sure as hell six other experts will turn up to contradict your guys, just to be contrary. But you've still got your tigers behind you, so you go to auction."

"Auction," Galmoy repeated, squinting with the effort of following Pearse's exposition. "And what could we expect to get, Michael? That was my question, all I really wanted to know."

"That's what I'm trying to tell you, man," Pearse said, with exaggerated patience. "Nobody's got the faintest goddamn idea. Look at the last big out-of-the-blue sale—the Mozart manuscript—finally went for three and a quarter, but it could've been twice that, or half. You've got to pick a price out of the air . . ." He moved to where he had a better view of Galmoy's pained face, and slowed down. "Let's say you go in with a reserve price of a couple million dollars, and maybe you get it. But if you don't try to sell right away—hold the letter, and publicize it, till you win over a solid majority of authorities—after a while it'll be accepted as gospel. The sky really is the limit here, if you've got the patience. And if the damn thing's real."

"All right," said Galmoy, looking a little less deathlike. "That's the first letter, the long one. What about the other?"

"Ah, there it's *much* more complicated," said Pearse with

relish. "Half the world already accepts the idea of Mary as an accomplice in Darnley's murder. But no one, not since Darnley himself, has given much thought to the idea that her baby might have been fathered by another man. And certainly no one's ever considered Mary's half brother for the job."

"Why not? From all I've heard in the last few days, those precious kings and queens were just a pack of alleycats."

Pearse considered for a moment the complex character of James Stuart, Earl of Moray, and decided not to attempt a serious explanation. "He should've been king, Mary's half brother. And he knew it—but he loved her. He was into theology, too: very puritanical. Very patriotic."

"That kind slip the farthest, when they go," Galmoy replied. "But never mind. Say we have the same panel of experts agree that this letter's real, too. What would it be worth then?"

"Christ, who knows? Say ten million for openers, on account of the shock value of the accusation. It's just my guess, of course, but I'd bet that royal incest would be worth even more than royal murder. The trouble is, even if the letter is proved to be Mary's, the accusation itself can still be dismissed—one last hysterical attack by a vengeful woman, against Moray, who couldn't defend himself because he was dead, and King James, who'd let his mother go to the block without a serious protest. That would bring down the price, on the open market."

"What are you saying, then?" Galmoy demanded. "Is there another market?"

"Well," Pearse offered, "the Queen of England's said to have—what?—three and a half billion dollars of her very own. And these are her ancestors we're talking about. If someone approached Her Majesty properly, she might be receptive to making a takeout bid—"

"Are you out of your mind? The Queen dealing with *me?*"

Pearse, who had given rein to his own enthusiasm, pulled up short. "Why, of course not," he said, watching Galmoy narrowly. "That would be up to Sarsfield, wouldn't it?"

Galmoy's face, lit by greed, closed up tight. "Wouldn't it?" Pearse repeated gently.

Galmoy was silent.

"Well," Pearse went on, as if he had not noticed, "all that's none of my business. I need to know what you want me to say to Diana Speed. She'll be calling for a preliminary report anytime now, unless I miss my guess."

"Oh," said Galmoy. Pearse could almost hear his mental gears shifting. "Why, tell her just what you've told me: that the handwriting and the spelling and the rest look promising, but you absolutely have to have the originals."

"There's no problem with getting these originals, I hope," Pearse said. "Without them, you've got nothing. Zero."

The pale, mushy face opposite suddenly seemed to harden, but before Pearse could be sure, it had sagged back to its original state. As if conscious of Pearse's intent gaze, Galmoy forced a smile. The effect was awful. "When you talk with her," Galmoy said, "for God's sake don't tease her, the way you did with me. We want to whet her appetite, so do try to emphasize the hopeful side."

That was interesting, Pearse reflected, as the door closed behind Galmoy. If Mr. Vaseline once referred to our noble cause, I sure as hell missed it. On the desk behind him, the phone began to ring.

Ten: Diana

She set the telephone down gently, as if a jolt might break it, and remained staring into the middle distance for several minutes, replaying Pearse's end of the conversation. She was willing to swear there had been genuine excitement under the cautionary disclaimers, a barely controlled exultation. He might not be ready to acknowledge the letters, but he was privately convinced.

Diana looked down at her watch: nine-thirty, and not a sound from the bedroom. She had forced herself to lie quietly next to the softly breathing Marie until the glowing red digits on the bedside alarm clock read six, when she slipped from under the covers. The room was almost completely dark, and she felt her way out, leaving the door behind her slightly ajar. A single cup of coffee had sustained her till seven, after which she'd made breakfast, taken a shower, and washed the dishes, to the accompaniment of a steadily increasing volume of incidental sounds that concluded with a wholly deliberate crash when she dropped the frying pan.

To no avail: Marie slept on. At nine, when it seemed to Diana that watching another vapid TV interview might cause her brain to liquefy and run out her ears, she called Wild-Freeman and picked off Cathy O'Donnell.

"Are you all right, Miss Speed?" the girl said, the edge of

her concern dulled by a mouthful of Danish. "Shall I tell people you're reading at home?"

On any given morning, presumably, some tiny fraction of the publishing executives who were *reading at home* were not in fact taking their kids to the Bronx Zoo, or in bed with other editors, or simply too hung over to face the day. But the excuse—as Diana had quickly learned—was sacrosanct, not to be questioned. For that reason alone she never used it. "I'll be in later," she told Cathy. "But I don't know exactly when. What's on the list for today?"

Paper rustled in the background, and the girl's voice returned, unencumbered: "You're going over the ad budget with Mrs. Epstein at ten; meeting with Mr. Rose and Mr. Thomas at eleven about sales conference; lunch with Miss Aaron at twelve-thirty; meeting with Mr. Ellison at three, to talk about outstanding royalty advances; four to five you've got down for correspondence; five-thirty . . ." Catherine took an audible breath ". . . your calendar says 'stroke Princess Astarte.' And you have dinner with Mr. Troubridge—" The words *as usual* hung in the air, but Diana ignored them.

"Okay," she said, considering. Ellen Epstein, the new advertising manager, had the melting brown eyes of a Disney doe, the figure of a fashion model, and, Diana suspected, the soul of a tarantula. She was Maury Thomas's latest protégée and also his current quarry, and Maury would be double-checking her work until he had either bedded her or been conclusively refused. "Ask Mrs. Epstein to leave the budget with you. I'll review it over the weekend and get back to her if I've got any questions."

Wild-Freeman's twice-yearly sales conferences, which had been organized for the last twenty years by Maury and Haskell, had become as ritualized as an Ivy League commencement exercise, and very nearly as dull. The schedule for the Spring List meeting, to be held as usual in a run-down hotel on the Jersey shore, was an almost exact duplicate of last year's, which Diana's predecessor had approved without comment. It seemed reasonable enough, aside from the venue—Asbury Park in January would be an anteroom of hell, all creaking wicker porch furniture and wind-driven sand. "Stet the eleven o'clock meeting, but tell the gentlemen I may be a little late, and if I am, we'll have sandwiches in my office. Tell Miss Aaron I've had to cancel," she added, with real regret.

Next? Oh, yes—Brand Ellison at three. What in God's name had possessed her to schedule Brand for a Friday afternoon? Or for any afternoon? She knew perfectly well, of course, and hated what had to be done. Over the years, the rest of the editorial department had conspired to hide the managing editor's almost surrealistic incompetence by informally dividing his functions among themselves, with the result that some of W-F's simplest procedures were now incredibly circuitous.

The only responsibility that remained on Brand's desk (because no other editor would touch it) was that of policing the advance royalty payments made to Wild-Freeman's authors—making sure, among other things, that writers delivered the manuscripts for which they'd received advances, or else returned the money. Predictably, W-F's list of unmet, unreturned advances had become a financial black hole. Today, after many postponements, was the reckoning. It could not be put off. "Stet Mr. Ellison."

Princess Astarte, née Florence Miller of Towanda, Kansas, was one of Haskell's prospective authors, a psychic who had parlayed her combination of Druidical costume and Nostradamic interpretation into a medium-sized Southern California fad. She was now about to give birth to a book that would (Haskell promised) "knock crystals right on their ass." Diana had less than no interest in the supernatural, but she had a long-standing fascination with really first-class charlatans, and the Princess sounded like someone worth meeting. "Tell Mr. Rose I'm desolated that I won't be able to make it. See if you can reschedule for next week, and tell him to take the Princess to Barbetta, on my account, this evening."

"And Mr. Troubridge? Do you want me to call him?" Cathy asked, her tone clearly expecting a no.

"If you would," Diana replied. "My apologies, but something's come up and I'll call him as soon as I can." She thought for a second, and added: "Cathy? If he asks, you don't know what it is that's come up."

"But Miss Speed, I really don't."

"Well, that should make it easier, kiddo. Now get on your horse."

Why had she fobbed Troubridge off on Cathy? It was an instinctive decision, though the reasons prompting it had not yet revealed themselves. With everything else she had to think of today, Troubridge was one complication too many. And yet, Diana reminded herself, she usually reveled in complication. No, there was more to her reluctance than a desire to keep her day uncluttered.

Her musing was interrupted by the buzz of the front door, but Troubridge was still in the forefront of her mind when she pressed the intercom button. "Yes?"

The click of footsteps on concrete, the breathing of someone whose mouth was too close to the mike, even the sound of a sportscar shifting gears half a block away—all these came through the speaker with perfect clarity, but only two years' experience enabled Diana to translate the confused rasping that represented a human voice: "It's me. Patrick Sarsfield. May I come up?" Her own reply, she knew, would be as completely garbled, so instead she merely pressed the front door release, heard its distant buzz abruptly cut off as Sarsfield opened the latch.

He came bounding up the carpeted stairs like a man half his age, bringing with him an aura of damp, cold air and exhaust fumes. "Top o' the mornin' to you!" he cried. His face was gleaming with sweat, and Diana guessed he must have walked all or most of the way from the hotel. "Is she still asleep, then?" he asked, looking down the hall at the bedroom door.

"She is." Diana replied, taking his coat. "Coffee?"

"That'd be glorious," he said, beaming. When she returned from the kitchen with two steaming mugs, he was standing at the window, looking down into 50th Street.

"Thank you," he said taking the cup. "It's the gem of the world you've got here."

"I like it," Diana replied, folding herself easily on the couch, one foot tucked beneath her. "Did you fall among Gaels on the way over? You weren't talking that way yesterday."

Sarsfield's eyes widened with what looked momentarily like dismay, and he reddened to his collar. "You caught me," he admitted, grinning boyishly. "It's just my County Mayo accent, I'm afraid. Keeps the natives off balance." He took a quick gulp of coffee, spluttered desperately, and managed at last to get it down. "Jesus God," he gasped, staring into the cup with watering eyes. "My dear, you must have a throat lined in steel. Still on the boil, and strong enough to dissolve a sheep."

"It has got authority," she agreed, realizing as she spoke that she was quoting Troubridge. "I suppose you want to know what happened after you left last night."

"I would that," he said, dropping heavily into an armchair. "Did you ever get her to speak?"

"As a matter of fact, yes. Patrick, that child is really from outer space."

"I'm not surprised," he replied. "If you'd seen her mother. A perfect—what d'you call it?—bag lady. A bag lady with royal pretensions. And that house . . ." He shuddered, took a cautious sip of his coffee.

"I did see the house," said Diana. "So did Marie. It was on the eleven o'clock news last night."

Sarsfield's head snapped up. "Did they say anything about—"

"No. The usual death-of-a-recluse kind of thing. I gathered that nobody was about to go back inside until it airs out."

"I don't blame them," Sarsfield muttered. "I hung my coat out the hotel room window last night."

"You forget, I had the girl herself, the prewashed version. Not to mention her clothes."

"Lord, yes." He glanced nervously about the room. "What became of them?"

"God willing, they're in a Sanitation Department barge by now," she replied. "I gave Marie a nightgown, but we'll have to get her something to wear outside—we're almost the same height, but I can't compare with her in the chest or hips."

"I've always preferred greyhounds myself," Sarsfield said, and she returned a cool, one-second smile. "But we've got to get the child out to Queens and into that house, and soon."

"You've no idea where the letters are?" Diana asked, noting and mentally filing her impression of extreme urgency driven—understandably—by greed, but no less by fear.

"No, damn it," he replied. "From what the old lady said, I'm pretty sure they're hidden someplace. But I haven't a clue where. I'm counting on the girl."

Diana got up and moved just far enough so the light fell plain on Sarsfield's face, before she spoke: "Oh, she knows. And she'll tell us, when she's ready. But I was thinking," she added, addressing her cup and watching Sarsfield from under her lashes, "it might be safer to let things cool off out there, for a little. I expect the place is still swarming with cops. They did mention on TV—I forgot to say before—that they were looking for two people, a man and a woman, who left the house shortly before the body was discovered."

She paused, weighing the expressions that flittered across Sarsfield's ruddy features. "No descriptions?" he asked. She shook her head. "Well, that's a relief. But look, Diana, what if someone stumbles across the letters, or they tear down the house? Christ, we're so close . . ." He was sweating again, she saw.

"A few days can't make any difference," she said airily. "We'll pick up your expenses in the meantime, of course. I just want to avoid any tangles with the law, anything that might get the letters impounded, till Mrs. McIntyre's estate is settled."

"Oh, Jesus," he said, his face going gray. "I never thought of that." He drank off the rest of the coffee without noticing it and set the cup down. "Look," he began, and then stopped.

"Would you like a drink?" said Diana. "I know it's early, but—"

"By God, I would," he interrupted. "Irish, if you've got it. No ice." Behind her, as she knelt at the liquor cabinet, she heard his fingertips drumming on the coffee table.

"No Irish, alas," she said. "How about Chivas? Scotch seems appropriate." She turned as she spoke.

He managed a desperately weak smile. "Scotch would be grand." He took the highball glass in both hands and buried his face in it before he noticed her expression. "I'm not usually this jumpy," he said.

"I hope not," she replied, sitting down across from him. She watched as he took another long swallow, draining the glass, and only then did she speak. "You're scared, Patrick. Petrified. What is it?"

He opened his mouth, perhaps to deny everything, but closed it again and shook his head, staring down into the empty glass. She picked up the bottle and poured until the glass was half full. "I never lived overseas before I bought my place on Clew Bay," he said. "It was harder than I thought it'd be. Ireland's different, you know. It's . . ."

"Another country," she offered.

"Exactly," he agreed eagerly. "That's just it. And you want people to like you, so you start off buying rounds in the pub, contributing to the Life-Boat Fund, that sort of thing." He picked up the glass and took what might charitably be called a sip. "Anyway," he continued, "sooner or later you're asked if you'd like to 'help the lads.' And if you don't seem to understand what lads they're talking about—I didn't—they'll say that surely an American with an Irish name would understand their position, what they were trying to do."

He seemed to be running down again, and Diana jogged him with a soft "I see."

"So you try to slide past by talking about how you're against violence. 'Voiolence, is it?' " Sarsfield went on, sliding into his imitation brogue. " 'Let me tell you about voiolence, me bhoy.' And then they give you Oliver Cromwell, for Christ's sake, or Henry fucking Strongbow. And pretty soon you find you're sitting next to some kid—some nice, polite kid—and the guy in the corner's singin' 'Who fears to speak of '98,' and the first thing I know, I've got a bomb factory in my cellar and three cases of Uzis in the attic. Jesus."

So that was it, she thought, and voiced the question in her mind: "How'd they manage to get a piece of this project?"

Sarsfield snorted, presumably at his own foolishness. "That was the price to buy myself out. Ten percent of my advance payment from Wild-Freeman. It seemed cheap enough, and I didn't realize that things would be the same here. I mean . . ."

By now she could complete his thought without difficulty: "You figured their power stopped at the water's edge, back there in Mayo. But when you got to New York, here they were, waiting. And now they're impatient."

"That's about it." He seemed about to go on, then pulled himself up.

"What makes you think they'll be satisfied with ten percent?" she asked.

"They will. They'll have to be," he replied. She did not believe it for a moment, and neither, she saw, did he.

It was certainly a new factor, one that was hard to balance, and it raised another point: "These people—they are the IRA, right?—how did they hear about the letters?"

"I was showing off," Sarsfield said ruefully. "They couldn't see how a mere writer could make enough money to buy a brewery. That's what Castle Orme used to be, you know: a brewery. I wanted to show them what a big man I was." His laugh had only a little bitterness in it. "That always gets me in trouble. Got me married twice."

It was not a subject she wanted to get into. "I don't suppose," she said slowly, "that you ever found yourself showing off—as you put it—to Englishmen."

"Englishmen?" He looked surprised. "There aren't many English around Clew Bay."

"No, I meant while you were researching. In Scotland, or

when you were plowing around in the Public Records Office."

"Never." He was, she saw, more than a little drunk, but he seemed positive enough. "It was a different kind of thing, like a treasure hunt. Nobody knew what I was looking for, I made sure of that."

"How?" asked Diana, from the sideboard. She returned the Chivas and went to the kitchen to get some more coffee. "Go on. I can hear you."

"Well, I had that genealogy from Mrs. McIntyre," he said, raising his voice. "But I didn't just follow it straight through. Oh, no—I'd skip two, maybe three generations, then go back a month later and fill in the gap. Thanks, I'll have a little milk in it this time." He sipped noisily at the coffee. "Had only one real problem, when the line seemed to break at Culloden. But mostly it was easy enough—easier than I'd expected, sometimes."

"As if somebody was smoothing your path?" asked Diana, trying to keep her voice neutral.

Not neutral enough, apparently: He looked quickly up at her. "Who, the Provos? They didn't know a thing at this stage."

"Actually," she offered, "I was thinking of the British government."

For a moment he looked thunderstruck, then began to laugh. "Oh, come on!" he said. "I mean to say!" The laugh petered out and left him wiping his eyes. "Why should they want to help me—an American—find the Casket Letters?"

"Why, indeed," said Diana. "It is silly, I guess." Unless they were letting you help them. "I don't suppose the Brits would really want those letters to surface publicly," she added, as if thinking aloud. "Especially the last one. Makes the royal family look like characters in a checkout-counter newspaper—you know those headlines: 'Nun Gives Birth to Racehorse on Subway Platform.' How about 'Incest in the Palace'—"

"—or 'Queen Has Child by Brother, Then Pays Off His Assassin.'"

"She did, didn't she? I'd forgotten."

"She could hold a grudge, Mary Stuart . . . Oh." He was staring over Diana's shoulder, his eyes ludicrously wide. "Good morning, my dear," he said, lumbering to his feet.

"Hello." Marie stood in the doorway, blinking. Her red hair smoldered in the watery light from the window, and her skin had a thick, creamy whiteness that was set off by Diana's black nightdress, straining its seams at breast and thigh. She looked, even to Diana, utterly sensual—all the more so for being completely unaware of it.

"Let's get you a bathrobe, love," Diana said, seeing Sarsfield's expression.

"It's all right," Marie said sleepily. "I'm not cold."

"No, but you're a public menace, popping out of my nightie like that." From her father Diana had inherited an unlikely salmon-colored terrycloth robe with a monogram on the lapel, and she swathed the girl in it. "Sit down, Marie, and I'll fix you something to eat."

"Eat?" Marie repeated blankly.

"We're scheming, and you can't scheme on an empty stomach," Diana said firmly. "Fried eggs, bacon, juice, and coffee—coming up."

"Make that two orders," Sarsfield said.

•   •   •

"Then it's settled," said Diana. "Marie and I will cut a swath through Saks on our way to the office, where I've got some things to clean up. Patrick, you'll go back to the Algonquin and sit tight, and we'll pick you up in the Blue Bar around five-thirty." Sarsfield, his mouth full and a small yellow trickle of egg running down his chin, nodded importantly. Food and Marie's agreement to show them the letters seemed to have restored his confidence, but Diana could see there was still something nagging at him.

"What shall I wear, Diana?" Marie demanded, distracting her.

Through breakfast, a small part of Diana's mind had been considering the problem. "There's a track suit—gray pants and top with a black stripe—hanging behind the bathroom door, love. It ain't elegant, but it'll accommodate your salient points until we can get you something more restrained." The shoes had seemed an insoluble problem until Diana remembered a pair of Troubridge's brown suede desert boots in the back of the closet. They were perhaps a size too large for Marie's callused feet, but nothing of Diana's looked (she was delighted to note) remotely big enough. At the prospect of clothes, Marie gulped down the rest of her juice and vanished into the bathroom.

"Something's on your mind, Patrick," said Diana, as soon as the door had closed behind the girl. "Spit it out."

"It's just a suspicion," he replied. "Not even that, but . . ."

"I won't hold you to it," she said impatiently as she began gathering the dirty dishes.

"My contact here in Manhattan—"

"The Irish contact," she interrupted.

"Yes, but I don't think he is himself. Irish, that is. Anyway, some of the things he said made me wonder if he—they—might not have an ear inside your office."

She set the tray down slightly harder than she'd intended. "Things like what?" she demanded.

He wanted to leave it at that, she saw: "Oh, I can't really remember. It was his manner. As if he'd known what was going on at Wild-Freeman before I did."

" 'What was going on'? He must've been more specific."

"Well," he squirmed. "It was about my advance check." Having let slip the first detail, he suddenly seemed eager to spill the rest: "We were talking about the money I'm supposed to give them. And he said—this was yesterday afternoon, right after I left you and Judith and what's-his-name in the lobby—he said that I owed his people fifty thousand dollars already. Ten percent of the advance on signing."

"Yes, I know," Diana put in.

"And I said that if he knew about that, then he must also know that I couldn't cash the check." His solemn face was lit for an instant by a mischievous grin, which as quickly vanished. "He said he did, and then he said—this is the important part—he said he'd know when I was free to cash it, probably before I knew myself."

She felt her face go rigid and her stomach knot, both at once. The curious thing, she realized at once, was that Patrick's revelation was no revelation at all: At some level her brain had been expecting just this.

"Are you all right?" Sarsfield was saying.

"Just a touch of paranoia," she replied, as lightly as she could. In her mind's eye she saw again Cathy O'Donnell's round, loyal, worried face. She'd never betray me (what a strange word, *betray*), but she might let something slip. That was it; that must be it.

The bathroom door opened and Marie appeared, beaming. The sleekly sober track suit was stretched taut over her unconfined breasts. "I'm ready," she said, flinging her arms wide with exuberance.

"Jesus Christ," said Sarsfield.

"Try Mary Magdalene," Diana snapped.

"Why not Mary Stuart?" said Sarsfield.

Eleven: Sarsfield

By three in the afternoon, the hotel room felt like a cage and by three-thirty a trap. Each time the phone rang—and it seemed to ring every few minutes—Sarsfield saw his hand go out to it and then quickly jerk back. Twice, someone knocked on the door, despite the DO NOT DISTURB sign he had hung from the knob; the second time, a muffled voice called out something about room service and, when there was no response, tried the knob. It was the slowly turning knob, first one way and then the other, that finally got to him.

Grabbing up his Burberry and his porkpie tweed hat, he peered cautiously down the hall. Seeing a couple standing by the elevator, he slipped out and fairly sprinted to join them. Even with them as protection, he felt his heart pause when the elevator door slid open, but none of the occupants remotely resembled the dough-faced man with the breathy voice.

As always, the narrow space in front of the desk was teeming with people even Sarsfield could spot as non–New Yorkers, and he slid past them, head down, toward the unobtrusive door that led from the lobby to the dimly lit little bar where he was to meet Diana. The place was nearly empty when he entered it and sat down at a corner table, with his back to the wall and a field of view that commanded the only entrance. A good choice, he thought, surveying the obviously innocent people present, and by way of reward ordered a double Bushmills, no ice, and a newspaper—no, he didn't care which one—to bury his face behind.

Two hours and three doubles later, he looked up to discover that the room had become so crowded he could no longer see the entrance. Drinkers were standing two deep along the bar and leaning over their seated compatriots at every table. At one point, the second chair at Sarsfield's table simply vanished, and its disappearance made him realize how easily someone—anyone—could come up on him without being seen.

The brash confidence that eight ounces of whiskey had fueled was oozing rapidly out his pores, leaving him dazed and apprehensive, when the tightly meshed crowd of drinkers standing near the door rippled and parted, and he saw Diana Speed's unmistakable fine-boned profile, eye to eye with the taller men and half a foot above the women around her.

Alongside her was another young woman, equally tall, equally striking, equally self-possessed. After a moment, he realized it was Marie, with her red hair pulled up at one side and tucked under a dramatically wide-brimmed green hat that glinted with raindrops. For a moment the two stood, the focal point of the room, as they scanned the audience, until Sarsfield came to himself and waved to catch their eye. Diana smiled tightly in return and began to work her way through the crowd toward him; Marie gave the older woman a sidelong look, threw Sarsfield a warmer smile, and followed her, dropping immediately into a creditable imitation of Diana's eel-like progress among the jammed tables.

Watching their approach, he called a greeting that got lost in the echoing babble around him, and cast about him helplessly for more chairs.

"Sorry we're late," Diana said, undoing her raincoat. "It's been a hell of a day, so we decided to have our hair done by way of therapy. I called your room, but you didn't answer." Her face looked drawn, but her controlled elegance was emphasized by a pearl-gray pinstriped suit with an explosively frilled blouse. Her only jewelry was a heavy gold watch fob seal that hung from a lapel pin. A man's seal, Sarsfield noted; father or lover?

He had managed to get halfway to his feet, wedged against the table and the wall, when a man at the next table rose and offered Marie his chair. The girl, clearly nonplussed, looked to Diana, who said, "Thanks, terribly, but we're not staying." And to Sarsfield: "You ready to go, Patrick?"

"Oh, yes," he said, flustered. "Maybe I'd better ask for the check . . ." Before he could get further, Diana pinned the waiter with a glance, followed by a practiced writing-on-air gesture.

"Why did you do that?" asked Marie.

"It means you want him to write up the check—the bill for Patrick's drinks—so we can pay and get going," Diana replied; from her tone, Sarsfield had the feeling it was not by any means the first such question she'd answered, but part of a day-long crash course in urbanity. The waiter reappeared almost immediately and handed Diana the tab. Her left eyebrow rose as she inspected it, but she signed it without a word.

"*En avant,*" she said.

Sarsfield didn't fully appreciate the whiskey's impact until the three of them had carved their way back through the crowd and were standing on the brink of the lobby. As he struggled into his coat, he felt the sweat spring out on his forehead and his knees go rubbery. "A little woozy?" Diana asked.

"You're awfully pale," said Marie. She turned to Diana. "Is he sick?"

"Just boiled, love."

Marie looked baffled. "Because it was so hot in there?"

Diana laughed. "Never mind, Marie. We'll get to idioms tomorrow. Can you walk, Patrick?"

"I'm perfectly all right," he replied, pulling his shredded dignity around him. Western Ireland might produce the not-so-occasional termagant, but he was unprepared for this kind of briskly antiseptic handling. Abruptly, he remembered what he had wanted to tell her, and he blurted it out: "They were looking for me. They even came to my room."

She knew instantly what he meant, and threw him a warning glance coupled to a meaningful look at Marie. "They might try to follow?" she asked, at the same time drawing the others into a corner, out of the lobby's traffic.

"They very well might," he agreed.

Her gray eyes were cool and thoughtful, but he could see no trace of fear in them. "How about leapfrogging us—Is there any way they could know that address in Queens?"

He was surprised to find her no-nonsense competence acting on his brain like a cold shower. "I'm almost certain not," he replied. "Believe me, I've been trying to remember. But she, Mrs. McIntyre, gave me the address on the phone, the second time I spoke with her—"

"Your phone? In Ireland?" Marie was watching them closely, concern in her eyes.

"As a matter of fact, no." He grinned at her. "That's the beauty of it: I called her from a motel in Durham, North Carolina. It was the night I finally managed to trace the last link in her genealogy."

She seemed to relax slightly. "And your address book. It's never gone missing on you, even for a few hours?"

"I don't use one." He saw the disbelief on her face. "It's true, though. I have a trick memory, especially for numbers. I never wrote her address down until yesterday, for the cab driver."

"Were you followed then?"

Stunned, he could only stand silent.

"Let's get out of here," she said.

"You're still going to Queens?" Part of his spirit was carried along by her; but part of it remembered what people had said behind their hands about the Provos, back in County Mayo.

"Damn straight I am," she said. "Maybe they still don't know about Marie's house, and even if they do, they may not have found the hiding place yet—the fact they're still after you suggests it."

"Then going there could be dangerous," he said. "For Marie, I mean."

"For all three of us," she said, with a sardonic smile. "You coming?"

What choice was there? He began to button his coat, thankful his fingers were reasonably steady. "I'm in this up to my ears," he said. "What I don't see is why you're taking the chance."

She was staring out the hotel's front door at the rain-spattered street, and he thought for a moment she hadn't heard him. "Greed," she said lightly. "Ambition. Stubbornness. All the worthwhile reasons. If I can pull this off, it could be the biggest publishing coup in years. Maybe ever." She saw Marie's frightened face and smiled at her. "Don't take me too seriously, kiddo."

"What about someone following us?" Sarsfield interjected. "Do you think—"

"If he exists in the first place," she said. She pushed open the hotel's front door and stepped out into the chilly night. "You just leave followers to me," she called over her shoulder.

"Taxi, ma'am?" the doorman asked, hastening after her. On 44th Street an icy drizzle had brought the pre-theater traffic to a standstill.

"No, thanks." Sarsfield pulled the Burberry's collar higher around his neck. Next to him, Marie stood expectantly. Diana looked up and down the street, where traffic inched past them toward Fifth Avenue.

"Something wrong?" Sarsfield inquired innocently.

She didn't look at him but continued her rapid scan of the street, the sidewalks, the passersby. "A long time ago," she said absently, "I had to take a course called Municipal Evasion Tactics. Trouble is, those things are always phony— the final exam was in a suburb of D.C., and the bad guys stuck out like yaks in a herd of deer." Squinting into the drizzle, Sarsfield decided that everyone in sight looked like a potential yak. "Okay," said Diana, crooking her elbows: "Each of you take an arm." When they had rearranged themselves and were standing poised on the edge of the curb, she flashed him a ferocious grin, her damp face gleaming, and squeezed his arm against her side. "Straight across the street," she said. "Ready, set, *go*."

He was bewildered but game, allowing her to drag him right in front of an immense truck, whose driver merely rolled his eyes up to heaven at the folly of pedestrians. On the truck's far side, a woman at the wheel of a Cadillac with Jersey plates was inching her way along the curb. As Diana, Marie, and Sarsfield popped into her field of view, she gave a porcine squeal and tramped simultaneously on the gas and the brake. The car leaped straight up in the air and stalled. Diana ignored the woman, gibbering behind the windshield, and held up an imperious hand as she and her companions stalked past. Safely on the far curb, she yanked at their arms: "This way, quick."

Trotting dutifully in her wake, they dodged into a huge parking garage, where an elevator to the upper levels was waiting with its door open. Inside it, Diana punched all the buttons, to the muttered irritation of the other occupants. At the first level, she pulled Marie and Sarsfield off. "You have a car here?" he asked.

"What? No." She was looking for something, he saw. "This way," she ordered, urging them toward a dark tunnel that angled steeply downward. Above it was a sign, EXIT TO 43RD ST, and below, a larger one: NO PEDESTRIANS.

"Hey, lady!" called an attendant from behind her, but he was too late. Down the ramp, slippery from rain and oil, they skittered; past an astonished cashier in a glass booth, and out onto the pavement.

Sarsfield found he was beginning to get into the spirit of it. "Do you do this often?" he asked, panting, as she dragged them on the dead run past a sleek, anonymous building with a stuffed tiger in its lobby—the Princeton Club—and then a nineteenth-century blockhouse he recognized as the Century Association. At the corner of Fifth Avenue, the light was still green, but the DONT WALK light was blinking at them. Diana stopped quickly, waited till the traffic signal facing them turned yellow, then dashed across the avenue with Sarsfield and Marie in her wake, pursued by a chorus of car horns.

She paused on the far curb, not even breathing hard, and looked behind them at the steel torrent that flowed downtown. "Anybody . . . tried it . . . under a bus," Sarsfield gasped. She linked arms with them again and led them eastward on 43rd at a fast walk. "Where are we going?" asked Marie, her face shining with excitement.

"Grand Central Station. The big building up ahead of us."

"Splendid," said Sarsfield. "Are we going to scamper on the tracks?"

"Not unless you insist. I thought we'd take the subway out to Queens."

"Really? You don't look like the sort of person who takes subways."

Diana had settled into a pavement-devouring stride, matched by Marie, whose long legs were emphasized by dark slacks and boots. Not quite alongside, Sarsfield was walking as fast as he could, with a hop-and-skip every few yards to keep pace. "I do, sometimes," Diana said. "Just to keep in practice, and to remind myself what it was like being a poor working girl."

As they crossed Madison, they were picked up by a subsiding tidal bore of commuters which carried them through a side entrance and down a flight of marble stairs into the station. "Oh!" said Marie, her eyes shining. And then "Ow!" as Diana dragged her forward. Ahead of them, the stream of suited and briefcased figures divided to flow around a filthy lunatic, hair matted and eyes blazing, who was shrieking imprecations at the arched ceiling high above. A big railroad cop, his gut hanging grotesquely over his gun belt, watched without interest.

Diana, Sarsfield saw, kept one eye on the screamer as she fished in her shoulder bag and produced a leather coin purse. She allowed the moving crowd to herd them down a steep flight of steps as she sorted three brass tokens from the purse and passed them out. Marie was still engrossed in hers when they reached the subway turnstiles, and seemed momentarily reluctant to surrender it to the slot, but Diana urged her through, with Sarsfield bringing up the rear. Ahead was a sign that indicated the IRT line to Queens, and Sarsfield picked up his pace, only to have Diana stop without warning and turn in her tracks.

"What—" he began.

"Just checking for turnstile jumpers," she replied. "The real trick to losing a tail in New York is always carry half a dozen tokens. We're clean," she added, after a moment. "Let's go."

The crowd had thinned enough so they were able to huddle together in the car, sharing a pole. The train dived below the East River, and he saw that Marie was looking a little frightened as the flat roar of the wheels, echoing off the tunnel walls, rose to the pitch of an artillery barrage. Sarsfield leaned forward, over a middle-aged woman who was seated in front of him reading a paperback. He stared at the colored subway map mounted on the car's side. "I think our stop is Jackson Heights," he yelled to Diana, after several minutes' concentration. "Or maybe Elmhurst Avenue." He looked helplessly at her. "Until yesterday, I'd never been in Queens."

The paperback reader looked up at him with surprise and suspicion.

"Does you credit," Diana called back, and the seated woman glared at her. "But we'll get off at Queensboro Plaza, just in case."

He located it, after searching the map, under a smeared graffito. "We'll never get a taxi," he said. "And it's a hell of a long walk."

Ten minutes later, Diana settled back into the cab seat with a sigh of pleasure. "Taxis are just a knack," she said firmly. "Give the man the address."

Sarsfield said it off, and turned to her. Marie, he noticed, was looking at her with an admiration that was almost embarrassing to see. "You're a remarkable young lady," he said. "Have you always been like this?"

"Not so you'd notice," Diana replied. *"Maman* is the forceful one in our family."

"A terrifying thought," he said. "She's French, your mother?"

"Utterly." She smiled reminiscently. "Ancien régime besides. To her, the Bonapartes are still upstarts."

"Why doesn't that surprise me?" he asked the taxi roof. "And your father? He's not French."

"No, he wasn't." He thought she was finished and was readying his next probe, when she unexpectedly added, "He was sweet and dear and not, I think, entirely there. She ate him alive."

"Ah." He gave the silence a second, then plunged ahead. "I suppose she arranged your marriage."

"Yes," she said. To his amazement, he saw she'd been expecting it. "I suppose Judith told you I'd been married?"

"As a matter of fact, no," he replied. He groped for a second and then went on: "There's a . . . a wariness that gives you away. *Touch not the cat but a' glove,* if you know what I mean."

She laughed, and then seemed surprised at herself. "I like that."

On Diana's far side, Marie was looking perplexed and concerned. "What is it?" he asked her.

"I was just wondering if everybody gets married," she replied slowly.

Diana saw through the question before Sarsfield did: "Not unless you want to, Marie. And that's something worth remembering."

The silence that followed endured until the cab swung north off the main thoroughfare and began to thread its way among secondary streets lined by brick apartment buildings, interspersed with depressed-looking two-family houses. "That man in your office today," Marie said abruptly.

Sarsfield felt Diana, on his far side, stiffen in her seat, but the casual tone of her reply—"You mean Mr. Ellison?"— would otherwise have fooled him.

Marie nodded. "He was crying when he left," she said. "Did you . . . discharge him?"

"He's been discharged for years, in the electrical sense." In the dark, Diana's voice was level, then the quick flash of a passing streetlight showed Sarsfield a twisted, unnatural smile. "No, it's called early retirement. Not early enough, sometimes."

"But it was painful for you, too," Marie said.

Diana leaned forward and tapped on the Plexiglas shield between them and the driver. "Turn right at the next corner, please. And don't signal the turn."

"What you mean?" The driver glanced back at her nervously.

"Just do what I say," she replied. "Now."

"Okay, lady." He swung the wheel without braking, and the cab heeled giddily.

Sarsfield slid into Diana, who was looking intently out the rear window. "Is something behind us?" he asked. There was a sudden hollow feeling under his rib cage.

"Know in a minute," she said, and to the driver, "Now turn left, at the traffic light." The streets behind them were dark, wet, and completely empty of moving vehicles. "How much farther?" she asked.

"Little more," the driver called over his shoulder. The street they were on, lined with small homes, looked to Sarsfield exactly like the one he had visited the day before. In the wet glow from the street lamps, the neighborhood was cold and secretive.

"Should be halfway up the next block, and over one," the driver announced. "But this is Queens—who knows for sure?"

"Okay," Diana replied. "We'll get out here, please." She turned to Sarsfield. "I don't think we want to advertise our arrival."

"You're probably right," he said. The easy give-and-take of only seconds before seemed to have vanished; she was leaning forward, eyes narrowed as she surveyed the empty street. Sarsfield could feel the apprehension coming off himself in waves, wondered if she could feel it, too. "Here," she said, pushing bills into the slot. "Keep the change."

Outside, the rain had stopped, and the air was chill, wet, and heavy. Sarsfield looked wistfully after the retreating cab. "Couldn't we have asked him to wait?"

"Waste of time," Diana replied. "He'd be crazy to hang around here in the dark, on the chance we might come back."

He remembered the day before. "I guess you're right," he said, knowing she was. Marie was looking around her with nervous jerks of her head. The light from a street lamp caught her face. The whites of her eyes made Sarsfield think of a frightened colt.

"Come on," Diana said. She took the girl's arm and led off up the street, her heels clicking loudly on the pavement, as Sarsfield hurried behind them. Now that they were out of the cab, he found he was more aware of light coming from the houses they passed: a glow through a drawn shade, a brighter streak where two curtains failed to meet; here and there a faded strand of multicolored Christmas bulbs that swung listlessly from a gable or twined around a stunted evergreen.

At the corner Diana turned left, and when they reached the next intersection she paused and surveyed the block ahead. Many of the small houses had attached, single-car garages, but nearly all of them also had one or two vehicles parked in front by the curb. From where they stood, Sarsfield could see no sign of life on the street or in the parked cars. They crossed, and his eye was caught by an illuminated sign next to a doorway:

THE CARROWAY'S
139-21

He made a quick calculation. "It should be that one, three houses down."

"Don't point," Diana replied. "Keep moving—we'll walk past it." Someone—probably police—had knocked out the single pane in the front door, and someone else had slapped a patch of raw plywood over the hole. In the small front yard, the thick weeds were trampled into the mud. The absence of life was tangible; by comparison, the tightly shut houses on either side looked to Sarsfield almost festive. Diana pulled him and Marie around the corner before she allowed them to stop. To his surprise, he felt Marie grope for his arm. She was shivering.

The street they had come down was still deserted, Sarsfield saw, but who might be watching from behind those drawn blinds? Unexpectedly, Diana's hand grasped his shoulders, halting him. He looked quickly around. She was standing on one foot, pulling off her shoe with her free hand. The pavement under her stockinged feet must be like ice, he thought. Ice with frozen pebbles in it. "What're you doing?" he asked, under his breath.

"These damned shoes," she explained between gritted teeth. "I sound like a tap dance class. Lord, that's cold!"

They set off again, and the only sound he could hear was the faint squeak of Marie's boots. Twenty yards from the house, Diana stiffened. "What?" Sarsfield whispered.

"A light. Down by the ground, behind that little shrub. See it?"

At first he could barely define the edges of the house. "Your eyes are a hell of a lot better than mine. No, I see it now. What—"

"Basement window," she said. "Marie, isn't that where you told me the letters were hidden?"

The girl gave a stifled whimper that might have meant anything. Her shivering seemed to Sarsfield almost out of control. "Are you going to take a look?" he asked Diana.

She considered for a moment. "See that little flick of light from next door?" she whispered suddenly. "Somebody's watching us. Keep walking down the street—we'll be screened by the house in a few more yards." He counted twenty-three steps before she tugged at his sleeve.

"Over this little fence," she whispered. "Keep close to the house."

"What if the door's locked?" he said, but he followed her, pulling Marie behind him.

She was tiptoeing gingerly through the icy mud alongside the front walk stepping-stones, and he wondered how badly her feet had been lacerated by the sidewalk. The front door was not only unlocked but unlatched, and she pushed it open and stepped through. "Whoof!" she gasped. "That's awful."

It was not, he thought, half as bad as the day before, but next to him he could hear Diana swallowing convulsively. The room ahead was dark, a tangled litter of shapes only slightly silhouetted by a slash of light from the open door. Diana took a step forward, and something at floor level emitted a furious screech and shot past her. "Oh!" cried Sarsfield.

"It's just Campbell," whispered Marie. "He always gets under your feet." She had stopped shivering, and her voice sounded quite calm.

Sarsfield's eyes were adjusting to the thicker darkness. The room looked as if it had been attacked by madmen with axes, the shabby furniture smashed, the books hurled from the shelves and ripped apart. On the far side of the room, a faint, thin line of light showed. "Is that the cellar door?" Diana whispered.

"Yes." Marie moved forward, stepping high over the ankle-deep wreckage. "Who did this?" she asked, wondering.

"It looks like firemen," said Diana. "They love to bust things up. But it was probably your neighbors."

Marie pulled the cellar door open against a grating heap of debris until they could slip through, heads bent. A flight of rough, uncarpeted stairs led downward into a low, empty room with a dirt floor and walls formed of large, uneven stones painted white and cemented into place. The light was coming from a single bulb suspended by a wire from the beams overhead. As Sarsfield cautiously followed Diana down the creaking stairs, he saw that the brown earth of the floor was marked by hundreds of overlapping footprints that covered every inch of ground.

Marie had gone straight to one wall, where she seized a large, protruding stone and seemed to be wrestling with it.

"I'll give you a hand," Diana said. As she stepped forward her head grazed the hanging bulb. The sharply etched shadows leaped crazily as the bulb swung, and Sarsfield felt himself momentarily disoriented. Suddenly stone grated on stone, and the painted rock toppled to the dirt with a heavy thud.

"It's way in the back," said Marie, reaching past Diana. "A heavy box."

"D'you need help?" Diana said. Her voice was flat and tense, the planes of her face exaggerated in the harsh light.

"I can get it." Marie braced herself against the rough stone and heaved. A heavy scraping sound came from the dark cavity, and then it emerged—a cube more than a foot on a side, wrapped in gleaming, dirt-streaked white cloth. Diana took a half step forward, but Marie grasped the object protectively in both arms, turning to interpose her shoulder between it and Diana. Carefully she lifted it clear of the hole and set it down in the scuffed dirt.

The two women were for a moment motionless in the sharp chiaroscuro of the light. Marie was crouched over the container; a strand of red hair that had escaped from under her hat hung down along one cheek. Standing over her, Diana cast a huge, looming shadow. If he lived another hundred years, Sarsfield knew, he would never forget this instant. With the realization, his heart missed a beat and then raced madly ahead. "Shall we have a look at what's inside?" he said, his voice trembling audibly.

"Not here," said Diana. As Marie looked up at her, she added, "We're pressing our luck as it is."

"Diana's right," Sarsfield agreed. "Let's get out of here. We can open it at the hotel."

"No." Marie looked startled at her own vehemence, and hesitated. She pointed to Diana. "We'll go back to your house."

Sarsfield shrugged. Perhaps it was better that way. "Anything you—"

"Quiet!" Diana's whisper cut through the room. Then he heard it and so, from her expression, did Marie. A heavy creak from overhead, and then another. Sarsfield felt as if his legs had turned to water, and he sagged against the stone wall. Stepping between Marie and the staircase, Diana reached into the pocket of her raincoat and drew out a nondescript black object that looked like a flattened, elongated flashlight. From the way she held it before her, Sarsfield knew it was some sort of weapon.

Now Marie was standing up, the cloth-wrapped cube clasped tight against her breasts. "What're we going to do?" she whispered.

Diana's lips were drawn back over her perfect teeth in a humorless smile. With a feline grace Sarsfield had not seen in her before she eased across the dirt floor toward the stairs. She placed one foot in its torn and dirty stocking on the bottom step, close to the wall, and set her weight on it. Then the other foot, stretched out so it touched the next step close to its outer edge. She shifted the odd-looking device to her left hand and reached for the string that served as a primitive light switch. As she did so, a tremendous crash resounded from just above their heads, followed almost instantly by a piercing, eldritch shriek, a human yell of pure panic, and an unmistakable gunshot.

"Christ, it bit me!" shouted a very young male voice Sarsfield didn't recognize. "Let's get the fuck out of here!" Feet—several feet—clattered across the boards overhead, and they heard the front door slam.

Diana was still at full stretch on the staircase, but her head was bent and her shoulders were heaving. When at last she looked up Sarsfield saw she was laughing. "Campbell strikes again?" she said to Marie, her voice nearly steady.

"Oh, no," the girl replied, with complete seriousness. "Campbell wouldn't bite. That must have been Atholl."

"*What* did you say?" It was the first time he had seen Diana completely at a loss.

"The Duke of Atholl," Marie explained. "He's very territorial."

"Oh," said Diana.

Twelve: Diana

Running on nervous energy and sheer momentum, Diana didn't realize how much the evening had taken out of her until, sitting on the edge of the bed to pull off her ruined stockings, she felt a nearly uncontrollable desire to climb under the covers and pull them over her head. From the living room she could hear Sarsfield's mellifluous voice rolling on and on—a different kind of release from nervous tension—but not a sound from Marie. Come to think of it, the girl had said practically nothing during the two-hour scramble back from Queens; had just sat on the edge of whatever seat—bus, subway, taxi—she'd been thrust into, clutching the silk-wrapped container as if it were a life preserver.

Diana closed her eyes, took a long, deep breath, and willed herself back into control. *So much to do, so little time:* In the years she'd been working for the Rajah, it had become almost a mantra, and now it worked again. Quickly she removed everything but her bra and slipped into her father's old dressing gown and a ridiculous pair of fur-lined slippers that soothed her bruised and aching feet. A quick glance in the mirror reassured her; heightened by cold and rain, her complexion could compete with salmon-pink terry cloth though not, admittedly, as well as Marie's refined pallor did. She picked up the hair dryer, decided against it, and went out to the living room.

161

Marie was poised on the edge of the beige armchair; she had set the cloth-wrapped cube down on the coffee table in front of her and was pretending, without much conviction, to listen to Sarsfield's anecdotes, delivered in his excruciating brogue. He had enthroned himself on the sofa, and his bristly tweed suit looked as if it might rend the smooth leather upholstery, but he looked both relieved and pleased with himself. Diana turned in on him long enough to realize, from the disjointedness of the story, that he wasn't nearly as self-possessed as he seemed. When he paused for breath, she leaped into the silence: "Drinks. Marie?"

"Nothing for me, thank you," the girl replied. "But if I could have a knife? These knots are too tight to undo."

"Of course," Diana said. "And for you, Patrick?"

"Scotch, I think." He was looking hard at Marie, so he must have heard it, too—an assurance that was quite new and, after Marie's almost rabbitlike behavior, quite unexpected.

When Diana returned with his highball and a glass of Orvieto for herself, he was still silently watching Marie, who seemed wholly oblivious. "Here's the knife," said Diana. Marie, her eyes on the chest, put out her hand. "It's very sharp. Be careful."

Marie slipped the blade under a fold of silk. She seemed to hesitate for a moment, then her hand jerked and the knife slashed effortlessly through the cloth. Beneath the wrappings, the box looked crude and battered and old. It was secured by a rusty hasp, but no lock. Marie fingered the hasp, as if trying to remember something, then lifted the lid, which came up with a muted groan from the hinges. Sarsfield, his drink forgotten, leaned forward. His cheerful, ruddy face had paled and set. Marie, in contrast, looked as composed as if she were opening the mail. One by one, she removed three packages, each shrouded in dusty plastic sheeting, and laid them side by side on the coffee table.

"The heavy ones . . ." Sarsfield's voice cracked. He cleared his throat and tried again, two notes below his normal pitch: "The heavy ones must be the Bibles."

"Yes." Marie's fingers were working at the wrappings that sealed the smallest package. She was looking down at her hands as if they belonged to someone else. The topmost sheet of the small stack of papers was rough textured, and the once-black lettering had faded to a pale gray, but even from where she stood, beside Marie's chair, Diana could make out the words: "Tomorrow I shall see my God face to face." She sank to her knees, drawn by the strong, stark lettering; the woman who had held the pen knew what she was facing and disdained it.

"We've got them," Sarsfield breathed. He started to reach across the table and then drew his hand back. Marie lifted the first sheet by its edges, set it aside. Beneath was a page in a hand that was different yet essentially similar, a burst of passion to an unnamed addressee.

"I wouldn't touch those any more than I had to," Diana said. "We know they're what we want, and that's the important thing now." Marie looked at her and nodded silently. Without a word, she replaced the first page on top of its stack.

"Your expert, Pearse, will go mad when he sees these," Sarsfield said. His voice was slightly hoarse.

Diana rocked back on her heels. "I'll give him a call," she said, glancing at her watch. "Even if it is after ten."

She went into the bedroom and took her address book from her bag. The answering machine, she saw, had registered four calls, but she stuck out her tongue at it and dialed Pearse's number. He answered on the first ring, his voice tense, expectant.

"Mr. Pearse? Diana Speed."

"Yes," he said. "I mean, how are you?"

"Fine, thanks. Sorry to call you so late, but we have the originals at last."

A sound that might have been the release of held breath rattled the receiver. "You're sure?"

She felt almost light-headed. "That's supposed to be my line. Well, they look the same as the photocopies I gave you, only you know, *original*." My God, I haven't sounded that air-headed since the junior prom.

He seemed not to notice. "When do you want to bring them over?"

"First thing tomorrow? How about nine?"

"Nine o'clock's fine," he said. "I'll have everything ready. Listen," he added: "You got a safe place to keep them tonight? A vault or something?"

"Don't fret," Diana replied. "They'll be safe. And we'll be there at nine." But she set the phone down thoughtfully. On the answering machine's face, the numeral 4 still glowed green. "Oh, well," she said aloud, and pressed the playback button. The tape reel whirred for nearly half a minute—someone had been running off at the mouth.

"Speed, Troubridge here. Eight-thirty." He hated the answering machine, and it showed.

"Diana, it's Judith." And sounding as if she'd just run the hundred in 9.5. "Did you get them? Call me, dear." A long pause, and Diana waited for the end-of-message click. Instead, Judith spoke again, this time in the honey-and-acid tone she reserved for serious office gossip: "What *did* you do to Brand, darling? He's *devastated*. 'Bye."

Diana felt her stomach knot, but before the memory of her interview with the managing editor could take shape, the next message began.

"You black-hearted bitch." A man, of course, but not the usual opening gambit. "You heartless cunt." The voice—a thick and, she thought, fake Southern accent—was shaking with apparently genuine rage. "Somebody ought to . . ." It went on for some time, detailing exactly what somebody ought to do to her. It sounded extremely painful, and she had to force herself to listen.

Diana's acquaintance with obscene calls was considerable, though no wider than the average New York single woman's, and there was something unusual about this one. A young voice, and, behind the accent that came and went, an educated one. Nothing so odd about that. No, it was the words themselves: Not only did they sound like a prepared text, but a text she was sure she'd heard before.

The recorded phone slammed down hard, and as she stood looking at the machine with narrowed eyes, another man's voice, flat and without accent, came on. "Plaza three, eight-six eight-two. Tomorrow." It was one of the Rajah's people, of course: They always called from different numbers, with the same minimalist messages, and the only clue to the caller was the use of the old New York City exchanges—Gramercy, Trafalgar, Chelsea. It was, she knew, inevitable, but a twinge of apprehension tightened her stomach, and reminded her at the same time that she'd missed dinner.

Going over to the night table, she opened the drawer and removed the automatic pistol that lay inside and the full clip next to it. With confident ease she slid the clip into the butt, slapped it home, and checked the safety. The pistol, an army .45, had belonged to her great-uncle Julian, who carried it unused through what he always called The War. It arrived in Diana's mail, fully loaded and with the safety off, the day after she had moved out of her husband's Georgetown town house and into a sixth-floor walk-up in Hell's Kitchen. Uncle Julian died during an asthma attack a week later, so she never learned exactly what he meant, though the general message seemed clear enough.

Because of its provenance, the gun at first seemed like a joke to her, until a drunken friend to whom she was showing it pulled the trigger and not only exploded a fifth of quite good New York State champagne, but also put impressive holes through the door and back of the refrigerator in which the bottle was chilling. The friend fled while Diana was inspecting the damage, and the next day she looked up the entries under "Gun Safety & Marksmanship Instruction" in the Yellow Pages.

At that period in her life, shooting holes in black paper silhouettes of male figures provided a certain emotional satisfaction; before it wore off Diana found herself an adequate shot, and even when the gun was no more interesting to her than, say, an electric can opener, she kept it by her bed, a habit that horrified Troubridge when he found it one night while looking for a Kleenex.

She slipped the gun into the pocket of the dressing gown, and felt the weight of it drag at her waist. In the mirror the bulge looked obvious, and she put the .45 back in the bedside table drawer before returning to the living room. Sarsfield had finished his drink and was pouring himself another, while Marie seemed immersed in a copy of *Vogue*. The chest, reclosed and without its silk cover, looked merely sordid. "Pearse sounded quite excited," Diana said. "We'll take the papers over to him in the morning."

"Excited? He bloody well ought to be," Sarsfield replied. "The biggest thing he's ever dealt with. He'll be famous."

"If they're—" Diana began, as the extension phone at her elbow burred softly. "Damn. I forgot to turn the machine back on." The three of them sat silently as the phone rang.

"Maybe it's Pearse," said Sarsfield. "Maybe he forgot something."

The phone rang four more times. At last, Diana sighed and picked it up. "Yes?"

"So you got through your busy day at last," said Troubridge's voice.

Oh, God, she thought. I'm not really up to this tonight. "I'm sorry about our dinner date. I trust Cathy got hold of you."

"She did indeed. Made it sound quite dramatic."

Without warning, a picture of Brand Ellison's stricken face flashed in her memory. "Part of it was," she said.

"A little Veuve Clicquot's all you need. Put the spring back in your step. And by great good fortune, I've got some right to hand."

Was he plastered? His voice seemed crisp enough, but jollity on the phone was completely unlike him. "That's sweet of you, Troubridge, but not this evening."

"Then I shall drink it all myself. What about tomorrow night?"

"What? Oh, I don't know . . ."

". . . or the next, or the next. I'm quite relentless, so you may as well give in."

"Tomorrow night?" Marie had looked up from her magazine and was watching her with interest, while Sarsfield, listening no doubt just as closely, was studying the ceiling. "I guess so," Diana said, as Troubridge swung into full spate. "All *right*, I said." Silence at the other end. "Look, I'm sorry to be ungracious, but I'm dead on my feet."

"And I'm sorry to be so persistent," he replied. Paused, and added in a hesitant tone she had not heard before, "I rather missed you this evening, Speed."

Damn you, she thought. You know where the chinks are. "Drink up your old Veuve Clicquot then, and I'll see you tomorrow . . . right. Seven. Good night." She hung up, feeling slightly warm around the ears. "Apologies," she said.

"I think we're all exhausted," said Sarsfield equably. He indicated the scarred chest on the table in front of him. "Where are we going to stash this thing for the night?"

"At quarter to eleven?" said Diana.

"I'm sure the Algonquin has a vault . . ." he began smoothly.

"I'm sure they do," said Diana. "But I for one don't want to risk taking that box out of here again tonight." She turned to the girl. "It's up to you, Marie, but here's my suggestion: I'll put the letters and things in my safe, here in the apartment. Patrick can toddle off to his virtuous bed without worrying about being robbed along the way, and we'll all meet here in the morning for breakfast, then go off to see the manuscript man." Marie looked uncertainly from Sarsfield to Diana and back again.

"An apartment safe?" he said dubiously. "One of those little tin things?"

Tired as she was, Diana felt her ears prick up. Could he be planning a midnight flit? Or a meeting with friends? Is paranoia reversible? She went to the mirror above the mantel and lifted it free, exposing the steel door behind it. "Not exactly tin," she said, setting the mirror on the rug. "And I have burglar alarms on the windows and the front door."

"Doesn't it get awfully hot in there?" Marie asked. "If you light a fire, I mean?"

The knob gave a series of well-oiled clicks as Diana spun it. "No fear," she said. "You can't use the fireplace; the flue was sealed years ago, like most New York apartments. This way the space is good for something."

The safe door, impressively thick layers of metal, swung open. Inside, the safe was empty except for a few small boxes. "Jewelry," Diana said. "*Maman* leaves some of her things with me. She's too cheap to rent a safe-deposit box of her own. Mostly I use it for company papers."

Sarsfield's smile was a little thin, but he shrugged his acquiescence. "I'm sure it'll do splendidly." He picked up the box and handed it to Diana, who slid it into the safe. The heavy door shut with a solid thud, and she spun the dial. "There. It's not a vault, but it'll serve. And now for bed—I don't know about you, but I'm knocked out."

She felt there were lead weights on her heels, and it seemed as if Sarsfield would never get his Burberry buttoned, but finally he was out the door. Diana shut it behind him and shot both the bolts, set the chain, and flipped on the burglar alarm switch. Turning, she saw Marie watching her wide-eyed. "Welcome to Manhattan, kiddo. The cultural capital of the world."

* * *

As Diana came out of the bathroom, she saw Marie standing by the bedroom window, looking out into the night. That nightgown looks obscene on her, Diana thought. Wish it did on me. "See anything out there?" she asked.

Marie turned. Her smile was warm and somehow support-ive; not a child's smile at all. "I was thinking of you, Diana. It must be very hard sometimes, being alone as you are."

Her words so precisely echoed Diana's own thoughts while washing her face that she paused in mid-step. "Alone," she said at last. "That's very perceptive, Marie." And very patronizing, Diana.

"But you go on," Marie continued, as if she hadn't heard. "That's the important thing, of course. It's something I must learn again." A teenage girl's grin erased her thoughtful look, and she leaped on the bed, slid beneath the covers with a flash of white skin. "You want to sleep next to the night table."

"I do?" said Diana.

"Of course, silly. Next to where you keep the gun."

SATURDAY

Thirteen: Pearse

By the time the downstairs bell rang, Pearse was unable to restrain his impatience. Leaving his apartment door ajar, he walked down to the elevator and stood staring up at the backlit numbers on the floor indicator, felt himself urging the car upward. When it finally clashed open, he found himself confronted by not one tall, striking woman but two. "This is Marie McIntyre," Diana said. "The papers belong to her."

Pearse had always considered himself a leg man, but the chest on the big redhead was impossible to ignore, especially in the green sweater it was fighting to escape. "Mick Pearse," he said, with open admiration. "Very pleased to meet you, Marie."

"And Patrick Sarsfield," Diana was saying.

Pearse had not even noticed the chubby, red-faced man behind the two women. "Hi, Patrick." The name didn't register with Pearse until they were halfway down the hall; so this was the guy—the other guy—Galmoy had under his thumb. Pearse wondered if his belated double take had showed. "Everything's all set up," he said.

Diana was carrying an attaché case whose chocolate-colored leather looked good enough to eat. It must have run her five hundred bucks if it cost a cent, Pearse decided. And the quietly elegant overnight bag in Marie's hand could hardly have cost less. Both, he saw, were stamped D. D'A. S. in small, heavy gilt letters.

"You have the papers with you?" He tried and failed to keep his eyes off the two containers.

Diana's voice was cool, businesslike. "As I said," she replied. "But I don't like doing business in the hall."

"Oh. Sure—come in." He pushed the door open and stepped aside, and Diana led the way into the apartment. Now that he knew what the women were carrying, he barely noticed Marie's frankly appraising look, the twin to the stare he had just given her.

"Can I see them, please?" Pearse asked. He had tidied away the stacks of papers that had been on his desk, replaced them with the two single photocopies of the library's Stuart documents. "These are authenticated," he said, following Diana's look. "I have more coming."

"But what's this?" cried Marie, stooping to retrieve a sheet that had fallen partway under the desk. She held it up, a plain white sheet with *Marie R*. inscribed a dozen times, large and small. And in the corner, sprawled across the width of the page, *Marie Royne dEcosse*.

Shit. "I was just fooling around," he said. "To pass the time." His face, he knew, was scarlet.

"It's wonderful," said Marie, beaming at him. "They're exactly like my own."

Diana gave the younger woman a sharp, almost suspicious look. "Mr. Pearse—Mick—used to be employed doing that sort of thing," she said. Her tone made his spine prickle as much as her words did. "You were at Fort Meade, weren't you?" she added. The hint of a smile flicked across her face.

Surely Galmoy would never have told her that. Pearse felt as if the floor had dropped from under him, but he forced the corners of his mouth into a stiffly artificial grin. "You've got some well-placed friends," he murmured.

If she heard him, she didn't show it, but set the attaché case down on the glass-topped surface and unlocked it. "These are the letters."

"And this?" indicating the overnight bag that Marie still held.

The girl—what was she? eighteen?—put the second case next to the first and opened it, so that he could see two thick rectangles wrapped in smudged, dirty plastic. He extracted one of them and hefted it. "A book?" he said, looking into Marie's expectant eyes.

"A family Bible," she agreed. "So's the other one."

Of course. "The two genealogies," he said. "One inscribed in each." She nodded delightedly. "In the back, I bet."

"Why don't we save them for later," said Diana. "Look at the letters first."

"Whatever you say," he replied. He replaced the wrapped book and shut the case. As the others watched, he took a thin-bladed knife from the drawer. "May I?"

Diana looked to Marie, who was standing silently beside her. "Go ahead," said the girl.

Pearse flashed her his most engaging smile, saw her color to the neckline of her sweater. He slit open the plastic and removed the first letter with a pair of oversize, padded tweezers, set it down carefully on the clean glass. He took a second piece of glass, about a foot square, and laid it over the paper. He would not allow his eyes to focus on the writing yet, but concentrated on his hands, moving with confident precision, as they swung one of the desk lamps and the frame-mounted magnifier into position. "There," he breathed at last, when everything was exactly as he wanted it. "Now let's have a good look at you."

An hour later he straightened up from the last of the letters, switched off the light, and blinked at his visitors—he had, he realized, completely forgotten them. He felt both numbed and triumphant, and his facial muscles seemed uncertain what was expected of them.

"How about it, Mr. Pearse?" Sarsfield demanded, his voice loud after the long silence. "What have we got?"

Pearse ignored him. "Where did you find these?" he asked Marie.

She appeared quite calm, though her eyes—funny greenish brown eyes—shone with triumph. "My mother had them, and her parents before her. Since the time they were written."

Pearse shook his head in wonder. "Well, I guess it does happen."

"You mean you think they're real," Diana said.

Pearse turned to her. He felt high as a kite, but without the blurriness. Quite the opposite, in fact—everything seemed to be clearer, sharper than usual. He tamped down his rising glee with a will he didn't know he had. "Look," said, measuring his words, "I still have—"

"—to do your chemical tests," Diana interrupted. "I remember. Pending those, tell us what you think, so we can stop holding our breath."

It was more than anyone's professional reserve could withstand. To hell with caution, he thought, and let the emotion that was welling up inside him overflow. "Shit, yes," he said. "They're real." Once the words were out, hanging in the air, his face split in a grin so wide it was painful.

Sarsfield emitted an inarticulate bellow, his face going purple as he groped for words. Diana, beside him, said nothing, but her eyes first opened wide and then went from the letters to Marie, who looked quite pleased, if unsurprised.

"That is to say," Pearse went on hurriedly, taking in their expressions, "I'm confident these are all real sixteenth-century. But they weren't all written by the same person."

"What—" Sarsfield began, but Marie cut him short.

"Of course they weren't." The other three spun around to stare at her. The tall girl's voice was coolly contemptuous, richer and deeper than it had been. Looking past her, Pearse was struck by Diana's expression, which combined affection, eagerness, and (he thought) deep apprehension.

"Let me see them," said Marie. She had turned instantly into an imperious woman. She stepped to Pearse's desk—she even seemed to be walking differently, he noted—and began sorting through the pile of fragile papers.

"Hey," he cried. "Take it easy. Those things are four

hundred years old." He took one step forward, froze in mid-step at the command in her eyes.

Marie picked up a sheet, holding it by the edge. "This one," she said, her eyes hard. "His Danish slut wrote this to him. Anna Throndsen. With so little English, she should not have tried love letters." As Pearse watched, unable to move, she tossed it aside and picked up another. "From Lady Jean. Illiterate, like all the Gordons, but sweetly innocent. For those who like that in a woman." She glanced up at Diana, looking right through her.

Pearse came to himself in time to catch the letter as Marie released it. "Please," he begged. "Don't chuck them around like that . . ."

Marie was holding yet another, staring at it, her brow wrinkled. At last her perplexed expression changed to one of disdainful amusement. "Walsingham," she remarked, and let the sheet fall. "A great fellow for letters, but free with the names he signed to them." She reached for the next piece and then, seemingly aware for the first time of the three pairs of eyes locked on her, paused. She glared around her, and as she did the tension went out of her body and her blazing eyes dulled. "Is something wrong?" she asked, her voice hesitant.

"No, Marie," replied Diana gently. "It's all right now." She stepped forward and took the girl by the shoulders, led her to the couch. Marie sank down on it and began to sob, while Diana stood uncomfortably over her, patting her shoulder and murmuring.

Sarsfield let out his pent breath in a snort of relief, and Pearse looked up from the papers he was re-sorting with meticulous care. "For Christ's sake, get her out of here," he snapped to Diana. "I can't do anything with her around."

Even though his nerves were stretched like guitar strings he hadn't meant to sound so harsh, but clearly it put Diana's back up: "As I recall, we're the clients, Mr. Pearse. We can always find another expert."

He felt as if he had been blindsided, shock succeeded by quick anger, followed by dismay. "I apologize," he said. "That was dumb of me. I'm sorry, Marie."

Diana was stroking the girl's neck. "Apology accepted," she said. The corded muscles in his own neck began to relax. "We want your considered verdict as soon as possible, and no one likes to work with three people looking over his shoulder."

From her place on the couch Marie looked up at Pearse, her tear-streaked face bewildered. He felt a wholly unexpected pang of remorse, but shook it off and forced himself to address Diana. "I appreciate that," he said. But the temperature in the room was still chillier than he liked, and he groped for a change of subject: "Now, what about these two Bibles? Where do they fit in?" He opened the overnight case as he spoke, extracted the larger of the two bundles it contained. With the knife he slit open the plastic to reveal the massive leather binding. "Oh, my," he breathed, as he turned back the covering. "This is something else." And to Diana: "Books are a whole different area, you realize. I really couldn't give you a respectable opinion on this."

"What about the pages of genealogy?" Diana replied. "What can you say about them?"

As he gently opened the volume, he saw from the corner of his eye Marie, sitting bolt upright, wince at the creak from the stiff leather. Diana, standing beside her, still had a protective—or was it proprietary?—hand on her shoulder.

"So," said Pearse, as he came to the handwritten pages. He lifted the book and set it under one of the lights. For several minutes he let the thicket of long-ago inscriptions flow over him. "This is wild," he said, to no one in particular. "This is really fantastic."

"You see what it means, of course," demanded Sarsfield, his voice hoarse and loud. His face had reddened and he was sweating slightly.

Pearse glanced up at him. "I see what it *says*," he corrected. He turned to Diana and Marie, speaking at both of them: "You want this tested, too? It'll be a brute—there must be a dozen different inks on this page alone. It'll be hard to get enough samples without destroying the whole thing."

Marie gave a wail and leaped to her feet. "No!" she cried. "It's mine! I won't let you!"

To Pearse's surprise it was Sarsfield, not Diana, who looked stricken. "But Marie," he said, "it's *vital*. Don't you see? This shows who you are, the unbroken line from you back to . . . to her."

Pearse, who had dropped his eyes in the face of the girl's anguish, was adjusting the magnifier over the book, and he continued to toy with the setscrew. "I know who I am," Marie was saying, "I know those names are real." Suppressing his strong urge to look up, Pearse continued to inspect the page as if he were alone in the room.

"But if we can prove they're real," Sarsfield insisted earnestly, "think what it'll mean to you. How much more . . ." He pulled himself up short, and his voice faded away into inarticulate rumbling.

Pearse risked a glance. Marie was standing in front of Sarsfield, shaking her head stubbornly. "All right," said Diana. "This isn't getting anywhere. We can deal with the Bibles later—the letters are the important thing, and we're just in Mr. Pearse's way."

Now he straightened up, closing the book gently. He kept his expression blandly neutral. "It'll still be a few days," he said to Diana. "I've laid in the chemicals I'll need, but there's several tests for each letter, and with material like this, I want to be super-careful."

"We want to be super-careful, too," Diana said. "In fact, just to be on the safe side all around, we decided that it's unfair to ask you to take responsibility for all these documents." As she spoke, she took a quick step forward and interposed herself between him and the stack of letters.

Before he could stop himself, he'd made an involuntary, instantly aborted gesture toward the papers she had begun to sort. "I don't understand," he said. "What's the matter?"

"Nothing," Diana replied, placing about half the papers into their original nest of plastic wrapping. She beamed sweetly into his angry, baffled face. "We're leaving you quite enough to get started on: the beginning and the end pages of the very long letter that begins 'Having departed from the place where I left my Heart,' the entire poem that starts *'O Dieux, ayez de moy,'* and these other papers that may or may not have been Mary's at all. The rest will stay with me." Deftly, she resealed the plastic over the remaining letters and slid them into the attaché case. "They'll be in a safe place, along with the two Bibles, till you're ready for them." The locks clicked shut.

"Listen," Pearse said, "those papers have to be kept cool and away from too much light. I have a climate-controlled box here—" He was talking too fast, he knew, and even Marie's visible warmth seemed to have chilled slightly.

"Monday morning, they'll go in a vault," Diana interrupted. "Till then I have a perfectly good safe." Looking at her, Pearse knew he had lost any chance of changing her mind.

"They'll be fine," Sarsfield echoed, looking closely into Pearse's face. "But what about the stuff we're leaving here?"

Pearse rounded on the stocky man, his frustrated anger boiling to the surface. "You don't trust me, is that it? Well, if I was the kid here"—indicating Marie—"I'd keep a close eye on you, mister."

Pearse was slighter than Sarsfield, but he was also two inches taller and twenty years younger. Sarsfield took a step backward, his face reddening. "I discovered her!" he snarled. "This has been my project, from the beginning. Two years' work—you think I'm going to run off with bits and pieces of it now?" He was about to go on, when a peal of silvery laughter cut through the air.

For an instant Pearse thought someone else had slipped into the room, but the laughter was coming from Marie, her head thrown back and her face flushed. For a long moment, the three of them stared at her. At last she mastered her amusement, but it was still in her eyes when she spoke: "Gentlemen, gentlemen!"

Pearse caught a glimpse of himself in the hall mirror, head lowered like a bull about to charge, and his fists clenched at his sides, but Sarsfield seemed relieved at the interruption.

Diana, who had not moved from her position by the desk, was watching neither of them; her eyes were fixed on Marie's face, and she looked tired and deeply concerned. Marie let her oddly light-colored gaze play over them before she went on. "This is all so foolish. Miss Speed will hold the documents in her briefcase"—she inclined her head toward Diana, in a gesture that should have looked artificial but didn't—"Mr. Pearse obviously requires to keep the papers he has. And Mr. Sarsfield can stay here . . ."

"Stay *here?*" exploded Pearse, and heard Sarsfield echo his words a split second later.

". . . and protect him. With the gun Miss Speed has in her shoulder bag. A perfect solution, *n'est-ce pas?*"

The silence in the room crackled. Diana broke it with a strained laugh. "Madam," she said, sketching a bow, "King Solomon could have done no better."

Fourteen: Diana

As a rule, Judith made it a point of honor to arrive late for meetings, but the clock on Diana's mantel showed two minutes short of five when the street doorbell rang.

"I came, too," said Haskell Rose, towed in Judith's wake. "Hope you don't mind."

"Where is she?" Judith demanded, looking around Diana's living room.

"Asleep," Diana replied. "We spent the afternoon in Saks, mostly. She's a good kid, but she never hit pre-Christmas shopping crowds before." Diana was being less than completely honest: Marie had scarcely noticed the surging, snapping mob around her as she allowed herself to be led from department to department, lost in some private dream. Diana first put it down to bewilderment or even shock, but after an hour of Marie's polite, detached acquiescence, it was clear that the girl's mind was not galvanized by shoes, lingerie, or even jewelry.

Such an attitude seemed perfectly reasonable to Diana—she herself could face a full afternoon of shopping only if it was broken midway by tea and cinnamon toast at the Plaza—but she was becoming desperate for an indication of normal teenage behavior from Marie. By three, the game was clearly up; there was nothing for it but to head back to the apartment. On arrival, Marie had politely declined to try on the few things Diana had bought for her, tumbling instead into Diana's bed, where she fell instantly, deeply asleep.

"Asleep?" said Judith. "It's five o'clock in the afternoon." A thought wiped the disappointment from her features. "At least we can see the letters you didn't leave with Pearse."

"I think, under the circumstances, it'd be better to wait for Marie to wake up," Diana replied.

"And anyway," said Haskell, brightening, "the sun—if it were out—would just be clearing the yardarm."

"Scotch?" said Diana. "Martini? What for you, Judith?"

"A little sherry, please," said Judith. "And nothing for Haskell. But don't let that hold *you* back, dear."

Diana and Haskell digested the instruction in silence. Haskell's expression showed his opinion, while Diana out of pure contrariness opened a can of diet soda for herself and set it prominently on the coffee table, next to Judith's sherry.

"I—we were going to let it wait till Monday," said Judith, "but since what's-her-name, Marie's, still asleep, why don't we get it over with now."

Haskell's visible dismay deepened, but Diana, who had a good idea what was coming, nodded pleasantly. "By all means."

"It's about Brand." Having plunged in, Judith seemed at a loss how to go on. Diana crossed her legs, idly arranged the fabric at the knee of her slacks, and waited. "He's terribly upset," Judith said at last. "In fact, I'm very worried about him."

"We all are," Haskell put in earnestly. Judith, momentarily derailed, tossed him an irritated glance. "Tim Mark's afraid he might . . . you know . . ."

"Kill himself?" Diana asked. She took a sip of diet soda; it was fully as dreadful as she had expected. So much, she thought, for gestures. "I doubt it. Once he gets over the initial shock he'll realize"—if he can still add and subtract—"that the company's giving him a very generous deal."

"Deal? What was it?" asked Judith.

"You'd better ask him," Diana replied. "As for putting him out to pasture, there wasn't any choice. And you people in Editorial——" More annoyed than she had expected to be, she was about to add a few remarks about the responsibility of people who used a decrepit colleague as a stalking horse, when a voice behind her said, "Hello?"

Marie, wearing her brand-new robe and, quite obviously, nothing under it, stood in the living room doorway; she looked barely half awake. Haskell, his eyes intent, was on his feet. "You must be Marie. My name's Haskell Rose. I'm delighted to see you."

"Yes," said Diana, standing. "And this is Patrick's editor, Judith Sanders. Both of them were anxious to meet you."

Judith had not risen; given the disparity in heights, Diana thought, it was probably an intelligent tactical decision. She did, however, seem to be sitting unnaturally erect, her chest thrown out like a pouter pigeon's. "Hello, Marie," she said. "We didn't want to wake you."

"Oh, that's all right," said the girl. Her voice—she sounded not a day over sixteen—was a marked contrast to her figure, and, Diana reflected, to her manner earlier in the day.

"Judith was wondering if she could see the famous letters," Haskell said. "The ones you have here, that is."

Marie looked to Diana. "Is it all right?"

"No reason why not," Diana replied. "I'll just get them out of the safe." She lifted the mirror off its hook and set it on the floor and had just spun the dial the first time when she saw Marie's face from the corner of her eye. The sleepy, abstracted look had vanished, to be replaced by an expression fully as intent as Haskell's, and a set hardness that seemed completely out of place on so young and unlined a countenance. "Oops," said Diana. "Missed it that time." She began again, entered all four numbers and turned the handle, felt the bolt pull back. "There, that's got it."

Marie was at her side when the door swung open. "I'll take them out." Diana stood back as Marie removed the package of letters and the two Bibles. "Would you get those things off the table?" she asked.

Diana removed Judith's glass and the can of soda—both nearly untouched—to the sideboard, and stood there quietly as Marie unwrapped the letters and spread them out for display. "Please don't touch them," she said, a velvet-wrapped command that arrested Judith's hand in midair.

Over the previous year, Diana had taught herself how to sense the emotional temperatures in a packed conference room without ever raising her eyes from the papers in front of her. But how much easier it was, she thought, when you were free to stare at preoccupied people as hard as you liked.

Judith's face, as her eyes devoured the letters laid out before her, was possessed by a greed so complete it left no room for any other expression. Haskell's attention, on the other hand, was clearly split between the fragile scraps that might bring him his longed-for blockbuster and the V at the front of Marie's robe that gaped a little wider every time she bent forward.

Marie herself was the one who held Diana's eye, however, as she explained the salient points of each document, her manner a nice combination of didactic and what could only be called regal. No trace at all of the sleepy young girl of five minutes before; was it the physical presence of the letters that did it? Diana found herself abstractedly sipping Judith's sherry—a drink she loathed—as she watched.

After a few minutes, Diana saw, Haskell's attention had left the papers completely. He was sitting back from the glass-topped table, his head cocked slightly to one side and his eyes on Marie's face. Haskell might drink too much, and he was in most respects an intellectual lightweight; but like most good acquisitions editors he was more sensitive to writers than to writing, and he was clearly struck by something in Marie's manner.

Not so Judith, whose stable of authors was exclusively male and whose modus operandi seldom varied: vamp the writer till his eyes were crossed (as Milly Aaron had once remarked), and then cut his manuscript by a third. Judith had become aware of Haskell's interest in Marie, and it was not the sort of aberration she forgave in an escort. She looked pointedly at her watch, mimed elaborate surprise, and, when that failed, cut right across an observation of Marie's: "Haskell! It's nearly seven. We've got to run."

She broke his concentration, Diana saw, but her leaden hint sailed right past him. "Run where?" he said. "We weren't going anyplace." His eyes were still on Marie, whose face had frozen at Judith's interruption.

"I guess we weren't," Judith replied, with the slightest emphasis on *we*. "I guess I'll go home and make myself some dinner."

Marie's small mouth curled into a smile. "Surely you don't have to leave, too, Mr. Rose."

Judith's face went dark, and her already formidable breast seemed to swell. For a moment, Diana thought she might explode into one of her notorious tantrums. Haskell appeared to think so, too: He began to sputter excuses. But Marie looked so oblivious that Diana decided to take a hand. Scooping up Judith's coat from where she had tossed it on an armchair, she advanced on the other woman. "Then it's all settled," she said brightly. "Haskell will have dinner with Marie and me." She held the coat out for Judith, who regarded it with baffled fury and then snatched it from Diana's hands.

Even with the apartment door closed, they could hear—and feel—the slam of the building's front door. "I'll pay for this on Monday," Haskell murmured, ostensibly to himself.

Diana, returning from the kitchen with a bucket of ice cubes, decided it was best to pretend she hadn't heard. "Martini," she said.

"Straight up, lemon peel," Haskell replied automatically. Coming to himself, he turned to the girl, who was still sitting on the couch. "What about you, Marie? What'll you have?"

"I don't really know," said Marie. "Would I like what you're drinking?"

"You're too young for martinis," Diana said flatly. Handing Haskell his, she reached into the sideboard and produced a fat brown bottle and a highball glass. As she poured the dark, syrupy liquid over ice she observed, "I have a friend who tells me this is a hopelessly debased American taste, so I hope you're a debased American like me."

Marie took a cautious sip. "It's delicious," she announced. "Chocolate and oranges, isn't it? I could drink the whole bottle."

"Well, before you get too far into it, why don't you put the papers back in the safe, while I consult the kitchen and see what we've got to eat."

Five minutes later Diana was standing in front of the freezer, wondering when everything inside had turned to frozen chicken curry, as Marie appeared in the doorway. "How do I lock it?" she asked.

"Close the door tight, turn the handle all the way to the left, and then spin the dial two full turns either way," she said. "And Marie"—halfway out the door the girl paused—"maybe it'd be a good idea to put something on under that robe."

"What? Oh." She looked down, and her face turned scarlet. "Oh, I see."

"So does Haskell. That's the trouble. Or could be, with a couple more martinis in him."

When she returned to the living room, Marie and Haskell were deep in conversation. Marie had changed into dark slacks and a blouse of Diana's, and had attempted, without great success, to do something to her hair. Even from the doorway Diana could tell she had reverted to her hesitant, childlike manner. "But that's how *I* feel," she was saying. "Just that way."

"Just what way?" asked Diana. She went to the mantel, checked the door of the safe, and replaced the mirror. Marie was still groping for a reply as Diana turned back to her.

"As if . . ." She seemed to be nerving herself up, but Haskell stepped in.

"As if there were another person in her mind," he said. "It's not that uncommon, especially among people who've spent most of their lives alone." His smile was disarming. "Humans are social animals: If you don't have a person to

talk to, you supply one. It's very different from true possession."

"Possession?" Marie did not look reassured. "I've read
about it. In books. Does it really happen?"

Haskell opened his mouth to answer, caught Diana's
warning look. "Well," he replied, "that's hard to say for
sure. Lots of people think so, me among them." He matched
Diana stare for stare, and she remembered that this was his
great enthusiasm. Every W-F list had at least two of what the
catalogue listed as "Occult Interest" and what the sales force
privately referred to as Rosenuts; when Diana had checked
out the books' collective track record she had been depressed
to find that all of them at least made a profit and some did a
good deal better than that.

"You remember the case of Sylvia Merdling," Haskell was
saying. "No less than seven distinct personalities. And all of
them . . ." He paused for effect, and Diana noted with
interest that emotion was fogging the upper half of his
bifocals. ". . . every single one was a real historical personage."

Marie's round face had set in a rapt expression that Diana
found faintly unnerving. "Real like Napoleon and Cleopatra,
you mean?" Diana said, letting the acid seep into her voice.

"No, no," Haskell responded impatiently. "That's con
game stuff. These people were ordinary folk, like Sylvia
herself, but there were records of them: birth certificates,
contracts, mentions in other people's letters."

In the course of her intelligence career, Diana had supervised the creation of false trails that sounded a lot more
impressive, but she knew from dreary experience that
Haskell's obsession was impervious to mere reason. "Why
her?" Marie demanded, leaning forward as if to draw the
answer from Haskell. "Why did they choose this Sylvia?"

"Ah, that's what we don't know for certain," Haskell
replied. "There are gaps in the historical record, you see. It's
perfectly reasonable—some of the personalities came from
very small villages, very long ago." Now he leaned forward
in his turn, until his face was only inches from Marie's. "But

where they could trace the records, all the personalities were Sylvia's own forebears."

"Of course!" Marie cried, and then clapped her hand across her mouth.

Oh, Christ, thought Diana.

"I've heard about the two genealogies," said Haskell. "Is it someone from either of them?"

Marie regarded him wide-eyed. She shook her head. A long minute passed, and she lowered her eyes. "Maybe kind of," she admitted.

Haskell removed his glasses, something Diana had never seen him do. Without them, his face seemed to narrow and age. "You know who it is, though," he said gently.

Marie lowered her eyes. "I think so. I didn't at first."

"Wouldn't you like to be certain?" he asked.

"I'm not sure." She paused. "I'm afraid."

"Of course you are. It's a great responsibility."

She looked stunned. "You know?"

"I can guess," he replied. "Who else would it be?"

Diana had watched the interchange with a growing sense of alarm. "I think this has gone far enough."

"No." Marie's voice was steady, though her lower lip was trembling. "It's why I'm here, isn't it?" she said to Haskell. "The purpose of my life."

"How can I say?" But his expression told Diana that he was about to try: "Sometimes we can't see the larger pattern, Marie. We simply have to go forward."

"I suppose you're right," she replied.

"Trustfully . . ." My God, he's worse than TV, Diana thought.

"Yes," the girl said softly.

"Acceptingly . . ." He put his hand over hers.

"Oh, *yes*." She covered it with her own.

In a minute we'll need a bucket of cold water to get them apart, Diana thought. And a copy editor. "Just what're you getting at, Haskell?"

The whiplash of her voice made him jump. "I was about to tell Marie there may be a way," he replied.

"Exorcism?" Diana made no effort to hide her contempt.

"You've got it backward," he said, coloring. "We don't want to drive out whatever it is. If Marie is harboring a . . . let's call it a spirit"—he glanced at the girl, who nodded her encouragement—"we want it to come forward. That is," he added, "if Marie's willing."

"I am."

"There is some risk."

Seeing that Marie was about to dismiss it, Diana jumped in: "What kind of risk?"

"If I'm correct, we're dealing with someone who remains a very powerful personage, even at several removes." My God, Diana thought, he really believes this stuff. But before she could interrupt, he went on: "The shadow of a queen can be dark and long," he intoned, and Marie nodded solemnly, her eyes wide. "I'd like to put you under hypnosis, Marie. For your own protection," he said.

"You?" Diana was frankly incredulous. "Haskell, you're an *editor*, for God's sake."

"Believe me, I've done this before," he said earnestly. "I've had training. And I think Marie would be a perfect subject."

Diana bit off her reply and took a deep breath. "What do you say, Marie?"

"I want to try it. Now." As if to emphasize her words she picked up her glass and drained it off.

• • •

Marie sat on the couch, breathing slowly and evenly, her eyes nearly closed. Her face was calm but pale, and her tousled hair gleamed darkly in the tightly concentrated light of a single lamp. "Is she under already?" Diana whispered, from the shadows behind the couch.

Haskell, who was sitting on the straight-backed chair directly in front of the girl, nodded absently. The room was cool, even chilly, but from where she stood Diana could see the drops of sweat on his forehead. Without taking his eyes from Marie's serene, vacuous face, he shrugged off his jacket and wrenched at the knot of his tie.

"Are you all right?" Diana asked, speaking quietly.

"Oh, sure," he said impatiently. "Just nerves." Deliberately, he reached out and snapped his fingers in front of Marie's eyes. She blinked, but gave no other sign of wakefulness. He let his breath out slowly, and Diana guessed he had been holding it. He looked up at her.

"What now?" she asked.

"You have the first Bible—the older one?"

"Yes." Standing just outside the circle of light she felt a little like a spirit herself, but it might have been nothing more than helpless anger and two glasses of Orvieto on an empty stomach.

"Bring it around here where I can see the list of names. The last page." She dropped to one knee beside him; the acrid smell of tension came off him, cutting through the odors of dusty paper and ancient leather and battling with Diana's own light, astringent perfume. "What are the last two names?" he asked.

Creak of leather as she opened the heavy cover, and then the thick crackle of pages turning. Marie's head moved slightly, and Diana saw Haskell tense. When the girl was still again, Diana read aloud: "Mary Hunter to Patrick Donovan. No," she corrected herself, "Mary Ogilvie, until her first husband was killed."

"And after she married Donovan, they came to America?"

"You're right. How did you know?"

He nodded at the silent figure on the couch. "She told me. The only near break in the line, so a good place to begin."

"Begin?"

"Be quiet." He took a hoarse, deep breath and let it out slowly; then again. "Mary Hunter," he said. His voice sounded quiet, assured. "Are you there?"

Nothing. Or perhaps the slightest shiver running over Marie's frame. Haskell glanced at Diana beside him and then turned his attention back to the girl. "Mary Hunter," he said again, and she could hear the strain. "Are—"

"—Aye. What d'ye want of me?" A harsh, anxious voice, quite unlike Marie's own. But it had definitely come from the girl's mouth. Diana felt an icy tingle run the length of her spine.

"Free passage through your spirit."

"No' tae find Ogilvie," Marie snarled, her accent so heavy Diana could barely understand the words. "I'd no' sell him quick, and I'll no' sell him deid."

"Let him rest in peace. I want to speak with your mother."

Marie's face contorted in a rasping, humorless laugh. "Auld witch. Ye'll hae no guid o' her."

"Even so," Haskell persisted.

"On yer ain heid, then."

As Diana watched, horrified, Marie's face seemed to collapse in on itself, and she slumped to a shapeless huddle—an old, old woman. A screech of mad laughter echoed off the walls and Diana felt the hair on the back of her neck rise. "Good God," she heard herself breathe. The laughter stopped as abruptly as it had begun, and was followed by a torrent of hoarse gabble in no language she had ever heard.

"Stop," Haskell said, and then louder: "Enough. Go back." Silence again. Marie was breathing in short, stertorous gasps, and drops of saliva gleamed on the front of her blouse.

"What was that?" Diana demanded, her voice unsteady.

"A madwoman. I think," Haskell replied. He sounded as shaken as he looked. Marie stirred and moaned. "This is taking too long," Haskell said. "What's the first name in the book? The first female name?"

Diana held the page under the light. " 'Marie filz-Iames'— must be Fitzjames—'callit Balfor,' " she replied. "Unless you mean—"

"Don't say it!" Haskell snapped. Diana had the feeling he was very close to panic. What would happen to Marie if he flipped out? She felt the muscles knot at the pit of her stomach.

"Now or never," Haskell muttered. "Marie Balfor," he called softly.

Marie moaned again. Gradually she straightened up and as she did her cheeks seemed to fill, her mouth to lose its pinched look. "Marie Balfor," Haskell repeated, more urgently. Marie's back arched; she opened her mouth as if trying to speak, and then fell back.

"One thing left to try." Haskell's eyes gleamed with desperation. He leaned forward until his mouth was at Marie's ear. "Marie," he whispered. "Marie Fitzjames."

"No. She will not come. Silly man, you'll not stalk me through my children." Marie's mouth formed the words, but the voice—deep yet very female, and accustomed to command—was certainly not hers.

"What's going on?" Diana cried, hearing her own fear. "Haskell, what the hell *is* this?" He seemed to be trying to say something, but no sound emerged.

"You thought to take me by surprise, Master Rose. Why?" Marie's mouth smiled indulgently, but her eyes were dead. A trill of silvery laughter echoed through the room. "Ah, I see: You want me to prove I exist? How shall I do that, little man?" Marie bent forward stiffly, as if she were hinged at the waist. Her hand extended slowly, awkwardly, and picked up the steel letter opener with which they had slit the plastic wrappings of the Bible. "Perhaps this would convince you."

Before Diana could move, the tip of the blade was at the base of Haskell's throat, where the opened collar of his shirt revealed a thick vein throbbing just under the damp skin. "I kill, therefore I am." In profile, Haskell's face was a death mask already, until a muscle jumped in his cheek. "Oh, I suppose not," said the silvery voice, and the blade fell away. "But don't tempt me again." The laugh had the same silvery ring, but a half tone lower and warmly amused this time. "You know my reputation: Temptation's the one thing I never could resist."

Marie's eyes rolled up in her head until all Diana could see were the whites. She gave a small, exhausted moan and toppled sideways to the floor. As she did so, Haskell cried

"No!" in a loud, frightened voice and scrambled to his feet, kicking over the chair. As Diana knelt beside the unconscious girl, the heavy Bible still in her hands, the apartment doorbell rang, echoed by an angry buzz from the kitchen.

"Oh God, the chicken," said Diana, and burst into helpless, uncontrollable laughter.

Fifteen: Troubridge

The wild-eyed man who answered Diana's door was streaming with sweat, the outline of his flabby torso clearly visible through the shirt that looked pasted to him. "Who the devil are you?" Troubridge said, and without waiting for an answer pushed past him down the short hallway. In the darkened living room, spotlit by a single lamp, Diana was kneeling over another woman, who lay crumpled next to the coffee table. Troubridge dropped the white cardboard box he was carrying; three long-legged strides and he was standing beside them.

Diana looked up blankly; she was holding a huge, leatherbound volume open in her two hands, and she seemed to have been crying. Troubridge knelt beside her. The unconscious woman—as tall as Diana, he saw—had her face turned away from him. She was clutching a wicked-looking letter opener in one hand, but he could see no sign of injury on Diana or, for that matter, on the woman herself.

Troubridge put his fingertips to her wrist; the blood was pumping hard in her veins, but the beat was steady. He turned her gently, so he could see her face. She was, he saw, very young, and something about her was familiar, though he couldn't immediately place it. Her breathing was regular if a bit shallow.

Behind him, he heard footsteps and he spun on one knee.

The sweat-soaked man, unsteady on his feet, was watching him without expression. "Is she all right?" he asked.

Troubridge rocked back on his heels. "Seems to be," he said. And to Diana: "What's going on here?"

"You wouldn't believe me if I told you," she said. To his utter amazement she giggled, but he saw a spark of fear back in her eyes. "Help me up, will you? I feel a little wobbly."

"Well, you look like death's pale horse," he said, bracing her to her feet. "Speed, you need a drink."

"Now that's for damn sure," she agreed. "Maybe we all do. Oh," as she remembered, "this is Mr. Haskell Rose, editor and amateur hypnotist. Haskell, may I present Alan Troubridge, a culture vulture from Her Majesty's consulate here in Manhattan." On the point of nodding to Rose, whose name he already knew, Troubridge glanced at Diana sharply, but she was looking down at the unconscious girl. "And Sleeping Beauty, there on the floor, is Marie McIntyre."

The girl's name gave Troubridge the second's warning he needed: So this was the Cinderella who was giving them fits back in Westminster. He forced himself to toss her a merely casual glance, and a remark so automatically innocuous that he never heard it himself. "Can you wake her up?" Diana asked Rose. She turned back to Troubridge: "She's not passed out, you know. Just a . . . a parlor game that went sour."

The editor, who had been regarding the unconscious girl apprehensively, said to Troubridge, "Let's put her on the couch." They propped her in a sitting position, her head lolling back openmouthed. Rose reached out and took her chin, turning her head toward him. "Marie, come back," he said, in a conversational tone, and the girl's eyes popped open like a doll's.

"I must've been asleep," she said. From the corner of his eye, Troubridge saw Diana look quickly at Rose, who shook his head. "I don't know you," Marie was saying. "You're very tall."

"Alan Troubridge, Miss McIntyre," he replied, shaping a professional smile. "At your service." The sidelong look she threw him from beneath her lashes was probably mere shyness, but it made him catch his breath: For an instant the teenage American was gone, replaced in his mind's eye by the portrait of another young woman—a woman in the formal mourning white of the sixteenth century, but with the identical rounded face, almond-shaped eyes, and small, considering mouth. In the stark clarity of shock, he could remember not only the portrait's subject but even its peculiar appellation—*Deuil Blanc*.

A yawn caught Marie by surprise, breaking the likeness. Troubridge could feel his mouth still frozen in an artificial grimace, but his mind was reeling. Bring back the letters or destroy them, they'd told him; discredit the girl's lineage, in case she—or others behind her—have disturbing ambitions. But what did papers matter now? Properly costumed and coiffured, this Marie would be her own prima facie case. In the age of instant celebrity, she could be the most famous woman in the world . . .

"You have a funny way of speaking," Marie remarked, and colored in embarrassment. Her own way of speaking, Troubridge thought, was mostly lower-middle-class New York, over a background drawl he could not place. But the timbre itself was pleasant enough; a good voice coach could make her sound as much like a princess as any of the real ones did.

"He can't help it," Diana said. Her composure seemed to have returned, and she was looking at him quizzically. "Troubridge is your first Englishman, Marie."

Her face lit with interest. "Really? I've read lots of English books, and I always wondered how they spoke. Differently from us, that is."

The coquettish smile was, he decided, quite unconscious. Heaven knew she came by it legitimately. No, wait a minute, he reminded himself, I'm supposed to be on the other side. "And how *do* we speak, Miss McIntyre?" he asked her, wondering if he sounded as heavily avuncular in her ears as he did in his own.

"Well . . ." She cocked her head to one side, consider-

ing. "Quite nicely. I like it." Her sudden grin was wholly
unroyal, and wholly disarming. Troubridge could see her
doing it in front of the world's television cameras. "Are you
a friend of Diana's?" she asked.

The necessary answer stuck in his throat, but Diana
supplied it: "Yes, he's a friend, Marie. Just a good friend."
She was looking oddly at him, and he knew at least some of
his thoughts must be reaching his face, knew he had to get
command of himself. But before he could frame a suitable
double entendre, Diana gasped: "Oh, no! I totally forgot."

"Forgot what?" asked Marie.

"Our date. Troubridge, I'm devastated: I've *never* done
that."

Her dismay was so genuine—and so engaging—that he felt
an unexpected jab of affection. Then he remembered why
he'd come. "No harm done," he said heavily. He retrieved
the cardboard box from the floor and presented it to her.
"We've plenty of time, happily. Just leap into something that
goes with this, and we'll be off."

Dead silence. Diana took the box and opened it, but her
mind was obviously elsewhere. She took out the corsage—
the single white bud he always brought her—without apparently seeing it, and Marie broke the spell with a cry of
delight: "It's a rose, isn't it? May I smell it, Diana? I've never
smelled a rose."

"Of course," Diana replied, handing Marie the corsage.
"She hasn't, you know: smelled a rose," she said to
Troubridge. To his amazement, her eyes—the clear, gray-
blue eyes he so admired—were moist with tears. She saw his
surprise, blinked twice, and launched into an incoherent
explanation of Marie's background: sequestered by a
madwoman . . . never allowed out . . . never went
shopping . . . never even saw TV until yesterday.

"—And now she's out of Eden," Troubridge interrupted.
"You can tell me the details over dinner: I've booked a table
at the Côte Basque. And we have to hold to schedule if we're
to make Bobby Short's ten o'clock show at the Carlyle."

Her eyes darted to the coffee table. The book she had been

holding was sitting there, a huge, tatty dinosaur. Without knowing why, he was instantly certain it had something to do with Marie. He realized Diana was watching him, realized as well that it would be far too obvious for him to ignore it: "Going in for first editions, Speed?" he asked, as lightly as he could. "Lord, what a monster."

He felt Diana's tenseness back off a notch, but her expression was still concerned. "Look, Troubridge," she began, "I hate to say this—you know how I feel about Bobby Short—but I just can't go out. Marie's staying with me, and I've already started dinner for her and Haskell." The obvious answer struck her, and her face brightened. "Why not join us? Just cancel the reservations, and I'll put some more curry in the microwave."

He was flabbergasted. The whole plan, carefully contrived by the odious Carr, depended on her apartment being empty for at least three hours. He glanced surreptitiously at his watch; Carr would be arriving anytime now, assured that Diana would be gone. Pray God he didn't blunder in. Troubridge saw Diana was waiting for some kind of answer, and he cudgeled his brain for a way out. "To hell with haute cuisine," he said. "We can go to . . . to Sloppy Louie's, down at Fulton Fish Market. All four of us," he added quickly. "My treat. I'll call the consulate, have a car sent round."

"That's sweet of you Troubridge, but—"

"Think what an experience it would be for Marie," he said in desperation. At the sound of her name, Marie stared up at him.

"Oh, don't worry about me," she said. "After all, the dinner's *cooked*. There's no reason to go out at all." She looked meaningfully at Diana, then down at the large volume, then up, past Troubridge, to the mantel behind him. It was almost as if she knew, Troubridge thought. But that was impossible. And unnecessary, he reminded himself: By now even this unworldly child must have some notion of the value of those letters; of course she and Diana were unwilling to leave them unguarded.

Impasse. By Monday the papers would surely be in a vault. Out of reach. Spurred by that fact Carr would insist on a coup de main tonight. And in terms of both their missions he would be right. But there might still be a way to retrieve matters, without bloodshed. "Here's what we'll do," said Troubridge, thinking fast. "Mr. Rose, you take Marie to the Côte Basque and then on to hear Bobby Short at the Carlyle. The reservations are in my name and the consulate's, so you shouldn't have any trouble." He turned quickly to Diana, before she could conjure up an objection. "You and I will dispose of the food." He sniffed the air appreciatively. "You know how I love my own curry, especially when it's slightly burnt."

"Well . . ." she said, wavering.

There was something between her and Haskell Rose: Troubridge could feel it. Sexual? No, that was ridiculous; a sort of mutual repulsion—she wanted to see his back, and he wanted to be gone.

It was Marie who saved the day for him: "Who *is* Bobby Short?"

"There, you see?" said Troubridge. "Speed, your duty is clear. This young lady must not be deprived of such an experience."

She gave in with a smile. "Oh, all right. Okay with you, Haskell?"

"Why not?" Rose said. "But I'm kind of a mess."

When Diana was presented with a merely tangible obstacle and the opportunity to organize others, Troubridge knew, she could always be relied upon. She shifted smoothly into what he thought of as her field marshal mode: "What time are those reservations of yours?"

"Seven-thirty and ten, respectively."

"And the Côte Basque is 55th off Fifth, isn't it? Right. Marie, you hop into that blue dress we bought this afternoon. I'll help you with your makeup and your hair. Haskell, give Troubridge your shirt. He'll run it through the dryer while you shower. Don't just stand there," she snapped at the bemused trio. "You've got exactly twenty minutes. *Allez.*"

On the face of it, her take-charge manner was officious, intrusive, unfeminine. Why did he also find it endearing? There was a possible answer, as he well knew, but now was not the time even to consider it.

• • •

"This is very generous of you," Rose said, as Marie climbed into the taxi twenty-one minutes later.

"Not at all," Troubridge replied. "It's not as if I were paying for your evening." From the corner of his eye he could see the unobtrusive sedan parked across the street and fifty yards down, looking just like all the other parked cars except for the figure hunched behind the wheel.

Rose slid into the back seat of the cab, next to Marie. "You were going to get wine, weren't you?" he asked Troubridge. "Can we drop you at a liquor store?"

"No, no," he answered. "It's right around the corner. You two go off and have a splendid time. And Rose," he bent forward confidentially, "you needn't hurry back, you know."

"We'll get to know each other, Marie and I," Rose replied. To Troubridge's bottomless disgust, he even winked. Two of a kind, that's what we are, he said to himself, carefully not slamming the cab door.

He waited till the cab had crossed Second Avenue, and glanced up at the curtained window of Diana's living room before striding across the street. As he came abreast of the parked sedan, the passenger door swung open, and he jackknifed himself into the seat. "You're bloody late," Carr said. "Who were those people?"

"The tall girl's your Cinderella princess," Troubridge said. "The man . . ." He paused; there was no time to explain Rose, and no need. "Forget him. But Diana Speed's still inside."

"What?"

"She won't go out. It's the papers: She's not going to leave them unguarded."

"Shit," said Carr. "Well, it's on her head, then. We have

to get hold of them tonight." Perhaps sensing his companion's opposition, he half turned in his seat. "That special letter you told me about, the deathbed accusation—she's got it in that safe of hers," he said. "We don't have a choice: We have to go tonight."

Go. What a silly synonym for flat-out assault. He and Carr didn't have that kind of training: Someone—almost certainly Diana—would be injured, or worse. "I won't do it," Troubridge said.

"Won't? What d'you mean, *won't?*"

"Just that." No, not just that: If Carr intended to try a raid by himself he'd have to be stopped, and there was only one person to do it.

Perhaps Carr saw his answer in Troubridge's expression. His face went dark with anger, and the fat little body tensed. Troubridge's own body was poised to defend itself, but his mind was still curiously detached. It watched as Carr visibly took his emotions in hand, and it considered with respect the iron self-control required. After a silent minute Carr shrugged. "I can understand how you feel," he said. "She's a woman of . . ." The word he wanted eluded him, if it existed. His eyes met Troubridge's, and for the briefest moment they shared a perfect understanding. "You have to choose: *Tout pour le Roi*—or something less."

"Not necessarily," Troubridge said, and explained the idea that had come to him in Diana's living room, and that had been elaborating itself ever since.

"You're barking mad," Carr objected, halfway through. And: "Bonkers. Absolutely bonkers," when he had finished.

"It'll work," Troubridge insisted. "And no one gets hurt. Remember what you said: Once the banks open Monday, those papers'll be locked up in proper vaults." He saw the point had registered and pressed in: "If you want my help, this is the way it's got to be."

"You're sure you can drink her under the table?" Carr asked. He was wavering; Troubridge felt sure of it.

"That's not a problem," Nor was it: Diana was temperamentally incapable of refusing any challenge, however

veiled. She had a hard head but not, as he remembered with
bitter amusement, as hard a head as she thought.

"What about the safe, then? I have plenty of plastique, but
it'll make a hell of a noise."

"You won't need it," Troubridge assured him.

"You said you didn't know the combination."

"She hasn't told me it, no. But I've seen the dial, and I've
watched her open it a dozen times: four single-digit numbers,
right-left-right-left. You mark my words: It'll be four-five-
five-six."

"Four-five-five-six," Carr repeated. "How can you be so
sure?"

"It's what everyone uses," he replied, hoping he sounded
more confident than he felt. "Some familiar number: Birthday, license plate, address. She doesn't own a car, and her
address is five digits, not four."

"And it's safe enough," Carr mused, "except from close
friends." He looked sidelong at Troubridge, and his knowing
smile died at birth. "All right—we'll try it. Nothing to lose,
I suppose. As long as she's really unconscious."

Troubridge opened the sedan door. "Leave that to me," he
said. "Me and Poire William."

"I may be able to help matters along," said Carr, fumbling
in the pocket of his ill-fitting coat. His hand reappeared with
just the random assortment of trash Troubridge had half
expected: a tangle of dirty white string, a matchbook with the
cover torn off, a couple of coins, and a small plastic
container. Carr tugged off its top and tipped a capsule into his
palm. "Here," he said, handing it to Troubridge. "Open this
and pour it into her poire whatsit."

"What is it?"

"Just Nembutal. I've had trouble getting to sleep lately."
Carr's mouth twisted. "Don't worry. I won't poison your
lady. I realize it's hard to believe, coming from me, but I
don't want to hurt her. I just can't risk her creeping up behind
me when I'm working on her bleeding safe."

Carr's admission—confession?—was so unexpected that
Troubridge found himself swayed by it. Anyway, it would be

safer for Diana if she was soundly asleep when the pudgy agent was in her apartment. Troubridge slipped the capsule into the pocket of his suit jacket. "Remember," he said, "I'll drop the keys in the dustbin by the curb. Wait half an hour after I come out of the building. You'll still have plenty of time: Marie and her escort won't be back till well after one in the morning. I'll be waiting for you in the White Rose—it's a bar, about five blocks north on Second."

"Getting yourself noticed by the customers," Carr agreed. "Just don't do anything foolish."

"I'll have my alibi, never fear," Troubridge said, levering himself out of the sedan. He shut the door and started toward First Avenue, resolutely putting from his mind what he was about to do. He was committed—had been committed all his life. Duty was properly the highest of priorities, and he'd known from the start that the possibility of betraying Diana was built into their relationship. Somehow, the knowledge failed to assuage him.

Sixteen: Diana

When she opened the apartment door, Troubridge handed her a brown paper bag. "Here," he said. "An after-dinner drink that really *does* taste better cold." She took it, feeling the slender, long-necked bottle inside, and stepped back to let him in. "What's the matter?" he asked, as the hall light struck her face.

"I want you to hear something," she said. She put the bag in the refrigerator and led the way to her bedroom. "Happened while you were out." She was pleased that she could keep her voice level without an effort. Her hands, she noted, were steady as she hit the answering machine's rewind key. "There was another call like it last night. Different voice, same tune."

As she pressed replay, though, she felt a premonitory stab of revulsion. "You there, bitch?" Definitely a different voice, but somehow similar. How? "Listen up, you cold whore."

Troubridge's face had gone still, intent; what she thought of as his suspended-animation look. The caller took a raspily audible breath and launched into his litany: the painful, revolting things that were going to be done to her, and soon. This time, the list of prospective atrocities was punctuated repeatedly with her name; somehow, it made them seem less personal rather than more. When the caller signed off, Troubridge was silent for about fifteen seconds and then looked at her. "He's reading it. Everything after the genteel salutation."

Of course, she thought. Why didn't I catch that? "So was the other one. And the text sounded familiar to me."

"Not to me," he replied. "My mama didn't let me look at things like that." He put his arm around her shoulders, and she was surprised at how reassuring it felt. "You appear to have pissed someone off, Speed. Scarcely conceivable, a sweet child like you."

"Someone young," she agreed, allowing his big, bony hand to cup her breast.

"Young, and I should say well-bred," Troubridge mused aloud. "Did you hear just a little hesitancy when he got to the fruity bits? Our Percy—I'll call him that for the moment—our Percy isn't really at home with X-rated language."

"Last night's caller seemed to enjoy it. A more personal performance throughout." It was amazing just how gentle his powerful, square-tipped fingers could be. Especially the finger that was ghosting back and forth over her nipple.

"D'you still have the tape?"

"It's been erased by this one," she said. "I didn't realize there'd be a repeat." She eased his hand away. "What else can you tell me?"

"Manhattan upper-class," he said without hesitation. "It's unmistakable; always makes me think they've burnt the tip of their tongue. Good school, maybe amateur theatricals. Literate but not literary," he continued thoughtfully. "Young, as you've already said—mid-twenties, most likely." He paused, considering. "Here's a wild guess for you, Speed: This lad's doing a favor for a friend; it's not his idea at all."

"By God, I think you're right," she said.

"Which suggests—"

"—that whoever's behind it has a voice I know," she exulted. "Troubridge, you're a wonder."

"I've been telling you that for months," he said blandly. "Got any ideas?"

"Yes." But this was something she'd handle herself from

here on. On impulse, she pulled his head down, and her opening mouth met his.

• • •

So where, she wondered two hours later, had the evening gone wrong? The kiss had not carried them to bed, and she was still unsure which of them had failed to ignite. Even so, she was left in a comfortably self-congratulatory mood that extended easily into dinner. The chicken curry was not burned after all; its spicing was properly inflammatory, the beer at just the right temperatures (cold for her, lukewarm for him), even the goddamn poori bread had turned out right for once—delicate and airy as a cloud, but a cloud with a delightfully greasy substance to it.

She had been aware of the restraint that hobbled their usual badinage; he was treating her like one of his damned VIPs, which only brought out the acid in her. And he seemed to have an almost skittish reluctance to let the conversation go down any track for more than half a dozen sentences, as if he feared some kind of trap. And that was too bad, because it left several nicely hidden traps unsprung.

"More coffee?" she asked, lifting the china pot. "Or another beer?" Troubridge shook his head, pushed his chair back from the table.

"I think not, thanks. I'm at the exact pitch of gassy stupefaction. Be a shame to ruin it."

"Port, then. I've chilled it off for you."

"Stuff yourself, Speed," he answered comfortably. "We'll drink the present I brought you."

"The brown bag in the fridge, right?" She got to her feet, picking up her plate and his. "I'll get it—you look too comfortable to stir." She put the plates in the dishwasher, added the empty casserole. For no reason at all, her mind flicked to Marie: Of course there wasn't—couldn't be— anything to that hocus-pocus of Haskell's, but what on earth was going on inside the child's head? The two of them should have finished dinner by now; had it been a good idea to let

Haskell be alone with her? Have to take the kid aside and warn her about middle-aged wolves. And Troubridge: Just for a second he'd looked at Marie as if he'd seen the Second Coming.

She shook her head irritably and opened the refrigerator. The brown bag proved to contain not the dessert wine she had half expected but a rather menacing bottle of thick, clear fluid with a pear lurking at its bottom like an undersea mine. Her eyebrows rose as she deciphered the handwritten label. She pulled the cork, took a quick, appreciative sniff, and grabbed up a couple of crystal wine glasses as delicate looking as cobwebs.

"Pear William," she said, as she poured his glass. "I'm in the big leagues at last."

"Don't be vulgar," he said. "I wanted to be sure you were up to it." He took a noisy sip. "Splendid. You eat the pear, you know."

She toasted him silently. It *was* good, she decided. But not the liquid dynamite he'd been threatening her with. "Eat the pear, do you? How do you get the damn thing out?"

"That, my girl, is the secret. Wild horses wouldn't drag it from me."

Well, they might see about that later. She refilled his glass, and her own. Three mutual refills later she decided he was ready. "Troubridge, what's an equerry?"

He looked at her as if he doubted his hearing. "An equerry?" he repeated. "What is it, a crossword clue?" She said nothing and his expression slowly began to change. "What've you been up to, Speed?"

"I had to call friends in Washington, to check a reference," she began, finding it extraordinarily difficult to meet his eyes.

"Friends or cousins?" he interjected.

She attempted a smile, but it wilted as it emerged. "*You* might call them cousins," she admitted.

"And as long as the computer was warmed up, you thought you'd trot my name through it," he said. She had expected anger, not this watchful resignation.

"I didn't have to tell you," she said.

"No, you didn't." He picked up the liqueur glass, regarded it blankly, and set it back down. "Look, I can't blame you; might have done the same myself. It just takes the edge off one's evening."

"I'm sorry."

His smile had a bitter twist: "No, I'm the one who's sorry: I should have told you about her."

For a moment, Diana failed to make the connection; her train of thought was well down another track: "Your wife, you mean? Oh, I'd always assumed you were married."

She had not really surprised him, she saw. "I wasn't aware it showed."

"Don't worry—you're unmarked. No, it was just the law of averages. Anyway, our . . . arrangement has always been no questions asked. If anybody broke the rule, it was me."

She expected relief. What she saw beneath it, she was almost sure, was disappointment. "Now you know everything," he said; it sounded like a question.

"Not yet. You still haven't answered me: What's an equerry?"

"As in Sir Guy William Aske Troubridge, K.C.V.O., equerry to His Royal Highness Edward, Prince of Wales?"

"The very man. Right."

"A personal attendant, of sorts. Smoother of difficulties. Confidant, on occasion . . . There isn't any American equivalent, really."

"Why aren't you one?"

"It's not hereditary, Speed. Some things in England aren't you know."

"Well, you certainly are," she said. "You're related to absolutely everyone." He seemed to have relaxed slightly, and she took another cautious step forward: "Did you ever meet the Prince? Afterward, when he was the Duke of Windsor?"

"No." The word ricocheted off the walls. After some time, he said, "I didn't know you were interested in royalty."

"I'm not, as a rule. But I was reading about the Duke of Windsor. He was different from your usual run of royals. Colorful."

"He was that. Frankly, I'm surprised at you, Speed."

"Because he married for love?"

"Because he abandoned what he'd been bred to do." He seemed to see the puzzlement in her eyes and added, in a smoothly savage tone she had never heard him use, "Perhaps I find it difficult to be fair about the man who broke my grandfather's heart."

She was taken aback by his barely controlled emotion, but he scarcely seemed to notice.

"I realize that's out of bounds for you and me, a phrase like *broken heart*," he went on. "It happens to be true, though. Grandfather Guy was never the same after the abdication. He died two years later. We had no word from Windsor, of course."

"How awful, a man who loved him so much."

"That's not it at all." He picked up the glass again and emptied it. "Impossible to explain."

She could see that at least a part of him wanted to. "Try," she said, and refilled his glass.

"You see, it wasn't the man Edward my grandfather loved, it was the Crown, the institution. As Grandfather Guy saw it, Edward's failure was grandfather's, too. The Duke realized that much, anyway. He would never have dared to write us."

"I don't see how you can fall in love with an institution," she said. "Especially when it's occupied by such a dreary collection as your Windsors. They're so . . . so goddamn *thick*."

He turned on his tolerant look for her. "Well, consider the gene pool they have to draw from: It's a wonder the poor dears can even tie their shoes."

"Can they?"

"I have it on the very best authority, Speed. No princeling is allowed out of Buck House until he can tie his own shoes, in the dark and with his eyes closed. Princesses, of course, wear slippers, not shoes."

"Glass slippers, I suppose," she said. Explaining the exotic aspects of England always seemed to restore his good humor.

"That Princess? She was a very different case. It's not a talent hunt, choosing a queen-to-be."

"I'd have thought it was almost the opposite—an antitalent hunt."

"This from an American!" he replied, in mock dismay. "Have some more Pear William, you're falling behind."

"Okay," Diana said, not allowing herself to be deflected: "You people used to have kings with charm *and* intelligence: either Charles, for example. And queens, too, like the first Elizabeth—"

"—granted—"

"Or Mary Queen of Scots. Though of course she never ruled England," Diana added hastily, watching Troubridge's face from under her lashes.

"She scarcely ruled Scotland," said Troubridge. "An utter disaster. If one wanted the perfect example of what the throne doesn't need on it, she'd do admirably."

"Oh?" He seemed almost angry, she thought. Or was it just the booze? You couldn't tell from his articulation—that was always the last thing to go.

"Let me try one last time to penetrate that thick colonial head of yours," he said. "A British king or queen has only one function, to provide an example to his people of the qualities they ought to have but don't. The problem with us English is that we're dreadful romantics—Don't interrupt, Speed, it's quite true: Left to ourselves, we'd start every day by riding off in all directions, chasing the Grail. The royal family gives an example of solidity—"

"Don't you mean stolidity—"

"Often. The two qualities tend to merge. It's a defense mechanism. You couldn't imagine what it's like to be a modern-day royal. It'd drive you round the bend in an afternoon. Having to stand about for hours muttering inanities to idiots. Looking absolutely self-possessed, while wearing a succesion of costumes that would make Sigmund

Romberg cringe. Your every gesture watched and weighed by people eager to take offense. Always surrounded by flunkies telling you what to do—and telling you so respectfully that you can't possibly object. And every time you go out the door, the possibility of some lunatic pitching a bomb at you. You can't even really resign; Windsor realized that, toward the end: Just look at the photographs of his face. The only escape is to die." He pulled himself to a stop, with a visible effort. "Sorry, Speed. I'm being tedious."

"Not at all," she said. "It's a side of you I never suspected—the passionate patriot."

"Colonel Blimp, we call it."

"I'd have called it frustrated equerry," she said lightly.

"Yes, well, you may be right." He regarded her steadily, and she had the sense he was on the verge of a confidence. "May be right," he repeated. "We've been at it a long time, my family; like the English lawn. You know the story about the English lawn?"

"You told it to me." Five different times.

"Oh." She was afraid she'd broken the thread, but he went on. "Soldiers of the king. Or queen," he bowed toward her, "as the case might be. Not always soldiers, of course, but servants. Not necessarily a bad word, *servant*." He seemed, she thought, to be talking less and less to her and more and more to himself. "You Yanks have the saying, *My country right or wrong*. Well, with us Troubridges it's always been *My sovereign right or wrong*. And God knows there've been enough wrong 'uns. The thing is . . . " Suddenly, he seemed to see her again. "The thing is, I've got to make a call. 'Scuse me."

My God, she thought, he's drunk as a skunk. "Phone's right by the couch," she said, as he lurched toward the hall door.

"Consulate," he said. "Official business. Sorry." She heard a muffled thump as he bounced off the bedroom doorjamb, then the sound of the door shutting.

His own booze, and he can't hold it, she thought. Might as well do the dishes while I wait. Oh, dear: As she rose, the room simultaneously spun and swayed. She stood with her hands braced on the table until her surroundings steadied, then walked with exaggerated care into the kitchen. What's happened to the damn dishes? She opened the washer. Oh, there they are. She caught a glimpse of Troubridge marching back down the hall, straight as a tree. Do I love him? Do I love him not? I don't know, but I hope he doesn't want to finish up in bed tonight.

She went out into the living room, to be met by a cup of black coffee. "If I need this—and I do—so must you," said Troubridge.

She didn't particularly want another cup, but she knew he wouldn't drink it if she didn't. She downed it without thinking, and made a face.

"What's wrong?" he demanded.

"Don't look so worried," she replied. "It's not poisoned or anything, just been around too long. Here, give me that cup—I'll make you some fresh."

"No, no, it's fine," he insisted. "Only one thing lacking to make it perfect . . . "

"Not a cigar. Not in my apartment, ever."

"Never known anyone get so worked up over a little tobacco," he muttered.

"And the more they cost, the worse they smell," she went on, ignoring him. "Besides, it's time for you to go."

"It is," he agreed, just as she realized she very much wanted him to stay.

"Though I suppose," she said, "you could show me how to get the pear out."

"No, you were right," he replied. "We'd best postpone the extraction of the pear. It's a very long and complex procedure."

Well, damn you anyway, she thought. That's just what I'd like—a long and complex procedure. But she was not about to beg. "Here's your coat, Troubridge."

He pulled it on and opened the door. The coffee seemed to have sobered him up remarkably, but it had done her no good at all; if anything, she felt dizzier than before she'd drunk it. "Good night, Speed. Remember to lock up behind me."

"I was born in this town," she replied. How drunk did he think she was?

He stood in the doorway looking down at her, and she thought how nice it was to have a man tall enough to do that. "Give us a kiss good-bye," he said.

The force of his embrace knocked the breath from her body; she could not remember a kiss so intense. When she finally, reluctantly let him push her away, she could barely stand. "Come back in," she whispered. "Come back in or get out."

"*Arrivederci*, Contessa," he answered, and closed the door behind him.

Seventeen: Marie

All through dinner Marie had felt as if she were split in two. Half of her basked in the restaurant's warm, pastel glow, reveled in tastes that transcended mere food, preened in the attention heaped on her by Haskell, by the uniformed waiters, by the other diners. But beneath there was the other, darker half that struggled desperately against the encroaching power of—what had Haskell called her? Yes: the shadow queen.

She wondered if he had any idea how apt his phrase was. The queen still stood in the shadows of Marie's mind, but she was almost completely revealed now. Her face was Marie's own, her body the same, only their souls were still separate. Marie remained herself, just able to fend off the intruder who beckoned so enticingly, but it was such an unequal battle.

On the one hand, the knowledge of power and the memory of glory; the strength to face down a nation or heaven itself; a ruthless, unconquerable spirit. Against all that, the girl Marie, her only armor a pitiful ragbag of misinformation—Victorian place settings and faulty translations from the Greek. More than once, lulled by Haskell's endless babble, she found herself on the verge of giving in; what pulled her back, curiously enough, was the recollection of a supportive strength that veiled itself in banter; a cool detachment that concealed a realer warmth than men like Haskell or Mr. Sarsfield would ever know: Diana Speed.

Why me? Why not her?—surely the shadow queen would feel more at home in Diana's mind, with Diana's spirit and Diana's memories to draw upon. All she shared with Marie was the accident of blood.

"Marie? Marie?"

She pulled her mind back to the brightly lit room, the attentive waiter. Haskell was holding her left hand in his right. "What?"

"Would you like anything else?"

"Oh. No, thanks." Yes, her mind cried out. Yes, I would: freedom, happiness, someone to love.

"Then I think we'll have the check, please," he was saying. He had to release her hand to take out his wallet—smaller than Diana's but filled like hers with brightly colored plastic oblongs. He was speaking to her as he wrote: "You wouldn't be afraid to do it again."

"I guess not." Do what again?

"Super." He repossessed her hand and squeezed it. "There's something I've always wanted to try, but I've never found the proper subject. Not until this evening." She didn't like his smile at all, she decided. Or his moist hand.

The waiter pulled the table out for her and she got up, feeling self-conscious again as most of the heads in the restaurant swiveled around. She thought of Diana, and straightened her back. At a table near the entrance, watching Marie approach, sat a youngish man with a raw complexion, a straggly mustache, and a small, compressed chin. When he saw he had caught Marie's attention, he slowly wet his lips with his tongue. She let her eyes unfocus, as Diana had instructed her earlier; it worked: The man dissolved to a globular, pink blur that might have been anything.

Worked too well: Without warning another set of features superimposed themselves on the blur. Curly hair, darkly alert eyes, a rakehell grin that caught at her heart. A face as familiar as her own. Bothwell.

"What did you say, Marie?" She knew it was Haskell who'd spoken but for a second could not remember who Haskell was.

The face vanished and she was seeing the man with wet lips. Only now uneasiness glinted in his eyes, before he quickly looked away. "Nothing," she said.

•　•　•

In the cab Haskell took her hand again and put it on his thigh. "We don't really have to go hear Bobby Short," he suggested.

She pulled her hand free without a word.

"Carlyle Hotel, driver," Haskell called out. "Madison and 76th, I think it is."

•　•　•

The big, low-ceilinged room was filled with tables and a low anticipatory hum of conversation. Without asking her, Haskell ordered Marie a drink whose name she didn't catch, and a double martini for himself. He was talking at her, his voice low and urgent; the words "help realize your true potential" sifted through the crowd noise, and his hand was creeping over the table toward hers. She lifted her drink to her lips; as she considered the taste—lemon, with something metallic under it—she noticed over the rim of the glass a man with a long, florid face and a neatly trimmed black beard who had half turned in his seat and was regarding her. Disapproval was written harshly on his downturned mouth, but she knew he still wanted her, in spite of everything.

"Who's that man you're staring at, Marie?"

"My brother Moray," she heard herself reply. "I thought he was dead."

Haskell's chair scraped back from the table. "Maybe we'd better go," he said.

"No. Sit down." At that moment the lights dimmed to black, leaving only the space around the piano illuminated.

•　•　•

They stood on the curb, waiting for an empty cab. "How do you feel, Marie?"

"I feel fine," she replied. "Why?"

"Oh, I just wondered." He seemed to be nerving himself up for something, and she hoped he was not going to take her hand again. "Tell me, the man you saw . . . " he began, and stopped.

During the music, Marie had figured it out: "*I* didn't see him. *She* did."

"I get it." He waved at an approaching taxi, and a sign on its roof lit up: OFF DUTY. "You mean, she can make you see things."

Clearly, he did not get it, whatever *it* was. "But you saw him, too: the man with the beard."

"Yes, but he wasn't really your brother, was he?"

"Why not? He was hers."

"Oh, God. Listen, you just said it was she—Mary Stuart—who saw him as her brother Moray." This time, his frantic wave brought results. As the taxi swerved in toward the curb, he said, "What *you* saw was just a man with a beard."

She wriggled into the cab, wondering why any vehicle so large on the outside had to be so small within. "Did you hear me, Marie?" he said, clambering in after her. "What you saw was just—"

"I heard you," she replied. "But he was Moray, too."

"You mean he was two people at once?"

"Listen, Jack, you wanta go somewhere?" said the driver.

Haskell rattled off an address, but it was not the one Diana had made her memorize. "Where are we going?"

"I thought we'd continue this discussion at my place," he said, a little too easily. "When you're under, perhaps I can talk to . . . both of you. Simultaneously."

She could sense the other thing in his mind. Silly little man. "If you think you're going to fuck me, you're quite mistaken."

A strange, choking sound came from behind the driver's partition, and the taxi leaped ahead to a squeal of rubber. Haskell stared at her, his mouth gaping. "I never . . . " he sputtered, his voice a squeak of outrage. "How could you think . . . " And finally, conclusively: "You're not even my author."

She leaned forward to the hole in the partition. "We're not going where you were told."

"Whatever you say, lady." The driver was grinning, looking straight ahead.

She gave him Diana's address and sat back. The cab rolled down Park Avenue and then swung left on 50th. They crossed Lexington, and Haskell gave an unconvincing snicker. "Your friend Diana won't thank you for breaking in on her little tête-à-tête."

Marie tried to picture Diana in bed with the tall Englishman Darnley. She remembered his desperate passion, like a man drowning, and shivered. That had been before he got the pox, of course, and he was a different tall Englishman, anyway.

At Third Avenue Haskell said, "I think you need professional help, Marie."

She would have known from his voice what the euphemism meant, even if she had not read it in a dozen bad novels. They stopped for a traffic light at Second Avenue. Pulled back as far from her as he could get, Haskell had become small, mean, inconsequential. The light changed and they moved across the street, slowed as the driver scanned the numbers on the nearly identical brownstones, stopped. "I'm getting out," Marie said, "but this gentleman isn't."

"I was only telling you for your own good," said Haskell.

She had to bend nearly double to squeeze out, but once she was on the sidewalk she leaned back in, holding the door open. In the light from the street lamp she saw him recoil. "Thank you for a lovely evening," she said.

Standing on the sidewalk in the chill, damp air, Marie looked up at the yellow oblongs of Diana's living room windows. She was aware, behind her, of the taxi rolling slowly away, but it ceased to interest her. She could see no movement behind the curtains; was Diana really in bed with him?

Marie had no difficulty picturing the bed, or even Diana's long, slender body naked among the covers, but somehow she could not recall what Harry Darnley looked like, or see what he was doing to her. His cheeks, she remembered, were very smooth, quite unlike Bothwell's. She wanted to see what they were doing, and was terrified by it.

In the street there was no breeze at all; the smell of the cab's exhaust hung in the air. Sour exhaust and another smell: penetrating, bitter, familiar. The right-hand window above her was slightly open at the bottom, and as she watched a coil of gray smoke puffed out. So Diana had lighted a fire, and perhaps she and—what was his name, her long lad?— perhaps they were lying in front of it.

Recollection cut like a knife through the fog of Marie's thoughts: Diana's fireplace was blocked; if there was a fire, the apartment must be burning. Marie's feet were moving before the implications had completely formed, and she found herself in the little vestibule, stabbing again and again at the black button below the neatly printed white card: "3rd Floor—D. d'A. Speed."

Break the door pane, said the voice at her side. *The one next to the knob*.

"Where did you come from?" she gasped. "I thought you were dead long ago, in Norway." *Takes more than jail to kill a man. Or miles, or years*. Better even than the beloved face, it was the wild, fearless spirit she remembered. *Now break it, quickly*. Marie drew back her fist; her eyes watched it in fascinated horror. "No!" she heard herself cry, but it was too late. Her bare hand drove through the glass of the inner door, and the crash was echoed almost instantly by the furious pealing of an alarm bell. Marie was groping for the lock, found it, and pushed the door open.

She drew back her hand, blood welling from several deep gashes. Thick, scarlet drops fell to the white tile floor. Her stomach felt hollow, but there was no pain at all. *Up the stairs*, he whispered. *She needs you*.

A door on the ground floor hallway opened to the limit of its chain, and a frightened face stared through the gap. One look at Marie's face, at the blood now running down her forearm, and the face vanished behind a slammed door.

Two steps at a time she hurled herself up the stairs. She hammered on Diana's door, but no sound came from inside. She dragged a deep breath into her lungs, conscious of the acrid smell, faint but stronger than it had been outside. She pressed her nose to the crack at the edge of the door: The smell was definitely stronger. *Try the knob, love,* he said, right at her ear. Without much hope—she had seen those locks of Diana's—she twisted it and pushed; the door swung inward.

The hall light was on, slightly veiled by smoke, but she could not see where it was coming from. Behind her, she heard a quavering voice call from the next landing up: "I've called the police! Whoever you are, the cops are coming!"

Footsteps on the carpeted stairs below, a different voice: "Call the Fire Department! Quick!"

Marie's cheeks felt wet; she tasted salt on her lips. She pushed into the living room, her bleeding hand held in the air. "My letters!" she gasped. One look told her enough. The mirror was on the floor, leaning against the wall, and the safe door gaped open. Papers and jewelry were strewn across the floor. A tall bottle of something colorless lay on its side on the glass-topped table, with two liqueur glasses next to it.

The smell of smoke was stronger now. Marie took a step toward the papers. *Not now,* he said. *Remember your friend.* She wavered, pulled in both directions, then with a choked sob turned on her heel and dashed down the corridor. The bedroom door was closed and, when she tried it, locked. *Knock it in. Hurry!* She had taken two steps back, ready to throw herself at it, when her eye caught a metallic gleam from the floor: Diana's leather key case, wedged between the edge of the carpet and the wall, its contents fanned out.

When Marie flung open the bedroom door the smoke rolled out chest-high, in a thick, greasy wave. Through it, she could see a deep red-orange glow from where she knew the bed was. *Go on, brave heart,* he urged. You make me brave, she thought. You always did. She took a deep breath, put her head down, and ran into the smoke. Two steps into the room, and she stumbled over something inert, heavy. Staggering, she caromed into a bureau, lost her balance, and reeled into the curtains, smashing the glass beyond. A second alarm bell, shriller and louder than the one downstairs, began to clang somewhere near.

A puff of cooler air from the broken window parted the smoke and fanned the glowing bed into small tongues of flame. She could see what she had tripped over, halfway to the door. She turned back, dropped to one knee. Diana was lying on her stomach, her clothes torn, her long legs moving as if she were still trying to crawl.

SUNDAY

Eighteen: Diana

The uniformed police—two very young patrolmen from the nearby 17th Precinct—had stayed the longest. It seemed to Diana like the better part of forever before they left, but when she looked at her watch, it was only a little after two. The bedroom was a perfect wreck, sodden and reeking of smoke, but the rest of the apartment was relatively unscathed. Marie, wrapped in a blanket, had cried herself into exhausted sleep on the couch, her bandaged hand thrust out at an odd angle. In sleep her face was calm, untroubled.

The telephone at Diana's elbow rang softly. It was probably Haskell again, and Diana was wholly unwilling to lift the receiver and find out for sure. The triple-proof armor of shock had enabled her, groggy as she was, to face down cops, fire fighters, two physicians, and the ambulance attendants who wanted to cart her off on a stretcher. When the interviews became repetitive, and then importunate, she simply retreated to the bathroom, where she washed the smoke from her hair, tried to brush the awful taste from her mouth, repaired her face (to hide the bruise over her left eye and the other along the angle of her jaw), and considered the situation.

Now, with the intruders gone, she could—as soon as the damned phone shut up—put her deductions together. The cup of coffee on the side table next to her was cold, but one of the detectives had given her a handful of his cigarettes, and she watched a smoke spiral ascend into the still air.

The telephone stopped in mid-ring, and Marie's eyes opened. "How're you feeling, kiddo?"

The girl blinked several times. She looked tired and confused, and she was certainly entitled to. "I'm all right, I guess," she replied slowly. She sat up on the couch, regarded her bandaged hand with surprise, then looked over to the mirror, restored to its place over the mantel. "They're really gone, aren't they?"

Dreading another outburst of tears, Diana nodded. "Books and letters," she said. "Every one of them, and nothing else."

"Why didn't you tell the police he did it? Because he's your lover?"

So much for my once-private life, Diana thought. Aloud, she replied, "I suppose you mean Troubridge. I'm not sure he took the letters and the Bibles. And if he did, I don't think the police are the ones who'll get them back."

"But he beat you and tore your clothes," said Marie. "He tried to kill you." Her voice was detached, almost bemused.

"That's what it looked like," Diana agreed. "And if you hadn't saved my life, there'd be nobody to see the holes."

"Holes?" Marie looked about her as if searching for them. "Where is he?"

"Where's who?"

"Bothwell," she replied absently. "He's the one who saved you, not I."

Perfect: She's flipped out. Punctuating Diana's thought came the peal of the downstairs bell. Marie looked up, visibly startled. "Isn't that the door? Should we let them in?"

"I suppose so," Diana said. "There's nothing left worth taking." She made as if to get up, decided against it. "You want to buzz the door, love? Probably just a cop who forgot something."

It was Haskell, talking fast even before he was all the way into the hall: "Is she all right? I'd have been here sooner, but I had to call Judith." The moment he entered the living room

Diana knew, from the way he slid past Marie, that something lay between them. I shouldn't have left him alone with the kid, she was thinking, as Haskell turned to her: "It's all gone, right? The Bibles and the letters, too?"

"That's right."

"Has anybody called Sarsfield?"

"Not unless Judith did," she replied, suddenly feeling the strain of the past hours fall over her like heavy canvas. Stubbornly she forced herself to sit upright. "Find yourself a chair, Haskell. Marie, you can be the bartender."

"Oh, don't bother on my account," he said, shrugging out of his coat.

"I wasn't. Marie, I'll have some more coffee. In the pot on the stove." As the girl went out to the kitchen Diana sat back and waited for Haskell to begin.

"What happened?" he said. "You weren't all that coherent on the phone. Understandably."

"Basically, somebody broke in, opened the safe, and took Marie's papers." She saw Haskell's eye dart to her bruised face and then away. "Knocked me unconscious, set fire to my bed, and locked me in the bedroom," she added. Spat out like that, it was something she could handle. But she was not willing to allow the memory of it into her head.

"Tried to kill you," he said, nodding. "Dreadful. But you saw him? Before he knocked you out?"

"Not exactly," she replied. "I was asleep. I felt somebody slug me"—her hand went automatically to her jaw—"and I woke up enough to see a man, standing over my bed. Then he hit me again."

"So your friend Troubridge had left, obviously," he said, seemingly to himself but watching her sidelong. "And you didn't hear him break in?"

"It wasn't Troubridge," she said, her voice flat in her own ears. "And he didn't *break* in, whoever he was," she added. "He must've just walked in somehow."

He stared at her, clearly baffled, and then his face cleared. "You forgot to lock the door, you mean."

"No, it was locked." In her memory she could see her own

hand, awkwardly careful, working the knobs. "I definitely remember: three locks and the alarm switch." She grimaced, recollecting. "I had to hold on to the door frame while I did it; I was somewhat shelled. Troubridge and his goddamned Poire William." Marie reappeared, carefully holding a cup of coffee without a saucer. Diana took it gratefully. "Shock takes a while to wear off," she said. "I'm still a little spacey." Marie had forgotten to heat the coffee, but she swallowed it anyway.

Haskell was looking at the mirror. "What about your safe? Was it forced?"

"No. And it was locked, too."

"I remember your doing that." He seemed lost in thought, then looked up at her. "Whoever got in here had it all taped: He knew what he wanted and where it was, and how to get past the locks and the alarm."

It was an abrupt reminder that a man could be an ass about a lot of things—women, for instance—and not about others. "That's about it," she agreed. "He didn't even touch the family jewels."

"So why did he try to kill you?" Haskell asked innocently. "You weren't even a witness. And roughing you up like that. There was no point to it," he added, "if that was all he did."

She regarded him with cold hostility. "That was all. Absolutely."

"Of course." He got up and went to the sideboard, picked up the tall, nearly empty bottle that stood there. "This was what you and Troubridge were drinking? Poire William," he read aloud. "Eighty proof." He took a sip, rolled it on his tongue and swallowed. "Quite a kick." Marie's eyes followed him, but she looked as if she were trying to remember something.

Diana twisted around to watch him. "What're you getting at, Haskell?"

"Well, it's nearly gone," he said slowly. "I mean, just two people . . . How much of it did you account for?"

"You think Troubridge got me drunk, you mean?" So far, Haskell's thinking seemed to be tracking her own, but she was not ready to admit it yet. "I already told you I locked up behind him. And I have the only keys."

"The keys," said Marie. Haskell and Diana turned to stare at her. Without a word she held up a familiar brown leather case.

"Where'd you find those?" Diana snapped.

Marie winced, and Diana kicked herself mentally, but before she could say anything, the girl was speaking, slowly and hesitantly. "They were on the floor in the hall. That's how we unlocked the bedroom door. The apartment door was unlocked."

We? Oh, yes: Marie's phantom boyfriend. But Haskell seemed to have missed the pronoun. He had the foxy look Diana remembered well from editorial meetings, when it meant he'd just thought up another way to diddle the company finances. "Tell me something," he began. "Did Troubridge remind you to lock the door when he left?"

"He didn't have to," she said. And then more slowly, "But you're right: He did. Why?"

"Misdirection," Haskell replied. "He already had the keys, I'd bet—lifted them earlier in the evening. I'm not prying, Diana, but he knows this place and he knows your habits. When you come home, what do you do with your purse?"

He was being unusually delicate, for him. With her head beginning to throb she appreciated it. "My bag? Toss it on the bedroom bureau," she replied.

"Keys in it?"

"Always." So that was how he'd done it. "He was in there alone, too. Had to make a business call. On the bedroom extension."

"Hey, presto," said Haskell triumphantly.

She managed a chilly smile. "What about the safe? I never told him the combination."

"You never told it to me, either," he said. "And I was standing across the room the one time you opened it. But I could tell it's four numbers, and they're close together: You made nearly complete turns on the dial every time. It's a number you remember automatically—no hesitation—so I'd bet it's one that's woven into your life. Like . . . " He paused, waiting.

" . . . my birthday," she whispered. "That son of a bitch." She straightened up and took a deep breath. "You've got some unexpected talents, Haskell."

His offhand shrug was a model of false modesty. "My authors get the credit. You deal with writers a lot, especially occult types, and you see a lot of con artists. Though most of them," he added quickly, "are completely honest."

"Completely," said Diana straight-faced.

"I don't think any of this comes as a big surprise to you," he said.

"I had been working it through," she admitted.

"Then how do you make sense out of what he did to you—the rough stuff?" he asked.

"You tell me."

"I can't, not all of it," Haskell answered. Idly, he poured the last inch of the Poire William into a glass and held it to his nose, then set it down, before he continued. "I can see where your friend Troubridge might decide the alibi he'd arranged wasn't good enough. Or he might have thought he heard you wake up. Whatever. So he panics and decides he has to kill you. That's understandable . . . " He grinned quickly at her, and she could see how he succeeded with some women. "But slugging you? And then setting your bed on fire—that's not easy, setting a bed on fire."

"It was soaked in cognac," said Diana. "My cognac." The words cost her less than she'd expected, and she pressed on: "That's not all. He ripped open my blouse, pulled up my bra, tore off my slacks and my—" Suddenly she found herself too close to the edge of self-control. She put her nose into the coffee cup for a moment, while she collected herself. "Why would somebody go to all that trouble and then not . . . finish the job? It's kind of insulting." She hardly recognized the harsh sound she made as a laugh.

"I think you know," he said quietly. "If you want to tell me."

"There was this, too," she said, holding out a tiny hemisphere of colored plastic. "I found it in the kitchen drain." Her fingers were shaking, and she set it on the table quickly.

Haskell held it up to the light. "What is it, a contact lens for a rat?"

"The end of a capsule, cut off with a sharp knife." He looked at her with surprised respect; it was like a tonic. "A sleeping pill for my drink, I guess," she added. "That'd account for how I feel."

"It does make a complete picture," he said, nodding.

"I don't understand." Marie had been sitting so quietly that Diana had forgotten her presence. "You mean Mr. Troubridge *did* take my letters, and tried to kill you?"

"That's what the evidence says, love," Diana replied.

"Then you'll have him arrested."

"Someone hopes we will," said Diana. Haskell looked quickly at her, and she felt his thought jump the gap between them.

"It's too much, isn't it?" he said.

"Unless Troubridge is a bigger fool than he seems," Diana agreed. And an amateur, she added to herself.

"Someone hopes?" Marie repeated, slightly out of phase. "You mean someone else? Someone pretending he was Mr. Troubridge?"

"Could be," Haskell said, his mind still obviously exploring the possibilities. "But your friend is in on it."

"Too true," Diana agreed. "And maybe our mysterious someone wants him out."

"You said it was a man," Haskell mused aloud. "It wasn't me; Patrick and what's-his-face Pearse are watching each other; we've eliminated Troubridge—who's left?"

"I have the feeling Marie's letters aren't as much of a secret as we thought," Diana said. "I wonder if they ever were. A secret is one person; two are a conspiracy; three or more, it's a press conference."

"And is *who* that important?" Haskell went on. "It's what they'll *do* next—"

The telephone at Diana's elbow cut him off. "Yes?" The other two watched her anxiously, unable to hear the attenuated gabble that came over the line. Diana knew her face was setting like concrete. "We'll be right over," she said, and hung up.

"Who was that?" demanded Haskell and Marie together.

"You wanted to know what next? That was Pearse. Somebody broke into his apartment, tried to steal the letters we left with him. No"—she cut across their expressions of dismay—"they're safe. But Sarsfield's been killed."

Nineteen: Pearse

He forced himself not to rush out and meet his visitors in the hallway, but nervousness sent the words tumbling out of his mouth before the door was fully open: "I tried to call you earlier," Pearse heard himself saying. "Nobody ans— My God! What happened to you?"

"Later," Diana said, stepping inside. As she moved from beneath the hall light, the dark bruises along her jaw faded under a thick layer of makeup. "You remember Mr. Rose and Marie."

"Sure. Come on in." Rose, who looked drawn and apprehensive, brushed past without a word, but the girl Marie took Pearse's hand and searched his eyes with hers, as if expecting a more intimate greeting. He led them into the living room, where furniture had been shoved aside and then pushed not quite exactly back into place. On the floor the chalked outline of a sprawled figure, partially erased, drew their eyes. Its legs were drawn on the living room rug, and it stretched through the open door so that its torso, arms flung wide, was outlined on the kitchen linoleum. A reddish brown smear gleamed faintly where the figure's sternum would have lain. "I was just cleaning it up," Pearse said, as he held out the stained sponge. Damn it, stop babbling, he told himself.

"The letters . . ." said Marie, and stopped. Both she and Diana Speed seemed unaffected by the chalked outline, though Rose had paled when he saw it, and the expression on his long, sheeplike face made Pearse wonder if he were going to be sick.

"The letters are okay," Pearse replied quickly. "He didn't get them."

"He?" Diana turned suddenly.

Pearse dropped his eyes at the intensity of her stare. "Maybe I better start at the beginning," he said. "Can I get anybody a drink?" He turned away to the cupboard, still talking: "I've got beer and Irish and some other stuff that's been here forever."

"A rain check, thanks," Diana said, lowering herself carefully onto the sofa. "It's been a long night, Mick, so maybe we could just have the story."

"Just the facts, ma'am," Pearse agreed. He busied himself pouring the half tumbler of whiskey and perched on the arm of the couch. "Okay. It's just like I told the police: I was asleep in the bedroom, through that door over there, and Sarsfield was sacked out here, on the couch. I heard a noise in the kitchen, a kind of scratching. It must've waked me up." Not too fast, he reminded himself. And don't add anything unnecessary. Tell it straight.

"When?" asked Diana.

"Twelve-fifteen. The digital alarm's right by my bed," he added. "I lay there for a couple of minutes, trying to remember if I left any food out." He saw Rose's puzzled look and explained: "Figured it was rats. Then I remembered Sarsfield was in the living room, and I thought it might be him, so I got up. I didn't like the idea of him poking around."

"Fair enough," Diana said, into the silence that seemed to call for some comment. "But it wasn't Sarsfield."

"No. He was still asleep. The kitchen door was a little open, and I could tell the noise was somebody opening the window." He paused. From here on, he had to be very careful. Far more careful than he'd been with the cops. "There's a fire escape outside the kitchen window," he said. "Come out here, I'll show you." Dutifully, the three trooped out to the kitchen behind him, stepping wide to avoid the chalked image on the floor.

The kitchen window was closed and locked again, and Pearse went over to it. He pushed the catch back and raised the window slightly, until the frame rasped in its channels. "Like that," he said. "That kind of noise."

Rose stepped to his side and peered through the glass into the night beyond. "Where does this go?"

"The fire escape? Down to the side street, off Second Avenue," Pearse replied. "And up to the roof, of course."

"It looks pretty deserted down there," Rose observed, his cheekbone pressed to the glass.

"Well, it's three in the morning," said Pearse. "And people can't get by on this side of the street, since they started renovating the building next door."

"So you heard the window opening," Diana said. She was leaning against the refrigerator, looking very pale, but her blue-gray eyes were alert. "It doesn't make much noise."

"It does if you've been robbed that way before," Pearse said. The cops had made the same point, and he was ready this time.

"Oh?" Did she sound suspicious? Maybe he'd answered too quickly.

"Everyone in the building's been burgled, one time or another," he went on. "Any tall guy with nerve can jump up and grab the bottom rung of that fire escape ladder and haul himself up. Or come over the roof from one of the other buildings. They won't let us take the fire escape off, though." He shrugged. "The City."

"You never considered a burglar alarm?" Diana asked. "You must have valuable things here, from time to time."

Pearse had opened his mouth to answer, when Rose did it for him. "There is an alarm," he said, pointing. "An electric eye, isn't it?"

"That's right." Pearse, who had been concentrating on Diana, glanced quickly at Rose, whose cheeks had regained their color. Two inquisitors were more than he had bargained for. "See, it doesn't do anything till somebody breaks the beam, which they have to do to get in."

Diana blinked twice, and he realized she was nearly out on her feet. Besides, her jaw must hurt like hell. "Okay," she said slowly. "You're in the living room, Patrick's asleep. You figure out that somebody's trying to get in. What next?"

"Well, first I thought it was dopers, like the last time. I don't know about you, but dopers scare the shit out of me." Diana nodded, with a trace of impatience, but Marie looked puzzled. "A lot of them'll kill you as soon as look at you," he explained, projecting all the sincerity he could muster directly at her; she reddened slightly, but her eyes were steady on his face. "They don't care, dopers. And then I remembered your letters. Tell you the truth," he said, with what he hoped was a winning smile, "that didn't make me feel a whole lot better."

"So what did you *do?*" Diana demanded.

"I keep a gun by my bed," he said. "You said before: I've got valuable things here sometimes. I tiptoed through the living room—Sarsfield was still asleep—and I was looking through the kitchen door"—he mimicked himself in a half crouch—"and I had the gun in my hand. Waiting for the guy to show himself. If the alarm didn't scare him off, it'd at least attract his attention so I could get the drop on him."

"But that didn't happen. Obviously," Diana said.

Christ, she was a cool one, he thought. No empathy at all, though Marie's eyes were wide and trusting. He nerved himself to press on into the part of his story that he disliked remembering. "I could see the window, about halfway open, and this shape outside. An outline—no, more like a silhouette, with the streetlight from below. He opens the window some more, and I figure he's getting ready to come inside . . ."

"A big man? Or could you tell?" Rose asked, in a mild voice that Pearse did not quite trust.

"Tall, not big," Pearse said, then caught himself, and added, "but I didn't see that right away." They were all intent on him now, and he forced himself to look Diana right in the eye. "All of a sudden, somebody comes up behind me, shoves me out of the way. It was Sarsfield. I never even heard him get up. He turns on the kitchen light—the switch is right behind the door." The kitchen light was already lit, but Pearse flicked it off, to show them the dark, and then back on. "I was off balance," he continued, "but I hear Sarsfield shout, 'It's you!' real loud. And he shoots, with that gun you gave him. The hole's under that piece of tape, alongside the window; cops chewed the plaster all to hell, prying the bullet out."

"And?" said Diana, who was clearly not to be deflected.

"And the other guy shoots back. One shot, right in the breadbasket. Sarsfield goes down like a tree. The other guy runs down the fire escape. That's it."

Diana looked across the room at Rose, but Pearse could read neither of their expressions. She turned to him and said, "The other man was tall. What else did you see about him?"

He paused, forcing himself to picture what he would have seen, and not the memory that thrust itself before his eyes. "Thin. Very thin. Long face. Bony. I think a double-breasted suit." He had thought Diana looked bad before, but she suddenly went an ugly yellow-gray, and the purple bruises stood out more sharply then ever.

"What was it he said?" Rose asked.

"Just—" Pearse pulled himself up short, saw he was trapped, and forced a bemused smile. "I'd forgotten till you asked. Didn't even tell the cops. He just said, 'You bastard.' Right after he shot Sarsfield. 'You bastard,' that's all."

"What was his voice like?" Diana's own voice was tired and flat, almost uninterested, as if the question were accidental, but Pearse saw Rose's narrowed eyes suddenly sharpen.

"Like?" He repeated, playing for time. What was the right answer? God damn that son of a bitch Galmoy anyway. "Just a voice . . . what can I tell you?"

"Deep? Harsh? Accent?" The three words came from Diana in rapid fire, no helpful emphasis on any of them.

"Not deep," Pearse replied. "An ordinary kind of voice.

Middle range, like mine." Gaining confidence, he added, "Of course, maybe it would've been lower, if he wasn't excited."

"Any accent?" Diana repeated.

"Nothing I could hear in two words."

"And you're sure that was all he said: 'You bastard.'"

He'd said something wrong, something about the tall man's accent. But it was too late to catch. "That's right."

"And ran away."

"Down the fire escape, like a shot. By the time I got to the window, he was in the street, running like a deer." Diana was pointedly not looking at Rose, and Pearse spoke quickly, before she could say anything: "Now, what happened to you?"

The smile that stretched her mouth was anything but humorous. "Somebody broke into my apartment, too. Only he tried to kill me."

Pearse's astonishment was complete. "It happened tonight?"

"Tonight. And he got the letters."

"God damn." He could feel them waiting for him to say something else, but he was out of his depth, knowing only that another word might betray him. "You said *he*. Did you see him?"

"Not really. Somebody spiked my drink: I was halfway passed out. *He* is just a manner of speaking."

"Oh. So it could've been the same guy."

"The same tall, thin guy," she agreed, looking not at Pearse but past him, at Rose.

"The letters," said Rose, in the tone of a reminder.

"Right. We'll take them with us, Mick," said Diana.

"You sure?" He hated even the idea of letting the letters go, but his brain told him that they would be safer away from here. Galmoy had panicked and fled; he'd be back, and he wouldn't leave without them a second time. "You will put them in a vault?" Pearse said, with real earnestness. "They're more valuable than ever, now."

"As soon as the banks open Monday morning," she agreed.

"Could we have them now, please," Marie put in, turning Pearse's attention to her. For the first time, he noticed her bandaged hand, which she held at her side, in the folds of her skirt. She looked a little bedraggled, he thought, but still a lot better than the first time they'd met; not pretty, but there was something about her. She was watching him with a fixed, unblinking stare that suddenly made him more nervous than Diana's pointed questions or Rose's fake mildness.

"Sure thing," he said. "Coming right up." His hands fumbled with his key case and then with the double locks on the portable vault, an oversize box that took up most of the floor in his tiny bedroom. Damn Galmoy, he thought again, his mind flashing back to the muted tapping on his bedroom window.

When Pearse had raised the shade, he'd seen Galmoy leaning perilously over the edge of the fire escape to reach the window. Behind him, the second man was only a lumpish shadow on the metal-framed platform. Galmoy had pointed urgently over his shoulder, at the kitchen window. Pearse could still see the motionless figure of Sarsfield on the couch, entangled more than wrapped in an old quilt, and snoring softly. He had looked so peaceful, so completely asleep that Pearse had put him immediately out of mind once the kitchen door was closed between them.

The moment Pearse had unlocked the window and raised it, Galmoy started to climb in, hampered by the silenced revolver in his right hand.

"Christ, man! Watch the alarm," Pearse had said, just in time.

Galmoy drew back quickly, revealing the figure who knelt on the fire escape behind him. A tall, thin man—just as Pearse had told the police and Diana—swaying slightly. His face, when it caught the light from the kitchen, was pale and glassy-eyed. "Never mind him," Galmoy had snapped. "Get me the letters. The ones she left with you." The pudgy man was clearly in a state, his voice vibrating with tension.

Though it was only a few degrees above freezing, his face ran with sweat.

"What—"

"Get the damned letters," Galmoy repeated, teeth gritted.

"But I haven't finished—"

"Can't be helped. I need them now."

"What'll I tell Diana? Miss Speed?"

Galmoy's laugh was an angry bark. "You won't have to tell her—" He pulled himself up, glanced quickly over his shoulder at the tall man, who seemed to be concentrating on merely staying upright. When Galmoy turned back to Pearse, he dropped his voice. "*He* did it," with a quick nod. "That's what you tell anybody who asks. Stuck you up, made you give him the stuff."

"Who the hell is he?" Pearse had demanded.

"Never mind. A guilty bystander. But his dabs are all over your ironwork, aren't they?" For the first time, Pearse had noticed the tight-fitting leather gloves on Galmoy's fat little hands.

Pearse had sensed the danger of arguing. He stood back carefully, keeping his own hands in plain sight. "Whatever you say. Wait here; I'll get them out."

That was when everything had come unglued. No sound from the kitchen door, just Sarsfield's blurry voice behind him saying, "Who's that, Pearse?" As he saw the bulb-shaped muzzle of Galmoy's pistol swing up, Pearse threw himself to one side, heard Sarsfield shout, "It's you!" Heard—and felt—the hot blast of his gun, deafeningly loud in the small room. Saw the silenced pistol buck in Galmoy's hand . . .

"What's keeping you, Mick? You lose the key?" The impatient voice was Diana's, pulling him back to the present.

"Here," he said, holding out the carefully wrapped box. "All present and accounted for. You want to check?"

"Thanks, we'd love to," she replied. She compared each piece with a list drawn from her shoulder bag. "Complete," she said to Marie, who was eyeing the papers with a look that Pearse could only think of as hungry.

"Be careful," Pearse said. "I'd give you back your automatic, but the cops took it. My gun, too. They want to test them."

"I suppose," said Diana vaguely. She seemed about to add something but didn't.

"Whoever took your letters is going to have a hell of a time selling them, as long as you have this package," Pearse said. "He'll be back."

"Yes," Diana replied. She pulled herself to her feet. "I think we've taken enough of your time, Mick. You must be exhausted."

She herself looked to be beyond exhaustion, holding herself upright by will alone. When the elevator's open-worked iron cage lurched into view, Diana's gaze was fixed on it. But Marie had half turned to face Pearse. Her face was level with his, her half-closed eyes smoldering. "So you did come back," she said, her voice low. "I knew you would. Sleep well, James." He was caught flat-footed as much by the open invitation in her tone as by the unfamiliar name; he could only stare openmouthed. But once the door was shut, locked, and chained, she went out of his head like smoke in a breeze, and his mind turned irresistibly to Galmoy.

"That four-star cocksucker," he heard himself say aloud. He really put me on the spot this time. And what the hell is he up to, anyway? A dumb question, he realized. He knew perfectly well what Galmoy had in mind. What he didn't know was how to stop it.

He drank two more glasses of Bushmills, warm and straight, before he felt numb enough to go back to bed. When he did, he surprised himself by falling asleep almost instantly. He moved through swirling dreams, populated by hazy, threatening figures, and always the beckoning shape just ahead of him, her body almost visible through her sheer nightdress. The girl, Marie.

Twenty: Troubridge

By the time dawn finally grayed the window, he would gladly have accepted a full-blooded nightmare as a change from the recollections, interspersed with uneasy dozes, that had kept him turning and heaving on the lumpy couch in Carr's minuscule living room. Troubridge was not one of those people who drew blank after an evening's heavy drinking, and this morning he regretted it. Every foolish word and ill-considered act of the night before was etched on his memory in high relief. The previous twelve hours, the worst in his life, presented themselves as a starkly backlit procession of mistakes, leading up to that inevitable moment on Pearse's fire escape.

With a groan, he rolled himself into a painfully upright position. Too-hot curry and half a bottle of Poire William had left a sticky varnish over the inside of his mouth, varnish with a strong garlic underlay. And the brandy that had followed made his head ache as if someone had drilled it from temple to temple and filled the hole with molten lead. He wondered how Diana was feeling this morning. If she had discovered the robbery yet. He reached down to scoop his watch off Carr's scrofulous rug, and then quickly sat back up before his eyeballs could fall out and break like eggs. Eight-thirty: later than I'd have thought. She must be up.

Diana. No point to wallowing in guilt; what was done

couldn't be recalled. Face it squarely: He'd betrayed her, no other word for it. The betrayal, unpleasant enough to contemplate, was less painful than the prospect of what was yet to come. This wretched mess wasn't over, not by a long chalk. He'd have to see her, today; confront her disaster with smooth, hypocritical consolation. She would, he knew, be either flippantly brave or openly raging. He'd shared both moods with her in the past, and now he could not. Even if he pulled off this last masque, they were finished. That much he had known since he'd reminded her—with her keys in his pocket—to lock her door.

Would that line make her suspect him? No, he was worrying too much. She'd suspect him to some extent anyway. Her Washington training would see to that, even if her emotions conspired to shield him. And he did have a perfect alibi, though it hadn't worked out quite as he'd planned. (What began as a small disagreement, designed to fix the bartender's memory of him, had ended with Troubridge being tossed physically onto Second Avenue, half an hour ahead of schedule.)

He got to his feet, still a little loose-jointed. Carr's apartment was a horrible place to wake up in, he decided. Peeling paint; dirty windows with gratings over them; a few sticks of soulless, impersonal furniture, and those on a scale slightly smaller than life-size. Even the ceiling seemed unnecessarily low, so that he found himself half crouching under the lintel as he stepped into the kitchen. It was no smaller than Diana's, but Carr had left it as he'd found it, complete to the half-inch crust of grease baked onto the burners of the gas cooker. There was something liquid and black in the dirty pot; Troubridge poured himself a lukewarm cup and sluiced it down before he could reconsider. Weak, as he had known it would be, but not as bad as he'd expected. He struck a match and turned on the gas under the pot.

Carr was gone, of course; he'd left around seven, to move the stolen documents to a safer place until they could get hold of the rest. Troubridge looked in the refrigerator, hoping to find the tin of coffee, but the only thing in it was a bottle labeled *Maalox*—a name that always suggested some ill-natured minor deity from the Old Testament. He opened the cupboard beneath the counter. It was filled with oddly familiar-looking crates. Idly, he pulled one out, opened it—"Christ Almighty!"—and hastily shoved it back. What on earth was Carr doing with fifty pounds of plastic explosive in his kitchen? And where did he hide the damned coffee?

A sudden wave of vertigo swept over Troubridge, an ugly sensation that triggered his memory, pitching him back onto the fire escape. Even drunk, he'd been acutely aware of the ladder thumping and clanging as he climbed it. Why no one on the lower floors had called the police was a mystery. Or perhaps just another instance of the New Yorker's world-famous ability to dismiss what was happening next to him.

Pearse hadn't even heard them coming: His face, when it appeared in the bedroom window, was blank with surprise. And red with anger two minutes afterward, as he opened the kitchen window. Troubridge had stayed well back on the fire escape, as Carr told him to, but the light from the kitchen fell across his face, and he knew Pearse would be able to identify him.

Why in hell had he gone up the ladder in the first place? Why hadn't he stayed with the letters, in Carr's ugly American sedan? The exact sequence was blurred in memory—oh, yes: Troubridge's great height was required to grasp the metal ladder's lowest rung, which was hung well above a short man's reach. And then he had somehow found himself climbing, ahead of Carr. Once they reached the metal balcony on the first floor—the second, as Americans persisted in calling it—steel stairs led upward to the floors above. Carr had gone first, and Troubridge had followed his wake.

The echoing roar of Carr's pistol. No, that was Sarsfield's: He remembered now. Carr's silenced gun had made an odd sound, like a clap of cupped hands. Troubridge had seen his share of violence, but he would not soon forget the look on Sarsfield's face as he slammed backward off the door frame, stood a moment, and folded slowly forward.

In Carr's living room the telephone jangled, and Troubridge

started, spilling coffee onto the narrow counter. Two rings and it stopped. A moment later it began to ring again. That was the signal, he remembered: Carr wanted to talk to him. He took five strides into the living room and managed to pick up the phone just before the fourth ring. Don't say anything, Carr had told him. He waited, his heavy breathing exactly in time with the throbbing ache in his temples.

"You've been identified," said the breathless voice at the other end.

"What?" The exclamation was unstoppable.

"It's in the late edition of the *Post*. Not your name. Just a description. Pearse must've panicked." Troubridge's mouth was open to speak, but the voice went on: "Stay put. I'll be back in a couple of hours."

At the click of the receiver, Troubridge felt his stomach turn over. He replaced the handset, reached out again to pick it up, and his hand halted in midair. If it's tapped, I've already had it; if it's not—what the hell. He dialed Diana's apartment. No answer, but at least he didn't have to talk to her damned machine.

Well, of course she's not home: Sarsfield's death must have hit Wild-Freeman like a bomb. Never mind Sunday. Diana was doubtless on her quarterdeck, directing operations. He dialed Wild-Freeman, using Diana's direct line instead of the switchboard number. She always picked up herself, but this time it was Catherine O'Donnell, her voice trembling badly. He ignored it. "Is she there, please?"

"I'm sorry, she's . . . Is that you, Mr. Troubridge?"

"It is." Every time he called Diana's office, he first reminded himself to be pleasant to the O'Donnell child. And every time his ear was assaulted by that atrocious accent (especially awful, now that it lay in ambush behind a flimsy screen of speech lessons), his soul-deep disapproval froze him into the caricature of a British snob.

Yet the further Troubridge would retreat into icy reserve, the more puppylike the O'Donnell's ingratiations would become, as now: "Wasn't it awful, Mr. Troubridge? Poor Mr. Sarsfield, and losing the letters, too. And if that wasn't bad enough, what happened to Miss Speed! I've been trying to make her go home, but this place would fall apart without her. How could anybody do that? I can't believe it."

It was like trying to wade upstream against a torrent of treacle, but he broke in at last: "What's awful? What's the matter with Diana?" The child seemed overstrung even for her, but Troubridge was thunderstruck by the blow when it fell.

"The fire, and Miss Speed being attacked—you didn't know? She's been trying to get you since she came in . . ." She sniveled on, Cassandra with an adenoid condition, as Troubridge tried to pick a few facts out of the cataract. What in God's name had gone wrong? And why hadn't Carr told him?

He became aware that Cathy had run out of breath, and he pulled his wits together before her gasps evened out. "Let me get my mind around this," he said. "Someone broke into Miss Speed's apartment, beat her senseless, and set the place on fire? Is that what you're saying?"

"Yes, Mr. Troubridge. And stole the *letters*."

Was he supposed to know about them? He could hardly ignore Cathy's portentous tone: "The letters?"

"*You* know . . . oh, dear. Maybe you don't. I guess I wasn't supposed . . . I'm sorry. I—"

"Never mind. How did this burglar get in? Past all those locks, and the burglar alarm." The phone was slipping in his hand, and the sweat was sluicing down his spine. So much for alcohol dehydration.

"He had *keys*"—hell, he thought—"and she was *drugged*. He tried to *kill* her." She paused, clearly determined to get off a final shot, yet uncertain how to phrase it. "But at least she wasn't, you know, *raped*."

"Oh." That maniac Carr. He's gone right off the rails. Unless . . . "Look, Miss O'Donnell, just tell her I called, will you?" He groped for a conclusion, some way of escape. "Tell her I'll call again later, when things calm down."

My God, he thought, as he hung up. I've been framed. Twice in one night.

Twenty-one: Diana

The letters should've been in a vault," Judith was saying. She had been saying it for the past five minutes, her voice rising with each repetition. Soon, Diana hoped, only bats would be able to hear her.

Pacing her, an octave down, Haskell was muttering, "We should call the police; we have to call the police; let the police handle it."

Maury Thomas, a tight smile on his rubicund face, provided the obbligato murmur, variations on "Wait till the Rajah hears about this."

Milly Aaron's lips were moving, but not a sound could be heard. Given her normal speaking voice—anthracite rattling down a steel chute—the absence was unusual enough to make the other three gradually trail off and watch her in silence. Only then could they hear her rasping whisper: "The sky is falling. Oh, dear, the sky is falling." She stopped and cast a level, malignant glare around her. "Just wanted to be part of the chorus, folks."

It was Diana's moment to intervene, and she took it. "One, this isn't over yet: What was stolen isn't saleable without the half we still have. Two, I'm not calling in the police because I want whoever took it to come to us, not go into hiding. Three, I'm taking responsibility for everything that's happened, as far as W-F is concerned, and you can quote that to

Mr. Channing. Just in case"—she smiled gently at her colleagues—"you happen to speak to him before I do."

"You're going to have your hands full, Diana," Milly said. "What do you want us to do?"

"The obituary for the *Times*. Maybe a memorial service," Haskell put in. "You'd better get on that right away, Milly." Taking in the blank stares that greeted his remark, he added: "Well, Sarsfield was our author, as Patricia Orme—and under his own name, too, even if this book was on hold. Now he and it are both dead."

Milly and Judith began to speak at once, but Diana cut them off: "Patrick Sarsfield may be dead, but the letters—and the project—are very much alive. And why do we want to kill Patricia Orme, anyway?"

Haskell looked scandalized. "What choice do we have?"

"Wild-Freeman owns the name," Diana said. "Judith made it up, and we registered it." She saw Judith's expression change as the possibilities began to register. "How about it—any potential successors in your fiction stable?"

"Right off, I can think of half a dozen," she replied. She seemed to be perking up with remarkable speed. "And two of them would probably skip royalties just for the chance to write in drag."

"Okay, that's your assignment," said Diana. "Milly, I think a very discreet obit would be in order—are there any relatives we have to contact?"

"A sister someplace." Milly flipped rapidly through an overstuffed file folder, paused to read: "Akron. She lives in Akron, or she did eight years ago, when Sarsfield filled out this questionnaire."

"That's for you, then. Also fielding any questions from outside." Haskell was, Diana saw, on the verge of a sulk, and she turned her most dazzling smile on him, ignoring the twinge that ran right up her jaw into her temple. "You've got the really delicate job, Haskell. Telling the employees—but only the ones who have to know. Since we're going to keep this in the family, as it were, it'll be up to you to make sure the secret doesn't get out. No all-hands memos: You'll have to phone them at home, one by one. It'll require a lot of discretion."

Haskell appeared to inflate slightly with each successive sentence. When Diana had finished, he nodded curtly and pulled a staff roster from his desk drawer, setting it before him. "You'll want us out of your hair," said Diana, getting to her feet. "I'll be in my office, if anyone needs me."

In the hall outside Haskell's door Judith stopped and turned. "You know, Diana, you can think just like an editor, when you try. You don't have to be stuck on the business side all your life." With a quick, vulpine smile she patted Diana's arm and hurried away, her hips swinging.

"I'll be damned," Diana said.

"It was a compliment, dear," put in Milly, from behind her. "Just accept it graciously. And remember what they used to say about Philip the Second."

" 'His dagger followed close upon his smile'?" said Diana, who knew Milly's taste in quotations.

"Something like that. You want me to call this sister of Sarsfield's, assuming she's still around?"

"If you would."

"And the funeral?" Milly asked. "You want me to take charge of that?"

"Oh, God." Without warning, imagination produced a dead, boxed Patrick Sarsfield: the coarse, ruddy features cosmeticized to a pink blur; the complicitous grin sanded to vapidity; the man himself completely gone. In an unexpected way the awful vision helped. But the effort required to put her emotions down nearly drained her, and she wondered if she'd have the strength to do it again, with a stranger. Besides, it was becoming harder to focus her mind on even the simplest thought. After what had happened last night, five hours' uneasy sleep in a second-rate hotel was just not enough. "Tell Patrick's sister we'll handle it. And pick up the tab, of course."

"I suppose the police—or the coroner—still have the body," Milly mused aloud. Her head was cocked to one side, and she reminded Diana of a wrinkled parrot. Diana recognized the look in her eyes.

"I'm okay, Milly. Just a little out of focus," she said. "If you could be an angel and call the cops, I'll take it from there."

"You're certainly not okay," Milly snorted. "You look like me on an average morning. Well, maybe not quite that bad." She gave a theatrical sigh of despair. "I can see I'm just talking to myself. But can't you set the world down for a few hours and get some sleep?"

"In a while, dear," Diana said. "I promise. Right now, I'd better get back to the store before Cathy goes into hysterics." On Sundays the elevators were even more lethargic than usual, and Diana hurried down the inside stairs to the fifteenth floor, emerging at the end of the corridor that led to her own office. Ahead of her, Cathy stood halfway out her door, grasping the moulding as if for support and staring in the opposite direction, toward the reception area. Presumably the dreadful pink dress was what she'd worn to Mass. At least it wasn't jeans. Hearing Diana's footsteps, the girl whipped around.

"Oh, thank God you're back!" Cathy's eyes were on the point of overflowing and her nose was already running, but she was not yet in what Troubridge called full spate. Tears were Cathy's one habit that Diana had failed to dent, but today the girl seemed to be trying to hold herself together. Still, there was something out of the usual about her manner, something Diana was too exhausted to pinpoint.

"What's up?" she demanded, hearing the flatness in her voice; so, to judge by her alarmed look, did Cathy.

"The phone hasn't stopped ringing since you left, Miss Speed," Cathy whimpered, lowering her reddened eyes. That's interesting, Diana thought: she won't look me in the face. How come? Cathy cleared her nose with a gooselike honk and pressed on: "Someone from the FBI called. They want to talk to you about Mr. Sarsfield."

"Why?" Diana stalked into her office. Next to the telephone was a heap of phone messages, in a barely controlled version of Cathy's normally precise hand.

"Oh," the girl replied, nonplussed. "They didn't say." She stood shuffling in the doorway, her round face etched with misery. (And what besides? Guilt?) "I guess I should've asked."

Diana dropped into her swivel chair. "Never mind," she said. "Who else?"

Cathy glanced quickly over her shoulder, and Diana knew what was coming: "Mr. Channing," she said, her voice dropping to a stage whisper. "He called twice."

Diana felt a sharp, hot stab just below her rib cage. Across the room, in the small mirror that hung over her second desk, her face looked like a mask. "Is that all?"

"Miss McIntyre. She wanted to lie down."

Not half as much as I do. "Where'd you put her?"

"In the little room."

It was Wild-Freeman shorthand for the dank, windowless chamber on whose sour-smelling vinyl-covered couch female employees could stretch out when overcome by cramps or extended lunches. At the moment, it sounded to Diana like heaven.

"Well done," she said. As she spoke, the direct-line phone rang. She eyed it for a second, took a deep breath, and picked it up. "Diana Speed."

"What's going on over there, anyway?" The Rajah's voice was deep and vibrant, an instrument of amazing power and range. Even in ordinary conversation it could be felt as well as heard; raised in anger it could set the facets of a ballroom chandelier jingling. Right now, it sounded only mildly inquiring, which meant nothing. Cathy, recognizing the sound from across the room, blanched and fled to her own desk.

"Things are a little . . ." She had to search for the precise word: "Confused. For the moment."

Silence. "Sure you can handle it?"

"Yes." The one word he hated was *maybe*, and *no* was unthinkable.

"If you need help, I can loan you Vandevoort. Or Hoskins."

A Dutch thug or a Harvard MBA; it said a lot about the Rajah's enterprises. But the offer itself said more: He doubted her. Her spirit wavered, but her instinct was what spoke, "No, thanks. I'll cope."

"I hope so." Not a threat—he wouldn't be bothered threatening. "I'll be back in the States tomorrow. I'll look forward to seeing . . . everything."

So he knew. Of course he knew. "I'll have them back," she said, but he had already hung up. She sat down in the desk chair and closed her eyes, listened to her heart thumping. When she looked up, Haskell Rose was standing in the doorway.

"Are you all right?" he asked.

"I've been better," she admitted. "How about you? I must say you look remarkably lifelike on so little sleep."

"It's all done with mirrors—or uppers, in this case. I can go a few more hours yet." Haskell was a master of the circuitous approach, and he was clearly ready to sidle around the edges of his errand until he judged the moment had arrived. Today, Diana decided, she might easily die like a dog before he got around to spitting it out.

"You wanted?"

"Well . . ." He tossed a meaningful glance over his shoulder, toward the outer office.

"Why don't you come all the way in and close the door behind you?" He did, and dragged a chair to within a foot of hers before plunking himself down in it.

"It's about Marie," he said, his voice barely above a whisper.

"What about her?" He shifted in his seat, collecting his thoughts, and Diana suddenly knew, without the possibility of doubt, that he had made a move on Marie the night before. And that it had failed.

"She's very important, Diana. More so than you can possibly realize."

"I told you, Haskell: We'll get the letters back."

"The letters are the least of it," he snapped, then looked nervously over his shoulder at the closed door.

"As long as you don't yell, we're reasonably private." She keyed the intercom. "No interruptions, Cathy, except for Miss McIntyre. And send out for more coffee. About a quart; black, with lots of sugar."

Eager as he had been five seconds earlier, Haskell now seemed tongue-tied. Diana found herself unwillingly fascinated.

"What happened last night . . ." he began, and stalled.

Maybe shock tactics would work: "Between you and Marie?"

"Exactly," he replied, then saw her meaning in her face. "Oh, not *that*. It wasn't anything, anyway. No, I mean before, when she was under hypnosis. Do you remember what we heard?"

"Pretty well," she said, mystified.

"It was incredible," he breathed. "I've read about that phenomenon, hundreds of times, but I've never seen . . ." He shook his head in stunned admiration. "She's a perfect channel. And to a *queen*, Diana."

So that was it; she might have known. "Haskell," she said wearily, "what we heard was weird as hell. I wouldn't deny it for a minute. But——"

"Don't you see?" he interrupted. "She's a window to the past. To *history*. If we handle her right, the possibilities are unlimited!"

She had seen him get worked up, in editorial meetings, about his preposterous crystals and sacred mushrooms, but never to this degree. One thing was certain, though: There was no point in arguing with him. If he'd convinced himself that they'd seen history's own Directory Assistance in action, nothing she could say would budge him.

"Haskell," she replied, "you may be right. But without those letters we've got nothing. Or nothing that sets her apart from the rest of your . . ." The words *sideshow acts* trembled on her tongue, but she was able, barely, to suppress them. And it would be a cold day in a very hot place before she let Haskell Rose play games in Marie's mind again.

"I guess you're right," he was saying, crestfallen. "But I don't see how we're going to get the letters back." He brightened. "What about a medium? Or I could hypnotize Marie again—it'd be perfectly logical for her spirit to be in touch with something so important to her."

Another time she might be able to enjoy Haskell's version of perfect logic, but now it just made her head ache. "What we do is wait," she said firmly. "Wait for them to get in touch with us."

At least he saw what she meant: "How about your friend Troubridge? You heard from him yet?"

She was completely unprepared for what the sound of his name did to her. I am not going to self-destruct over that bastard, she told herself. And certainly not in front of this bastard. "No," she said evenly. "I phoned his apartment twice this morning, long before he's usually up." She touched the intercom button again. "Cathy, if Mr. Troubridge calls—" She heard the girl's gasp clearly and so, clearly, did Haskell.

"Oh, God, Miss Speed. I forgot to tell you . . ."

"It's just not your day. What did he say?"

"It was about half an hour ago, just before the man from the FBI. He—Mr. Troubridge—told me to tell you he'd call back later, when things had calmed down."

"If he calls on your line, put him through." It was not so bad now; she could handle it. Diana looked across the desk at Haskell, who was staring thoughtfully out the window. "He didn't shoot Patrick, you know," she said.

He turned back to her, surprised but not, she saw, all that surprised. "What makes you so— Oh, the accent that Pearse didn't hear."

"Exactly," she agreed, pleased at his confirmation. "If you had to pick one word no Englishman says the way an American does, *bastard* would be a strong contender. *Bahst'd.*" She considered her mimicry. "Well, not quite, but he couldn't put an R in it, no matter what. If you ever heard

Alan Troubridge say *bastard*, you'd never mistake him for anything but a Brit."

"The description, though," Haskell offered. "That fit."

Diana shrugged. "Supplied to Pearse by whoever's behind it all?"

"Maybe. But I think it would've had more detail if it was a fake: the classic pooh-bah error."

With her brain laboring in low-low gear, it took her a moment to make the connection. "You may be right," she said. "A little verisimilitude goes a long way."

"It's a thing some of my authors never learn," Haskell agreed. "Too much detail trips you up, sooner or later."

Haskell seemed to have discarded his psychic preoccupation, she was relieved to note, and she decided to toss his ego another snack: "So what do we know?"

"We don't *know* much," he said slowly. His hands formed a steeple in his lap, and he regarded them for several seconds before continuing. "We can be pretty sure that Troubridge is tied up with whoever slugged you and took the letters . . ."

"Yes." There was no other conclusion. "And my guess is that Troubridge was with this other guy when he visited Pearse."

"Who's also in it," Haskell put in.

"For sure," she agreed. "Then why are they shooting each other?"

From the look on Haskell's face, he had not considered that side of it. "Thieves falling out?" he offered.

"Could be."

His brow furrowed as he considered. "Can I ask you a personal question?"

"Why not?" Diana was sure her expression never changed, but Haskell, from his sardonic grin, had felt her defenses go up.

"How long have you known Troubridge?"

She'd been making that very calculation: "Oh, eight months. Maybe nine."

"How'd you meet him?"

"We ran into each other at the Met. It could have been set

up, though." Mozart, she remembered. He had got to her with Mozart; that was really unforgivable.

"And where did you find Pearse?" Haskell asked, breaking the silence.

"That's what I can't explain. I picked his name myself, off a list of handwriting experts." She glanced up at him, and he nodded slowly.

"You know the next question, don't you?"

Incredulity gave way to disgust and then to weary sadness. "Cathy," she said.

"If she gave you the list, you're probably right: Who better to stack the deck?"

"But she's just a kid," Diana protested. "From the *Bronx*. She wouldn't know how."

"She wouldn't have to," Haskell replied. "Somebody did it for her." His smile was wryly sympathetic: "I've been gaffed the same way, by fake mediums."

"Why would she do it?" Diana was hurt and baffled. "I hired her, sent her to school . . . I could have sworn she was devoted to me. If *devoted* exists anymore." She found herself blinking angrily.

"Everybody has a bunch of different loyalties inside," said Haskell evenly. "You never know which one's going to come up on top."

"I guess not," Diana replied. She straightened, taking a grip on her emotions. "So the question before the house is what do we do now. If I don't get some sleep soon, I'll fold up like a cheap tent."

"You really don't plan to go to the police, then?" Haskell asked.

It was the sensible, obvious course. "Not a chance."

"We're withholding evidence. In a murder case," Haskell said. "We could go to jail."

"The only thing we're really withholding is the name of the guy we're sure didn't do it," Diana snapped. "No. That's sophistry, of course. But I still think we have a better chance of getting Marie's letters back if we don't have the cops running things."

"And that's your top priority? Getting Marie's letters back? It doesn't bother you that a man was killed last night—that *you* were damn near killed last night?"

"Look," said Diana, putting her elbows on the desk and propping her chin in her hands. "If those letters are real, and it looks as if they are, then they're worth millions. Millions to Marie, and that's great. But also millions to Wild-Freeman, and thus to my boss, Roger the Rajah."

"No millions for you, Diana?" Haskell was watching her narrowly. "No hopes of heaven? Right here in the house?"

"President?" At the sound of the title he'd wanted for so long, Haskell actually licked his lips.

"Don't try to tell me you do this kind of thing for exercise," he said.

"Haskell, there's only one person who runs anything the Rajah owns. If you work for him, you accept that." Even, she thought, if you sometimes bridle a little. "I don't care who has the title, because the Rajah sees to it that I get opportunities that turn me on. Some of those opportunities entail risks, that's all."

"Risks to other people rather than him," said Haskell.

So that's what's worrying him. "Those are his rules, and I accept them. But you don't have to."

"What about Marie?"

"Nobody's going to arrest her. She doesn't even know what we're talking about. And you're clear."

"Well, I'm not so sure about that," said Haskell uncomfortably. "We're kind of back to the beginning: What now?"

The digression had allowed her to work it out in her head: "The way I see it we have three leads into this: my secretary, Troubridge, and Pearse."

"Agreed."

"Pearse is on the sidelines for the moment, now that he isn't holding the letters. If we had enough people"—she was amused to see how nimbly he avoided her eye—"I'd say we should keep an eye on him. But we can't."

"And your Miss O'Donnell?" he asked, lowering his voice.

"If you were the brain behind something like this, how much would you tell her?"

"As little as possible." His laugh was a humorless bark. "Even less."

"Which leaves Troubridge, and he's trying to get in touch with me. Why, do you think?"

"Well, even if he just wants to talk, that's something," said Haskell. "Maybe he's figured out that his partner, whoever he is, has been setting him up, and—" The buzzer on Diana's desk cut him off, and she reached for the telephone.

"That must be Troubridge," she said. "Funny he'd use Cathy's line." She picked up the receiver. "Yes?"

"Miss Speed, I'm terribly sorry, but it's a Special Agent Murdoch, from the FBI . . ."

"I'll call him back," Diana replied.

"He's outside, Miss Speed. In the *reception* room. He wants to talk to you about Mr. Sarsfield; he says he'll wait till you're free."

"The FBI," she said to Haskell, her hand over the mouthpiece. "Something about Patrick." And to Cathy: "Oh, hell: Bring him in."

"The Feds? That's heavy." Haskell occasionally dropped a chunk of slang into his conversation, but his samples were invariably several years out of date. It was something Milly found endearing. "I'm glad you've decided to talk to them. It's the right thing to do."

"Sure," said Diana.

•   •   •

"Is there anything else you can think of that might help us, Miss Speed?"

She sipped her coffee while she weighed Special Agent Murdoch's words. Back in Washington, Diana, like most of her colleagues in State, had found the people from the Bureau unimpressive: invariably white, male, earnest, humorless, and just a little too thick in the middle for their three-piece suits. Except for his skin, which was almost the same color as her coffee, Murdoch matched her recollection exactly; maybe too exactly: For the past fifteen minutes, her suspicion had been growing that she was watching an act. And if that were the case, Special Agent Murdoch might be a lot smarter than he was letting on.

Even so, Diana had learned about interrogation from a master, an elderly gentleman who taught her that you could learn as much from being questioned as from asking the questions yourself. Thus far, without giving Murdoch any information he hadn't entered the room with, she had found out that the Bureau was aware of Sarsfield's donations to the Irish Republican Army, but they didn't know him as Patricia Orme, they didn't know about the Casket Letters, and they didn't know about Marie. What they wanted was a believable source for Sarsfield's money, and with a mental apology to Milly Aaron, Diana decided to give it to them: "I'm going to tell you a secret, Mr. Murdoch."

Was that the smallest hint of a smile? Too bad they couldn't have met in a different setting. "I'm all ears, Miss Speed," he said solemnly.

"Does the name Patricia Orme mean anything to you?"

Delighted recognition lit up his pleasantly ugly face, followed almost instantly by embarrassment, and then the rueful awareness that Diana was reading him like a headline. "Don't tell me: You're a fan," she said.

"I spend a lot of time on aircraft," he replied. "Patricia Orme sure beats in-flight movies."

It was a better epitaph than most novelists got. "Well," she said, "Patricia Orme is—was Patrick Sarsfield."

"You mean a man wrote those books?" He looked startled; then the obvious explanation occurred to him: "Or was he a little . . ."

"Not at all."

"Well, I'll be damned." He shook his head in wonder. "Patricia Orme. But I guess he must have done pretty well for himself, over the years."

Smoothly done, my friend, Diana thought. She sat back and prepared to let Murdoch winkle out of her just how well

Patrick Sarsfield had done, while leading him far away from Sarsfield's last and greatest expectation.

• • •

"That's about it," Murdoch said, closing his pocket notebook. "I do have one question, though it's not really about Mr. Sarsfield."

"Shoot."

"You said Sarsfield only got half of the money his paperback publisher paid, and that you—Wild-Freeman—got the other half. Is that the usual thing?"

"Invariably," she replied.

"That's amazing," he said, shaking his head. "How come, if you don't mind my asking? I mean, how come writers put up with that?"

"Actually," she said, giving him the battered remains of her ingenue smile, "it's because we've got them by the balls."

He could not have looked more shocked had she tossed a dead mouse in his lap, and she was still savoring his expression as the direct-line phone rang at her elbow. "Yes?"

"Contessa, I've got to talk to you."

"To tell me what?" Her voice sounded controlled in her own ears, but Murdoch was so pointedly looking away that she knew she must have betrayed some of the numb emptiness she felt.

"There's no excuse for what I did," Troubridge said. He sounded terrible. He deserved to. "But I didn't try to kill you."

"That's reassuring." Murdoch had got to his feet and was staring intently at the display of Wild-Freeman's latest titles that Cathy had set up on a table by the door.

"Look, I'll be at the bar we went to after we saw *Figaro*. In an hour. You can send the police, if you want."

"Sorry for the interruption," she said, replacing the receiver. "If you see anything you'd like, just help yourself."

"You're very generous," he replied. "What's this one about? The cover's really wild."

The book he was holding had a scarlet jacket that looked as if the color might come off on your hands. *FIEND!* shrieked the title, in jagged black lettering. "Oh, that," she said. "I can't recommend it. Another juvenile novelist who thinks he's discovered a new way to shock the readers."

Murdoch set it back down. "And how does he do that?" he asked.

"Same old raw language, and lots of it." Her tired brain gave a nearly audible click, and she blinked. "Son of a bitch."

"Oh, everybody knows that one," he said automatically, then saw her expression. "Is something wrong?"

She picked up the book, riffled rapidly through its pages. "No," she said, sampling a clotted slab of prose. "Something's right. First thing today." She tossed the book on her desk. "You've done me a favor, Mr. Murdoch."

"Maybe you can do me one," he said. "Is there a Miss Sanders around here anyplace?"

"Patrick's editor? She was here a little while ago. I'll call her office."

"I'd appreciate that. And your secretary—I didn't catch her name—I'd like to talk to her, too."

"Her name's Catherine O'Donnell, but she never even met Patrick Sarsfield."

"Maybe not," he replied. "But those photos over her desk intrigue me."

"The sad young men?" Diana smiled condescendingly. "Whoever they are, she doesn't know them, either. Poor child doesn't know any men at all."

"I don't suppose she knows these," Murdoch said. "They're all dead. The Irish Republican Army's more recent martyrs."

Twenty-two: Troubridge

The White Rose Bar & Grill on Second Avenue had ridden out the first wave of East Side gentrification with an absolute minimum of concession: Two young, muscular bartenders with curly hair, a cocktail menu that included piña coladas and margaritas, and the restriction of cocaine deals (retail only) to the rest rooms. Further than that a reluctant management would go only by millimeters, so that the Rose was always two brands behind in the imported beers merry-go-round, its recorded music ten decibels below what the trendiest ears had numbed themselves to endure.

But the place survived and even prospered. Troubridge attributed its success to its resolute lack of any atmosphere whatever. For patrons exhausted by the dramatic decor of midtown watering holes, the Rose's vinyl-sheathed booths and pictureless, mustard-color walls seemed to induce a soothing sense of relief; it was a place where you could just get drunk, and most of its customers did so, with the same obsessive efficiency they applied to their regular occupations.

Right after opening on a Sunday morning, however, the place was deserted and silent. Paul, the owner and daytime bartender, was hunched over the *Times* crossword, sucking the end of a soft-lead draftsman's pencil while a cup of black coffee sat untouched at his elbow. He looked up as

Troubridge entered. "Unh," he grunted, without removing the pencil.

"Good morning," Troubridge responded, slightly relieved to see that news of his violent expulsion the night before hadn't reached the day staff; or perhaps Paul did know and simply didn't care. "I'll have a brandy and soda. No ice."

Paul made the drink, took Troubridge's ten, rang it up, and set down the change, all without a word.

"I'm expecting a lady. Rather tall, short blonde hair. I'll be sitting in back." He left a dollar and walked into the near-total gloom. He chose a booth that had views of both the main entrance and, in the mirror over the bar, the only other door to the street, and lowered himself gently to a seat. He was intellectually certain that Diana would come, but his stomach was not nearly so sure. He took a sip of brandy—or whatever it was; the taste suggested pennies boiled in methylated spirit—and tried to construct an opening gambit.

He was still trying when the front door opened and she stalked in, alone. Paul glanced up and inclined his balding head toward the row of booths where Troubridge was sitting. She nodded an acknowledgment to Paul, and turned toward Troubridge as he rose. She was wearing a sweater, dark slacks, and a short jacket, and the bartender's eyes followed her retreating rump, as well they might. When she was just beyond arm's length from Troubridge she stopped and regarded him steadily. For the first time, he saw the bruises on the side of her face, and he felt the muscles along his jaw tighten.

"If I'd known this was going to happen . . ." he began and dried up, shaking his head as he groped for words. "You've got to believe me, Contessa: I had no idea."

"Don't call me that," she said, her voice coldly contemptuous. Her level gaze fixed him. "Okay, so you didn't try to cremate me; I already knew that. You didn't even punch me out; I knew that, too. But you let in whoever did it. And you were there when Patrick was shot."

Troubridge had forced himself to meet her stare; it was less painful to see than what she almost hid behind it. "Will you sit down?" he said and, when she had slipped into the seat across from him, asked, "How did you know? About Sarsfield?"

"Pearse described you," she explained. "He's in on it, isn't he?" Troubridge nodded. "But he didn't kill Patrick, either."

"No."

Her stony indifference was unrippled by visible feelings. Troubridge knew her well enough to guess what it was costing her, and dreaded her inevitable next words. "Cathy, too."

Pride was what held her together. The slightest hint of regret from him would sound to her like condescending pity. He realized that he would sooner die than hurt her again. "Cathy, too," he acknowledged. "But bamboozled by emotion."

"I don't know which I resent more," she observed, addressing the air between them, "being betrayed by you and her, or being suckered by the two of you." She sounded as if she were discussing three people she barely knew. She even managed to look detached, dark-rimmed eyes and all. Unless you noticed the tension in the gracefully clasped hands on the tabletop. Troubridge quickly lifted his eyes from them.

"What do you want me to do?" he asked.

"Here's what I figured was supposed to happen," she said, ignoring his question. "Haskell and Marie would come back at about one-thirty, maybe just in time to see the medics carry me out under a sheet. They tell the cops that you were with me when they left for dinner. Your prints are all over the place. Probably on my key case, even. Somebody finds this in the kitchen drain . . ." She fished a tiny lacquered pillbox from her purse, opened it and spilled the half capsule onto the table. Troubridge, who had been listening in silence, his head back as if waiting to be struck, said "Bastard!" under his breath, but Diana went on: ". . . and the contents in my gut."

She paused, but Troubridge knew she was not waiting for him. She reached out and took his half-empty glass, emptied it down her throat. She coughed, and her reddened eyes blinked. "Awful," she said. "Where was I? Oh, yes: my body. Maybe the bruises would show up in the autopsy, and maybe not. But if your . . . friend's plan had worked, there would've been other traces of you. Inside me."

Troubridge's breath hissed through his teeth, a sound he hadn't made since he was ten, under the housemaster's birch.

"Poire William—or was it guilt?—wrecked that little detail," she continued, and he felt himself go scarlet from collar to hairline. He could hear the strain in her voice, and found himself wondering how long she could sustain the performance, and how long he could force himself to submit to it. "Never mind: There was lots of other evidence lying around. And what it boils down to, Troubridge, is that you're the fall guy. Even if I don't go to the cops, you're buried under so much shit you'll never dig yourself out."

He held up his hands in surrender, but she had, he saw, come to the end. "God knows you're entitled to bite, Speed. If you want to turn me in to the coppers, I won't try to stop you."

. "With diplomatic immunity, why should you?" she said.

Troubridge winced, covered it with a bitter smile. "I doubt if you can imagine the kind of reception I'll get back home. On the whole, it might be easier to take my chances here." He took a deep breath and went on. "Look, I'm not trying to salvage my career. That's beyond recall. Nor am I trying to salvage any of our . . . whatever it might have been." He put his arms on the table, his hands a carefully calculated distance from hers. "I want to make amends. Truly. That's all there is to it."

Diana's face colored slightly. "Ain't we civilized? I hope someone's taking notes."

"They're being etched on my liver," he replied, as neutrally as he could manage. "Why don't you just tell me what you want me to do?"

"Put you out of your misery, you mean?" She looked down at the surface of the table, visibly collecting herself, before she went on. "Okay, Troubridge, here it is: I don't care what kind of game you and Pearse and your mystery boss are playing, but I want it to stop. I *do* care about what happens to the kid—Marie—and me. I want this project to fly. You know who took those letters, and I want them back. You help me and I'll stay off your case. If you can weasel your way out of the Sarsfield thing, that's all right with me. But if you won't get me those letters, I'll tear you to bits—here in New York and back across the water, too. And if I can't do it, the Rajah can." By the time she had finished, her voice was trembling with barely suppressed anger, and her face was white.

"All right," said Troubridge quietly.

"You'll get the letters?" Diana pressed. "You know where they are?"

"I'll take you to the man who stole them," he said carefully.

"And then?" Some of the tension seemed to have gone out of her, but Troubridge sensed she had only channeled it into watchfulness.

He shrugged. "I'll do my best." He saw the objection in her eyes, and after a couple of seconds he continued: "You have to understand that I can't order this person around. No one can anymore. He's run amok."

"But he was working with you."

"In a manner of speaking." How much could he tell her without putting her on the spot, right beside him? "He seems to have gone into business for himself."

Diana regarded him in silence; he could almost hear her tired brain whirring. "You two weren't free agents before?"

Troubridge shook his head.

"Or working with the Irish terrorists?"

"Lord, no!" Though of course Carr had been, as a double.

"So. That leaves just—"

Even exhausted, she was quite capable of working at least part of it out. "You said you didn't care, remember?" Troubridge interrupted.

"I think you just told me," she replied thoughtfully.

"You don't seem surprised," he said.

"Why should a spook be different from a diplomat?" The

cold, hurtful smile looked as if it were physically painful. "A man sent to lie abroad for his country—or his queen. Isn't that how it goes?"

"Frequently," he replied, drawling out the word in a self-parody of his usual accent. She saw through his screen of unconcern, of course; it was a mark of how close they'd been that each could cut the other to the bone so efficiently. "Look, Speed, time has a certain importance here. My own people will be after me by now, and they're not dolts. If you want me to help, you'd best use me while you can."

She nodded. "You're right. Let's get rolling."

"My erstwhile associate has a pied-à-terre in Brooklyn. Just maybe we can snag him there."

"After we pick up Marie," said Diana, slipping out from behind the table. Still astonishingly graceful, but he could tell she was aching as well as exhausted. "I'm not going to leave her where I can't keep an eye on her."

"This may be dangerous," he warned.

"Then you'll have to protect us," she said. "Two helpless dames and a British gentleman."

• • •

"I can't believe it," Diana said, through clenched teeth. "I absolutely cannot believe it, Haskell. You just let Marie walk out of here with that . . . that Grand Concourse Mata Hari."

"How could I know?" Haskell Rose replied. His look of injured innocence was right out of silent film, complete to the eyes cast up to the ceiling. Diana took a step forward, and for a second Troubridge thought she might knock Haskell flat. He clearly thought so, too, and scurried behind his desk. "You didn't tell me," he spluttered. "You didn't say you were going to meet Troubridge"—the well-known murderer, his expression added—"you just vanished. And how was I supposed to stop Marie anyway?" In utter desperation, he turned to Troubridge. "*You* tell me: What could I do?"

It was not a fight Troubridge planned to join. From his

vantage point behind Diana's left shoulder he gave Haskell a
shrug which said as much, and a mildly supportive expression of sympathy. Diana, bracing herself with both hands,
stared down at Haskell's desk top, took two deep breaths, and
looked up. "You're right," she said. "I left you in the dark.
It was my fault completely."

Haskell's mouth, caught forming a new excuse, dropped
open in astonishment. "Well, I . . . that's all right. I guess
I should've stopped her," he said sheepishly. "It all happened
so quickly."

"All what?" Troubridge put in.

"What?" Haskell still seemed stunned by his reprieve.
"Oh, the phone call," he said at last. He turned to address
Diana: "I sort of wandered around to your office. The FBI
person was inside, talking to your secretary. The door was
closed, but I could hear her crying." I expect you could,
Troubridge thought; it's a wonder you didn't bruise your ear
on the wood.

"Could you hear what they were saying?" Diana asked.

"Not really. She was rather incoherent." He paused.
"Anyway, that was when the phone rang."

"On Cathy's desk," said Diana. "Not the direct line inside
my office."

"Right. The ring surprised me, and I just sort
of . . . picked it up. The way one will."

"And?" Diana prompted.

"Well, apparently your secretary did the same thing, and at
the same moment." He looked sidelong at Diana. "I wasn't
about to hang up."

"No," Diana agreed, deadpan.

"It was a good thing I didn't," he added defensively. "I'm
sure you'd agree."

"Maybe I will, when you tell me what you heard."

"Oh. It was a man's voice. Familiar." Troubridge wanted
to reach out and shake him. He saw that Diana's fingertips
were white against the desk top, but she waited silently for
Haskell to go on. "I think it was that man Pearse, but he
sounded different from last night."

"Different how?" she asked; only someone who knew her as well as Troubridge did would have heard the edge on her voice.

"I'm not sure. Scared."

"What did he say?"

"That's the trouble: not much. He asked your secretary if she were free to talk, and she said no. So he gave her a number, and asked her to call him back as soon as possible."

"That's all you heard?"

He had the grace to look apologetic. "Well, a couple of minutes later your office door opened and the two of them came out. She'd been crying, all right, and she was as white as a . . . as—"

"—a sheet?" Troubridge said innocently.

Haskell threw him a poisoned glare. "Whatever. Anyway, she asked me if I'd show the FBI man where Judith's office was; I could hardly say no."

"So you weren't there when Cathy called Pearse back," Diana said.

"No. In fact, by the time I disposed of Mr. FBI, she'd gone. I just caught a glimpse of her and Marie, getting in the elevator."

"Why Pearse?" Troubridge mused aloud.

"One way to find out," said Diana. "You coming, Haskell?"

"Actually—" he began.

"Never mind," she cut him off. "*En avant,* Troubridge."

"Just a moment," he said, putting his hand on her arm. She stiffened, but she didn't pull away. "Rose, you said that Pearse gave Miss O'Donnell a number to call. D'you remember what it was?"

"Well, no." He seemed almost annoyed at being asked, and then his frown was wiped away by a dawning surprise. "But it couldn't have been Pearse's home phone: It was a 718 prefix."

"Brooklyn," Diana breathed. "Good catch."

The stab of pleasure was absurdly sharp, and he was careful not to let it show. "Now I think we'd better go, Speed."

Twenty-three: Diana

Without warning, Troubridge pulled her into a doorway. "That's the place," he said. "Fourth one down on the far side, with the dead vines over the door."

Diana surveyed the building, one among a row of small, nondescript apartment houses. Caffeine and sugar from three containers of coffee had sanded her nerve endings raw and made her eyes feel as if they were on stalks. "He's got a view of the street, of course."

"The two left-hand windows on the top floor."

"If we go back around the corner and cross there," she said, thinking as she spoke, "we can come up in dead ground."

"Dead ground?" he repeated, his eyebrows shooting up. "Where on earth did you pick that up?"

"Never mind. Come on." He had not tried to take her arm again, nor did he now. A silly thing to notice, she told herself. Once they were across the street, hugging the buildings, she said, "What about the front door?"

"A very basic lock," he reassured her. "Mother Bell's credit card should deal with it easily."

"*Ma* Bell," she said. "We Americans call her Ma." Cut the camaraderie, Diana. Remember what he did last night. And, remembering, she stopped and turned on him. "If you double-cross me, Troubridge, I'll kill you."

270

"I know," he replied calmly. "In the meantime, would you trust me enough to let me use that bloody great cannon of yours? If my ex-colleague's here, he's got a revolver."

How could she have forgotten? "It's gone," she said. "I loaned it to Patrick, and now the cops have it. All I've got is this." She drew her hand from her coat pocket just far enough for him to see the black plastic oblong nestled in her palm.

"The stunner? Against two pistols?" He looked dubious. "Rather long odds, Speed."

"One pistol," she said. "The police took Pearse's. And anyhow, it's the only game in town." Heaven knew where the adrenaline was coming from, but she felt a manic exaltation sweep over her.

She heard Troubridge mutter, "This is how people get themselves killed," but he was a half step ahead of her when they reached the front door. The lock was no more difficult than he'd said; she could have opened it herself. He led the way into the dim, echoing lobby; the small tiles underfoot were dirty, and some of them had cracked. "There's no lift," he whispered. "Stairs are over there." She had her foot on the second step when she felt his hand on her shoulder. "The flat's 4-A, straight ahead at the very top," he said, his mouth close to her ear. "The door's just matchwood: I'll knock it in, but you may have to deal with Carr—with my colleague."

Carr. Given a name, he was suddenly real, though she had yet to lay eyes on him. She realized she had frozen, poised with one foot on the stair. If she didn't move now, she never would. "Go," she said, and took the step.

A bicycle was chained to the heavy, scarred banister on the second-floor landing, and a smell of liniment took Diana by the throat. She shook her head and attacked the next flight as she had the first, two steps at a time, her rubber-soled boots squeaking softly against the tiles. At the third floor she heard the rhythmic thump of a bass from behind one door, saw a panic-stricken cockroach scuttle across the step in front of her. She broke her stride momentarily, and Troubridge, moving silently in his crepe-soled shoes, sped past her, three steps at each bound.

Her breath was rasping in her throat, but she ignored it and matched his stride. At the top he threw a glance over his shoulder, saw she was close behind. He took an odd little half step, lowered his shoulder, and drove into the door still moving full tilt. It flew open with a rending crash, and he went sprawling on hands and knees as Diana leaped past and over him, her momentum carrying her through the entrance hall and into the small living room, the stun gun at her side. "My God!" she heard a breathless voice cry out, and realized a second later it was her own.

Pearse was on the floor, slumped against a small, ratty couch; still-damp blood had streamed down the side of his head and soaked the shoulder of his heavy turtleneck sweater. Across the room, Cathy was propped against the old-fashioned iron radiator, her hands behind her back and her pink dress, torn and dirty, rucked up around her fat thighs; her head hung forward, and she seemed to be unconscious.

Diana stood dazed, trying to put a meaning to the scene in front of her, but Troubridge, still on his hands and knees, scrambled past her and began fumbling desperately at something half concealed by Pearse's body. She saw what it was as Pearse toppled sideways—a small box, crackle-finished gray metal, two knobs and a dial on top and wires running from the back—and knew she should recognize it, but her mind seemed to be waterlogged. "What—"

"Detonator," Troubridge said. "Three minutes on the timer. Get the girl out."

His urgency slashed through the fog in her head. With no notion of having crossed the room, she found herself on one knee, pulling Cathy's inert form into a fireman's carry. "Damn! She's handcuffed to the radiator. Can't you just tear the wires off?"

He was rocked back on his heels staring down at the innocent-looking box. "I don't know. There's one model that goes up if you try that. Can you get her loose?"

With Cathy rolled on her side, Diana could see the handcuffs, see the raw flesh where the girl had tried in vain to pull herself free. Diana emptied her bag on the floor—

compact, keys, change purse, pencil, checkbook . . . there had to be something she could use on the handcuff lock. "Don't they teach you people about your own bombs?" she demanded.

"I must've been playing hockey that day," he said, but his big, square-tipped fingers were working at the box's cover.

"Hooky, Troubridge," she said, trying and discarding a mechanical pencil. "It's called playing hooky."

"Actually, it was hockey," he replied. "On ice, you know. There, you little bugger." The top was off and she caught a glimpse of wiring.

The nail file point was far too blunt to fit in the lock, and she tossed it aside. "Can you defuse it?" she asked.

"I'm trying," he replied. "Haven't you got those bracelets open yet? Surely they taught you how to do that."

"With a hairpin," she agreed. "Only in Washington do they think women still have hairpins."

"When I was in training," he said, "it was nutpicks. Governments are all the same." He set the box down gently. "Look, Speed, I think you'd better run for it—there's enough plastique under that couch to put the top of this house in orbit."

"And you're just going to sit there . . ."

"No, I'm going to pull a wire free," he snapped, his exasperation finally showing. "Maybe it'll be the right one."

"If it's not, I hope I'll have time to say 'I told you so.' "

The wire he chose was bright red. He took two quick turns around his finger and looked up at her; his face was white to the lips. " 'Come then, let us to't pell mell,' " he began, and with a strangely crooked smile. " 'If not to heaven—' " Diana drew herself up; she could meet his eye, but a smile was beyond her. " '—then hand in hand to hell,' " he finished, and tugged the wire free.

The end of it, vibrating in Troubridge's grasp, was shiny. She couldn't seem to take her eyes off it, until finally the silence was broken by a groan from Pearse.

•   •   •

Diana's hands were so unsteady that she gave up trying to pick the lock on Cathy's handcuffs, and in the end Troubridge did it, using a piece of stiff wire from the detonator. The girl lay still as he worked, her eyes staring straight ahead of her at the blood-smeared couch. Diana had gotten Pearse back into a sitting position and was sponging the blood from his face and head, to a chorus of groans and curses from the patient.

"There," she said at last. "Just a crease along the temple, you big sissy."

"Crease?" he said. "Christ, it feels like a goddamn trench." He turned his head cautiously, saw the wreck of the detonator and blanched. "Holy shit. What's that for?"

Troubridge tossed the handcuffs on the floor. "To blow you up with, my lad. What else?" While Pearse digested the remark, Troubridge and Diana helped Cathy to a chair. She was whimpering quietly, and her skin was chilly and damp.

Diana picked up Troubridge's raincoat from the floor and threw it over the girl's shoulders. "Shock," she said to Troubridge, over Cathy's head. "She must've just sat there, waiting to die."

"Why didn't she call for help, then?" Troubridge replied. "Silly creature."

"I did," Cathy said suddenly. Her voice was so faint and hoarse Diana could scarcely hear it. "I did, over and over, and nobody came." She burst into dry, racking sobs. "Oh, God, I was so scared."

Pearse was staring at her, clearly bewildered. "I don't understand," he said. "What happened?"

Maybe he really didn't remember, Diana thought. It was a head injury, after all. "You phoned my office this morning, talked to Cathy. D'you remember that?" He shook his head. "You told her to bring Marie here—"

"No," Cathy put in, snuffling. "He asked for the letters. When I told him they were in the office vault, that was when he said to bring Miss McIntyre."

Informed horror lit up Pearse's face. "Marie!" he said. "Where is she? And where's that prick Galmoy?" He tried to rise, sank back on the couch with a moan. "Oh, Jesus, my head."

"So Cathy and Marie came here," Diana continued. "And you were waiting with . . . now who's this Galmoy?"

"Guy who pushed me into this," Pearse said. "Fat little bastard—no, not really fat; kind of soft looking."

"That's not his real name, though," Cathy said. "It's Swallow. Mr. Swallow."

"My ex-colleague Carr, I think," said Troubridge quietly.

"A busy little bee, whatever you call him," Diana said. "And you went along with his idea to kidnap Marie."

"No!" cried Cathy and Pearse together. "I never even thought—" she went on, but Pearse's voice was louder: "We were going to make a deal with her. Buy her out."

"But she wouldn't sell," said Diana, as Pearse's face flushed red. "And so you and Galmoy decided to put the arm on her."

"It wasn't like that," said Pearse sullenly.

"He's telling the truth," Cathy cried. "When Mr. Swallow said he was going to take Miss McIntyre away, Mick tried to stop him. Only he got shot." She turned to Pearse: "I thought you were dead."

"For all the good it did . . ." Pearse shrugged. "I was a fool."

"There's a lot of it going around," Diana said. "Okay, you were out cold. Cathy, what happened then?"

"It was awful," she said, beginning to cry again. "He grabbed me and put those things on me. He said if I yelled he'd shoot me in the . . ." She turned scarlet. "Up there. You know."

"What did Marie do while this was going on?" Diana asked.

"She was holding Mick's head, trying to wipe the blood off, only she kept calling him James . . ." She stopped short and turned to Pearse: "Your name really is Mick, isn't it?"

"Michael Matthew," he affirmed. "But you're right. I didn't pass out right away, and I remember her calling me James."

Cold dismay knifed through the fog of exhaustion in Diana's brain. The poor kid had gone over the edge for keeps. But who had she thought she was calling to—Moray or Bothwell? "Don't worry about that," Diana said. "What happened then?"

"He went to the kitchen," Cathy said. "Mr. Swallow. Brought back all that stuff like clay. And the box. He said Mick was going to blow me up. At least that was how it was going to look." She shivered. "Then he went away. Miss McIntyre went with him. He told her Mick was dead, and she just went."

"Did he say where he was taking her?" Diana asked.

She shook her head; she was sobbing again, wrenching spasms that shook her whole frame. She tried to say something and failed, then took hold of herself and tried again: "He's going to sell her."

She couldn't have heard right. "What d'you mean, Cathy?"

"To *you*, Miss Speed," the girl sobbed. "For the other letters." She drew a long, whooping gulp of air into her lungs. "He doesn't care about Ireland at all!" she wailed. "He's only doing it for money."

It was just what Diana had feared. The whole structure of her ambition in ruins, and no way out. She had never been so tired, but there were still a few odds and ends that had to be untangled. "Mick, I want you to take Cathy home."

He looked up at her. "I guess so. Sure. Just give me a hand up." On his feet, his face pale, he turned to Cathy. "Come on. It's time to get out of here." Troubridge took his own coat to the hall closet and returned with the two that had been hanging there.

"What's going to happen?" Cathy bleated, as Pearse awkwardly crammed her into her coat.

"Nothing," Diana replied, answering the unspoken part of her question. "You're out of it. Home free, kiddo. Be grateful."

Pearse took the girl's arm, but it was not entirely clear who was supporting whom. He started toward the door, then stopped and turned back to Diana. "You will get her back, won't you?" he asked. "You won't let him . . ." Unable to continue, he started to shake his head and grimaced with pain. The bleeding had mostly stopped, but the wound was a raw track through his black, curly hair.

"You leave it to me," Diana said. "Now vanish, the two of you, before I change my mind."

She listened to them lurching heavily down the stairs, then closed the door and set her back against it. Troubridge was sitting on the blood-spattered couch, watching her. "You don't need me anymore," he said.

He was right, but she found herself surprised. And sharply disappointed. "No, I guess I don't." She began to button her coat. Her fingers moved stiffly; at least they'd stopped trembling.

"He'll double-cross you, of course," Troubridge said.

"He'll try." She saw her bag on the floor, leaned forward to pick it up, and almost lost her balance. "You know, I really could use—"

"—some sleep. You certainly could."

I was going to say *a hand*. And he knew it. There's a reason he's staying here; why won't he tell me what it is? "Well, so long, Troubridge."

"*Adieu*, Speed." He didn't get up from the couch.

She opened the hall closet door; his coat was on the hanger. "Oops, wrong one," she said over her shoulder.

By the time she reached the lobby, the last of the adrenaline had evaporated; she stumbled out the front entrance, blundering into a couple of men who were coming up the steps. "Sorry," she said, but she didn't hear a reply.

Twenty-four: Troubridge

The two men didn't knock—just walked in and sat down on the couch, avoiding the spatter of Pearse's blood. Troubridge had found a bottle of Scotch in the kitchen, and he poured a second glass and handed it to the smaller of the two, a soft-faced man, who was clearly in charge. "Welcome to Park Slope, Peter," Troubridge said. "I wondered when you'd catch up."

"We'd have been here sooner, Alan, but Willingden lost his way." The slablike man sitting beside him rumbled something subterranean and uncomplimentary, in which the words *bloody maze* were just recognizable.

"It's got rather out of hand, hasn't it?" Troubridge offered, slipping easily into the speech pattern he always thought of as Whitehall Diffident.

"Debacle," said the soft-faced man, "isn't too strong a word, I'm afraid." He shook his head at Troubridge, plunged his nose briefly into the whiskey, and set the glass down with a sigh.

"Bloody disaster, if you ask me," muttered his companion. "Documents vanished, principals missing, dead Yank to explain away. A total cock-up."

The soft-faced man glanced quickly at his companion and, without moving an inch, gave the strong impression of having distanced himself by a foot at least. "The question, of course," he continued, in the gentle, abstracted tone he had been affecting since he and Troubridge were schoolboys, "is what do we do now. Poor Willingden has spent a dreadful afternoon with the Americans—"

"Cleaning up," Willingden put in angrily. "Cleaning up messes that shouldn't have happened."

"And doing it beautifully, I'm sure," the soft-faced man said. "You have an incredible rapport with colonials, Willingden. I've noticed it time and again." The square man looked at him sharply, but the other rolled smoothly on. "The point I was making, though, is that even with the American authorities as it were tamped down, they've hamstrung your operation. I dare say the street—the avenue—outside the consulate is positively teeming with unmarked police cars."

"That's why we're talking to you here," said Willingden. The square man's presence was an ominous note but, Troubridge realized, scarcely unexpected. Willingden had made his name tidying up operations that went astray, and his passage was often marked by the sudden removal of the unsuccessful personnel involved. Ever since his arrival at Carr's flat, he had been surveying Troubridge like a butcher deciding how to carve a side of beef.

". . . has to be done quickly," the soft-faced man was saying. "And, of course, unobtrusively."

"Well, there's no one more unobtrusive than you, Peter," said Troubridge, and it was true: When the Honourable Peter Crichton-Laing entered a crowded room, most of its occupants would have sworn someone—they wouldn't be sure who—had just left. In the Foreign Office his rise had been at once imperceptible and extremely rapid, marked principally by the startled expressions of senior functionaries wondering why the devil Prince Peter (as he was invariably known) had turned up at *their* elbow. They soon discovered there was nothing to be done about it: Peter's diffident politesse smothered all opposition, and he was related to more people than Troubridge himself. Even his considerable competence had not held him back, and lately he had begun to be referred to, in Whitehall circles, as the Inevitable Crichton.

Though he and Troubridge were distant cousins, they had first met at school, where the twelve-year-old Peter quickly recognized the utility of a larger companion as a sort of ambulatory lightning rod. When Troubridge had comprehended his role in Peter's life, he had been first furious, then baffled (even the most ferociously physical snubs had no effect), and finally amused. He had retained that amusement over the years, as he observed Peter's career from a middle distance and, lately, from below; with time, Troubridge discovered—it unnerved him at first—he had actually come to like the man.

"Our problem," Peter was saying earnestly, "is that this whole thing has nothing to do with the F.O. Nothing to do, actually, with any official department at all. We simply can't understand what it's all about." His voice, Troubridge reflected, was the voice of concerned responsibility, but his bland expression was that of a cat who knew exactly what was in the cream dish.

Willingden, however, did not. "We're just the fire brigade, you see. Nobody's told us what caused the bloody fire." He paused, waiting for Troubridge to speak.

"I wonder if *cause* is really important," Peter said, offering the remark so hesitantly that it scarcely seemed to exist. "As I understand the brief, I'm supposed to smooth the Americans' ruffled feathers, and get Alan out of here unlynched. The rest is your business, Willingden, not—thank God—mine." A look of deep depression slid into place. "I'm not at all sure government ought to be involved in this, Alan. Far better to leave it to the evanescents like yourself."

Willingden was no fool. He could see that Peter had moved his conversation with Troubridge to a dimension they shared and he did not. As the nuances pattered around him like invisible snow, he sat and glowered silently.

"A dreadful shambles," Troubridge said. "I suppose I'm for it this time."

"I'm afraid so," Peter replied. "No way out that I can see. You're to go straight home this afternoon."

"And not on the Queen's Flight, I expect," Troubridge

said, but he was weighing the phrase *that I can see:* a little leeway, perhaps.

"Oh, dear, no," said Peter, with a sad, sympathetic look. "It's Cunard for you, old boy. Probably steerage."

Willingden growled something under his breath, and Peter glanced at him, surprise painted across his unremarkable face. "Oh, was that security? Dreadfully sorry." Apologies flooded the room, but Troubridge barely heard them. The hint had been plain: His superiors wanted him out of New York, but were in no hurry to get him back to London. Did that mean Willingden was going to inherit the case? Very likely. It was a possibility that made Troubridge uneasy. There was the memory of a rumor he had heard about Willingden. If only he could recall the details . . . No, it was gone.

"I hope no one's planning to do anything silly about the innocent parties," he said.

Peter looked quite shocked: "Her Majesty's government are not Bulgarians, Alan." But Willingden said nothing at all. Still, Troubridge reflected, Diana at least was very well connected, if the Rajah decided to protect her . . .

He was brought back to the present by Peter rising to his feet. "Have to run," he was saying to them both. "Willingden will keep you company till it's time to go." And pointedly to Troubridge: "See me to the door, there's a good fellow."

Behind him, Troubridge could sense Willingden's compelling desire to overhear his superior, but Peter's confidential murmur had been perfected in the highest echelons of government. Troubridge had to strain his own ears to the utmost in order to hear the man beside him. "He was wished on me, of course," Peter was saying as he buttoned his elegant tweed topcoat.

"Of course," Troubridge replied. "Would you keep an eye on Diana Speed for me?"

As Peter tugged on his gloves he muttered, "I'd like to help, but I'm on the wing tonight . . ." His glance darted quickly past Troubridge, toward the living room. "In your place, I'd jump at any chance that offers." At the open door, he bade a conventional farewell, then called past Troubridge, "Take care of my friend, won't you? Good care."

Peter's departure threw a pall of silence over the living room and its remaining occupants. Willingden had brought the front section of a Sunday newspaper with him and immediately retreated behind it, holding it up like a shield. Troubridge stood irresolute in the doorway. There was, he knew, no point in trying to run; Willingden had both the physical equipment and the training to stop him before he reached the stairs. And even if Troubridge succeeded in getting out of the building, he had, aside from highly traceable credit cards, perhaps a hundred dollars in his wallet—not nearly enough to get him any distance. And what about Speed?

"They never should've given the job to Carr," said Willingden suddenly, from behind

SCREEN QUEEN'S
LUST REVEALED

"Obviously not," Troubridge agreed. "But what makes you say that?"

Willingden lowered the paper until his small, bright blue eyes were just visible over the top. "Too much money in it. Herbie Carr was all right dealing with the Provos' funds— they expect a little skimming, anyhow. But all of a sudden he had these millions under his nose, and him a poor man. Not to mention he must've known he couldn't tunnel into the IRA forever without getting caught." Willingden's iron face assumed an almost sympathetic expression. "I expect it looked like a chance to get clear once and for all. Waste of a good man."

An obituary, Troubridge thought. I've just heard Carr's obituary, and from the mouth of his executioner. He saw that Willingden was waiting for a response. "He did seem to be strung a bit tautly," Troubridge said, remembering as he spoke the dough-faced man's blind panic on Pearse's fire escape. "By the way," he went on, "since I'm going by ship . . . Cunard, you said?—"

"I didn't."

"—I'll need clothes. Can't appear on deck in these, and they'd be no good in Bermuda at all. Assuming we are going via Bermuda." Troubridge's descent into prattle turned Willingden's face to stone, just as he'd hoped. "Someplace warm, at any rate. And that means whites, if we're going to keep our end up."

"Don't count on being there long."

"Just long enough to get from the pier to the airport, I suppose?" said Troubridge. Nothing in Willingden's expression changed, but Troubridge felt as if someone had just run a long, sharp fingernail down his spine. "Mind if we stop off at my flat, to throw some things into a suitcase?"

"No," said Willingden. Perhaps the refusal sounded excessively brutal even to him, for he went on: "They're to pick you up downstairs. It's all arranged." He looked down at his wristwatch. "In fact, we'd better start down now." He heaved himself to his feet, followed Troubridge into the minute hallway at exactly the prescribed distance. To Troubridge's intense disgust, he found himself shivering from fatigue as well as the chill of the underheated apartment, but he saw Willingden's contemptuous private smile and knew what he was thinking. Angrily, he pulled his raincoat off the hanger, shrugged it on, and thrust his hands in the pockets.

What the devil? It couldn't be the wrong coat—there was only one in the closet. But something was in the right-hand pocket that hadn't been there when he hung it up. Something made of plastic, cool and oblong, smaller and much lighter than a gun. Something whose shape felt familiar, though he knew he had never touched it before. As his fingertips translated the details, Troubridge felt the blood suddenly course hot through his veins.

"What is it?" Willingden demanded. "Feeling sick, are you?"

Try as Troubridge might to restrain it, the excitement was

obviously visible on his face, but Willingden must have put another meaning to it. "Here," he said, taking the taller, thinner man firmly by the shoulder. "Just put your head down between your . . ."

Shielded by his own bending body, Troubridge's seemingly empty hand pressed hard against Willingden's hip as he triggered Diana's stun gun. The big man tried to move back, but he was against the wall. "Bloody hell!" he roared, as his legs folded under him. He grabbed at Troubridge's shoulder, but received instead a knee in the groin. He was still trying to get to his feet when the immaculate toecap of a hundred-and-twenty-dollar shoe took him right in his solar plexus. Willingden sagged back against the wall of the hallway, gasping for breath, and Troubridge kicked him, with meticulous care, in the right temple. Downstairs, the bass had stopped playing and the whole building seemed to be listening.

"Let's get you back inside, my large friend," Troubridge said to the unconscious heap at his feet. "I've got a debt to repay."

Twenty-five: Diana

At first she dreamed she was lashed into the dentist's chair, his drill driving its way into her unanesthetized jaw, but as she fought her way up into consciousness she realized the insistent burr was coming from the downstairs doorbell, and the pain was merely last night's bruise. "Oh, all *right*," she muttered, rolled over, and fell off the couch. She got up painfully, pulling the blanket around her shoulders, and staggered across the darkened room. "Yes?" she snarled into the intercom, hoping the hostility she felt was coming out clearly at the other end.

"It's me. Mick Pearse." The volume nearly took her head off: He must have his mouth right against the speaker.

"What do you want?" She glanced at her watch; nearly seven P.M. Why didn't she feel more rested?

"Got to talk to you. I can help."

She tried to pull her thoughts together, but no useful pattern seemed to form. On impulse she stabbed at the buzzer, and repented in the next second. But already she could hear him on the stairs, awkward and heavy-footed. As he reached the landing, she opened the door to the limit of its chain and braced her foot against it. "You can talk from there," she said. "And stand under the hall light."

Whoever had bandaged Mick's skull had not known when to stop, and the ludicrous navy watch cap pulled down over

the gauze made his small, neat head look like a blue wool
basketball edged in white. His hands were thrust into the side
pockets of an expensive-looking ski jacket, but his feet were
in a pair of the cheap, old-fashioned sneakers that New York
cops used to call Felony Shoes; altogether, he was the sort of
apparition you didn't want on your doorstep, especially after
dark. But there was an earnest, appealing urgency in his eyes
that made it impossible for Diana to slam the door in his face.
"I took Cathy home," he began. "She said to tell you
good-bye."

It was probably better that way, Diana reflected. Mick was
waiting for a reaction; she gave him a neutral "And so?"

His face, already pink from the cold outside, flushed
deeper. "About Marie. I want to help you get her back."

"I bet you do. And the letters, too."

He shrugged. "Sure. Them, too. But her mostly."

"Why on earth should I trust you, Mick? And what could
you do to help?" She kept her tone derisive, but she
recognized she was dangerously ready to hear a good story
from him. *Damn it, I like him—I can't help it.*

"I was trying to think how I could convince you to trust
me," he said. "It wasn't easy. But there's two things we both
want: Marie back safely, and that prick Galmoy on ice." He
flashed a pale vestige of his infectious grin. "And I want
Marie to have her letters back, even if you don't believe me."

Strangely enough I do, Diana realized. "But why wouldn't
I just want to take the letters for myself?" she asked.

His jaw dropped. "You want that?" His cheerful face
darkened with anger. "Well, damn you to hell, Diana Speed.
I'll go save the kid myself."

"Wait!" *He could be acting,* she thought. *No, I'd bet my
life against it.* And then the stark realization: *That's what
you're about to do.* "Not so fast, Mick." She unhooked the
chain and opened the door quickly, before she could change
her mind. "I was just checking."

"Oh." He regarded the doorway with reluctance. "The
thing is, I've been in over my head right from the start. I
don't know who to believe anymore."

"Come on in," she said, giving him a weary smile. "We can start with an armed truce and see where things go from there."

He nodded. "That's all right." Inside, as she snapped on the lights, he looked around the living room with frank curiosity. "A nifty place," he said. "I can smell the fire, though. Take some doing to get that out."

"You're telling me." She opened the liquor cabinet. "Help yourself, and there's food in the fridge. I'm going to clean up."

•   •   •

Fifteen minutes later. "Good: you found something to . . ." The words died on her lips. "What in God's name *is* that?"

"Peanut butter'n ketchup sandwich," he mumbled through a scarlet-streaked mouthful of it. "Not as bad as it looks. You want some?"

"I ate earlier, thanks." She dropped into the armchair and regarded him thoughtfully. Without the watch cap, she decided, he looked considerably more human. "I still don't know why I let you in here, Mick."

"I'm probably not as useful as Troubridge," he agreed cheerfully, picking off her thought. "Where is he, anyway?"

"Gone." She saw he realized the subject was closed. "It's just the two of us."

"Galmoy hasn't called, I guess."

"Not yet. I got my answering machine working again, so we can monitor the incoming calls." A recollection struck her: "You said something about being in over your head. Did that have anything to do with Galmoy's hold on you."

His boyish face wrinkled with disgust. "Damn right. I did some work for him a while back, kind of on a dare." He apparently saw the question in Diana's eyes and decided to risk the explanation: "A bomb. Not to blow people up, you understand. Some stupid protest, I don't even remember.

Anyhow, it went off too soon and . . . hurt a couple of guys."

Hurt spelled *killed*, she thought. "You weren't there when it happened."

"No, but Galmoy told me all about it." And you believed him, you big pussycat. "So he had me by the short and curlies. That was how I got dragged into this." He grinned suddenly. "Not that he could've kept me off with a spear, once I had a look at those letters."

"What about after we get the letters back?" she demanded. "What's your interest then?"

He seemed bewildered. Could he really not have thought that far ahead? "I don't exactly know," he said, after several seconds. "It's funny, but I feel as if they're behind me. That job's done. What I'd really like . . ." He stopped, and his face turned red.

"Yes?" prompted Diana.

"It's Marie. I know she's a little strange, but when she turns those funny eyes on me—" At his elbow the telephone rang, jarring him out of the confidence he had been on the point of sharing. I'll never know, Diana thought. Whatever he tells me later, it won't be the same.

The answering machine clicked twice, its microphone came to life, and a man's voice said, "You listening, bitch?"

"What the hell?" Mick gaped at the black box, and Diana waved him to silence.

"Give it a minute," she said; even so, she could hardly contain herself.

The voice cleared its throat and launched into a barrage of stilted hatefulness. The same very young voice as the night before, and even more nervous. Diana recalled Troubridge's diagnosis, decided he had been correct in every particular.

She waited, one hand on the receiver; across from her Mick's fascinated gaze shuttled back and forth from answering machine to Diana like a spectator watching a tennis volley. At last the caller paused to take a breath, and Diana snatched up the receiver. "Tell Tim Mark—" The gasp at the other end was a hoarse explosion in the amplifier. "Tell your buddy to pick his quotes from some book he didn't edit," she said, and slammed the receiver down with a crash.

Mick's awed respect was as refreshing to her as eight more hours' sleep. "Jesus. What was that about?" he asked.

"No big deal. A little internecine battle," she replied.

"Sounds as if you won it," he said.

With a little help from an absent friend. I wonder if he found the stun gun; I wonder if he needed it. The thought recalled her to the present. "I don't suppose you've got any kind of weapon, Mick."

"Oh, I forgot." He reached over to his ski jacket, lying tossed on the couch, and pulled a small pistol from the pocket. "It's about two steps up from a zip gun," he said apologetically, holding it out to her.

A six-shot revolver, she thought a .32. The frame felt rickety and, as she flipped the cylinder out and back, she detected a trace of looseness. "A lot better than nothing," she said, as enthusiastically as she could manage. "Where'd you get it?"

His smile was disarming. "This is New York, Diana. These things are under every bush."

For someone like him, they probably were. She handed the gun back. "I don't know if it'll scare Mr. Galmoy, but it sure as hell frightens me," she said. "Looks like it'd blow up in your hand."

"Yeah." He examined it closely, set it down on his jacket. "I wonder what that bastard Galmoy's doing."

To her, you mean. "He'll call," she said. "He needs time to set his trap."

Mick seemed unsurprised. "I suppose. How do you want to handle it?"

"I can't say. We'll have to play it by ear." How I wish Troubridge were here, she thought. I feel so rusty at this. Not that I ever really worked in the field. She clamped her racing mind shut: If you started thinking like that, you were half beaten before you started.

•　　•　　•

The phone rang at nine, and although Diana had been willing it do so for an hour, the soft jingle sent a stab of apprehension through her. Mick, who had fallen asleep with a book in his lap, was wide awake on the instant. "Miss Speed?" said a breathy, unfamiliar voice. "Are you there?"

Mick was nodding furiously. She picked up the phone. "Speaking."

"You know who this is."

"By reputation."

"You've got an item I want."

"You've got several items I want."

"Only one's for exchange. And it's perishable." She had never heard a voice at once so soft and so taut.

"Now, wait a minute—"

"Be quiet." Mick was shaking his head at her; he looked scared. "Go to the southwest corner of 53rd and Third. Next to the underground entrance. Be there in fifteen minutes and bring the merchandise. Come alone."

She sat holding the dead receiver. Mick was on his feet, pulling on his jacket. "Come on," he said.

"Wait a minute. I've got to think this out."

"What's to think? You heard his voice: He'll kill her for sure if you don't come."

"Maybe," she replied. She got to her feet and went to the safe, removed a padded book-mailer envelope.

"Are they really in there?"

"Oh, yes." She considered her dark slacks, decided on a short, quilted jacket for warmth. But no hat: He'll want to see my face. If he's there at all. "I guess that'll do." She turned to Mick: "You wait here."

"Fuck that," he snapped.

"—for five minutes," she went on, ignoring his outburst. "I'll walk over to Third and up. Even slowly, it'll take only ten minutes. You go to Second and move fast. Come west on 53rd. The subway entrance is just short of the corner." She moved to the door, drawing him in her wake. "If he's there—which I doubt—you stay clear unless I signal you in."

"How?" He seemed calm enough. Maybe he was better when he had orders to follow.

She felt in the jacket pocket and produced a pair of leather gloves. "If I drop one of these, you come running."

"Got it."

They were down the stairs. The street door, its opaque glass already replaced, was in front of them. "Stay back out of the light," she warned. One last proviso: "Listen, if I go down . . ."

Pearse's battered young face was hard. "So will he."

"Wrong," she said firmly. "Look, I appreciate the thought, but forget me and stick with him. He'll take you right back to Marie." It was a forlorn hope, and she saw from Mick's expression that he realized as much, but he nodded agreement.

•   •   •

Is Galmoy watching? Diana asked herself, as she stepped onto the top stair leading down to the nearly empty street. She felt light-headed with excitement but not, as far as she could tell, even a trace of fear. She paused to get a better grip on the padded envelope under her arm, turned her head so the streetlight two doors down caught her profile. Maybe he's got help, another blackmailed sucker like Mick. Could he know Mick's still alive? Too many things to consider. She squared her shoulders and set off westward.

By the time she reached Second Avenue, she had spotted two men who might be following, but one turned south at the corner. The other, pacing her on the far side of 50th, simply vanished halfway down the block. One moment he was there, in the corner of her eye, and then he wasn't. No, that was nonsense—he must've gone into one of the houses. That's what those doors are for, Diana.

At the corner of Third Avenue she was tempted by the DONT WALK sign: Sprint across and see if we flush a bird, she thought, then vetoed the idea. She crossed instead to the north side of 50th and waited with uncharacteristic docility for the avenue light to change. Except for one obvious tourist couple (the man clutching a green paperback guidebook, the woman gabbling at him in German), the other pedestrians ignored the red light as completely as Diana herself would normally have done.

Striding north along Third, she could feel eyes on the back of her neck; they told you never to ignore that feeling. But what could she do about it? She risked a fruitless glance over her shoulder. More people here, even after ten on a Sunday night: a middle-aged couple wobbling back from dinner, God's gift to pickpockets; a pair of frightwigged streetwalkers drifted north from Grand Central; more tourists—a whole family this time, with twangly Tidewater accents, arguing in front of a restaurant.

At the appointed corner a surprising number of people were still pouring down the steps into the subway, a trickle coming back up. There was a protective railing around three sides of the subway entrance, and she took a position with her back to it, so she could watch the uptown traffic on Third and the westbound cars on 53rd simultaneously. No one seemed to be taking any interest in her, but she shifted the padded bag under her other arm, to make it more visible from the street. As she did so she glanced down at her watch. Thirty seconds to go; is Mick coming up the street? Don't look.

A car swung around the corner within a few feet of her, making the turn onto 53rd, and the man in the driver's seat—square jawed, short haircut, looked like an army sergeant—stared right through her. Uh-oh, she thought. I've seen you before, and recently. But where? Somehow she associated him with Galmoy's Brooklyn apartment building, but she couldn't recall the exact context. In any case, he certainly didn't match the description of Galmoy-Carr-Swallow that Mick had given her.

Behind her, in one of the two open phone booths, a bell jangled. Of course, she thought. She stepped around the triptych partition that did nothing to mute the traffic noise and picked up the receiver. "Yes?"

"Quick reactions, Miss Speed."

Not as quick as they should've been, she thought. "It was pretty obvious, Mr. Galmoy."

Hissing silence in the receiver. What did I say wrong? When he spoke, his voice was even more strained than before, his English accent even more pronounced: "A straight swap. The girl for the rest of the letters."

"I'll pay you for the letters you've got. There's a lot of money behind me."

He hesitated for a half second. "How much have you got?"

"As much as it takes, and cash. By mid-morning tomorrow."

His regretful tone told her she'd almost had him. "Sorry, no. I haven't the time. The letters for Marie. Tonight."

"Now, look —"

"The Blarney Castle. It's a pub. Third and 55th. Five minutes."

She hung up, thinking fast. Galmoy probably wasn't watching her himself, but there remained the square-jawed man in the car. She spun around as if to go eastward on 53rd Street. Mick was standing in front of a fancy yuppie restaurant, inspecting the posted menu with visible distaste, while the doorman inspected him with exactly the same expression. Diana was thinking that no woman dressed as she was could speak to a man who looked the way Mick did, when he turned quickly away from the menu and shoved his hand in front of her. "You got some spare change, lady?"

"I gave at the office," she said loudly, turning back toward Third Avenue.

"Come on, lady," he whined, falling into step beside her. "You got a warm place to live, and I'm in the street." Dropping his voice so she could just hear it, he said, "That was him, right?"

"Place called the Blarney Castle," she whispered, and loudly: "Move off, buddy."

"On Third?" He pawed ineffectually at her sleeve. "Hey, lady."

"Stay outside. It won't be the last place." She stopped in her tracks: "Get away from me, creep."

Mick took a step backward, and a fat-faced woman in a doubleknit track suit pushed herself between them. "Here," she said, waving a folded bill in Mick's astonished face. "I'll buy you something to eat. And keep you company, too. Not everybody's like *her*."

Diana was three long strides down the street before she looked back. The woman had Mick by the arm and was trying to drag him into a hot-dog-and-soda joint on the corner. Abruptly, it hit her: *Galmoy*. She'd called him by the name Mick Pearse used, and she shouldn't have known it; couldn't have known it if Mick were properly dead. Damn. Be more careful, she told herself; this man's a professional. She turned up Third, stretching out her stride, and edging in toward the shop windows. As far as she could tell, no one in the sparse crowd reflected behind her was trying to keep pace, and she slowed to a normal walk.

Her heart was still pounding at a run when she stepped inside the Blarney Castle. It was an old-fashioned Irish bar, of the sort that had been succumbing in droves when Diana was buying her first legal drink. She shuffled through the green sawdust and up to the bar. The man behind it, thin and angry looking, had the classic broken-veined drinker's nose. He turned away, pointedly ignoring her, as the phone on the wall rang. A sodden troglodyte at the end of the bar looked up from the spilled beer in front of him and made as if to get off his stool.

"Never mind," said Diana, pressing him back into place. "It's for me."

"Now, where were we?" said Galmoy's voice. "Oh, yes: the terms."

"I want to hear Marie," said Diana. The bartender was watching her narrowly, but with eyes like his it was the only way he could. "I want to be sure she's all right."

"I'm afraid not," Galmoy replied. "You'll have to take my word for it."

"Not on your life," she said. "Put her on."

"Look, Miss Speed," Galmoy said, "it's not a good idea.

Believe me." He was nearly pleading, and Diana suddenly guessed the reason for his reluctance.

"I don't care who she is at the moment. I just want to hear her speak."

"Oh. You know then." A muted, inaudible squabble in the background, followed by a voice that was and was not the Marie she knew.

"Yes?"

"It's Diana Speed. Are you all right?"

"This is improper." Cold anger, not a trace of fear. "This person has treated me foully."

"Madam," said Diana. "Please calm yourself. Your friends will set you free."

Silence. The same voice, but more hesitant, more uncertain. "Is James with you?"

"He will be soon. Just do what Mr. Galmoy says."

"Galmoy?" The anger was back, with interest. "I know no Galmoy, but my cousin shall hear of this fellow Paulet."

"Paulet, then." The telephone was slippery in Diana's hand. "Do as he says, madam. Please. It's most important."

A cry from the other end, of pain or rage, and Galmoy came back on, breathing hard. "That's long enough. Northwest corner of 54th and Eighth. Half an hour from now."

Clear across town, she thought, as the receiver went dead in her ear. Why? Buying time, perhaps. She started toward the door, lost in thought, and the bartender called to her, his voice shrill and aggrieved: "Nothing to drink? Or maybe you'd like to use the ladies', too. While you make up your mind, like."

She stopped, turned deliberately, and surveyed the room. The bartender refused to meet her eye, but she heard him muttering "Rich bitches from Park Avenue" not quite under his breath. Without a word, she picked up an ashtray from the nearest table and shied it at his head. As it sailed through the murky air, leaving a cometlike trail of ash and butts, she turned on her heel; behind her, the crash of glass was echoed by a high-pitched squeal.

Mick was just outside the door. "Jesus, Diana, why'd you do that?"

"Because it felt good." The coldly bracing night air filled her lungs, and she took him by the arm. "Come on, Watson. The game's afoot." The tide was turning her way: She was positive of it, and she had learned to follow her luck when it started to run. She put up her hand, and an empty cab braked to a halt beside her. "Fifty-seventh and Eighth," she said as she climbed in.

"What's at 57th and Eighth?" Mick said, settling himself beside her.

"Damned if I know. It's three blocks north of where Galmoy told me to go next." She was looking out the rear window, trying to pick out a pattern of movement among the headlights behind. She leaned forward and tapped on the plastic partition. "Driver, you're going straight across on 57th, right?"

The man at the wheel didn't bother looking back. "Sure, lady. I'm not taking you on a ride."

"Fair enough." She sat back.

"You think Galmoy's having us followed?" Mick asked.

"I'm not sure," she said. "There was a guy in a car, back at 53rd . . ." She had a sudden picture of the driver's face, coming directly at her with another man beside him, and then it was gone. "Keep a sharp eye behind us when we turn, Mick. I've got to do some thinking."

If her memory was accurate, and the man in the car was someone she'd seen back in Brooklyn, then he almost certainly wasn't Galmoy's. Who else's then? The two remaining possibilities were equally discomforting. "Two cars made the turn behind us," said Mick. "But one of 'em's just an empty cab—I can see his Off Duty sign."

"Good," she replied, though it was not what she felt. If there was a follower, it wouldn't be Galmoy's man anyway. Galmoy already knew where they were going; he could send someone on ahead, if he had someone to send. No, the more she thought about it, the surer she became that the phone calls were no observation pattern, even if they were meant to look like one. The next jump would tell the tale. As she came to her conclusion, the taxi rocketed across Fifth Avenue on the cusp of the yellow light. "He still behind us?"

"I don't get it," he said. "They both ran the light—the car I was watching, *and* the cab behind him."

She twisted around in her seat, but the overhead streetlights made it impossible to see through the windshields of either following vehicle. Their own cab slowed to a halt behind a heavy truck. What was the likeliest answer? That what Mick had seen was just two cars running a light; it only happened five thousand times a day in midtown alone.

No, Diana told herself. Think paranoid: two deliberate tails. And it fit. Whoever Troubridge had been waiting for, probably in a Hertz or Avis sedan; and the Rajah's tiger, in the off-duty cab. The question was, when would somebody make a move? She had been counting out the fare as she thought, and she shoved it through the slot. "We'll get off here," she said. "Come on, Mick."

There was still more than enough time to reach the phone booth on foot; maybe Galmoy hadn't allowed for their finding a taxi right away. She jumped from the cab onto the yellow lines in the middle of 57th, pushing Mick in front of her. Up ahead at Sixth Avenue, the light had just changed, and the eastbound traffic was leaping toward them, the drivers galvanized by the chance of bagging two pedestrians at once. Behind her, Diana heard an engine roar and tires squeal.

She threw a look over her shoulder and saw a brown sedan pull out, apparently to make a U-turn. It was coming right at them, across 57th and gaining speed, its driver seemingly oblivious to the cars bearing down at him from his right. A half step ahead of Diana, Mick paused and grabbed her by the arm, whipped her beyond him with a strength she didn't dream he possessed. She felt something hard strike her out-thrust foot, and she was sprawling on the damp, cold asphalt as the world around her erupted in a series of rending metallic crashes punctuated by car horns and the pop-and-tinkle of breaking glass.

Mick was on one knee at her side. His anxious face was

gray in the light from the street lamps, as he helped her sit up. "Are you okay?"

His torso was blocking her view of the wreckage. A horn hung on a single deathless note, through which she could hear cries, curses, and now a distant siren. "Help me up," she said. He grabbed her outstretched hands and pulled her to her feet; a patter of glass shards fell from her clothes to the ground. Over Mick's shoulder, the brown sedan that had attempted the U-turn was lying on its side, with its right front wheel still spinning in the air. The two cars that had rammed it sat side by side, their bumpers neatly compacted back into their engines. Behind them, traffic was already frozen into a solid mass back across Sixth Avenue.

Diana picked up the padded brown envelope from where it had fallen. As she straightened, she saw the sedan's right-hand door pushed open from inside, and a man struggled to pull himself up and out. His face was streaming blood, but she was almost certain, from the shape of his head and the color of his hair, that he was the driver she'd seen back at the corner of 53rd. Beyond the smashed sedan, in the rank of westbound traffic ogling the shambles, sat a taxi with its OFF DUTY light on. The driver, a middle-aged man in an army field jacket, was placidly watching the show in front of him; there was no one else in the car at all.

A cop pushed his way through the gathering crowd, crunching heavily over the broken glass toward the wreckage. "Let's get out of here," Diana said. As she and Mick reached Sixth and turned south, she saw a last glimpse of the man with the bloody face, struggling feebly in the grasp of three burly policemen.

For some reason her left knee felt ice-cold; when she looked down she saw it was only a triangular tear in her slacks, with an ugly but so far painless abrasion beneath it. Her padded jacket seemed to have absorbed the rest of the sliding impact.

At Seventh and 56th, she pulled Mick into the doorway of a stationery store. From the corner of her eye she thought she saw a too-quick movement behind her, but when she looked again there was no one suspicious in sight, aside from a handful of prospective muggers, a ragged madman, and an immense bag lady clutching a length of pipe. "You go down Seventh and turn west on 54th," she said. "Wait at the corner and watch. I'll go across to Eighth and walk down."

"What am I watching for?" he asked. A little color had come back to his cheeks, but he reminded her of a balloon with half its air gone.

"I don't know exactly. Somebody watching me." She took a step and then remembered: "By the way, thanks. If you weren't so quick, I'd have tire tracks right across my behind."

The weak shadow of his grin flickered for a moment. "That guy was following us, wasn't he? Know who he is?"

"One less to worry about," she replied. "Go."

•   •   •

She quickened her stride at the now-familiar sight of a telephone half booth, then forced herself to slow down. The phone began to ring while she was still twenty yards away, and she threw reticence to the winds and sprinted for it. As she did so, a figure loitering on the far side of Eighth Avenue abruptly dived into the sparse traffic and darted across toward the booth. A weedy young man, she saw, with a narrow, determined face and long, pale hair flying behind him. She beat him to the booth by a step and snatched up the receiver.

"Been running?" said Galmoy's voice.

"Clear across town," she gasped. "I'm getting bored with this."

"Second and 59th," he replied. "In front of the cable car station."

She hung up and turned to go. The weedy young man was holding a gun, and it was pointed at her midsection. He looked terrified. "Where next?" he demanded.

"Get out of my way," she said, and started past him.

"Wait!" he cried. "You can't do that." He tried to step in front of her, a half second too late. Off balance, waving the pistol in her face, he caromed into the side of the phone booth. "I have a gun!" he yelled, as Mick rose up from behind a parked car.

"So do I," Mick growled, producing it. The young man stared at him wide-eyed for a second, dropped his pistol with a clatter, and toppled slowly forward into Diana's arms.

She lowered him to the ground and began to explore his pockets. Mick, who looked almost as surprised as the young man had, jammed his pistol back into the pocket of his ski jacket. "What're you doing?"

"Just checking identities," said Diana, as she found a thick wallet in his breast pocket. She flipped it open and scanned the contents. "Third assistant to the assistant," she observed to Mick. "Is that a storm drain next to your foot?"

"Yeah. His gun fell down it, worse luck." He watched in silence as she dropped the wallet through the grating. "Assistant to the assistant what?"

"At the British U.N. Mission. Somehow, I don't think this was his regular job."

He shook his head in admiration. "It could be yours, though. This is fun for you, isn't it?"

"Maybe a little," she admitted. "Look, there's a cab."

• • •

Above her, the brightly lit structure of the cable car station loomed like an oversize piece of steel-and-concrete abstract art. Paralleling the 59th Street Bridge, the shiny black wires stretched out over the East River until they were lost in darkness. "I wouldn't be surprised if this is the last phone call," Diana said to Mick. "In fact, I'd bet on it."

"How do you figure that?" Mick asked. He was leaning against the wall, his head down, panting heavily.

"All this jumping around is to buy time," she replied. "For some reason Galmoy needed half an hour and then another half hour. My guess is that he's moving, too."

"Moving?" Mick lifted his head slowly. "Moving to where?"

"Wherever he's planning to meet us. Not too far from here."

"I see." For the first time since she'd helped him out of the cab he looked around him. In the station above them a gate clanged hollowly, and she heard the liquid whirring of wheels on cable. The bright red car swung free from the platform and began its spiderlike progress eastward. "That's the thing that goes to Roosevelt Island, isn't it?" Mick asked, as if from far underwater.

"The cable car, right."

"Then I know where—" The telephone cut him off, and she reached for it.

Twenty-six: Troubridge

I can't stay here forever, mister," whined the driver, for the tenth time in as many minutes. Troubridge, crouched in the hired sedan's rear seat, continued to ignore him. On the far side of Second Avenue Diana and Pearse stood—or in Pearse's case slumped—silhouetted from above by the bright lights of the cable car station. Clearly they were waiting for another phone call, but Troubridge wondered if perhaps their quarry might not be setting them up for an ambush, here where the sight lines were relatively open in three directions and the escape routes, all of them nearly empty at this time of night, included the 59th Street Bridge to Queens, southbound Second Avenue, and the FDR Drive north—though not the cable car itself, which could be a perfect midair trap for a fleeing assassin.

"I'm telling you, the cops are gonna make me move this thing," said the driver hopelessly. Confronted with Troubridge's silence, he tried another tack: "I don't even know what you're up to, mister—how come you've been trailing this dame all night."

"I'm a mobile peeping Tom," Troubridge replied. "Why don't you just sit still and count the extra money you're getting." As he spoke, Diana turned quickly and picked up the telephone. In the seven-power eye of the binoculars her profile was sharp and clear. Action had somehow restored

ner, Troubridge saw, even as it was slowly wearing Pearse
into the ground. He saw her glance suddenly upward, then
hang up the phone and take Pearse by the arm. "I think you're
through for the night," Troubridge said to the driver, as the
two small figures entered the cable car station tower.

Once they were concealed inside the structure, Troubridge
paid off his chauffeur and loped across the avenue, nearly
certain there was nothing immediate to fear from his own
people. As he ran, the mental picture of Willingden climbing
from his overturned car into the arms of the New York City
cops made him smile in spite of his preoccupation; it would
have been amusing to hear Willingden exercising his cele-
brated rapport on that particular group of colonials. And the
poor boy from the U.N. Mission: How in heaven's name had
he been swept into Willingden's scratch team? Presumably
they were trying to cover all the bases and had simply run out
of trained men.

At the station entrance he pulled up sharply. Three people
were coming down the stairs; from their dress and their
slightly elevated manner he guessed they were returning from
dinner in one of the luxury apartments on Roosevelt Island.
Troubridge summoned up what he knew about the island, but
it wasn't much: a narrow splinter of land in the middle of the
East River, on which ziggurats of fancy condominia sat cheek
by jowl with glum state-run hospitals for the chronically
diseased; a peculiarly American juxtaposition.

From overhead came the metallic sounds of a cable car
leaving, presumably with Pearse and Diana aboard. He
checked his watch: fifteen minutes between departures; he
would be that far behind them. Even on foot, one could get
a considerable distance in fifteen minutes and, on Roosevelt
Island, in either of two opposed directions.

But why Roosevelt Island in the first place? It was a virtual
cul-de-sac in a city that teemed with more likely killing
grounds. As he thought, he pumped a subway token into the
turnstile and stepped cautiously out onto the platform. He
stood back in the shadows, watching the car diminish as,
from the terminal at the far side, the other car emerged and

began its westward passage. In the chill, damp wind off the
river, the cars swayed on their wires, wheels vibrating. He
stared through the small binoculars and thought he caught a
flash of ash blonde hair, but it was already too far to be sure.

Diana had got her second wind, all right, but her reckless-
ness seemed to have increased along with it. Troubridge
shivered as he recalled her racing across 57th Street, into the
very teeth of a three-car pileup; and saw again the set of her
chin as she'd elbowed aside the gormless young twerp on
Eighth Avenue. She'd used up two of her nine lives already
this evening, and now she was steaming blithely into a far
riskier situation. At least Pearse was armed—but could he
hold together even a few minutes more?

Troubridge shook himself mentally; this was getting him
nowhere. He had to concentrate on the problem at hand. If he
could work out where Carr planned his confrontation, it
might be possible to deduce the nature of it. Start with the
telephone trail: Three of the four stops had been at outdoor
kiosks—phones whose numbers weren't listed in any normal
directory, which meant that Carr must've researched the
ground himself, and with some effort. A further indication of
careful planning was the fact that each of the outdoor phones
was one of a unit of two or three: Even if one instrument was
vandalized, Carr would still have a fallback.

And three of the four locations were in a relatively small
area, seven blocks by three, which made the aberrational
crosstown trip stand out even more. The only reason
Troubridge could think of to account for it was that Carr
himself needed time—time to get from one place to another,
perhaps to set up his trap. Troubridge wondered if his
thoughts had paralleled Diana's, then realized that she might
well be in Carr's hands by now.

The approaching scarlet car was perceptibly larger, but it
grew with maddening slowness. Forget the cable car; think
about the phone calls. What else had they in common—the
three that he'd been able to witness? All were very brief,
which was merely a reasonable precaution against tracing.
And that suggested, if it did not prove, that Carr had been

calling from a phone whose location was worth tracing. A hotel or motel seemed most likely, a place where he could hold the girl Marie in privacy, and where he could put her on the line when Diana insisted—as surely she would've had the wit to do—that she hear Marie's voice.

God knew there were enough anonymous hotels in New York, but even the most carefree of them was not the sort of place one would choose for a showdown. Still, Carr had been setting up a meeting in a specific place; he had to be able to ensure that Diana was carrying the remaining letters before he killed her. That meant no prying neighborly eyes, and no pricked-up neighborly ears, either.

The cable car slid into its bay with a muted crash. It was empty, and Troubridge found himself the only eastbound passenger. He stood at the forward end, shifting from foot to foot as if impatience could make it leave sooner.

A meeting in a modern paper-walled apartment seemed unlikely, too, even if Carr had access to one. And a Roosevelt Island hospital, where nurses and orderlies crisscrossed the corridors at all hours of the day and night, seemed an equally dangerous place. What Carr needed was an empty building, one that he could count on being truly vacant; not just untended by its owners, but unvisited by addicts, squatters, or lovers.

As if to punctuate his thought, a bell rang and the car door slid shut. The cable car gave a premonitory lurch and was airborne, an unpleasant sensation. But something in it galvanized Troubridge's mind. He thought of the last time he'd driven the 59th Street Bridge, going to JFK airport. Diana had been with him, but he couldn't remember the occasion. As the car had crested the bridge's span, he'd looked down and to the right, where Roosevelt Island lay stretched below them; on its southern end sat a massively dismal pile of masonry, Victorian in its appearance. Most of the windows had been sealed with rust-streaked sheets of metal; its roof was partly collapsed. Diana had followed his eyes and, as so often, answered his unspoken question: "An old hospital.

Smallpox or TB or something. Too bad they let it go to hell
that way."

*   *   *

The burly woman behind the wheel of the bus looked up
from her paperback novel. "Don't just stand there," she said,
turning down the page corner. "Climb on."

"I beg your pardon," Troubridge replied. "But were you
here when the last cable car came in."

Deep suspicion clouded her face. "You from the dis-
patcher? 'Cause I don't have to go if they's no passengers and
there wasn't except for the tall gal and the guy with the hurt
head and they didn't want no ride anyway, just headed off
down toward the hospital, only I don' know why anybody
come all the way across the river to find a 'mergency room."
She stopped, but it was clear she was ready to inhale and fight
again.

"The hospital to the south?" Troubridge asked. "Down
that way?"

"Goldwater Memorial," she nodded. "That's the one."

"Thank you very much," he said warmly. "You've been a
great help."

"I have?" She looked aggrieved and closed the door in his
face.

He loped past the low, twenties-modern buildings of the
hospital at a silent, energy-conserving trot. Ahead of him,
behind a solid fence of corrugated metal topped with rolls of
barbed wire, the ruinous old building sat lurking, a black
smear blocking the lights of Manhattan downstream. The
chill breeze was fresher here, where it had a clear sweep up
the river. As Troubridge regarded the high fence, the gibbous
moon found a hole in the heavy clouds and lit the scene
brightly enough so he could make out a gate toward the
right-hand end of the barrier. The sheet-metal door was
secured with a heavy chain and an even heavier padlock, but
through carelessness or arrangement the chain hung loosely

enough to permit the gate to open about a foot—enough for a person to squeeze through.

Glancing quickly around him to make sure he was unobserved, Troubridge moved forward. A corner of the door's iron facing had been bent outward, and from the sharp triangle fluttered a bit of stained white cloth. He picked it off: a piece of gauze bandage, with a damp bloodstain. So Pearse had come this way, and not long before. Troubridge edged through the gate. Ahead of him on the ground level one of the tall windows stood partially open: The lower of the two metal sheets that had sealed it was lying flat on the ground outside.

The moonlight abruptly went out, but Troubridge was already moving. The windowsill was nearly at chest height, and he was just thinking of the problem it would present for a man as short as Carr when his shin struck the answer—a solidly built crate, half hidden behind a straggling bush.

He stood on it looking in, waiting for his breathing to slow and his eyes to adjust fully to the darkness ahead. A trace of light from the overcast sky showed that the whole ceiling had fallen in, leaving a jagged, burned-smelling maze of timber. The glimmer in the far corner, a vertical slice of light, was so faint he did not notice it at first.

He hoisted himself up, one leg over the sill, groping for the floor. Something scuttled through the roofless chamber with a patter of hard, clawed feet on wood. Troubridge slid through, lowering himself slowly until the uneven surface took his full weight with only the smallest protest. The faint light—a barely open door—was coming from directly ahead, but fallen roof beams and other, softer rubble he did not care to analyze required him to detour around two walls, where the floor was likely to be strongest.

So far, so apparently good, he thought. The door was open perhaps six inches; not enough for him to put his head through. He was debating the risk of unoiled hinges when a cry of fury came from the next room. "Swine!" Could that be Marie's voice? It was furiously angry, pitched like a trumpet: "Liar, cheat, thief!" Her ringing indignation covered the sound of the opening door. Cautiously he put his head around it.

The room was low and very large—how large Troubridge could not say for certain, since it faded off into darkness. At one time it had apparently been used for storage: One side was piled high with what appeared to be rusted metal bed frames and a miscellany of wooden furniture in various stages of disrepair. A three-legged table stood about twenty feet from Troubridge, the center of a small pool of light that came from an old-fashioned oil lantern in its center.

On the table was scattered the detritus of a man in hiding—a flashlight, half a loaf of bread, a six-pack of cheap beer, a dirty shirt. But what held Troubridge's eye was a thick package wrapped in plastic sheeting, and a padded envelope that he recognized all too easily. Beside the table was a heavy chair that had lost one of its arms, and in it, trussed like a fowl, was the girl Marie. Her clothes were stained and torn, her hair a wild tangle, yet she looked every inch a queen. Facing the table Diana Speed stood with her legs braced apart and one arm around Pearse, who was clearly at the point of collapse. In the ruddy, flickering light the bones of her face stood out in defiant relief.

But it was the short, pudgy figure of Herbert Carr that dominated the room. He was standing next to Marie, swaddled in an ankle-length brown coat and holding a pistol in each hand. The trumph that lit his face made Troubridge wonder how he could ever have thought of it as nondescript. "Swine, am I," he was saying. "You poor bloody nut case, you should see yourself."

Marie drew up to reply, but Diana spoke first: "You know who I work for, Mr. Galmoy or Carr or whatever name you're using. The Rajah knows what I'm doing, and if you kill us the world won't be large enough to hide you." Her cool, matter-of-fact tone carried a conviction that damped even Carr's manic grin.

"That's what you say, missy," he replied. "But what choice do I have now? You tell me that. Go back to Blighty like a good boy? I don't have friends in high places, like some

I could name. I'd never hear the birds sing again, and the Provos would get me for certain."

"With my boss behind you, you could disappear to where they'd never find you," she said, Troubridge could see the drops of moisture on her forehead, but her voice was sweet reason itself. "And once your government had their precious letters back, I doubt they'd care about having your head either."

"Never!" cried Marie. "Those letters are mine, to do with as I will."

"You see?" said Carr, with an oddly apologetic smile. "You'll never shut her mouth, except permanently. I'm sorry for it, but there it is."

"And the letters?" said Diana, the strain audible to Troubridge's ear. "They'll just be millstones. Who can you possibly sell them to?"

"Who? Why Her Majesty the bloody Queen, that's who. Like you said, that'll get the heat off me, and as for your rajah, I'll just have to take my chances. Besides, it'll be years before they find you in here, if they ever do." Diana opened her mouth to speak again, but Carr shook his head: "Sorry, Miss Speed. Truly."

As he finished, the silenced gun in his right hand came up and, at the same moment, Pearse toppled heavily forward. The long-barreled revolver wavered from Diana to Pearse, and as it did so she dived to one side, out of the lantern light. To Troubridge, the next few seconds seemed to pass in extreme slow motion, but with a supernatural clarity.

He saw Diana hit the floor rolling, half-hidden by a puff of dust. Carr's silenced pistol gave its hollow, muffled *pop,* as Troubridge, with a yell, hurled himself through the door. Five long steps separated him from Carr, five steps that might have been a mile. Like the caricature of a gunfighter from the American West, Carr swung halfway around, leveling the second gun as he did so. Troubridge saw the muzzle presented, realized in an instant out of time that he had no chance at all, saw a huge flash, and knew himself dead.

Except that he wasn't. Carr was reeling back, screaming,

his left hand a spurting shambles of bone and tissue. The silenced pistol fell to the ground as his right hand grasped instinctively at the awful wreckage of his left. Troubridge, in mid-stride, had a glimpse of Marie's face, mouth agape, laced with an arrow-straight line of red droplets. Then he hit the retreating Carr full in the chest, and the two men sprawled to the floor. Troubridge felt something crack in his ankle as he went down, and he grabbed instinctively for the gleam of gunmetal at arm's length in front of him.

His reach was perfect, his hand grasping the butt, but as he brought the weapon up he saw the cylinder was gone and the blackened frame bent out of true. Before his numbed mind had worked out what had happened, though, he was lining the gun up on the pudgy little man's retreating shoulder blades. "Stop!" he cried. "I'll shoot!"

Carr ducked quickly to one side, behind a stack of furniture that reached nearly to the ceiling. "There's a window back there!" Diana called. She was on her feet—the only one of the four of them—and started after the fugitive. Troubridge heard a heavy thump, as of a body crashing into a wall, followed by a scrabbling noise that was overlaid by a keening wail of agony which sounded as if it was coming through clenched teeth. He's climbing out the window, Troubridge thought, and then he heard the unmistakable shattering explosion of a sheet of glass.

He pulled himself up, tried his injured ankle, and felt a stab of pain so intense he almost cried out. "He's got away," he gasped to Diana, who was standing motionless. "But maybe you'd better check." She had already picked up the silenced revolver from the floor. Now she scooped the flashlight off the table and moved slowly into the silent darkness.

A minute or so later she returned. Her face was set in an expression he had never seen. "What is it?" he asked, but she only shook her head, and he saw she was swallowing hard, unable to speak. He set his weight gently on the ankle, decided he could just bear it. With the flashlight swooping its beam wildly from floor to ceiling, he hopped toward the back of the long room.

He heard himself grunt, felt his stomach turn over. He forced himself to hold the flashlight's powerful beam on the scene in front of him until his numbed mind had worked out the answer. It was a tall, rather narrow window that opened on to an interior courtyard, and apparently the lower half of the single huge pane had long ago been knocked out, leaving a convenient egress. Carr must have pulled himself up to the sill and crawled painfully through, feet first, his clumsy struggle shaking loose the hanging sheet of glass, so that it fell, straight and true, like a headsman's axe.

Carr's body lay on the withered grass of the courtyard, in a widening pool of dark blood. His head, wearing an expression of ludicrous surprise, lay on the floor just inside the window. "Behold the head of a traitor," Troubridge murmured.

PARTINGS

1. Fifth Avenue, Midtown

Judith came into Haskell's office without knocking, as she always did, and dropped into a chair. "Well, it's all wrapped up," she said.

Haskell, who had ostentatiously ignored her entrance, looked up from the pile of typewritten pages in front of him. "I take it you've settled on the reincarnation of Patricia Orme?" He knew his testiness was showing in his voice, but he was beyond caring. Credit for the triumphant return of the Casket Letters had naturally fallen to Judith, as their editor, while the promising novelist Haskell had discovered at the Bread Loaf Writers Conference had for some reason decided to change all his believable Westhampton Beach tennis players into the Vietnamese crew of a fishing boat in Southern California.

And to add to his frustration, Judith obviously didn't even notice its existence. "He's a published romance novelist," she was saying, "and he's been under our noses for simply years. He freelances for Sammy Lake in Copyediting—and he's actually *worked* on three Patricia Ormes."

Haskell found himself unwillingly impressed. Someone who'd published a novel—that was good. But no one was more familiar than a copy editor with the bird's-nest mess that underlay most novels. "Sounds promising," he admitted.

"But best of all, he's an amateur historian himself," Judith went on. "Diana and I are going to sound him out tomorrow, about the Big Project." With apparent irrelevance, she added, "He's unmarried."

Haskell weighed the undertone and decided that she was referring obliquely to the unknown writer's sexual orientation, not his prospects in her personal future. There was nothing he felt like contributing in either area, so he gave the subject a half turn: "The letters really are in the bag, after all?"

"They seem to be," Judith agreed. "Diana's got experts crawling over them like ants at a picnic, but all I've heard so far is enthusiasm." She eyed Haskell curiously. "I gather she had a little trouble getting them back—spent most of Sunday chasing them down. The mailroom boys tell me her secretary was the one who stole them. The fat O'Donnell girl."

"Oh, was it?" Haskell reflected momentarily on the little Diana had told him of her adventures. If this was going to be the official version, perhaps it was just as well—and a tribute to the primacy of rumor over mere fact. "Well, she certainly didn't look the type. Are we going to prosecute?"

"No, she resigned. Got off too lightly, if you want my opinion. But that's Diana's department."

He pushed the pile of manuscript away from him and regarded her thoughtfully. "You seem to be a lot friendlier toward our treasurer. Quite buddy-buddy, in fact."

Fraternization with the business side—even the head of it—was an accusation Judith could scarcely ignore. "She's not so bad, really. Reads a lot, and she went to Wellesley, which I didn't know. And now that she's got the letters in the house, she'll be our Maximum Leader's fair-haired girl."

It was ever Judith's way, he thought. Her usual line of approach wouldn't work in this case, though. But she'd think of something; she always did. "Nice for her," Haskell said. "By the way, what's come over your Young Lochinvar? He's been sidling about the halls as if he expected to be mugged."

"Tim Mark?" She looked vaguely surprised. "I haven't seen him all morning. Which reminds me: You want to share a cab to Patrick's funeral? It's in an hour, at Campbell's."

Haskell was already back in the manuscript, and Judith's question was nothing but disconnected words in his ear. "Patrick who?" he said.

2. East 65th Street

The Bar-le-Duc, on Sixty-fifth just off Madison, is one of those small, elegant, overpriced New York hotels that seem to be supported by the faithful patronage of ancient ladies with pale blue hair who can somehow afford to live permanently in them, and by out-of-towners who pride themselves on the cachet of a posh but obscure city address: Only a small brass plate announces the Bar-le-Duc to the world that hurries past. How Diana had found it Troubridge couldn't imagine, and he only dimly recalled being installed in its best suite at three o'clock in the morning. Seven hours later, he realized that he had already been subtly spoiled by its creature comforts, its staff's discretion, and the security provided by its nearly complete invisibility.

No one except Diana knew he was there, which was why he froze when he heard a key grate in the lock and saw the door swing open. He was groping under the pillow for Carr's revolver when he recognized that tall figure in the doorway. "Good morning, Mr. Troubridge," she said.

"Good morning," he replied, biting off the *Marie;* and it was not Marie who was standing there, casually imperious, in a rather formal suit that echoed Diana's style. He felt as if he should go to one knee but decided it was beyond him.

"I trust I haven't wakened you." She advanced into the room, not waiting for his answer, and suddenly she metamorphosed back into the shy teenage girl. "This is really nice," she observed. "Much better than where that man took me." A shadow of pain crossed her face and was gone. She had come with a purpose and, it appeared, a speech to go with it. "You saved my life, Mr. Troubridge—you and Miss Speed. Even though you at least were working against me."

He saw he was supposed to respond, but the best he could produce was a self-deprecating murmur.

It was enough to get her going again. "Miss Speed—Diana—told me what you gave up to help me."

"Not really," he objected. "It was out of my hands, you know."

"Nevertheless," she said firmly. "I've been thinking how to reward you—no, please don't interrupt me. I've decided you should have this." She was holding out a large manila envelope and he took it, noticing only that Diana must have got her to a manicurist. "Open it," she said, flashing her young girl's smile.

He felt his face turn to wood as he withdrew the fragile piece of paper. The single sheet, with the gallantly raked *Marie Royne dEcosse* at the bottom. He read the first line through three times before he actually saw the words: "Tomorrow I shall see my God face to face." He looked up at her, utterly bewildered. "I don't understand."

A child's delight was blended with a curious severity in her features. "It's for my cousin, your Elizabeth—how odd both our names should have come full circle, too."

"But why—"

"Two reasons. The more important is that this letter is false. Oh, it was written by . . . her. But in such a rage of bitterness and despair that she wove a black lie. What it says isn't true, so it must be destroyed before it does more damage. Yes," she said, to the question on his lips, "who else could know but me?" She believed it, Troubridge saw. Believed so absolutely that she carried him along for several seconds, before he took in the real lunacy of what she was saying.

"I was going to burn it myself," she continued, "but Diana said that if you bring home this letter, it might put you in your own queen's good graces, which would please me greatly. That's the second reason. My cousin has a loyal servant in you, Mr. Troubridge, more loyal than most I ever had." She colored, and quickly added: "I'm not supposed to say things like that anymore. Diana was very firm about it. But I knew you'd understand."

Mad as a whole battalion of hatters, he thought, then saw

she was waiting for his reply. With superhuman effort he managed to assemble one: "I'm overwhelmed," he said. "You're as thoughtful as you are generous."

"It's some small repayment," she said. "I wish I could restore the other thing you've lost."

Does my heart show in my face? He saw she understood his expression perfectly. "Perhaps I never had it to lose. We're speaking again, at least."

"She needs you," said Marie. "She needs someone."

This was too much, no matter who she thought she was. "I don't suppose you told her so."

"Oh, no!" She grinned at him. "She scares me."

Her smile was contagious; it made him feel a million years old. "She scares everybody."

"I wouldn't have known, you see, if I hadn't found someone of my own." He saw again Marie, released from her bonds, falling to her knees beside the unconscious Pearse, the tears that streamed down her face washing off the traces of Carr's blood.

"I hope you find he's . . ." There was really no way out of that sentence, he decided, but she rescued him.

"He will be," she said confidently. "Diana said she'd have a word with him."

3. Manhattan: Grand Central Station

"Fascinating," said the Rajah, turning the page. "So she really was in on Darnley's murder."

"Up to the hilt," Diana agreed, and took a sip of sauvignon blanc from a goblet shaped like a calla lily. They were in the salon of *Utopia Express,* her employer's private railroad car, which sat with its blinds drawn, hissing softly, on a secluded lower-level track. The interior decor was pure Victorian Ominous—immense, overstuffed chairs flanked by dark wooden side tables and tall, dim lamps with fringed shades. The insides of the blinds showed landscapes of classical ruins, in depressing shades of umber and sepia.

The result, to Diana's mind, was a claustrophobic masterpiece; she strongly suspected the Rajah had arranged it that way to unnerve visitors. Looming above the fussy knickknackery, he seemed even larger and craggier than usual. When he raised that heavy, shaggy head and regarded her with those unsettling eyes—yellow-pupiled, like a lion's—she felt an involuntary chill run down her spine. He must, she knew, be approaching sixty, yet he radiated power on every frequency, including the explicitly sensual. His appetite for women was legendary, but he never pressed the issue. From the moment of their first meeting Diana had known, without a word between them, that his offer was on the table; knew he accepted her refusal—though not as necessarily permanent.

He finished the last page, looked under it, and arranged the stack of papers in a neat pile. "A dangerous woman," he said, sounding almost wistful. "Knew what she wanted and went for it." He paused, and Diana felt her stomach tighten. "Wasn't there one more letter?"

She had considered three different responses to this question, but none of them emerged. "There was," she replied. "It was withdrawn by the owner."

"And you agreed?"

"I did." Dealing with the Rajah, lies or even evasions were pointless. Like most of his employees, Diana had at first been petrified by conversation with no room for maneuver. Now, she found it curiously liberating.

"I see." He sat seemingly lost in calculation. "Well, I suspect you were wise." It was as close as he would come to an accolade, but she recognized it, relished the absence of flattery. "You've still got enough material for the book, though."

"More than enough, with Patrick's notes on his research. And I understand we've signed an author, too. We'll publish a year from today—Mary Stuart's birthday."

"Miss Aaron's touch, I presume."

"Of course."

"It could put Wild-Freeman in the black next fiscal," he reflected.

"It will," she said.

"A year ahead of schedule," he added. It was luck, though—or mostly luck—so no further praise was called for. "And how are you getting on yourself? No problems with the editors? Young Mr. Mark, for instance."

How in God's name had he known about that? "Mr. Mark's getting one more chance," she replied. "Editors are easier than I'd thought. All you need is a whip and a chair."

"Having the checkbook doesn't hurt," he observed mildly. "I've put Editorial back on the short leash, by the way: All advances go through you again."

Now that was a true vote of confidence, she thought. And something even rarer: a tacit admission by the Rajah of his own mistake. Comment was unnecessary, even inadvisable, and she waited silently for him to go on.

His face gave nothing away, but she knew he was shaping another topic, wondered how he would ease into it. "The girl—Marie—is quite crazy, you know."

"So are lots of people. I think with a little time she'll be able to cope."

"A little time, a lot of money, and some supervised male companionship," he corrected.

"Mick is a presentable young man. Anyway, she thinks she's in love with him."

"And just how far do you trust Mr. Pearse?"

"Not quite as far as I could throw a Buick. But he knows where he stands." By the time Pearse had understood the exact depth of the precipice at his feet, she recalled, he'd been sweating like a pig, his eyes round as saucers.

"It makes an odd relationship," the Rajah suggested.

"It worked for Catherine the Great," said Diana.

"Catherine the Great didn't have a fairy godmother to keep her men in line," he replied, but the corners of his mouth hooked upward momentarily in the predator's grin some of his employees had not seen in decades. "Speaking of men," he went on, his tone suddenly neutral, "your friend has gone back home, I hear."

So there it was. "Left this morning," she agreed. The

knowledge had been clawing at her all day; she was damned if she would let her feelings show.

"It's probably for the best. I don't see a future for him here—do you?"

She wondered if the Rajah meant his question to be ambiguous; decided he did, and so what? He manipulated those around him as automatically as he breathed, and to take offense was merely a waste of spirit.

All the same, Troubridge was not a subject she could trust herself to discuss. His betrayal and her own pride stood like a wall between them, but it was a wall with unexpectedly shaky foundations. In Diana's purse was a single sheet of paper, twice crumpled and hurled away, twice retrieved and carefully refolded. She needed no handwriting expert to identify the arrogant script, and the two-word message exemplified its author—exasperating, yet precisely aimed to remind her of what they had shared:

Contessa: Perdóno.

Is that who he thinks I really am—a Countess Almaviva who'll forgive her man anything? And, realizing she might still do exactly that, she felt her face grow hot.

The Rajah was watching her, waiting for a response. With an effort she dredged up his last remark. "No future here?" She managed a shrug. "I can't say."

He sat back in the high-backed chair that was nearly a throne. From his expression—or the absence of it—Diana knew he had taken both her meanings. "I admire your generosity," he said. "I expected you to be . . ." He hesitated, and she realized he was actually at a loss.

"Distraught?" she offered. "Devastated?"

"Well, at least furious. And entitled to be."

"Furious was—let's see—day before yesterday. I'm past furious." Which was true enough, as far as it went.

The Rajah seemed not wholly convinced: "I don't suppose you'd feel up to a quick out-of-town troubleshoot?"

The required answer was, fortunately, the honest one: "Where and how long?"

"Los Angeles. Maybe two weeks." He lifted a thick manila folder from his desk and passed it over.

She riffled quickly through the contents—the usual corporate history of high hopes tarnished by honest error, and the inevitable descent, through self-serving memoranda to petty backbiting, grinding down into immobile hostility. A dismal chronicle, and she could see no immediate solution; even so, she felt her heart lift to the challenge.

"It's a mess," the Rajah warned. "Maybe unfixable."

That's not why you hired me, she thought. "I can fix it," she heard herself say. The confidence in her voice was absolute.

"Can you leave tomorrow morning?"

She considered the endless expanse of evening, in an empty, violated apartment that still reeked of smoke. "I'd as soon fly tonight," she said. "Descend on my victims with the dawn."

"As you wish. My office can book your flights and hotel."

"Please." She got to her feet, her mind already busy with preparations.

The Rajah rose, extended his huge, freckled paw. "Good luck. We'll miss you at the executive meeting."

"A week from today?" She retrieved her hand. "I'll be back by then—with my shield or upon it."

One tufted eyebrow arched in surprise. "You don't have to push so hard, you know."

But she did, especially now. Troubridge knew what she needed: "Most birds are happy in their little nests," he'd said. "A few, like you, can only perch way out on a limb."

"Just save my seat," she said, smiling. Though the ache was still there, she could ignore it for a little while.